SOLOMON'S DREAMS
PREYING FOR REVENGE

ERIC SUDDOTH

RISING SMOKE PUBLISHING

The characters and events in this book are fictitious. Any similarity to real persons, living or dead, is coincidental and not intended by the author.

Unless otherwise indicated, Scripture quotations are from:
Holy Bible, New International Version®, NIV©
1973, 1978, 1984, 2011 by Biblica, Inc. ®
Used by permission. All rights reserved worldwide.

Rising Smoke Publishing
ISBN 978-1-949869-14-9

Then Solomon awoke –
and he realized it had been a dream.
1 Kings 3:15

Monday
CHAPTER 1

The moon cascaded a sliver of light through the dismal low-hanging clouds scattered in the sky like fallen rose petals after a storm. He tapped his steering wheel rhythmically to the tune in his head as he cheerfully hummed along to the song he was spontaneously orchestrating on this prelude night. Glancing down at his phone, he saw 3:18 a.m. shine through the darkened confines of his midnight black Ford Fusion.

He casually drove the roads he had mapped out Friday afternoon while sitting in his three-wall cubical of tan laughable privacy panels. He had the map in the passenger seat but knew the path would change nightly. Working in the District Department of Transportation of Washington D.C., he knew which stoplights and streets had working surveillance cameras and which ones had the gimmicky knockoffs to deter those speeders who would be discouraged by such a thing.

Lowering his windows, he inhaled the springtime air, crisp and clean, unlike his afternoon walks through the city with the congestion of bumper to bumper traffic exhaust fumes. He felt like the last man on earth on the deserted streets of silent apartments and darkened storefronts where brightly lit streetlights shined their radiance every twenty yards along the pleasant sidewalk.

He couldn't help but smile at the tranquility of the Navy Yard area in southeast D.C. on this evening. Usually a bustling area in daylight with tasty restaurants scattered throughout, now it was like a city of one. He circled National Park where his beloved Washington Nationals destroyed their opposing teams on their good days at home and smiled at the memories of sitting in the grandstands with an overpriced hotdog and cup of beer. $16 had never tasted so good.

He watched with great anticipation as a blue sedan turned onto the four lane M Street with him. Looking into his rearview mirror, he saw the early twenty-something blonde come into focus in the driver's seat. He let off the gas, allowing his vehicle to coast, gradually decreasing in speed inconspicuous to the woman behind. He stayed in the left lane, allowing his guest to pull up alongside him.

Turn red, he hoped. *Come on light, turn red*, he pleaded to the traffic light as the green light slowly changed from the soothing yellow to the haunting glow of fiery red. He gently pressed his brake, coming to a stop, as the blue sedan slid in beside him. He looked over at the blonde who also had her windows down. He waited for her to look over at him, but she never did. She continued to watch transfixed on the red light as if following the light in a doctor's office, ignoring her visitor. The red light shined on his face as his anticipation started to build. He wanted to honk his horn to get her attention. But he knew. He knew in the depths of his core she was aware of him.

The light turned to an electric green and she hit the gas pedal, proceeding through the intersection. They drove side by side a few blocks until fate aligned with the traffic light, changing to the glowing red. He once again looked over at her, almost leaning his body in her direction, as if he wanted to ask her how her night was going. Once again, she looked straight ahead. Without losing contact with the red light, she released her tightened grip on the steering wheel and blindly felt for her electric window button, causing the protective glass to speedily rise.

Smart girl, he thought, leaning back comfortably into his driver's seat, *but not smart enough*. He glanced over behind his aviator glasses, fixating on her profile, memorizing the outline from the top of her forehead, down her slender nose, to her full painted lips. Suddenly, the red light changed to green. She slammed her foot on the gas, causing her wheels to spin as she shot off like a rocket.

Oh, you want to play, do you? he smiled to himself as he gently pressed his gas pedal to follow the speeding blue bullet from a safe distance. His fingers were relaxed around the steering wheel as his breathing became deep like a meditative exercise. He started to feel the adrenaline rush he had longed for the last year, but he was trying to control it. All the sleepless nights were coming to fruition. All the years of pent up rage were about to explode in a wrath of structured volcanic proportion. All the daily journal entries of retribution and retaliation, which he immediately burned to hide his true character, were coming into the headlights. His smile widened as he looked ahead and saw the next traffic light quickly changing to yellow. He waited for her brake lights to shine, but they didn't. Her speed didn't decrease, but increased instead.

Interesting, little girl, he thought as he watched her run the red light, trying to flee the scene of her traffic crime. *Lucky for you, the cameras are off…or unlucky.* He pressed on his brake pedal coming to a stop. He wondered what she was thinking. Were her thoughts jumbling together in fear? Was she looking for a new way home, even though he could follow her as long as it took? Or was she trying to decide who to call and who would even answer this early in the morning? He let out a faint laugh as the streetlight one block ahead switched from yellow to red. This time, she stopped. Was her fear gone? *It shouldn't be.*

His light turned to green and he casually caught up to her. He wanted to reel her into a false sense of security. He wanted to play. He wanted this feeling to last. He wanted to look over at her, but he closed his eyes and let the red stoplight bathe over him. *What are you thinking? Are you looking at me now?* Curiosity got the best of him.

He carefully lifted up the rifle he had stolen a few months ago, placing the barrel into his meticulously chiseled hole in the lock. He slid the rifle through the hole until the end of the barrel popped open the makeshift lock latch, unnoticeable to the untrained eye. A GPS

3

looking infotainment screen on his dashboard lit up with a camera image of the rifle's shot. A red dot shined inside the interior of the blonde woman's car on the screen, unseen by her. He stared at the camera image he installed, maneuvering his hand until the red dot shined on the side of her skull. He smiled to himself.

"Bang," he whispered, knowing he could have killed her and no one would have ever known.

He looked ahead of him and noticed he was four blocks away from where the traffic cameras would once again be working. He wanted tonight to be a trial run. He didn't even have any bullets in his rifle. This was just a test, and he passed beautifully.

Tomorrow was the real deal. When the light changed to green, he turned left as she continued straight ahead. *You're lucky. Very lucky.* She continued to drive home safely, but he had somewhere else he needed to go.

He needed to check on his scapegoat – the last pawn piece in his elaborate plan.

CHAPTER 2

Heavily-muffled breathing gradually increased in volume as an 80-year-old man in a pair of worn gray sweatpants and New York Yankees t-shirt exited a quaint golden brick ranch home. He slowly walked down the driveway to the sidewalk, stopping to look both ways before he crossed the subdivision street. A female voice projected over the panting as he proceeded to walk on the sidewalk. "Stephen Klein, 82, was last seen Monday afternoon around 2:30 p.m. by his daughter at his residence in the Kenwood area of Bethesda, Maryland. He has dementia and congenital heart failure and requires medication. If you have seen him, please contact the local authorities." The gentleman passed a Kenwood Avenue street sign as three bells chimed. He continued to walk along the sidewalk as the woman's voice spoke, "Stephen Klein, 82, has been missing for six hours. In most cases this would not be a missing person until twenty-four hours have passed, but since this person has dementia and congenital heart failure and requires medication, we have upgraded this status. Without his medication, circumstances could be dire soon. If you have seen him, *please* contact the local authorities." The gentleman continued to walk until he and his heavy breathing faded into the distance.

The suburban surroundings of ranch and cottage style homes morphed into a nighttime setting of a metropolitan city. A black and white video showed a brunette woman sitting behind a steering wheel. She was saying something, but all that was heard was a male British accent. "It's me, Stewart," the male said. "Yes, yes, I know it's soon, but I just wanted to let you know I was thinking of you." The woman smiled as she drove, casually twirling her fingers into her hair staring straight ahead. She appeared to be laughing and having a good conversation. Suddenly, a red dot appeared on the side of her head. "Bye," he said as a bullet pierced through the driver's side window

5

before lodging itself deep into her skull. Blood splattered onto the broken glass as she fell forward on her steering wheel. "Drive safe," he wickedly laughed as the video quickly left the coasting woman.

Elizabeth Hyde awoke, reached for her iPhone on her nightstand, and started typing out the details of her dreams in her Notes app. Elizabeth had the remarkable ability of dreaming future events. Six months ago she would have written these dreams in a journal, just to mark them off the next day when she discovered the dreams had actually occurred, a method she had used since she was a young girl. Now, she used these dreams as a way to help people. She was no longer going to be a mere bystander.

She typed the details like she had been doing each night over the last few months, straining to remember key details such as locations, times, names, or anything else that would be helpful in resolving or circumventing the situations. She had finished writing down her two dreams when a chill went down her spine. She went through her notes over the last few months, reading the routine dream of a black and white video of different women. Over the course of four months, she had dreamed a similar dream thirty-two times, except this one was unlike all the previous dreams in one major way.

"He's going to kill tomorrow."

CHAPTER 3

My hands were fidgeting, feet were shuffling, and eyes were darting around the courtroom like a squirrel looking for a quick getaway. But unlike a squirrel holding a nut, I was trying to hold in the breakfast I had just eaten. A nervous and semi-nauseous wave of uncertainty slammed into me, causing my center of gravity to become a little unsteady as I walked. I entered the crowded courtroom with news reporters lining the back wall as if a game of dodgeball was about to commence. And in a way, I too, felt like I was back in middle school about to be pummeled to death.

I stared around the circus of what we called our judicial system, trying to find an open seat as if I were attending a wedding and trying to decide whether to sit on the bride's or groom's side. I didn't know which side to sit on this pivotal day. I knew the defendant and defense attorney, but I desperately wanted a guilty verdict for all the pain and damage Jenny Ascot had caused the D.C. area, especially to my beloved friends.

Jenny Ascot and her estranged brother, Alexei Lechkov, caused a weeklong havoc last October by killing retired tourists while obtaining the infamous name Carbon Monoxide Killers. They would act upon unsuspecting, kindhearted couples to help an ailing father or sister at one of the subway stations in the metro area of Washington, D.C. and then knock them out with a powerful dose of chloroform before dropping them off in their vehicles in a deserted park to die from their exhaust fumes.

My heart fluttered as I watched the defense attorney confidently walk down the aisle, passing through the gate with her leather briefcase in hand. She was beautiful, intelligent, passionate, and if asked six months ago, I would have added cold, heartless, and a piece of work. Now, Veronica Hyde-Cooper was a little warmer towards me, allowing

7

blood to find its way to her heart. But Verny, a nickname I had secretly given her when she first started dating my brother-like best friend, Officer Winston "Wint" Cooper, was still a piece of work I was learning to love. The key word was learning, and it was definitely a work in progress; years of negativity didn't vanish overnight.

Veronica was defending Jenny, not because she felt it was her civic duty as a reputable defense attorney with the motto every citizen deserves a fair trial, but because Jenny and Veronica were childhood friends and eventually coworkers at the same firm, Manfield & Hyde. The firm had an impenetrable clause to defend one of their own no matter the cost. It was a nice tagline benefit in the employee manual, but the partners never could have conceived of this type of situation. They were thinking of cases more along the line of traffic violations, possible ethical issues with upper management, and the ever-increasing rate of divorces. They had never planned on defending one of their attorneys as a serial killer. Not only was Jenny a ruthless serial killer who killed people at random, but she'd had morbid intentions of killing Veronica's own husband, Officer Cooper with the Washington D.C. police department.

He had tracked down the killers to Huntington Station in Alexandria, Virginia from a mysterious and anonymous telephone tip I had given. While Wint was hunting down these horrible killers, I had started having elusive dreams nightly foretelling of various events that would happen during the next day. One of the recurring dreams was of the various murders Jenny Ascot, a girl whom Wint and Veronica had set me up to date that same week, was committing.

Jenny and I had just gone on our second date the previous day before I surprised Wint by helping him take down these killers, because once again I had a dream my best friend was going to be shot and killed by the murderous siblings. It still baffled me how strangely my dreams worked. During the last dream I could see all the tiniest details of the subway, even down to the group of girls blowing bubblegum, but I never once knew Jenny was the psychotic killer. I never would have conceived the woman I could have possibly fallen for would be so heartless when my wife, Chelsea, who had been killed by a gang drive-by, didn't have one angry bone in her well-intentioned body.

Verny, or Veronica as she preferred, calmly took out her legal pads and documentation, arranging them on the defense table for easy access. She appeared cool and collected, but Wint had told me earlier in the day she was a wreck. Who wouldn't be? She was defending a killer who had supposedly been her best friend, had tried to kill her husband, and to top it off had told Wint she wished she had killed Veronica. Now, Veronica would have to defend her client, the client who wanted her dead.

Wint and I argued with Veronica to not defend Jenny, but sadly, her hands were tied due to the unbreakable clause for their employees. Kent Yelton, a partner of Manfield & Hyde, pleaded with Jenny to have another creditable legal firm defend her, stating it would be in her best interest to go elsewhere. But she was adamant on having her own firm defend her. Veronica's father and managing partner of Manfield & Hyde, Luther Hyde, said he'd tried to offer some form of compensation for Jenny to go elsewhere, which seemed unbelievable seeing how money-hungry he was, but as Veronica recited verbatim with Jenny's cold blank eyes, "You can keep your money, Luther, because this is going to be worth more than all the gold in Fort Knox." If that wasn't chilling enough, Jenny had then turned her attention across the table to Veronica. "I'm not done playing with you yet, hon. The fun is just beginning."

I continued to watch from afar as Veronica made last minute preparations, scribbling and crossing out notations on her yellow legal pad when I caught a glimpse of her fragility shining through. Wint had

9

warned me Veronica only had one tell he knew of after six years of marriage when she was feeling distraught or frightened, and I just saw it. Most people would have thought it was nothing or would have even missed it, but I knew she was feeling like a skier trying to escape an avalanche. She turned around in her chair to scan the courtroom when her eyes connected with mine. I saw her smile with a slight nod and a long blink. These three movements alone would mean nothing, but in succession I knew she was hanging by a thread.

All I could do was reply with the same casual gesture. By the way she cocked her head, I was pretty sure she got the message. We stared in silence for a few seconds as all the commotion in the room seemed a light year away. We broke our gaze as I quickly said a prayer for God to help her as the guards brought in the defendant in her sleek, flattering black pantsuit and pixie haircut.

"Ready for some fun?" Jenny asked in a chipper voice that only Veronica could hear from the way she masked her face with her hand. The cheerfulness caused Veronica's spine to shiver. It sounded more like they were about to have a slumber party with pillow fights and makeovers than a somber murder trial. Veronica didn't respond, but continued to write a few notes. Jenny leaned down to whisper in her ear, "Dear, if you don't play nice, I can't guarantee I will either. Now, smile for the news cameras. They're watching."

Veronica laid down her pen and looked into Jenny's eyes -- the same pair of eyes she'd looked into on her wedding day when Jenny was her maid of honor. She noticed that the friendliness she once saw had a new jagged edge. "I will not."

"Honey, if you don't do your best to get me off, I may have to take matters into my own hands. And next time, no one is going to stop me. Now, do your attorney duty and smile at the cameras for your client. You have to look confident while I look sympathetic. Got it?"

"Yes, Jenika," Veronica said, hissing Jenny's Russian name with disdain.

"Never call me that again," she growled as she furrowed her brow. A surge of rage quickly filled her core as she started to breathe deeply, trying to remain eerily calm. The rage washed away like the evening tide, pushing it back into the blackened abyss to take shelter until the wrath would once again be unleashed as a single tear rolled down her cheek. "I hate that name. I just hate it," she quietly said under her breath as she wiped the lone tear away.

Veronica didn't know what to feel, watching her once best friend crumble beside her. This woman had threatened to kill the love of her life, yet she wondered if Jenny had been somewhat brainwashed and coerced by her wicked brother to commit these horrible crimes. If someone had told Veronica six months ago Jenny would be one of the Carbon Monoxide Killers, she would have thought they were nuts. How quickly life can turn on a dime. Once again, her emotions were spinning.

"Believable enough?" Jenny asked with a wink. "I thought so."

CHAPTER 4

"What's happened, Solo?" Elizabeth asked as she squeezed beside me on the already packed pew in the courtroom. Elizabeth Hyde, Veronica's younger sister, and I weren't the best of friends six months ago. To be honest, after our first meeting at Wint's birthday dinner, I wouldn't have held my breath to ever speak to her again. We had a slight disagreement during the dinner party. A disagreement I was unaware of since at the time she secretly had nightly dreams of future events, and I stated I didn't believe people still had revelations. By not believing in people's visions, I was unknowingly doubting her. That night I had a dream. A strange, chaotic dream with various segments of people I didn't know, doing things I didn't understand, in places that were unfamiliar. I chalked it off as just a strange dream until each of the dreams occurred the following day. Down to the tiniest detail.

I didn't believe, even though I knew in my gut these dreams couldn't be a coincidence. A man of faith as myself couldn't ignore mysterious and miraculous events as mere happenstance or luck. I couldn't brush off these visions because they happened the next night as well. I eventually contacted Elizabeth to discuss my newfound ability and ask what I should do with it. I had the idea of helping the people I was dreaming about, whereas Elizabeth had the notion of just watching from a safe distance and notating when her dreams came true. I couldn't sit back and watch people get hurt or die if I knew I could do something. So I started trying to help as many of the people I dreamed about as I could.

Luckily, Elizabeth changed her tune when one of her visions involved my death. A death I dreamed of as well but hadn't realized I was the intended victim. She, Wint, and Veronica came to my rescue before I fell into the Potomac River. I couldn't swim, so drowning would have been inevitable. After that day, Elizabeth and I formed an unlikely bond, mysterious to Wint, confusing to Veronica, and delightful to her boyfriend, Dr. Jeremiah Huffington. We never told anyone of our abilities, but we became partners in this strange way of living. We text each other our dreams and decide our daily plan on how to help as many people as possible.

Elizabeth was a trust fund kid, volunteering a few times a week at a local private school and moonlighting as the significant other of an up-and-coming author and well-known anthropology professor, Dr. Jeremiah Huffington. I was a measly theology student, living off the interest of my wife's life insurance policy and photography jobs I did for weekend weddings or whenever someone wanted my services. So, since our schedules were flexible, we had the ability to change many lives daily. Sometimes we were thanked, but often, the people never knew they were three steps away from death or a paralyzing accident. I didn't do our good deeds for recognition; I came to the realization there was a reason for me having these dreams. I may not have truly understood why I saw what I saw, but I knew beyond a shadow of doubt there was a reason for not having a restful night's sleep anymore.

"Nothing much," I answered. "They haven't even started questioning the potential jury. She has calmed down." I stopped and looked forward at the silent Veronica. "Well, I hope she has," I said as I scooted closer to the gentleman next to me who was sipping his coffee like it was a fine wine. "You're late."

"I know, I forgot to take my gun out of my purse and almost caused a scene at the metal detectors. So I had to run back to my car and stuff it there," she said annoyingly. "Come on, do I look like I'd shoot up this place?"

I looked at her questioningly and she read my mind.

"Rude," she snapped with an eye roll. "Just. Plain. Rude. I mean, if I'd shoot anyone, it would be Jenny. Not the judge. I mean, who

13

would blame me? I bet the judge would even let it slide. He probably has a golf tee time this afternoon anyway. I'd be doing him a favor."

"Favors have consequences," I said.

"Favors have consequences," she mocked in a cartoonish voice. "I feel unguarded without it," she frowned.

"You'll be fine. That bailiff has a gun. You'll be safe," I said pointing to the sixty-year-old man standing in uniform beside the witness stand.

"When's the last time he used it?" she asked snidely. "It's probably rusted out by now. You don't hear much about shootouts in a courtroom anymore."

"When did you ever hear of that as a common thing?" I asked baffled.

"Anyhow," she said, waving off my clearance rack comment with a flick of her Rolex-wearing wrist. "I keep telling her she could just quit her job and go back to work once this nut job goes to prison," Elizabeth replied, trying to control her anger, a trait all the Hyde women had unsuccessfully tried to perfect. She craned her neck to see her sister sitting beside Jenny Ascot. She was about to say something when her attention darted to the coffee-drinking man on the other side of me. "Excuse me, sir," she said as she snapped her fingers inches from his face.

The man in his late sixties and decades-old polyester suit blinked and pursed his lips, acknowledging her snapping fingers with a slight eye roll. "Yes?"

"You see that defense attorney up there?" she asked with a smile, pointing up at Veronica as he nodded condescendingly. "Well, she is my sister, and if you don't quit slurping your coffee like a rabid dog, she will have to defend me next for choking you to death."

"Well," he huffed as he got up from his seat to try to find another spot in the courtroom.

14

"Thank you," she said with a fake southern drawl that oozed charm and whimsy.

"Did you really have to do that?" I asked, slightly humiliated.

"What? We have more room now," she said as she wiggled around comfortably on the bench placing her Michael Kors purse between us. I cocked my eyes at her in disbelief. "What? Did you want Gomer Pyle sitting beside us all day? Just say, 'Thank you, Elizabeth.'" She dug into her purse and pulled out her cell phone. "You know you were thinking it. Good ol' Solo won't say what he thinks, but he was thinking it."

"Anyways," I said to change the subject causing her to smile with my overuse of the word *anyways*. "You know she can't quit her job. Something about a clause in the firm and a possible lawsuit. I don't really understand it, but any time I brought up just not defending Jenny, she tore into me like a lion ripping apart an antelope."

"Same. I've walked away hobbling after her tirade a few times."

"But there has to be something that can be done," I quietly demanded. "I mean, this is like a torture treatment. Defending the woman who wished she had gutted her when she had the chance."

"But you know Verny," Elizabeth smiled, saying the nickname I taught her last year for her older sister. "She's always up for a challenge."

"I just sometimes wish she would walk away."

"It's a pride thing, Solo. Women have to prove themselves more than men do," she kidded as she jabbed me in my side with her elbow.

"Really? Playing the woman card? The way Verny scares me sometimes, I would think she could pass as a drag queen."

"Oh no, she could never do that. No Adam's apple."

We both started to laugh as our coffee-drinking gentleman hissed from three rows behind. "Can you quiet down?"

15

"Who made you the theater police? No one." Elizabeth barked back.

"I'm sorry," I kindly turned around to smooth the tension. "We're just concerned about our friend."

"Yes, I see your concern in your smiles," he remarked snidely.

"Look Fido," Elizabeth barked, starting to whip around as I caught her shoulder to restrain her from looking behind as she uttered a word. It was clearly heard by him which caused his eyes to widen in disgust.

"Well," he huffed in shock.

"Well, I wish for once in her life, Verny would throw away her standards and tell Jenny to go screw herself," I said, trying to divert Elizabeth's attention back to Veronica.

"Well said, Solo. Learn that in one of your Jesus classes?" Elizabeth snickered with an approving grin and head bob.

"Not quite."

"As you would say, 'anyways.' You know the strange dreams I've been having?" Elizabeth asked.

"The black and white video?" I answered.

"Yes," she leaned over to whisper in my ear. "He kills tonight."

I looked up and saw Veronica sit beside the killer I helped catch last year only to realize the cycle was going to start up again. The way Elizabeth had been having these dreams over the last few months, this wasn't going to be a one-time deal. This person had been planning this for a while. "Really? Why couldn't you just dream about something nice," I started to say, but as I was saying it I knew it wasn't either of our decisions what we dreamed. Sometimes gifts have sacrifices. "Give me your phone," I said as I reached into my pocket to give her mine with the details of my dreams from the night before.

We traded phones and quickly devised a plan on who was taking which dreams. Tonight was going to be a partner stakeout. "Why did I have to save your life last year?" she asked with a wink as we returned our phones.

"You'd miss me, I suppose," I said. She lingered in thought for a few seconds as a strange expression overcame her. "What?"

"Oh, I'm just imagining my life without you," she stopped and dropped her phone into her lemon-colored handbag. "I should've let you drown."

CHAPTER 5

"So, how do you think our boys are going to do this year?" Grant Harper asked, speaking of the Washington Nationals, whose season just began a week earlier.

"I keep hoping this is going to be the year, but my family tells me I need to give up and cheer for another team," Collin Diaz said in a defeated frat boy tone sporting a navy polo that showcased his many bicep curls against his Latin-colored skin.

"If you say the Orioles, I will peg you with my stapler," Stewart Weatherby said with a British accent donning his normal button down shirt and bowtie, blue gingham today.

"Oh, I would never stoop that low. Even if I'm being water boarded, I would never say a good thing about the Orioles," Collin said as everyone laughed. "What are you laughing at, Grant?"

"Yeah, but didn't your sister switch?" Jordan Lee asked, walking up sipping a cup of hot coffee. Jordan used to have the typical Asian-American build, but when he started dating a woman with Italian roots, his waist line started to increase with the endless baskets of bread at dinner.

"She only wore the jerseys for fashion," Grant mocked. "She was never a true fan," he continued, stating his case as if his reputation was staked on it. "And she only switched because she married a guy from over there."

"Sure, bud. Keep telling yourself that," Stewart said jokingly. "Sounds like a broken home."

"No, my family bleeds red for the Nationals."

"Everyone's blood is red, you moron," Jordan laughed.

"But…" Grant tried to correct, but his defenses were down. He was usually more quick-witted, but he was off his A game today. Grant never liked to brag, but he was the glue that held the group together.

Whenever he agreed with someone, the other two would follow. Women were drawn to him with his boyish good looks that matured in college, but the guys still remembered him as the goofball they ragged in high school.

"We're just busting your chops, man," Collin said as he turned to leave. "Oh, are we still on for tonight?"

"Sounds good to me," Jordan responded.

"Me too," Grant echoed. "The wife's somewhere over the Atlantic now."

"I'm game," Stewart said getting up to get a refill of his morning joe.

They each parted ways to head to their own cubical or kitchen in the District Department of Transportation. Three of the four guys had been friends since middle school and Stewart Weatherby joined the mix his freshman year of high school when his father was transferred from the Air Force base of Lakenheath in Suffolk, Great Britain to the Pentagon. It was a promotion his father had been dreaming of for years. Even after a decade in the United States, Stewart's accent was just as noticeable as when he had first arrived.

The four of them were as close as brothers. They had been through the highs and lows of high school together. In high school they'd made a pact to always watch out for one another. What better way to do that than to stick with one another? They each went to the University of the District of Columbia and got their degrees in various fields. Jordan Lee graduated with a degree in computer sciences, Collin Diaz with a management degree, Stewart Weatherby obtained business administration and statistics degrees, and Grant Harper earned a degree in political science. They were each smart in their own fields. What one person lacked, another would pick up. They never dreamed they would be working in the same organization in their mid-twenties, but old pacts died hard.

The killer from last night had a pep in his step as he walked back to his cubical, almost humming a new tune. He didn't care about the six messages on his phone or the mountain of emails signaling a long day ahead. His plan was working out nicely. When they left the bar that night, the real fun was going to start.

CHAPTER 6

Elizabeth and I watched from the grandstand as the jury selection was underway. I felt nauseous and jittery remembering the process I went through with my wife's murder trial. Elizabeth must have seen my anxiety as she patted my knee and said a few encouraging words, "Chill man. You're not up there."

Well, maybe not that encouraging, but I knew that was as much sympathy I was going to get from the woman who, just an hour earlier, said she wished I was dead if not in so many words.

"So, how long could this trial last?" Elizabeth asked, looking at her calendar that commingled her volunteer days at St. Mark's Elementary, social gatherings at ritzy places unfamiliar to me, and lunch dates with her boyfriend, Dr. Jeremiah Huffington.

"Who could say? Could be a few days, could be a week, could be a month. Murder trials aren't all like O.J.'s that limp along like an injured dog."

"Well, he had the celebrity status," Elizabeth remarked. "And the TV coverage."

"And the money," I commented. "Money can play a part in the prolonging of a trial. Since Jenny isn't as, well…" I started to say.

"Rich as me," she bluntly finished.

"Yes, since she's not loaded, Wint told me this could be a speedy trial."

"Good riddance to her," Elizabeth said then grimaced.

"What?" I asked, confused by the depressing look on her face.

"Her," she said, pointing up at the defendant's table. "She's going to be a problem."

I looked up at Jenny, sitting quietly still, nodding her head occasionally, and glancing over at the possible jurors with a look of consolation on her face. "Yep, Jenny is--" I started to say as Elizabeth interrupted.

"Not Jenny," she snapped back with a look of annoyance on her face. "Verny."

"Why is she going to be a problem?"

"Solo, do you even know my sister? She doesn't like to lose."

"But, this, this is different," I said in a bewildered tone. "Isn't it?"

"It should be," Elizabeth said digging into her purse to pull out her phone again. "But if Verny treats this case like her career is at stake," she shook her head in disbelief. "She's stupid enough to get that psycho off so she can kill again." She glanced down at her phone and quickly changed topics and tone of voice like she was reading off her grocery list. "So, you're going to take care of the old geezer around three, I'll help the kid at the subway at five, and then we can play it by ear tonight since neither one of us has a clue where the kill is going to happen."

"I haven't had any dreams about a killing going down tonight," I said solemnly. I knew there was nothing we could do tonight but wait for the news report tomorrow morning to see a young brunette had been murdered behind her steering wheel. I could drive all over town tonight, but since we didn't know a car model, time, or even a location, our search would be useless. Who's to say it would even happen around us?

Poor girl.

CHAPTER 7

Veronica stood up and asked a few typical questions to possible juror number eleven when Jenny tapped the table to get Veronica's attention. "One minute as I consult my client," she announced to the court. "What?"

"I like him. Don't ask him so many questions that the prosecution will get worried, but don't ask too few that they will quickly dismiss him either," Jenny quietly lectured.

"I think I know how to do my job," Veronica quipped back.

"Yes, but we need him," Jenny hissed.

"Why? Why do we need that guy?" Veronica asked annoyed and looking up at the other possible jurors yet to be questioned sitting around the room like corpses, deathly bored or napping.

"Because he winked at me near the start of the jury selections."

"You've got to be kidding me," Veronica scoffed, but she knew in her past with jury selections to look for any type of sign to get a read on the juror to win a case. She was used to looking for religious symbols on necklaces and bracelets, name brand emblems on polo shirts, positive body language with eye contact and smiles, and the assertiveness in their tone of voice. She had learned from her father to never overlook anything, because one thing missed could cause a loss. There was nothing worse than a loss. Nothing.

But for the first time in her career, she wanted a loss.

She began her final questioning, moving the banter with possible juror number eleven like a waltz. Once she sat down, she knew she had done her job. He was juror number eleven.

That thought caused her to cringe. She sat and wondered. *Did I sell my soul when I became a lawyer? Or was it when I was born to my father?*

Neither question brought any comfort.

Neither would the answers.

CHAPTER 8

"Ready to head out?" Officer Winston "Wint" Cooper asked his partner of five months, Dakota Peterson.

"Ready," she smiled as they walked down the echoing halls of the Washington D.C. police station that resounded every telephone call and footstep like it was a stampede of wildebeests. Dakota Peterson had made a life-altering change six months earlier when she'd decided to leave her dispatch operator post with the police department and become a full-fledged police officer. The strange thing about Dakota was she had already gone through the police academy and was one of the top cadets in her class, but she'd said she merely went to snag a husband, not a career. When she returned from the police academy, she realized she would meet more male cops as the operator in the office than working the streets, so she'd heeded her mother's advice and traded in her gun for a headset. She flirted for years with Smith Young, a young, cocky detective who only received the title because his parents were friends with the mayor, or friendly with their checkbook during his last campaign. Last October, Detective Young announced happily he was engaged to his reporter girlfriend and it had woken Dakota up. He was just a player like everyone said he was.

Cooper, being the good guy everyone knew him to be, encouraged Dakota to branch out and reach her full potential. He even mentioned the idea of her becoming his partner since his had recently retired and the force had yet to fill the slot. So, after a minute of deliberation, Dakota jumped at the chance. Dying her hair or buying a new wardrobe wasn't the change she needed to fix her situation. She needed a dramatic change – a change to show she was independent and in control of her life.

This change allowed Dakota to shine in ways she never could have behind the headset of helping citizens over the phone. Now she was walking the streets, rubbing shoulders with good and bad civilians alike.

Cooper was eager for the change. This way, he was the trainer instead of the trainee. His dream was to move up the ranks, but apparently he wasn't moving up quickly enough for Veronica's standards. She had mentioned multiple times she could get her father to make a call and he could be promoted, but that notion was a slap in Wint's face. They'd had many fights over this issue because she saw it just as a friendly boost, while he saw it as marginalizing his masculinity and work ethic. "If I can't get a promotion on my own, I don't deserve it," he would say.

"But you do deserve it. You just have to get noticed," Veronica would reply back kindly as she choked down her true stubbornness. "That's networking."

"I will get noticed, and I will do it myself," he would say. "I don't need your daddy's help."

More recently they would have these discussions not at home, but in a therapist's office. Last year Veronica was on the verge of filing for a divorce. They didn't seem compatible. They didn't finish each other's sentences anymore, and the more they looked at one another, they saw resentment more than love.

Another brick in the divide was when handsome, athletic Officer Cooper partnered with the beautiful, newly confident, 29-year-old Officer Peterson. This pairing didn't bide well with Veronica.

"I have a strange feeling about today," Cooper said as they reached their patrol car and he sat in the passenger seat.

"How so?" Peterson asked turning on the car's ignition.

"It's the first day for the trial," he groaned. "It's not going to be a good day or a good week."

"Well," she looked at him trying to find some encouragement in the words she wanted to say. "One way to make it better is to catch the scumbags that make this world suck. You caught Jenny. So, we can catch another one."

Cooper couldn't help but smile sitting beside his partner. She had the personality that would cause everyone to love her, yet she had the skills and tenacity to prove herself as a valuable member of the force. Give her a gun and she could outshoot any man with ten years more experience than her. Other guys in his squad would talk raunchy about Peterson. Sadly, women always had to deal with pigs, but Cooper saw Peterson more like a sister than a lover. He saw the potential in her he wished Veronica could see in him.

No matter how many times he told Veronica there was nothing between them, she still felt like she had some competition. Men treated women like toys, whereas women treated other women like enemies.

CHAPTER 9

Honorable Julian Ogdon banged his gavel in his arthritic hand to silence the court room. He could overlook the pain when the feeling of pride and honor rained over him any time he commanded the room.

He had seen many murder trials in his time, first as a public defender when he was fresh out of law school. He viewed the criminal system cycle like a revolving door of misfits. Repeat offenders were the norm, even though they each claimed they were innocent.

He quickly got a reputation as a public defender for getting thugs off and back on the street. This was the American judicial system, innocent until proven guilty. He had a sinister way of making the guiltiest criminal look like a virgin bride on her wedding day. When he could get broke drug addicts off without a nice payday, the question arose what he could do for clients with a fat checkbook. He soon started his own firm with a lengthy list of high-profile clients on retainer with lots of zeros in their bank accounts. Soon his bank account had lots of zeros as well.

Finally after rubbing elbows with politicians, a few guilty ones he got off from prison time, he was elevated to judge. People said he was a fair judge, or at least the attorneys and criminals whom Judge Ogdon sided with said this, sometimes with a wink.

He enjoyed being a judge, but often wondered if he would ever know when it was time to call it quits and enjoy the rest of his life. He was only 68 years old, and many judges worked well into their seventies or eighties, but he wondered what life would be like without donning the respectable black robe each day. Could his need for admiration and awe be filled by his wife at home making him a grilled cheese on a boring Monday afternoon? Probably not. He continued to daydream of life in retirement as the bailiff swore in the jury.

The jury took their seats after answering the bailiff and Judge Odgon recited the judicial process to the newly appointed twelve jurors as he had done for the last twenty years.

"Members of the jury, your duty here today and during the length of this trial is to determine whether the defendant is guilty or not guilty based only on the facts and evidence provided in this case. Anything you have heard before today should not be used in deciding your verdict. We all know the damage of untruthful social media stories and news reports, so please disregard anything you know of this case. The prosecution has the burden of proving the guilt of the defendant beyond a reasonable doubt. This burden remains solely on the prosecution through the trial. The prosecution must prove a crime was committed and the defendant is the person who committed the crime. However, if you are not satisfied of the defendant's guilt to that extent, then reasonable doubt exists and the defendant must be found not guilty. Remember that this duty you are privy to should be considered an honor. We live in a land of freedom, a freedom that some in this world will never know. I insist each of you understand the process and know this decision is not to be taken lightly. I urge each of you to remain attentive throughout the entire trial." Judge Odgon stopped his speech as if he had given a soliloquy of *Macbeth* waiting for the audience to conclude their applause.

"Is the prosecution ready?" Judge Ogdon asked turning his attention away from the jurors.

"We are, your honor," Jill Stapleton stood up, answering confidently in a flattering navy pantsuit that accentuated her best features. Everything. It appeared the prosecution handpicked a Veronica look-alike to sit at their table and be head counsel to counter Veronica's beauty and charm in the courtroom. When it came to trials, there were always theatrics, no matter the case.

She sat down beside her co-counsel, Angus Staufferson, who gave an approving nod. Angus was a seasoned member of the district attorney's office with twenty years of experience but not the ambition or drive that radiated from Jill. She smiled appreciatively, whispering, "Thank you," before looking over at Veronica as if to say, "We meet once again."

"Is the defense ready?" Judge Ogdon asked, turning his attention away from the prosecution.

Veronica stood up and smiled to Judge Ogdon and the jury, "Yes, your honor. We are ready."

"Splendid," Judge Ogdon said as he glanced down at his watch and saw it was 1:25 p.m. "We will have a lunch recess and return here in one hour for opening statements." He banged his gavel and proceeded to rise as the entire courtroom stood to attention. He couldn't help but relish in the power as he towered over everyone from his bench, watching the crowd before him. He often visualized himself as an emperor at the Roman Colosseum with his arm stretched out and his aging fist clenched with his thumb sticking out. The act of turning his wrist to give a thumbs up or thumbs down sent chills down his back. Life or death hung in his final decision. The sweet nectar of holding the scales in his hands caused his taste buds to dance through his being from head to toe. Oh, how he loved that feeling.

CHAPTER 10

He picked up lunch from a hole-in-the-wall sandwich shop two blocks away from the District Department of Transportation. He didn't want any of his other co-workers to see what he had printed out this morning. It was too early in his day to get a few sideways glances or questioning eyes asking about things that didn't concern them.

Taking a bite of his roast beef sandwich, he let the horseradish cream sauce dance around his tongue. He looked around the deli, and making sure the scene was secure, he pulled out a tightly curled sheet of paper from his satchel. He unwound the paper, placed it on the recently wiped tabletop, and brushed it flat, placing salt and pepper shakers on the four corners.

A smile developed on his face as he looked down at the Washington D.C. map with blue dots placed sporadically on varying street intersections throughout the metro area. Each blue dot signaled unsafe areas. Each glowing blue circle marked the surveillance cameras that would be in use tonight.

Pulling out a red marker, he started figuring out the maze like a rat trying to find a piece of cheese at the end, except this maze was the path he would take tonight to steer clear of any possible video footage. But unlike most mazes, where there was only one true route, his map radiated multiple red lines each sprouting like tree roots from the same location. It would be a shame to get caught on the first night. His mother trained him better than that. But sadly, she never thought her years of teaching and planning would help him rid the world of spineless, shallow, corruptibles. She wouldn't be proud of the end result, but she would be very proud with the preparation spent before it.

He marked three bars within a block radius of his starting point for the night, but he had one in particular he wanted to get to tonight.

Luckily, in the city of democracy, politicians needed many nice watering holes to drown their regrets and remorse. It helped them forget about the constituents they vowed to protect when their own agenda and goals took limelight on their stage of ambition and power.

He flipped the map around, looking at his various paths from a different angle, making sure he didn't miss anything that could lead to an untimely end of his revengeful entertainment. This was just the first night. Hopefully, there would be many more ahead.

Many more.

CHAPTER 11

"What did she say?" I asked as Elizabeth returned from a quick word with Veronica outside Jenny's holding room during their lunch recess.

"Why are you here?" she questioned patronizingly.

"I, uh, I was just waiting on you. I'll leave to go find the old man in a few minutes. I still have time. Kenwood's not a far drive from here," I stammered confusedly, wondering why Elizabeth was being so rude.

"No, that's what Verny said to me, 'Why are you here?' She sounded ticked I came. Yet," she stopped and stared at me quizzically, "she was actually quite keen on you being here."

"Keen? Elizabeth, who says keen these days?" I laughed, already knowing the answer.

"I've been hanging around Jeremiah too much lately. He's changing me," she said in a scared tone. "And the scary thing is, I don't even realize it. It's like…" she stopped to come up with some analogy, but from the blank expression on her face, she couldn't think of one.

"Oh. My. Goodness. You're speechless!" I said shocked, with a playful jab. "You are literally speechless. I never thought I would see the day that--"

"Yeah. Yeah. Yeah. Whatever, Solo. Big whoop! You got me. I'm speechless. Is it really the end of the world?"

I stared at her wide-eyed, because in the last six months of knowing her, she'd always had a quick-fired remark and another one on the back burner ready to go in case the first one didn't sting enough. "Maybe not the end of the world, but certainly a paradigm shift."

"Erosion. It's like erosion, Solo. Jeremiah is gradually eroding away my self identity till nothing is going to remain except what he wants to remain. Like California."

"You're getting a little slow," I laughed.

"Didn't you like the California bit though? How the scientists keep saying California is eventually going to just fall off the west coast. That was pretty quick," she smiled fragilely, wincing a little in embarrassment. "I need coffee."

"Yeah, I liked that bit if it was true erosion causing that, but it's not erosion. It's the San Andreas Fault."

She looked stupefied I had corrected her. This little peon of a photographer and theology student had corrected an Ivy League-educated socialite. All I could do was laugh.

"Stop it, Solo. It's just not been my day. Hell, it hasn't been my month. And now I know someone is going to get killed tonight, figuratively on my watch, and all I know is she's a brunette in a car going to get shot in the head. Not the best way to go."

"I know," I tried to console, but I was still reeling from her California statement. "But you do know that's a myth. California isn't going to fall into the ocean one day."

"Why do you have to keep pecking away at that? You've already proven yourself to be right. Even though Jeremiah made me watch some documentary on it a couple of months ago. So, who's to say what's going to happen in the next million years?"

"Well, the men who came up with their cliff falling theory will never see it happen. So, right now, I'm the one that's right."

"Fine," she huffed in mocking defeat. "You are right."

"Was that really that hard to say?" I smiled as we took a seat outside the courtroom.

"Once! You were right once. Don't get all cocky about it. Geez, you would think you just found the cure for cancer or something," she said, rolling her eyes.

"But I discovered something new. You can be speechless," I said with a hearty laugh. "No, wait, I made two discoveries. Being speechless and being wrong. If that's not on the scale of finding the cure for cancer, I don't know what would be."

"You know what, Solo?" she looked at me wickedly.

"You know you love me," I winked as I looked down at my glowing Timex watch I'd had since middle school, noticing I had a little bit of time to get a quick bite before rescuing 82-year-old Stephen Klein. "Well, I'm off to save Mr. Klein. Do you think he's related to Calvin? I could use some new underwear."

"Calvin doesn't put Mickey Mouse on his briefs," she remarked with a grin.

"That's the girl I know and love," I smiled and walked away. I got about halfway down the courthouse hallway when I turned and shouted, "And they're Captain America now. Mickey was so two years ago."

CHAPTER 12

"Hey Wint, how's it going?" I asked speaking to him on my cell phone as I drove north toward Kenwood, a small suburban neighborhood in Bethesda, Maryland, famous for their cherry blossoms lining Kennedy Drive.

"It's just another day of paradise," he chuckled from the passenger seat of his patrol car as Dakota drove down Massachusetts Avenue. "How'd she do this morning?"

"I was a nervous wreck watching her," I started, speaking of Veronica. "When Jenny came into the courtroom, my stomach felt like it dropped ten stories. Veronica looked anxious, but in no time, she seemed like her old self. Unfazed."

"I've been thinking about her all morning," Wint replied like a compassionate, loving husband. "The nerve of her doing this to Veronica is just," he started, but couldn't come up with an adequate example.

"Bat-eyed crazy," a muffled female voice inside Wint's car shouted.

"Hey, Dakota, keeping tabs on my bud? Keep him safe now," I said.

"It's a struggle keeping up with Officer Cooper," she said very professionally.

"Oh, Officer Cooper," I remarked sarcastically impressed. "She's been your partner for how long and you still make her call you Officer Cooper? Really, Wint? Come on."

"You know me better than that, Solo," he replied.

"No, he's a real drill sergeant. I've already requested a transfer to someone friendlier, like Stalin," Dakota laughed.

"Yeah, yeah, yeah, keep driving, Officer Peterson," Wint said with a smirk.

"Sounds like a good time in your cop car. Next time I get picked up for petty theft or indecent exposure, I'm requesting your fun wagon," I said.

"So, what are you up to? Wint asked.

"Oh, leaving the courthouse. I had to run a few errands this afternoon and Elizabeth was going to stay back and watch Veronica."

"Not smart, Solo. Not a smart move," Wint moaned as he ran his fingers through his short hair.

"Why? What did I do wrong?" I quickly asked. How was Elizabeth staying back and making sure everything went okay not a smart move?

"Elizabeth is Veronica's younger sister. Elizabeth may have good intentions, but all Veronica can see is Elizabeth keeping tally marks for things she may do wrong and then rub them in her face later like an annoying brat."

"They really need to end their feud," I said, seeing a patrol car coming up in the distance on the opposite side of the road. "Elizabeth isn't the same person she used to be."

"Well, Veronica can't see that," Wint said as he stared out Dakota's window to see me driving by. "Was that just you we passed?"

"Howdy," I said jokingly.

"Why are you heading this way?" Wint asked.

"I, uh, I'm meeting a friend for a, uh, a group project for school," I stammered with the worst possible lie.

"Okay," Wint said unconvinced. There was silence on the phone for a few seconds before Wint continued the conversation. "Well, Jill called me a few minutes ago and said to be ready tomorrow. The judge appears to want to get this trial done quickly, so she will be calling me to the stand early tomorrow morning."

"Are you ready for that?" I asked. I knew he was ready. He was a cop that had to testify for cases all the time. Speeding tickets, disorderly conduct, intoxication and DUIs – he was used to being on the stand. It was just the thought of being grilled by his wife that was going to be new.

"I'm ready," he said nonchalantly. "We all know she is guilty. So what if I'm married to the defense attorney who usually tries to ruin my credibility? I don't see Veronica ripping me a new one tomorrow. I see her just asking enough questions to make it look like she's trying."

"I hope so, brother. I really do."

"Me too," Dakota chimed in. "Attorneys make me nervous."

"They're just like us," Wint rebutted.

"No. No they're not," Dakota sassed back. "They've lost a piece of themselves in their line of work. Have you ever heard someone say, 'He's just the nicest lawyer?' People only say that about the losing attorneys who haven't grown their new layer of reptile skin." She came to a red light and turned to look at Wint. "Read my lips. What happens in the courtroom tomorrow isn't your wife. It's attorney Veronica Hyde-Cooper."

I didn't say a word. There was silence from all three of us. I didn't even know how to respond. I was hopeful Dakota was being overly dramatic, but what scared me the most was my other thought.

Maybe she's right.

CHAPTER 13

"Your honor, ladies and gentlemen of the jury," Jill Stapleton started as she rose from behind the prosecution table and made her way in front of the seated jury. She was not new to this. She had been the top of her class at Georgetown. She was quickly rising up the ranks in the District Attorney's office, and some were already pegging her to replace the current district attorney when he retired. Yes, she had the entire package: the irresistible beauty and charm to appeal to the men and the intelligence and fashion to beckon the women to her side. She knew what her many strengths were, and she mixed them with flattery and an intoxicating seduction. She was hiding a few weaknesses, but she hid them very well.

"This case is pretty simple and straightforward. The defendant, Ms. Jennifer Ascot, is guilty of murdering nine people. That is nine mothers and fathers, grandmothers and grandfathers, brothers and sisters, aunts and uncles, friends and colleagues. Nine people lost their lives in one week due to the treacherous plans Jennifer Ascot and Alexei Lechkov devised and executed. Jennifer Ascot is the only one being tried for these murders because Alexei Lechkov was caught and killed as they were trying to abduct and murder another set of victims at the Huntington Metro Station.

"Eight of these deaths were first-degree murders, Burt and Pam Hamilton, Samuel and Marjorie Dunn, Mark and Margaret Hudson, and Ted and Betty Appleton. First-degree murder is when the killers had intentions of murdering these individuals. These murders were willful and premeditated. They were planned out and rehearsed. They wanted to kill them," she said menacingly, stating her case with a flare of entertainment. In a society of Netflix and television reruns, if *Law & Order* was what they wanted, *Law & Order* was what the jury was going to get.

"There is one case of second-degree murder, Mitchell Ebley, where they sadistically bludgeoned this park ranger to death just because he came upon their crime and they had to get rid of him before he could do anything. Second-degree murder means they intended to kill Mitchell Ebley, but it wasn't planned in advance like the other grizzly murders."

She took a step back to assess the jury. All eyes were on her. *Good.* "Ms. Ascot and her defense team are going to try to sway you that based on the evidence, you cannot, without any reasonable doubt, state she is guilty of these brutal killings. They may say her brother, Alexei Lechkov, was the one who killed everyone and she was just a scared accomplice. They may even say neither one of them killed anyone, and this was simply a horrific tragedy." She stopped and turned to look towards the defense table, staring coldly at Veronica, and then back at the jury. "Don't fall for it. She is going to play upon your emotions and her family history to contrive a story to poke holes in our case. Don't fall for it.

"We have police testimony, video surveillance footage, eye witnesses, and material evidence that back up our prosecution that Ms. Jennifer Ascot was a partner in these horrific murders. Don't fall for it! By time we are done stating our case, giving all our evidence, you should not have any reasonable doubt she is guilty on all charges. There are probably more charges we can claim against Ms. Ascot, but these are the charges we can prove without a shadow of doubt. So, as Ms. Ascot's defense attorney comes up and tries to spin a web of 'what ifs' or 'are you sures', remember these four words.

"Don't fall for it."

CHAPTER 14

Why couldn't all dreams be handled as easily as helping Stephen Klein back to his home? I pulled onto Kenwood Avenue and drove up and down the street until I saw the elderly man hobbling in his Yankees t-shirt. Quickly pulling over, I tried to get him into my car, but the stubborn old man didn't want to get in.

After I bribed him with a piece of cinnamon candy I found in my console, I helped him into my car and then proceeded to drive back down the street he was just on.

"Where do you live?" I asked, but he didn't respond. He sucked on the candy as if it was the first time he had tasted the fiery cinnamon hard candy.

"Well, my name is Solo," I began to talk as I slowly drove down the street looking for anything that may have stirred Mr. Klein's memory, but he stared out the window like a kid going for a car ride before naptime. "So, Mr. Klein, you like the candy?"

Once again, he didn't respond. He didn't even flinch at the sound of his name. He was oblivious to my existence. I got to the end of the street and turned around. "I know you live around here somewhere," I said, once again slowly driving past the homes looking for any sign of his home.

Immediately, I saw a frantic, middle-aged woman knocking on a front door of one of the residential homes, waving her arms wildly. It may not have been a burning bush type of sign, but the terrified look in her eyes was all the sign I needed.

Crisis averted.

She was a little freaked out by my actions. "How'd you know? How'd you know?" she kept asking, but she never let me answer. She quickly hugged me and took her father back home as I drove away.

Hope Elizabeth's subway drama is handled as smoothly as mine, I thought as I sat in a nearby coffee shop, waiting for Jeremiah Huffington to arrive.

Jeremiah Huffington and I had a friendship centered on mutual respect. As I sat, I reflected on the many interesting facets of Dr. Huffington. He was a well-known and admired professor of anthropology at American University. He'd authored many bestseller books on varying topics of his expertise, the most recent about dreams and revelations in cultures around the world. Not only was he brilliant, but he had a quirky sense of humor that caused Elizabeth's eyes to roll back into her head numerous times in one sitting, which I greatly encouraged with many thumbs up. He was warm-hearted and caring and yet he dated Elizabeth, which still bewildered my brain almost as much as trying to dissect and unravel the mysteries of the holy trinity. He was all these things and more, yet, when I saw him, I saw him first and foremost as my friend, the atheist. Was I judgmental? Yes. Whereas he saw me just as Solo. He was such a better person than I.

"Good to see you," I said as I arose from my table to welcome my friend.

"You too. Always a pleasure to meet with you, friend," he said with a tone of prim and formality. Elizabeth and I joked, mostly behind his back, but every time I met with Jeremiah, I always felt like I needed to kneel as if approaching a king on my way to be knighted. I didn't know why. He just gave off this air of nobility uncommon in our region, and yet he didn't see this trait in himself. Once again, he was a better person than me.

"So, how say you?" he asked.

I did a double-take with his wording, "How say you? Are you still in teacher mode?"

"Oh, dear me, so sorry, Solo. I've been working on researching my newest book on the various social class systems used in European history and how the class systems are still used today, whether we

41

admit it or not. Fascinating finds. Truly heart-stopping finds," he said with a gleeful smile and wide-eyed enthusiasm. "So, what did you need to talk about?"

"Can't a friend just text another friend for a coffee in the afternoon?" I responded in defense.

"But you don't drink coffee. So spill it," he said.

"Spill it? Has Elizabeth been teaching you again?" I laughed as he started to blush like a four-year-old. "But you're right," I finally admitted. "I wanted to get your take on a hypothetical predicament."

"Purely hypothetical is my third love," he relished as he quickly ordered a green tea with two sugar packets.

"Oh Jeremiah, somehow that doesn't surprise me you have your top loves numbered. I'm not going to ask where Elizabeth is on that list," I laughed as he looked at me suspiciously. "And by that look, you'd better not tell her either."

"You are too much," he laughed as he thanked the waiter who brought him his tea so quickly. "So, what is your situation?"

"Okay, let's say you know something is going to happen. Something that may affect one person or a million. You know it's going to happen, but you don't know the specifics such as where or when or why. Even though you don't know these answers, you still know it's definitely going to happen. Can you rationalize doing something about it or not doing something?"

He leaned back in his chair and rubbed his chin in deep thought. He stared up at the ceiling as if solving a mathematical equation. "I feel there could be other questions that need to be asked, but in a situation like this, the one question with the most lasting effect that is stemmed from your question is, how do you handle the guilt? Because if you are fully weighing the options in the debate of doing something or nothing, it appears deep down, you are trying to figure out which one will give you the least amount of guilt."

"I, uh…" I sat stupefied, as I usually did on the opposite side of the table from him.

"Let me give an illustration," he said as he stirred his tea. "Let's say there is a bomb on a plane. You know there is a bomb on a plane. The question is where is the bomb? When will the bomb detonate? Why is the bomber bombing the plane? If you spend time finding out where the bomb is, out of the millions of places in the world: Austin, Texas; Melbourne, Australia; Milan, Italy; Quebec City, Canada, will this help you with your guilt when you still haven't answered the other questions? If you then figure out the bomb is in Cork, Ireland, but the bomb could explode in ten minutes, ten hours, ten days, ten months, or ten years, you may have more guilt on yourself for narrowing down one of the questions but still not answering the other. This happens during all my tests," he chuckled. "The students always panic more in the last one minute of the test than the first, even though each minute is just as important. But in their viewpoint, the last moments seem the most important and stressful."

"Okay," I said, leaning my elbows on the table to give him my full attention.

"So, let's say for some reason you discover the bomb is going to explode in ten hours. But then you have the question of why is the bomb going to explode? Is it a terrorist killing innocent civilians? Or is it someone taking vengeance into their own hands and bombing a private jet of criminals that are about to wreak havoc on thousands of innocent sex-trafficked children? Would you still stop the bomb if you then thought it would be better to let the bomb kill one evil human?"

"Jeremiah, why do you do this to me? Why?" I groaned with my head spinning like tilting plates on a stick in a circus act. "Can't you just give me a simple yes or no answer?"

"On that question I can. No," he laughed whimsically. "I can't give you a simple yes or no answer," he smiled as he sipped his steaming tea. "I think you know it's never a simple yes or no answer to any question for you, because each answer leads to other ramifications down the line."

"Do you believe in absolute truth?" I asked, knowing this was something atheists had debated amongst themselves for years. "I don't mean to sound rude, but where do you stand on that spectrum?"

Jeremiah looked at me with a twinkle in his eye. "Are you sure you want to know what I think? Aren't you afraid you will look at me differently?"

"You have an uncanny way that allows me to open myself to you. It's like all my guards are down when we talk because I know I can be completely honest with you, and you with me, and we don't try to sway or prove one another wrong. So, I'm not afraid of whatever you tell me. I'm more fearful of when you don't."

Jeremiah sat shaking his head in disappointment. Suddenly, it was like a fragile wall started to build between us. I had just spoken of lowering my guard, and instantly, I felt like I needed one. "What? What are you thinking?"

"Whenever I speak with you, Solo, it just awakens my mind at how messed up the world is."

Another layer of the wall quickly went up. "I'm sorry I caused you to think that, Dr. Huffington, but…" I said as his look of disappointment quickly shifted to remorse.

"No, no, no," he quickly shot out as he shook his head. "I just wish there were more people like us in this world, Solo. We may not agree, but we can still speak without any reservations. Your friendship has shown me that. You have shown me the world can be a better place if people want it to be. Sadly," he stopped to take a sip of his tea, "sadly, most people don't want it. They are content staying in their comfortable circle of friends and family that act and talk like them."

I huffed, relieved. "You started to scare me," I laughed as I quickly shot up my arm to get the waiter's attention.

"Oh dear, did my comment rattle you enough to get a latte?"

"Not quite that much," I smiled as I ordered a ginger ale.

"Typical Solo," he nodded.

"So, you haven't answered my question," I asked, turning the conversation back to absolute truth.

He glanced down at his watch. "I need a little time to collect my thoughts on what I believe on that. Can we reconvene later this week?"

"Wow!" I shouted in astonishment. "I never thought I would ever cause you to need deeper reflection."

"You cause it more than you know, Solo."

CHAPTER 15

The courtroom quickly emptied after Judge Odgon dismissed the proceedings for the day after Veronica's opening statements. She walked back to Jenny's court holding cell, even though she wanted to unwind at home; but she was Jenny's attorney and she always checked in on her client to go over the following day's schedule.

"Well, how'd you think you did?" Jenny calmly asked as Veronica shut the door to give them some privacy.

"Given the fact that you are as guilty as sin, I believe I did a good job," Veronica answered as she took a seat across the table from Jenny.

Jenny stared at her attorney like a scheming lion tracking its prey in the savannah. "Oh, really? A good job?" She smiled snidely as if the words were painful to say. "The way I saw it, you sucked."

"Ms. Ascot," Veronica said, not able to say her childhood best friend's first name. She wasn't her friend anymore. She was a guilty client, just like all the other guilty clients she had defended in her past. "If you want to find another legal counsel, you are free to do so."

"Oh, no Veronica. You're not getting off that easily," she said in a sinister tone, as frigid and smooth as ice. She stood up and paced behind the table like a lion at the zoo in a ten by ten foot cage. Her feet lightly tapped the hardwood floor as a slight humming sound from the air kicking on overhead drowned out the silence. "Tomorrow is a brand new day," she said as she stopped dead at the center of the table. "And it's a day you better redeem yourself. Or else."

"Or else what?" Veronica snapped back. "You're going to fire me?"

"Oh, dear Veronica, are you that naïve to believe something so simple? And something that would alleviate your pain? Tsk-tsk. I thought you were smarter than that. Weren't you all our teachers' prized pupil?" she asked, baiting her subject with her questions. "What would they think of you acting so clueless?"

"Get off it. You can't pin your life's failures on my accomplishments," Veronica chimed in with self-confidence and authority.

"We have a different way of measuring success, Veronica. I had a father that loved me dearly up to his dying day. I had a brother that sought me out after years of separation. When's the last time your father looked at you with even an ounce of approval, let alone a look of love? When is the last time your sister came to your home for no other reason than to see you?"

"Ms. Ascot, I am here to discuss your case. Tomorrow is the start," Veronica stated to say as Jenny interrupted.

"No, Veronica, I don't want to discuss my case," she growled as she planted her hands on the table, leaning down within inches of Veronica's face. "I know what I want, and I'm going to get what I want. Even if I have to break you to get it."

"I don't have to stand for this," Veronica said as she stood up, grabbing her briefcase to leave.

"No, but you need to sit, or I will turn you in to the bar for ethical violations and strip you of your license faster than you can call your daddy, who probably couldn't even help with his guilty hands. Knowing him, he would let you take the entire fall," Jenny said with a cunning smile.

Veronica stopped and turned, "What ethical violations have I done? The firm is defending you based upon the clause in your contract. We aren't violating you at all!"

"Oh Veronica, why do you keep thinking it's about this case? Do you really think I haven't kept track of all our conversations through the years? Do you really think I won't use those conversations to smear your credibility? Do you really think I would let it all slide and allow you to defend me like a criminal off the street and not as an innocent client who has been falsely accused of these brutal accusations? Really, Veronica?"

"You have nothing," Veronica said as she turned to leave.

"Rosenburg," Jenny whispered, causing Veronica to freeze in her tracks. A wicked smile landed on Jenny's face as Veronica turned around to see her ferocious eyes. "Rosenburg."

"You--" she started to say as Jenny kept repeating the name into a haunting melody.

"Isn't that just a beautiful name? It's like music to my ears," she grinned as if she was a seven-year-old girl opening a birthday present.

Rosenburg.

CHAPTER 16

After riding the subway for the last six months with Solo, Elizabeth thought she would have gotten used to everything this mode of transportation had to offer by now. Unfortunately, she still gagged at the thought of the Petri dish colony sprouting freely over every surface of the subway car. It was fine to wear gloves and scarves in the winter months, but since spring was quickly approaching, her attire would soon cause ridicule or even possible alarm. She glanced up at her Gucci leather-gloved hand clinging onto the metal handrails, knowing in good conscience she couldn't be wearing these shields in the sweltering humid summer or she would only be facilitating the problem by giving the germs a nice moist hand to latch onto.

"Blasted," she uttered under her breath.

She exited the red line metro subway car at the Gallery Plaza Station to catch her breath before she had to endure another two stops on the yellow line metro subway car down to L'Enfant Plaza. She marched to the yellow line platform, gritting her teeth at her stupidity for not telling Solo to take this dream so she could have taken the decrepit old man. *How hard would finding a man in a subdivision have been?* Her blood started to boil as she thought how quickly Solo jumped on taking Mr. Klein. *We always split the dreams*, she thought. *You can do this, Elizabeth.*

A gust of wind entered the station as she hurried onto the southbound yellow line metro car. *Where do all you people come from?* she wanted to scream at the top of her lungs as she crammed into a packed subway car. A grungy looking man raised his arm to grab hold of the metal handrail as she caught a whiff of his scent.

She tried to control herself, but she lost.

"Oh, no," she said without any regret. "You put your arm down until you invest in some Right Guard or whatever you people wear."

49

"Excuse me?" he said with breath that hadn't seen minty mouthwash since the Bush administration. The first Bush.

"You need to purchase some deodorant. And while you are there, pick up some mouthwash. And maybe you should invest in some Q-tips as well, since I didn't stutter the first time I said it."

"You know lady, I should just--" he started to say as she pulled a bill out of her pocket.

"Here, get whatever you need," she said with a smile.

"I don't need your cash, lady," he scoffed offensively. His eyes widened when he didn't just see one zero, but two. He quickly grabbed the hundred dollar bill and lowered his arm to hold a nearby pole at his waist. "I'm not doing this because you said so, but it was hurting my arm," he bellowed on the train.

"Mmhmm," she said as she turned her face from his and found a pair of beady brown eyes from a middle-aged woman. "What are you looking at? I'm not giving everyone a handout today, but I will give you a piece of advice. That blouse went out of fashion when my grandmother was buried in it."

"Well, you little," she stammered with a huff.

The subway car came to her stop. "I would really love to hear your opinion of me, but since this is my stop, I guess I will just have to go the rest of my life not knowing. It's really going to keep me up at night." The doors parted and she exited the repulsive train. She turned and waved goodbye to her new *friend*. "Ciao."

Elizabeth pulled out her phone and reread the message from Solo on where to find the person to save. Her phone read 4:49 p.m. At 4:54 p.m. she would see a little boy with a sucker running around too close to the edge of the platform trip and fall onto the tracks. "Where are you?"

She walked up and down the yellow southbound platform, looking for the five-year-old boy to get close enough to catch him before he fell to his death. A train was supposed to arrive seconds after his plunge. Simple enough.

"Come out, come out, wherever you are," she whispered under her breath with a slight chuckle.

She looked up at the train station clock; the next train would be arriving in three minutes.

A ray of hope shined among the darkened station as she saw a gleeful smiling boy holding his mother's hand with one hand and a sucker with the other approach the waiting area. "Momma, is it coming?" he asked looking up at his mother who attentively looked down at her beloved little boy.

"Soon. Real soon."

Elizabeth walked toward the little boy, ready to catch him when he darted toward the ledge. She stood for a few seconds and thought something felt wrong. He was not a rowdy kid running amuck near the edge. They were a good twenty feet away from the edge.

"Momma, is it coming now?" he asked politely.

Elizabeth couldn't hear the mother's reply. The sound of a raging boyish laughter echoed off the station's arched ceiling. Her eyes darted up seeing another five-year-old boy running around with a slobbery, red sucker wrapped in his hand as he neared the edge of the platform.

On the other side of the tracks!

CHAPTER 17

Elizabeth ran away from the well-mannered child towards the stairs that bridged the two yellow line platforms. "Solo, you said southbound!" she yelled as she looked up at the electronic sign blinking that a train was approaching the station. "You said southbound!"

She reached the stairs and dashed up the steps three at a time. At the top, she ran across the bridge of the two sets of tracks. She looked to her side and saw a bright glowing light in the distance of the darkened tunnel. It was getting closer. The train was about to arrive in less than a minute.

She wanted to shout, scream, yell at the top of her lungs to catch the little boy, but she knew she wouldn't be heard over the oncoming train. She could already feel the rumble of the train on the bridge.

She made it across the bridge, running as fast as she could down the stairs when one of the heels on her shoes snapped. "Argh!" she screamed. *Stilettos aren't for running. They're for making you look good.* Tripping down the stairs, she quickly grabbed the side railing before her knees collided with the stairs. She didn't even think twice that she had already taken off her gloves and her bare skin was touching the unsanitized rails. All she could think about was ditching her heels behind and saving the boy.

"You okay?" a young man asked her, but she didn't have time to answer.

She slipped out of her heels as she straightened up. She caught sight of the boy about a hundred yards ahead of her and only inches from the edge. She ran! She had never been one to run and had always thought sweat was an unhealthy occurrence that should be frowned upon. Her heart was pounding as she ran like a life depended on it. The boy's.

She wanted to look behind her, but she knew since the boy hadn't fallen yet, she still had a few more seconds. She could finally see the young boy's face as he smiled. "Get out of my way!" she screamed to the waiting passengers who didn't budge but made rude remarks instead. *Where is your mom?* she thought as she felt a gust of wind coming from behind her. "Get your son!" she screamed, but no one came to his rescue.

The boy looked over at the mad woman running in his direction and his feet tripped. He started to fall down toward the tracks, throwing his red sucker in the air, screaming incoherently.

Not on my watch! Elizabeth thought as she picked up speed, reaching out her hand as far as she could stretch it. She saw the fear in the little boy's eyes and wondered if he could see the fear in hers. Elizabeth couldn't hear anything as a spotlight shined directly on the falling boy as his black hair was ruffled from the gusting wind. She closed her eyes; she didn't want to see what was about to come. She took one more giant stride and reached her hand forward.

It was then she knew the inevitable happened. She felt a sticky glob encase her hand before she tugged as hard as she could.

She didn't care about the goo on her skirt as she clutched onto the black-haired boy panting on her chest. "You're okay," she could barely get out before an ocean of tears flowed down her cheeks.

She didn't even care about her running mascara.

"You're okay."

CHAPTER 18

"Rosenburg," Jenny kept repeating to herself in the comfort of her holding cell for the night. She reclined on her ill-gotten bed that squeaked its rusted-out springs with every move she made. The sound annoyed her for the first month, but she'd gotten used to it. It now semi-relaxed her like her own personal white noise machine, but instead of ocean waves or grasshoppers' legs, the sound of clinking metal soothed her to sleep.

Jenny devilishly smiled as she closed her eyes, regaling in the memory of Veronica's terror-filled eyes when she'd turned around when Jenny said the name from her tainted past. Veronica may not have known what she was doing, but she'd had plenty of time to try to make amends, or even turn herself in. Jenny's heart fluttered with the knowledge Veronica desperately wanted to erase. The treacherous secret Veronica confided to her best friend in their early years of legal work.

"Just breathe," Jenny remembered telling Veronica. "Can you go to the authorities?"

"Who would I go to?" Veronica had asked. "I'm afraid of what he will do to me."

"He wouldn't do anything to you," Jenny had said. "Would he?"

The smile faded from Jenny's face as she realized she was all alone now. If someone had told her six years ago she would be on trial for multiple murders, she would have laughed in their face. She was once the embodiment of happiness and pristine living, even though under the untapped surface she was a swirling current of unbridled rage and revenge. She had swallowed her contempt with a spoonful of her adopted mother's homemade chocolate pudding, but that didn't mean it was going to stay down. All she had to do was remember her true family history.

Her beloved brother had returned after years of separation, since she had been welcomed with open adopting arms and he had been put in the foster care system. He was killed as they were attempting their last kill for the year in October. She had forgotten about her brother after years of costly therapy, but it only took a few minutes of seeing him behind the glass at his parole hearing two years ago to quickly remember their bond. A bond severed after their mother was murdered by their Russian father.

Jenny hadn't wanted to face the reality that her father was the killer, even though her mother's parents had proof. At the tender age of seven, she'd executed the plan her father had devised. She shot her grandparents from outside their home in the bushes, making it look like a drive-by revenge killing for testifying against Dimitri Lechkov, Jenny and Alexei's mobster father.

"Otlichno, Jenika," he'd mouthed to his daughter as he sat at the defense table after hearing of the brutal crime. *Very good, Jenika.*

"I miss you, Papa," she quietly moaned in her jail cell. "Alexei, why did you have to die?" She replayed the pivotal moment in the subway station when Officer Cooper somehow knew they were coming. *What if we jumped him sooner?* she thought. *And how did Solo sneak up behind me, as if he knew something was going down as well? It doesn't make sense.* She had dwelled on these questions each night for the last six months before falling sadly asleep. *It doesn't make sense.*

Jenny fluffed her singular, thigh-sized pillow and curled under the covers of her woolen blanket. She knew she needed to rest because the coming days were going to be packed, and she needed to be on the top of her game. She wiped the depressing thoughts of her deceased family from her memory and brought forward a new name. A name she clung to tighter than any other now. A name she believed was more powerful than God.

"Rosenburg," she said drifting asleep. Just another life that ended too soon.

CHAPTER 19

Sitting in the driver's seat of his Ford Fusion in a back alley off of South East Eighth Street, he smiled at the plan he and the other guys had created for helping Stewart pick up chicks. Each of them were either married, in a relationship, or playing the happy bachelor lifestyle with a different woman each week, all of them except Stewart. They had decided to help their unlucky-in-love friend tonight, helping him with his confidence and skills with the ladies.

But he had another reason for smiling tonight. Romance was not in the air for him. Tonight was going to be the first night to test out his months of preparation as an act of revenge.

He watched as various women walked up the sidewalk and headed into Scott's Sports Bar, but there was one woman in particular he was waiting on. When he was a sophomore in high school, he'd been googly eyes in love with the cutest brunette he had ever seen, Sabrina Latener. After a month of pining after the girl of his heart he got the nerve to ask her out. He still recalled the feeling of dashed dreams when, instead of politely declining, she'd ridiculed him in his sixth period history class.

"Why would you think I would ever want to go out with a boy like you?" Sabrina had laughed wickedly as the entire class joined in with her degrading humiliation. All but his three best friends.

He had sat frozen. How could the girl that embodied the perfect specimen treat him like that? How could she? That night, when he was in his bedroom, he started a list of names to never trust again. Sabrina Latener was on the top of that list.

Throughout high school and college, this list began to grow longer and longer with different colored ink and writing styles. It consisted of reasons for broken hearts from lost loves, backstab wounds from ex-friends, crushed dreams by elitist professors and ignorant bosses, and an ever-growing list of annoying co-workers that caused heads to hurt just by listening to them. It was a hodgepodge list some would say showcased a troubled past, but he thought the list stated empowerment.

He folded the tattered paper and stuffed it back into his wallet when he saw her pull up. He watched her park her beat-up once-white Toyota Camry in the employees' parking lot behind the bar. She walked, not with confidence anymore, but with the wear and tear of years of wrong decisions, like her vehicle. He knew not everyone grew up as privileged as he did and not to look down on others because of this, but he couldn't help but smile. *If she'd only said yes back then, her life could have been totally different now.* Instead of working as a bar waitress, she could have done anything.

Sadly, her obituary wasn't going to be one of glamour like she pretended to have in high school. She may have pretended to have it all back then, but he was about to take it all away tonight.

You should have said yes, Sabrina. I could have blown your mind.
Tonight...I will.

CHAPTER 20

The office was unusually peacefully quiet at Manfield & Hyde since it wasn't even seven in the evening yet. It was nothing to have someone working in the firm all hours of the night. Manfield & Hyde was one of the most sought after law firms for new attorneys because of their prestigious and remarkable history. Unfortunately, they also had a secret reputation that when those same new attorneys signed their employment contract, some said it was worse than signing the devil's book.

Almost everyone had gone home for the night, and Veronica needed a safe place to unwind and clear her head from Jenny's threat. *Rosenburg* echoed in her head faster and faster. She tried to shake off the twinges of fear with her own words, *She has nothing*, or *It was years ago and statute of limitations could apply*, or *Who would believe her, a killer?* No matter how many words she was telling herself to ease the pain, *Rosenburg* echoed twice as many.

She needed to relieve herself of her worries and doubt. She needed to unleash all the nagging thoughts she was having and hear words of encouragement and relief from someone else's voice. She needed to be assured everything was going to be okay. *Rosenburg.*

Veronica sat behind her computer, her hands on the keyboard, but she couldn't move her fingers. She didn't have the energy to work on poking holes in the prosecution's theories. She had theories of her own for Jenny's case. Sadly, she knew the theories were lies. *Rosenburg.*

Staring at the blinking cursor on the screen, she started envisioning letters being typed on the screen. *R.*

"No, no, no!" she told herself, shaking her head to erase the imaginary letter. It didn't work. *O.*

"Stop! Stop! Stop!" she muttered, rubbing her eyes, hoping the letters would disappear. They started coming quicker. *S.*

E.

"Veronica, snap out of this! She wouldn't do it!"

NBURGROSENBURGROSENBURGROSENBURGROSENBU RGROSENBURGROSENBURGROSENBURGROSENBURGROSE NBURGROSENBURGROSENBURGROSENBURGROSENBURGR OSENBURGROSENBURG filled the computer screen.

She grunted, pounding her fist on her desk. The glass figurine paperweight Winston had gotten her as a present for her first year of working at Manfield & Hyde, toppled and crashed to the ground. Veronica quickly ran around the desk and saw the most important piece broken off. Now it was just a horse. She picked up the horn of the magical creature and wondered if her legal magic was gone as well. *Could I carry on? Could I face all the upcoming dirt that may be uncovered from my perfectly cleaned life?*

She was scared, but she knew she needed to tell her superior. She left her spinning office and walked down the hall. She knew he would still be there. He was always working.

She came to his closed door and knocked. "Can we talk?"

His cold exterior bid her to come in with a nod of his head.

"It's about the case with Ms. Ascot," she started as he closed his eyes and rubbed his temples.

"Yes, I heard you blew it today."

"Blew it? Who said I blew it?" she snapped. She didn't blow it. She was exceptional with what she had to work with.

"I heard Jill's opener made your opening statement look like child's play," he said, still not looking at her.

"I did a good job, Dad," she said, raising her voice.

"Don't you dare talk to me with that tone. And I've warned you before that when you are here, you never call me Dad. I am Mr. Hyde to you," he scorned, opening his eyes to gaze upon his employee's weakness.

"Yes sir, I apologize, sir," she said after taking a deep breath. "It's just, she is guilty, sir."

"So," he nonchalantly replied.

"But she killed nine people."

"So, she still deserves a fair trial," he calmly said, shaking his head in disgust. "You've adequately defended other guilty people before and didn't have any regrets in helping them gain their freedom. You have to do the same for her."

"But I don't want to get her off," Veronica meekly said.

"What? What did you say?" His voice rose in a tone Veronica dreaded like she was seven years old again.

"She said she regrets not killing me, sir," Veronica said, her voice trembling with untapped fear. She had kept this emotion buried deep for six months, but tonight she picked up the shovel and started digging.

"But she didn't, did she?" he asked as if that solved the problem. "You look perfectly alive from where I am sitting."

Veronica stood wide-eyed and in disbelief. "But..." was all she could say as her defenses fell like a silk curtain along with the shovel.

"But what, Veronica?" he simply asked, folding his hands on his desk. "But what?"

"But if she is found not guilty? What if she tries to kill me then?" Veronica asked, opening her heart to her father.

"I sometimes wonder where I went wrong raising you," he said passively. "Not everyone thinks about you all the time, Veronica. You're not that important."

The words felt like daggers, not to the back, but to her chest. Words of how her father truly felt about her. *You're not that important* echoed in her head along with *Rosenburg*. The two painful statements swirled around, causing a whirlpool of self-doubt. She stood in the middle, tied to these words like they were an anchor. She felt like she was going to drown, drifting in the revolving frigid waters.

Both of her biggest fears were realized today as she saw the hidden truth in two people she used to trust. They had each disguised themselves for a lifetime. She couldn't tell her father about Rosenburg now. She didn't want to see his disappointment anymore.

"Thank you, sir."

She stepped out of his office with a decision to make. Become a sacrifice for her past regrets? Become a pillar for her future endeavors? Or become something new and unknown?

The sad thing was she didn't know what the third option was. She just knew she had to figure one out, and figure it out soon. She needed something miraculous. She needed something extraordinary. She needed a unicorn.

CHAPTER 21

A wall of smoke from the smoking section of Scott's Sports Bar wafted through the entire bar like a slithering snake. Those with cigars, cigarettes, and e-cigs were oblivious to where their fumes were spreading, but those with sensitive noses noticed once again a non-smoking section was a joke in a room with no barriers between the two.

People loved Scott's, but it was mostly a young crowd of college students and recent graduates who lingered for hours under the lights of fifteen big screen televisions, each showing a different game, unless one of Washington D.C.'s own teams was playing. Then all televisions were showing one of their own. This was not a place for a quiet evening of self reflection or poetry readings. No, this was a place to forget about worries and cares for a few hours. To leave deadlines at the door and pick them back up on the way out.

"What about her?" Jordan asked Stewart, pointing at a blonde woman sipping a Long Island iced tea alone in the back corner of the bar.

"She's cute, but I'm not sure about her," Stewart replied. "It just hasn't been my night," he said downcast. "I've been shot down more times than--"

"But look at all the numbers we got you," Collin interrupted, feeling a kick under the table from one of the other guys, realizing that might not have been the best line as he rubbed his wounded shin. "I mean, pick a few of these numbers and practice talking to the women. You'll get there."

"It just doesn't feel right," Stewart grimaced. "You guys pretending to be me to get their numbers. And now you want me to call these numbers and talk to them. What if they want to meet?"

"Well," Jordan looked around the table for someone else to answer. "I guess meet up with them. Charm the socks off them. You spoke to each of the women before we did, so maybe they'll think they gave you their number." He wondered if he answered correctly, and apparently he did okay by the approving nods around the table.

"Yeah, meet 'em," Grant agreed.

"Fine," Stewart huffed in surrender. "And I'm a little offended how you did your accent of me, Collin. When's the last time I said, 'ol' chap?'" he asked, laughing heartily.

"I don't know," Collin shrugged. "I don't know what Britain people say."

"I've been in America since the ninth grade. I don't even remember what *British* people say either. Just talk normally," Stewart laughed. "But I know I haven't called a bartender 'ol' chap' even once. Do I look eighty?"

"Are you sure? Because I thought I remembered you saying it before," Collin said, nursing his ale.

"I've never heard him say it," Grant chimed in before gulping the last bit of his beer in his defrosting mug. "Nor did he ever say, 'tally-ho', Collin."

"Is this pick on Collin night?" he growled and stood up. "Anyone else want a drink?"

"No, thank you," Stewart said with a wink, "ol' chap."

Collin grinned as he walked up to the bartender and ordered another ale. Stewart flipped through half a dozen phone numbers he received like he was a charity case accepting donations of used socks and underwear.

"Any of them standing out?" Grant asked, looking over Stewart's shoulder with names and numbers written on Scott's napkins. Even in the age of technology, there was nothing like a phone number on a used napkin.

64

"Ginger was," Stewart said, looking around the bar, trying to remember which one she was.

Grant peered his head around the bar, not seeing the attractive woman anymore. "She was the black-haired woman up at the bar in the Nationals jersey."

"No, that was Nikki," Jordan said looking around the bar. "Nikki wore the jersey and Ginger was the brunette who was standing near the back in a pair of tight blue jeans and a Georgetown sweatshirt."

"Yeah, that's right," Stewart smiled. "I remember her." He darted his eyes around the table to each of his friends. "She was beautiful. Said she wasn't looking for a relationship and turned me down." He stared down at the phone number and smiled playfully. "Well, she lied to me, so it's only fair if I lie to her, right?"

"No different," Grant agreed.

Stewart started separating the names forming two piles. Ginger's name was in a pile all by herself. "Who got Sabrina's number again?"

CHAPTER 22

"I don't know what good this is going to do," I said, looking down at my glowing Timex signaling it was too late for me after the long day I had.

"Just humor me, okay?" Elizabeth said behind the steering wheel of her newly purchased, sleek, atlas cedar metallic green 2018 BMW X5. "I've had a hard day too, and I'm just not ready to give up on this girl yet."

"Elizabeth," I replied, "you can't save them all."

She looked over at me with a look of dread. Suddenly, a flash of déjà vu hit me. It was an image just like this, except six months ago Elizabeth and I were in different positions. Elizabeth had been having dreams since she was a young girl yet did nothing with her visions except record them in a journal. When I started having them, I couldn't let the revelations be forgotten, but I had to step out into the unknown and take action. She tried to convince me to leave the dreams alone and let them be, but I couldn't. I couldn't do nothing.

She started to open her mouth when I stopped her.

"I know, I know," I said feeling the weight of the world on my shoulders as well, "funny that I just said that."

"Funny isn't the best word in my opinion," she said, turning her gaze from me and back to the windshield. "Ironic."

"Don't you think?" I smiled, reciting a line from one of her favorite songs.

"Yeah, I really do think," she somberly said in a state of deep contemplation. "What are we doing here, Solo? I mean, is all this a game? Some twisted ploy from the man upstairs? I'm not overly religious, but it sometimes feels like a sick joke, and He's just laughing at our foolish attempts."

"I don't buy that," I said. "Look at what else you did today," I quickly said, recounting the life saved in the subway station.

"But what if that stupid kid was supposed to die? What if he turns out to be a juvenile delinquent? Or a rapist? Or God forbid, a democrat?"

"Really? Why do you always have to throw them into the mix of your rag-tag bundle of unfortunates?"

"Because they are," she answered coldly. "But really, what if God meant for that kid to die? Maybe He knew he was going to be the next Hitler and this was his end game."

We passed through many intersections, looking out the window for anything that looked suspicious, but we were the only thing that looked out of place this evening driving around town with no means to an end.

"I don't think God works like that," I said, reclining my chair slightly to look up through her moon roof.

"Teach me then. How does God work?" she asked matter-of-factly.

The night was beautiful with a few sprinkled stars overhead when we left the city lights in the distance. I didn't know how to respond and I knew if I said anything, it would be wrong in her opinion and mine.

"Did I leave you speechless?"

I didn't answer. I think she knew I was speechless. I have learned sometimes not saying anything is wiser than trying to come up with an explanation or an excuse. My mind is too small to understand all the complexities of God's design. I may not understand it. I may not agree with it. But it doesn't mean it's not right. It just means I haven't figured it out yet. And I probably never will.

"So, are you mad at me now?" she asked as I sat with my eyes closed as she turned down another street, closer to the blinding street lights overhead. "I just don't understand why He would show me a dream and not all the pieces," she started talking as if I wasn't there.

I wasn't sure if it was a prayer or just a heartfelt ramble, but it sounded like one of my many prayers before.

"Can't you give me something helpful? A name, a street, a license plate number? Anything? Anything at all would be nice." She sat silent at a red light as I opened my eyes peering my head out the passenger side window as a flood of memories erupted in my head. "Hey, Solo! Are you going to say anything?"

I slowly turned my head away from the window and leaned back on the head rest. Closing my eyes, I took a deep breath and wished I was a million miles away from here. "Chelsea got shot six years ago tomorrow," I said. "At that corner."

CHAPTER 23

"I'm heading out," Stewart said as he pocketed the random women's phone numbers and bid his friends ado for the evening. "Don't stay out too late," he smiled as he patted Collin on the back and nodded at Grant and Jordan who were across the table.

"'Night, man," Grant yawned as Stewart walked away and shook off the tiredness, "One more round, fellas?"

"If you're buying, I'm drinking," Collin laughed as he watched Stewart exit Scott's.

Stewart headed to the closest Metro station two blocks away. He found himself alone in the brightly lit subway station, whistling a tune he had learned as a small boy in England. He loved America, but there was something about the fond memories from across the pond.

He boarded the mostly empty subway car, pulling out the list of numbers and names with descriptions of each woman he had written on the back. He didn't know what his problem was. He looked up and caught his reflection in the glass. He didn't think he was unattractive. Even Grant had grown out of his awkward puberty years and tuned into a fine specimen. He thought his sense of humor was just as good as Collin's, maybe even better since Collin's resembled that of a sitcom frat boy. Someone had mentioned online dating, but he wasn't ready for that yet. But if he didn't find a woman soon, he might be making a profile on Match.com fairly soon.

He exited the subway train and walked the dimly lit Dupont Circle Metro Station. He smiled at the woman in a glass cage to assist passengers, but she didn't look up from her sudoku puzzle. "Maybe next year women will notice me," he thought as he started walking home on P Street. He came to his three-story townhouse, punched in his passcode, and allowed his facial recognition security system to welcome him home. "Good evening, Stewart," a computerized voice said as the door unlocked.

He threw his wallet and loose change on the kitchen counter before grabbing a bottle of sparkling water from the refrigerator. He thought he may have had one too many drinks, so he tried to counteract the alcohol with some good ol' water.

Falling onto the couch, he turned on the television to see the recap of the day's baseball, since the bar hadn't been showing any games, unless it was the winless game of cat and mouse with single females. He looked up and noticed his interior security cameras. He often wondered why the person who lived in the townhouse before him had security cameras throughout his house, facing every random direction. He could understand putting a camera facing windows and doors in case of a robbery, but one facing the middle of the living room just appeared strange and the one in the bedroom seemed a little too kinky for him. There was one in the bathroom he kept a sock over just in case anything happened and the police ever needed to see his footage. He didn't want the cops to watch his vulnerable moments in the shower or on the toilet.

Rubbing his eyes, he knew he needed to go to bed, but he had to do one more thing before calling it a night. He pulled out the top name and dialed the number. He waited for a female voice. He heard one, but it was just her voicemail.

"Sorry I missed ya. Leave a message and I'll call you back real soon. Later," she said in a chipper voice.

"Hey, Sabrina," he said as he coughed nervously. "This is Stewart. We met tonight at Scott's, and I just wanted to see if you would be interested in meeting me sometime this week to get to know one another a little better. Call me. Once again, this is Stewart."

He didn't think she would return the call, but at least he'd tried. *I've got to start somewhere*, he thought. He pulled out the remaining numbers from his pocket and placed them in the candy dish on the coffee table. Maybe one of these numbers would reward him with something sweet.

Tuesday
CHAPTER 24

The remaining guys left the bar about an hour before last call. They weren't college kids anymore able to stay up all night and drink and sleep late the following day; they had responsibilities. They each parted ways, heading either to the nearest bus stop or metro subway station. All but one.

The lone man who walked the lonely streets slinked his way in the shadows to a location five blocks away at a free after-hours parking lot. He unfolded his map with red lines throughout the city and set it in the passenger seat. He had memorized the route Sabrina would most likely drive to get home, but he didn't want to be outsmarted if she was not going directly home. He had marked various other streets he could drive down tonight if need be without any city surveillance cameras recording him.

He pulled out of the parking lot and slowly drove the deserted streets towards Scott's Sports Bar. He looked down at his clock and realized it was still before closing time. He drove back to the nearby alley he'd hid himself in earlier in the evening to wait for Sabrina to return to her vehicle and leave for the night.

He turned off the ignition and sat in perfect stillness beside the trash bins and a family of rats. Glancing over at the passenger seat, he saw the rifle loaded and ready with the safety latch on. He slid the barrel into the unseen hole, protruding the muzzle out a quarter of an inch from the key hole. Suddenly, his infotainment console awakened with a camera image of where the rifle was pointing.

A tiny red light shined on the screen, showing where the bullet would go if it was fired into the brick wall. He maneuvered his right hand, moving the rifle in all directions, watching the red light dance around the screen like a laser show at Epcot. His technology was all set. When he pulled out his rifle, the video image quickly disappeared, leaving him to sit in darkness except for the light from the streetlight twenty feet ahead.

He pulled out his disposable phone and typed Sabrina's memorized cell phone number for when he was ready to give her a call. He glanced down at the map, making sure he hadn't forgotten the journey he would drive tonight.

He hadn't forgotten. He was ready.

He opened his glove compartment and put on his Baltimore Orioles hat and a pair of aviator glasses, taped on a thick brown mustache, and hung an evergreen scented air freshener around his rearview mirror. If his image was caught on a picture or video, they would not ever think this was him. They would think it was another man on the tattered page of names in his wallet.

Reaching under his driver's seat, he pulled out a magnetized license plate. He got out of his car and stuck this license plate on top of his. No one would ever know this vehicle was actually registered under a partnership in Nevada that only had this vehicle as an asset. For all they would know, it was registered under one of his backstabbing best friends from the tenth grade who drove the exact same vehicle, even down to the bent back fender. He stepped away from the rear of the car, returned to the driver's seat and thought, *You should've never done that to us, man. Never.*

Replaying his plan in his mind, he wondered if he would really do this. Last night was a trial run and he passed, but he wondered if he could really pull the trigger tonight. Could he take someone's life for something they did over ten years ago and frame another? Would he have regrets?

The questions continued to come faster and faster, causing doubt to quickly rise like a fever. "It's not too late to back out," he told himself, but as he said the words he watched Sabrina walk past on the sidewalk across the street to her car.

He watched as she walked under the streetlights like she'd strutted down the hallways in high school. She had always welcomed the whistles and hollers from the guys. That was how she got her kicks, apparently – always needing to be the center of attention, no matter whose dignity it cost. Suddenly, all the questions and doubts he faced dissolved like the last snowfall they'd had three weeks ago.

Spring was in the air. Spring was all about rebirth. He was ready to give in to his own rebirth. He didn't care who he took down in the process. They certainly didn't care about taking him down a decade ago, so why should he care now?

"The old, scared high school kid is gone, Sabrina. Your words aren't going to hurt anyone ever again."

He turned the key to start his ignition and waited for her car to leave the parking lot. He quietly glided his car forward without turning on his headlights. He wasn't ready to be seen yet. She looked both ways before pulling out and entered Southeast Eighth Street.

He took a deep breath, turned on his headlights and proceeded down the rest of the alley. He turned onto the same road, staying a safe distance behind Sabrina's vehicle. *I see you, Sabrina. Do you see me?*

"Turn left, turn left, turn left," he chanted to himself hoping the route he planned was the one she would drive.

It was.

She turned left.

CHAPTER 25

He continued to drive a block behind Sabrina. He didn't need to get too close that early. He always wanted to wait until there were no vehicles on the road when he made his final move.

He picked up the cell phone he had in the cup holder and pressed the small green button to send his call. He wondered if Sabrina would pick up an unfamiliar number, but if she was the same girl as in high school, any phone call meant someone wanted to talk to her.

"Hey Sabrina," he said in a British accent he had perfected from years of watching *Dr. Who*.

"Hey," she answered sounding confused. "Who is this?"

"Have you forgotten me already?" he laughed like an old friend. "It's me, Stewart, from the bar tonight."

"Stewart, yes!" she exclaimed like a cheerleader.

He rolled his eyes annoyed. She hadn't changed since high school.

"Hey dimples," she laughed as she tossed back her hair, forgetting she was on the phone and he couldn't see her. Or so she thought.

"Yes, yes, I know it's soon, but I just wanted to let you know I was thinking of you."

"Really? Aww," she playfully flirted. "You're so sweet. I was thinking of you too."

Liar, he thought as he slowly got closer to her vehicle. "No, you weren't. You probably get hit on by many fellows each night," he said charmingly.

"But none with as sexy a voice as yours," she replied, trying to hook him in.

As he, too, was dangling a bait of comfort in front of her, he started to smile as he thought, who's playing who now? "Sexy?" he quietly laughed. "You American women are always so kind," he said warmly, disgusted with his own words.

"Oh, yeah, I could listen to you for hours," she gushed.

Hours is what you don't have, he thought. "Oh, come on," he kidded. "I get tired of hearing my voice. You are just being too kind."

"Oh, no, there is something about an English accent that just does something to me," she added. "You could read the Scott's menu and I would listen to you."

"Well, I will have to remember that for when our conversations go dry," he kidded. *I really hate myself now*, he thought.

She came to a stoplight, still on the path he had planned as he pulled up beside her. He glanced over to see her smiling, checking her lipstick in her rearview mirror, and fluffing her hair.

"So, where are you? Want to meet up? It's still early," she said.

"Oh, I'm in the middle of something right now, and I've got work tomorrow. I'll take a, how do you say it, a rain check?" he lied, pushing his rifle though the keyhole as the video image magically appeared.

"But I really want to see you," she moped.

"Look to your left," he said.

"What?" she quickly asked in a confused and heightened tone.

"Get some rest. What did you think I said?" he smiled wickedly thinking she was too easy to mess with.

"Oh, I thought you said something else. I guess I do need to get home, but I would rather spend the night with you," she said defenselessly, almost begging.

The light turned green and they both proceeded up the road. He glanced around in all directions, looking down the roads in the intersections to see if any cars were coming. He was clear. No headlights were in his rearview mirror. No oncoming lights were up ahead. They had left the busier part of town of restaurants and clubs and entered into a quieter street of apartments and storefronts closed for the evening.

"Not tonight, Sabrina, but maybe another time," he said as he saw the stoplight ahead was red. They both came to a stop as he aligned the rifle. He lowered his hand to raise the rifle barrel up so the red light on the video shined on the side of her skull. "Sleep well," he said, watching the opposite streetlights turning from green to yellow. In a few seconds he would have a green light.

"You too," she said, not remembering his name from the beginning of the conversation as she ended the call.

"Bye," he said as he pulled the trigger. The bullet left the barrel of the gun, broke through her driver's side window, and smashed into her brunette hair. She didn't have time to react. She was dead. Her body slouched forward as it was restrained in her seatbelt as the streetlight turned green.

"Drive safely," he wickedly laughed as he turned his car left to casually flee the scene. He drove down two blocks as he watched her car slowly cross the pedestrian walkway entering into the middle of the intersection.

He quickly turned right, gunning his engine to get out of the area as quickly as possible. But before returning the secret car to the garage that had a spot on the fourth floor under the partnership's name with which the annual rent was paid for with cash, he needed to drive by his old friend's current home.

In case anything was seen, he needed to be seen driving to his scapegoat's neighborhood. Just as a precaution.

CHAPTER 26

Rolling out of bed, Elizabeth's head still spun from the discoveries of the night before. She felt an emptiness in her stomach from the number of times she'd hurled the contents of her stomach into her toilet throughout the night. She knew she needed to eat something, anything, but she couldn't. She had tried to keep a few crackers down, but within a few minutes, the cheddar Goldfish just came back up, swimming with vengeance.

She wondered what knowledge from last night made her feel worse, but deep down, she knew what it was. And it sickened her to the core.

She tried to shake off the events from last night and started typing the incidents in the dream she just woke up from. She'd had a few dreams last night and one dream in particular.

He's going to kill again tonight.

Racking her brain, she tried to remember any key details of the dream. "Come on, Elizabeth, there has to be a street sign," she said to herself, replaying the dream, but no matter where she looked, no street sign was found.

"A time? You have to have seen the time." She closed her eyes and she could see the inside of the killer's vehicle, but his infotainment console didn't show the time or date, just the image of the redhead in the car next to him.

"Okay, okay, okay," she started mumbling. "Landmarks? Any landmarks?" She scanned her fleeting memory for store signage, light posts, trees, or anything that could possibly give her an idea. Nothing.

"Come on!" she screamed as she dug deep into the trenches of her dream. "Why are you doing this?" she screamed at the top of her lungs when an image flashed and a pleasing aroma from the kitchen wafted into the room. "Starbucks! She had a Starbucks coffee cup she was sipping on."

She typed the little bit of information she had into her phone, but it didn't bring her any comfort. There were dozens of Starbucks in D.C. scattered around all parts of the city. She knew the coffee cup wouldn't do her any good. For all she knew, it could have been something she ordered earlier in the day, not moments before her death. *Hope Solo had a dream*, she thought as her stomach did another somersault.

She jumped out of bed, kicking one of her journals open as she ran to her master bathroom, ready to alleviate whatever came up, but she was empty. There was nothing else to throw up. She splashed some water on her face, gargling a little of the nasty taste away before walking back to her bedroom.

She saw one of her past dream journals laid open on the floor. She picked it up and felt the deepest remorse she had ever felt. She had prayed to God, speaking to Him with frankness like they were old acquaintances on her anxiety-sickened drive home last night. She'd ransacked her closets looking for her old journals through the years. Her hands still trembled as she held the one she'd been looking for – 2012. It was open to a page she'd stared at for hours last night.

April 10, 2012

A bear attacks a jogger in the woods. He won't die, just badly wounded. (Check)

A school bus crash injuring three elementary kids. (Check)

A newspaper reporter shot and killed by drive-by. (Check)

Elizabeth had dreamed about Solo's wife, Chelsea, the night before her death. She felt her stomach drop again. She could have possibly stopped it. She could have tried to save her. *Chelsea could still be alive if I had done something.*

Anything.

But all she'd done was check to make sure her dreams happened like all the other ones.

It did.

CHAPTER 27

"911," a female operator said in an aloof tone.

"There is a car outside my apartment that just ran up on the sidewalk," a drowsy man said peeking through his third-floor apartment blinds.

"Is there anyone hurt?" the operator asked, quickly running down her questions on the computer.

"I, I don't know," he yawned. "The car is still running, and I think I see someone in the front seat, but I can't be sure."

"Where are you?" she asked, getting ready to announce the call to a dispatcher nearby.

"On the Corner of Half Street and M Street Southeast," he answered squinting his eyes to get a better look at the situation. He couldn't see anything but a figure. He went back to his bedroom and grabbed a pair of glasses, seeing the world in focus. "Okay, I got my glasses," he said to the operator as he raised his window blinds, not caring if anyone saw him in blue briefs. "I can't tell for sure, but it looks like someone is leaning on their steering wheel. Probably too drunk to realize they jumped the curb."

"Sir, I have a unit on their way," the operator said. "They should be arriving in two minutes. Do you see anything else?"

"Not from where I am standing," he said looking up and down the deserted street. "Probably just a sleeping drunk."

"We get too many of those calls," she replied taking a gulp of her lukewarm coffee that had been sitting on her desk two hours now. "More than you would think. Will you please remain on the line until I get confirmation the officers have arrived?"

"Sure," he replied scratching his pillow-styled hair. "Do I need to go down and talk to the cops? I didn't see anything. I just walked by my window on my way to get a glass of water."

"Can you give me your name and contact information in case they want to speak with you? I think once they arrive you can go back to what you were doing."

"Oh, good," he said quickly giving her the information she requested. "Hey, the cops just arrived."

"Yes, I just received word as well. You have a good evening, Mr. Tisdale."

"You too," he said as he ended the call. He watched as the patrol car arrived on the scene with their red and blue lights spinning wildly on his quiet street. Curiosity got the better of him, like anyone else who would have called the police in his situation. He stuck around to watch the outcome, wondering if they were going to make the drunk wake up and walk a line like they did in the movies.

The police officers stood by the white Toyota Camry and quickly spoke into their two-way radios. By the expression on the two cops' faces, he knew it wasn't good. They wouldn't be waking up the poor bloke up any time soon. He went back to his bedroom only to return with a chair. He wouldn't be going back to bed.

CHAPTER 28

Detective Smith Young, a 33-year-old, slightly demoted member of the Washington D.C. police force arrived on the scene. He and Officer Cooper weren't the best of friends for multiple reasons. Whatever Officer Cooper epitomized as a police officer, Detective Young was the complete opposite. Detective Young was rumored to have only been made detective after his parents gave a substantial contribution to Mayor William Ernst's political campaign, a clear case of quid pro quo.

Detective Young was a semi-capable police officer, but he didn't have the experience or skills to make detective that quickly. His lack of knowledge and discipline was evident when he'd had a fiasco last October during the Carbon Monoxide Killers spree. He had tackled a woman he'd assumed to be one of the Carbon Monoxide Killers without getting any information. He went on his gut instincts, which were usually wrong, and once again, it led to an internal investigation of his actions on that night. The city was lucky they weren't sued, since the young woman was injured when his six foot three, blond linebacker build collided with her petite frame.

He was lucky he wasn't fired for his unprofessional outburst, but he got his pride wounded when he was switched to night shift duties.

"What do you have?" he asked as he approached Officers Utley and Parsons, who were the first ones on the scene.

"Crime scene has already cordoned off the two blocks from where the shooting apparently happened down there at the light," Officer Parsons said pointing a block away. "It looks like someone shot Sabrina Latener at the light from the pieces of glass found on the ground. Then her car must have driven through the intersection until it ramped up on the curb. There are no witnesses."

"What about any surveillance camera feed from the lights?" Young confidently pointed, trying to make the two officers appear foolish.

Officers Parsons and Utley had dealt with Detective Young multiple times before. They agreed with the rest of the force that he was useless. "The cameras on these lights weren't working this evening," Officer Utley replied. "We have already looked around the scene for any stores that may have had some security footage, but it appears most of the buildings around here were apartment buildings. Unless they have some nice security cameras, no one we have spoken with has seen anything."

"Well, have you asked all the residents in the area?" Young barked.

The two officers looked at each other and then down at their watches. "It's 3 a.m., detective," Officer Parsons said. "If someone had seen something, I think they would have called this in. Mr. Tisdale called this in thinking it was just a drunk driver. Most people were asleep when this happened. You can speak to him yourself if you'd like. He's up there watching from the third story window."

"I may do that later," Young replied. "So, does crime scene have anything yet?"

"They just arrived a little bit before you," Officer Parsons answered. "They are still taking pictures of the crime scene. The Medical Examiner's office is on their way too."

"Good, maybe they will be able to tell us something," Young stomped off, swallowing the last bit of his coffee before throwing his cup on the ground.

"Young, that's littering," Officer Utley shouted from behind as Young turned around annoyed and quickly picked up his trash, looking for a nearby trashcan.

"What is the medical examiner going to say out here?" Parsons snickered to Utley. "A girl was shot and killed a little while ago."

"Wish my parents were rich," Utley said smiling as they walked up to the crime scene unit to offer their assistance.

CHAPTER 29

Wint smiled, nodding his head and talking, but nothing was heard. He looked pleasant as he continued to talk, using his hands and pointing one way and then another. He was dressed in his police uniform as he sat, resting his hands on his thigh, his relaxation evident.

Suddenly, a state of terror flushed over his face. Wint froze, his eyes darting around the room like he was trying to follow a bee. His hands started gripping his knees in agitation, and he started talking, shaking his head in frustration. He was talking faster now. As if his life depended on it. He lifted his hands from his knees and clung onto a wooden railing. His lips started quivering as his eyes started to fill with tears. None of them fell, but they were on the verge. Suddenly, he closed his eyes and bowed his head. After a few seconds that felt like hours, he looked up and stared directly into the void and the silence ended.

"I didn't know."

The words lingered in the air as he continued to look forward. No movement. No more speaking. Only an occasional blink. Then another blink with one lone tear.

The scene faded to black and switched to a sunny park setting. The sound of a cracking baseball bat reverberated into a parked car of a white Cadillac Escalade.

"You a cop?" a male voice asked with a wad of gum in his mouth.

"No," another male voice answered, this one a little huskier. "But would they really tell you?" he laughed at his own joke as the other guy reached for his concealed weapon stuck into his waistband. "Hold up," he quickly said, raising his hands. "I was only joking."

"You got the money?" the first man asked, rolling his eyes at the kid.

"Yeah, you got the goods, Chuck?"

"Never. Ever. Say my name," he commanded.

"Sorry. Evan said you were the best."

He reached into his console, pulling out a plastic sandwich bag, a quarter of it filled with white powder.

The college kid took off his shoe and then his sock, pulling out a wad of hundreds. "Sorry for the smell," he kidded.

"Money is money," he said unfazed.

"So," the college kid started to say when the dealer stopped him.

"Get."

"Huh?" he asked clueless.

"Get out of my car!" he angrily said, looking up seeing two young boys with baseball bats and gloves heading their way. The college kid got out and walked carefree to his Ford F150 pickup truck.

"Who was that, Dad?" one of the kids asked, getting into the backseat of the SUV.

"Just a client, Ty. Just a client," he said as he made sure his sons were buckled in before he started to drive away. "You had a good hit in the third."

"Yeah, but they caught it," Ty answered with a frown.

"You'll get it. You just got to keep practicing," the dad encouraged as he passed a green park sign with white letters. *Guy Mason Recreation Center.*

"I will, Dad."

I woke up and quickly grabbed my phone next to the bed and started typing the details of the dream. I was confused why Wint looked so freaked out in the first dream, so I knew first thing in the morning I needed to give him a call. I started typing the details of the drug deal when my heart sank. Chuck seemed like a good guy with his two sons.

Even good guys do bad things sometimes. But then I thought. *Can good guys stop doing bad things? Could I get him to stop? For his kid's sake?*

I laid my phone down on my nightstand and tried to fall back asleep, but I knew it was an impossible task now that I was awake. This was going to be a hard day. Just like the last six April tenths.

This day never gets easier.

CHAPTER 30

Veronica woke up early. Although, she technically never went to sleep. She'd waited up for Winston to tell him what had happened, but when he arrived home, fear seized her. She couldn't tell the secret she had been hiding from him for six years. She wasn't ready to see that look of shame and distrust yet. She knew she would see it soon enough. Wint had walked through the living room with a smile, but Veronica pretended to be asleep.

She hated she once again hid from him, but she didn't want to see his smile. It would break her. She had reclined on the couch, with her laptop on her lap as she felt something hover over her. She'd wanted to open her eyes, but she knew it was Winston.

"I'm so lucky," he had whispered as he'd tenderly kissed her forehead. He had picked up her laptop, closed and laid it on the end table so she wouldn't drop it in the night. He'd found a cashmere afghan in their ottoman chest and gently placed it over her, tucking her in. "Good luck tomorrow, my love," he said as he bent down one more time to kiss her, this time on her lips.

She had wanted to throw her arms around his neck and tell him the same thing. The last few months of marriage counseling had been hard, but in these moments when she saw her husband for who he really was, when he didn't know she was watching, she fell even more madly in love with him. They may have their problems, what marriage didn't? But it was times like these when he showed his sincere self with no motive but to love his wife, that she solidified her realization she had a good one.

She'd lain on the couch for an hour with her eyes closed. She'd hoped she would somehow drift to sleep, but she knew she had too many demons chasing after her to rest easy last night. When she'd thought Winston was sleeping soundly, she reached over and grabbed her laptop. She didn't open it right away; instead, she started relieving the frightening words Ms. Ascot had said to her right before she left. If she thought Rosenburg was chilling, these words almost caused her heart to stop.

She tried to think of a way to please Ms. Ascot so she wouldn't mention Rosenburg to anyone, but also show dignity. She'd thought and thought, but no matter where the trail led, it always forked. She couldn't do both. She couldn't please both of them. She knew only one of them really mattered at the end of the day, but Ms. Ascot had too much leverage to ignore. Sadly, she knew what she had to do. It would be hard, but in the long run, it was the best option. She just hoped Winston would eventually see it that way.

She had opened her laptop and her eyes started to water. He had written a post-it note and put it on her screen, "I love you, always."

She'd pulled the note off the screen and clutched it to her chest. She hoped he could still say this the next night as the words Ms. Ascot said shouted in her head.

"You must crush him!"

CHAPTER 31

My ceiling looked more dismal than most mornings. I had stared at the chipped white ceiling for three hours until I thought the sun was up. It wasn't. It was turning into the start of a grim, grey, bleak April Tuesday morning as the sun was staying hidden behind the blanket of an overcast sky. I, too, was wishing I could tuck my head into the covers of security and wallow my sorrow into my pillow. Sadly, I knew life didn't work that way. Each morning we had a decision: make the most of our day or not try.

My ambition in life for the last six months had been to try to make the most of my day, each day. If I decided to take a day off, someone could get robbed, mugged, tripped, or stabbed. Selfishness or self-centeredness was on the negative side of the coin, where the other had generosity and kindness as its residents.

I reached for my phone, reading the dreams I had typed a few hours earlier and felt a sadness in my heart. I didn't see a happy ending for either of the dreams. But I knew what I had to do.

"Wint, give me a call when you get up," I said as his phone went directly to his voicemail. "I just want to check up on you."

I rolled out of bed, my feet hitting the hard floor with contempt. It was as if they were telling me, *Stop! Get back in bed! You don't have to do this today!*

The words were nice to imagine. I felt the words weighing on my shoulder as I started to lean back, causing my body to lie back down on my safe, comfortable mattress. I closed my eyes as I considered forgetting about the day and lying this one out.

My phone started ringing. "Hey, Wint," I said as a woman's voice chimed in.

"Oh, sorry, did I wake you?" my mother said with a sweet, apologetic tone.

"No, no, I was up. How are you, Mom?" I asked, snuggling my head into my pillow.

"I'm good. How are you, dear?" she asked with a sound that only a mother could utter when they wanted to console their hurting child.

"I'll get through it," I said unconvincingly. "I always do."

"Yes. Yes, you will, but it's okay if it's hard. You know I'm just a phone call away, honey. Even if you don't feel like talking, I am always here for you."

"I know, Mom. I know."

There was silence on the phone for a few seconds as she blew her nose. "I loved Chelsea like a daughter. I still miss her too. There is nothing wrong with missing her, son. There is nothing wrong at all."

I didn't know what to say. We'd had this same telephone call the anniversary of this day each year since Chelsea died. It was just comforting to know even when people passed away, they weren't forgotten. I knew my mom thought about Chelsea on other days as well. It was just, this day was the day we could grieve a little more than normal. "I love you, Mom," I said as I rubbed my wet eyes on my pillow. "Tell Dad I love him too."

"Love you too. You'll get through it. You're a strong, strong, young man." She stopped as I recalled her saying these same words to me as she'd helped me fill out the paperwork for my stay at the mental ward. "And you're not going through this alone."

"I know," I said, wiping my running nose onto my hand. "I know." We were about to hang up as I quickly added, "Hey, Mom."

"Yes, dear."

"She loved you like a mom too."

CHAPTER 32

People were herding into the courtroom to see the prosecution's evidence against Jennifer Ascot, the accused Carbon Monoxide Killer. News outlets were huddled around the door, trying to get comments from attorneys and Jenny herself, but they were unlucky today.

Jill Stapleton carried her briefcase and herself confidently past the reporters, wearing a flattering brown pantsuit with a rose-colored blouse. Her maintained wavy locks matched her pantsuit, her full lips matched her blouse, and the blue of her eyes would cause anyone who looked into them to lose themselves in the beauty, as if drifting on a peaceful brook down a country hillside. She was ready, and those who saw her knew it.

Veronica, on the other side, tried to look at ease and professionally assured, yet on the inside, she was churning more than the gears in a grandfather clock. She wore a smile that showcased her confidence like a beauty contestant, yet if she was true to herself, she felt unworthy. She wanted to escape this charade she was having to play, yet the only way to escape was to get Jenny an innocent verdict. She could escape, but it wouldn't come without repercussions. Bruises and battle wounds were nothing to Jenny. The outcomes would be much more ghastly.

"Are you ready?" Jenny asked Veronica compassionately.

Veronica nodded her head yes without saying a word.

"Well then, show it!" Jenny hissed in her ear. "If the jury sees your Pollyanna wallflower routine…" she stopped and blew hot air into her ear. "You don't even know what I'm capable of, darling."

Veronica cocked her head over to Jenny, who sat angelic. The image of a crucifix necklace resting on top of her fully buttoned silk blouse almost caused Veronica to want to gag. How quickly people turned religion into a weapon or a defense mechanism.

"I think you have already shown me what you are capable of, Ms. Ascot."

Jenny childishly smiled, fluttering her eyes at Veronica. She leaned over, grabbing Veronica's shoulder like a dear friend. "Those who think they know are the ones who realize they don't one second too late." Jenny leaned back and looked up at the clock beside the Ten Commandments. "Tick tock."

Veronica organized the table with the information she might need as the jury walked into the courtroom, quickly followed by Judge Odgon.

"All rise," the bailiff announced with forceful command.

Veronica scooted her chair back, realizing as she tried to stand, this was the second time in her life her knees were shaking in fear.

The first was when she realized what she had done a few years ago.   *Rosenburg.*

CHAPTER 33

"Good morning," Jordan said as he stopped by Stewart's cubical in the Traffic and System Management division of the District Department of Transportation. "So, did anyone stick out to you last night?"

"A couple. I called two last night after I left the bar, so we shall see," Stewart said with a smile. "We shall see."

"Well, the week is early. We should go out tonight and see what other names and numbers we can pick up," Jordan said. "You in?"

"Well," Stewart answered. "Couldn't hurt."

"What are you two talking about?" Collin asked, walking up from grabbing a donut and coffee in the break room.

"Tonight," Jordan grinned. "Hit the streets two nights in a row like we were back in college. You in?"

Collin had his mouth full of a chocolate glazed donut. "Fine with me," he said with crumbs flying out of his mouth.

"Maybe you should cut back on the sweets," Jordan laughed, patting Collin's stomach, not as flat as it was a few years ago.

"I'm in a healthy relationship," Collin said after he swallowed. "She loves me and my love handles."

"You haven't tied the knot yet though," Stewart chimed in.

"Let's give Collin a break, Stu," Jordan defended.

"Thanks," Collin said with a quizzical expression. He wasn't used to Jordan being the nice one in the group.

"Yeah, standing next to Collin, you'll look much hotter," Jordan quipped with a light smack on Collin's cheek. "Just helping you get that piece of donut off your face," he lied, being his playful jock self. There wasn't anything to remove.

"Well, she loves me," Collin resigned as he took another bite of his donut.

"But for how long?" Grant said as he walked up to the conversation, strutting down the hall in his khakis and polo. Of the whole group, Grant was the best looking, even though Jordan wouldn't ever admit it. Jordan may have been the better looking in high school, but his youthful good looks had slightly faded. His charisma and ego hadn't.

"Right on!" Jordan shouted with a high-five raised.

"So, you in for the night?" Collin asked after he washed his donut down with his sugary cappuccino.

"I don't know," Grant frowned. "I think Whitney is going to be home sometime tonight."

"She's a flight attendant," Jordan said back. "They get layovers and delays all the time. And then, when is she leaving again? Next week for another week of flights?"

"I'm not saying I won't be there, but I can't guarantee anything right now, okay?" he snarled.

"Oh, you miss your woman, do you?" Jordan moved in to put his arm around his bud. "She'll be too tired for anything tonight, so you can hang with us."

"I'll let you know," Grant said walking away from the group with a smile. "I'll let you know." He turned down a hallway past a few cubical stations to reach his area in transportation, Permits, or to be technical, Planning and Sustainability Divisions.

When Grant got out of earshot Jordan quickly said, "He'll be there. Since he's gotten married he always feels like he's missing out on the boys."

"He did get more numbers than you last night," Stewart reminded.

"I got a few extra I didn't tell you about," Jordan winked. "I'm single too, you know."

"This week," Collin said, wiping away the crumbs from his shirt. "Next week you'll have a new one."

"Jealous much?" Jordan asked with a sexy tone in his voice.

"Not one bit," Collin said as he parted ways with Stewart and Jordan. Collin proceeded to the end of the hallway to find his desk in the center of the IT Department.

"We'll get the plans at lunch, Stu," Jordan said as he walked the other direction to his cubical in the Street Maintenance division.

The plan was set, he thought. Last night was just the start and nothing was headlined in the news outlets about Sabrina. There were still many more names on the list. Sabrina may have caused a broken heart in the tenth grade, but there were other names to remove from the list.

Many more.

CHAPTER 34

Wint sat in the courtroom and quickly typed a text but was unable to finish it before he heard his name. "We call Officer Winston Cooper to the stand," Jill Stapleton announced to the court.

He walked through the galley, passing his defense attorney wife on his way to the stand. He felt calm and relaxed. He was seated by the bailiff and agreed to tell the whole truth as Jill asked him to state the facts in the investigation of Ms. Jennifer Ascot.

Wint explained each crime in detail. He told the jury of the brutal crimes Jenny was accused of – abducting retired age tourists by arousing their sympathy by pretending to be terminally ill and then killing them in an abandoned parking lot. He showed pictures of the deceased, video footage of their abductions, and crime scene pictures and video. He was cool, calm, and collected. Jill had prepped Wint many times before since this wasn't his first time as an officer on the stand. They had a good relationship of ebb and flow. When he would start to lose the interest in a few of the jurors, Jill would be there to set him up for a spike.

"So, how did you know they were going to be at Huntington Station on that Sunday evening in October?"

He looked at the jury and said his memorized line, "We received an anonymous tip from someone saying they had heard from Alexei Lechkov he was going to be at the Huntington Station at 7:30 p.m. to kill someone."

"Hearsay, your honor," Veronica slowly chimed in.

Wint stared confusedly at Veronica as the judge sustained her objection. He didn't expect her to rebut his testimony. Jill finished her questioning and returned back to her seat.

"Officer Cooper, did you find any DNA evidence of Ms. Ascot's at any of the crime scenes?" Veronica asked as she approached the stand to start her dismantling of the prosecution. "Any strands of hair? Bodily fluid of any kind? Anything at all that could show proof Ms. Ascot was there?"

"No," Cooper answered calmly. He was expecting this line of questioning, so this didn't surprise him.

"So, no DNA evidence of any kind from my client? Is that uncommon in these types of murders?"

"Ms. Ascot and her brother planned well," he answered.

"You didn't answer my question. Is this uncommon?" she asked once again.

"Evidence isn't always easy to find like on the television shows," he answered.

"Once again, answer my question with a yes or no. With all the crime scenes you have seen over your career, have you ever seen this many crime scenes without any DNA evidence by the same perpetrator?"

"I usually don't handle murder investigations," he answered, and right when he replied, he knew he had made a mistake as he saw his wife's eyes perk up.

"Oh, so this was your first murder investigation? That's a big leap from being a patrol cop to working a murder investigation. And you were the cop that killed Alexei and arrested the accused. Interesting."

"Your honor, is there a question?" Jill jumped up as Wint stared at her wide-eyed. "Or is she just playing theatrics?"

"Yes, Mrs. Hyde-Cooper, state your questions and not your opinions."

"Yes, your honor," Veronica said as she took a deep breath. "So, there was no DNA evidence?"

"No, there was not, but--" he started to say as Veronica interrupted him.

"Yes or no, remember Officer Cooper?" she said in a belittling tone. "Are you sure Ms. Ascot is the woman you saw on that grainy black and white video footage?"

"She fit the description of the woman on the video," he answered calmly, rubbing his thighs as he tried to control his breathing.

"But per the video footage, any woman in here that has the same build as my client could be responsible for these deaths. Even I could be responsible since we have a similar build."

"Your honor," Jill said, annoyed with the lack of question.

"Mrs. Hyde-Cooper, what is your question?" Judge Ogdon asked. "Don't make me remind you again."

"My apologies, your honor," she said as she smiled back at the judge and then the jury. "Were you aware when you shot and killed Alexei and arrested my client, they were on their way to a Halloween party, dressed as the Carbon Monoxide Killers? Bad taste, I know," she said to the jury with a frown.

"During our questioning of Ms. Ascot, she did mention she was on her way to a Halloween party."

"Did you verify she was invited to a Halloween party that night?"

"Yes," Cooper said, clinching his fists. "There was a Halloween party being thrown by one of Alexei's co-workers in Alexandria, Virginia that night."

"So, this could have just been a terrible mistake where Alexei Lechkov was shot and killed and Ms. Ascot arrested."

"No," Cooper said defiantly. "There was chloroform in the oxygen tank. The same chloroform used to aid in killing all the victims."

"But what if Ms. Ascot wasn't aware there was chloroform in the oxygen tank? She was just invited to a Halloween party with her long lost brother. Do you know if Ms. Ascot was aware of the chloroform in the oxygen tank?"

"No, I am not totally aware if Ms. Ascot knew there was chloroform in the oxygen tank, but she did mention she regretted not killing--" he tried to finish before he was interrupted.

"Officer Cooper, please answer only the questions I am asking you," she said, raising her voice forcefully.

"You," he said with an evil stare.

"Your honor, ask the jury to ignore the last statement for hearsay. I didn't ask Officer Cooper of his discussions with Ms. Ascot."

"But your honor," Jill started to say as the judge banged his gavel.

"Jury, please disregard the last statement," Judge Ogdon agreed. "Proceed."

Veronica turned her back to Wint and started to walk to her chair when Jenny's eyes blazed into hers as if telling her, *crush him!*

"Officer Cooper, did you get a promotion after you arrested Ms. Ascot?" Veronica asked.

"What does that have to do with anything?" Cooper asked, looking at Jill who tried to rebut, but the judge said for Officer Cooper to answer. "Yes," he answered.

"So, you were promoted after you got an anonymous tip, shot and killed Alexei, and arrested Ms. Ascot? Sounds like a nice reward for one crime solved. Did I leave anything out?"

"Yes, you left something out," he smiled. "I rejected the promotion."

Veronica was not aware he'd rejected it. She remembered when he came in from work and told her he was offered a promotion and she was ecstatic. He had failed to tell his pride-hungry, career-driven wife he had rejected the promotion.

"I didn't want this one case to be a reason for a promotion," he said glancing over at the jury and then back at Jenny. "I don't care about promotions. I care about getting criminals off the street."

Veronica took a deep breath. She didn't want to do this, but she had to for the sake of her and Winston's future.

"I just have a few more questions, Officer Cooper," Veronica said as he nodded. "Were you aware Ms. Ascot spoke to your wife the night before you arrested her, and she had swayed your wife to file for a divorce?"

"Yes, Ms. Ascot told me that while I was arresting her. But I didn't believe it."

Veronica's throat started to clinch up. "Are you lying, Officer Cooper?" she asked, rigid and unremorseful.

"No!"

"Are you saying you didn't arrest Ms. Ascot because she had swayed your wife to file for a divorce? Are you saying you didn't act out on revenge to kill the one family member Ms. Ascot had left, because she was tearing your wife away from you? Are you saying you were clueless to your failing marriage?" Veronica stood motionless. She knew if she moved even an inch, a tear would roll down her cheek.

Cooper lowered his head, watching his sweaty palms quickly grow cold. He closed his eyes and shook his head in disbelief. *This can't be happening. This is all a bad dream,* he was telling himself. His world was spinning and he couldn't hear anything. Not even the banging gavel from the judge.

"Officer Cooper. Officer Cooper, please answer the question," Judge Ogdon ordered.

Cooper lifted his head as a lone tear rolled down his cheek. "I didn't know."

"Relevance, your honor?" Jill jumped up. "What does this have to do with the case? Nothing."

"I agree," Judge Ogdon said. "Anything further, Mrs. Hyde-Cooper?"

Jenny stood up, causing the entire courtroom to come to a halt.

"Yes, Ms. Ascot," Judge Ogdon said in an astonished tone.

"I would like to request new head counsel for my case, your honor," Jenny said as Veronica was walking back to her seat, slightly shaking. "But I will keep Mrs. Cooper on as second chair."

Veronica didn't know what to think as she stood beside Ms. Ascot. She was angry at herself for ripping Winston apart and angry for doing what Jenny requested.

Jenny leaned over and whispered in her ear. "I didn't think you had the guts to go through with it. I'm really impressed, Veronica." She stopped and looked at Wint still on the stand. "When I saw your husband shed a tear, it got me. It really moved me." She looked up at the judge who was talking, but she didn't care. She enjoyed torturing Veronica a little more. "Too bad about your marriage. Not sure anyone's relationship could recover after what you just did. But good job, sis. You made me proud. I'm glad I didn't kill you when I could have. Watching that made your living worth it. Now breathe, Veronica. Breathe."

CHAPTER 35

"This is quite out of the norm, Ms. Ascot. Are you sure you want to do this? I will not extend you any additional time because of these changes," Judge Ogdon stated with a bewildered look on his face.

"No, I am quite aware of what I am doing," Jenny answered, looking over at Veronica wickedly.

Suddenly, a tall older gentleman in a gray tailored suit in the back row of the courtroom stood up and proceeded forward to the defense table. His icy white hair was parted down the middle, glistening from the hair product that caused it to look wet and unmovable. "Nothing further, your honor," he said in thick eastern Russian accent.

Jill Stapleton didn't want Officer Cooper to remain on the stand much longer, so she quickly went through the main points in the evidence as Cooper agreed. The evidence was good. The jury seemed attentive still. They even appeared sympathetic to Officer Cooper. *This may play in our advantage,* she thought. "Nothing further with this witness, your honor."

Wint arose from the stand and walked past Veronica without looking at her. She felt sick. She felt like a betrayer. She felt played. Once again, she was a pawn in one of Jenny's games, still trying to separate her and Winston.

"Given the time and this new change for Ms. Ascot, I will give you an hour recess for lunch," Judge Ogdon granted with a quick bang of his gavel.

"Veronica, please meet Miloslav Alexeev," Jenny said sternly.

Miloslav reached out his hand to greet his new legal partner. "I do recall we have met once before," he said with an uneasy smile and thick eastern Russian accent. "Remember?"

Veronica's knees clanked together like a pair of rusted out chains. She politely extended her right hand and held tightly to her chair with her left. Even if she wanted to run after Wint, she couldn't. Her legs couldn't hold her weight.

Third time's the charm they say, but for Veronica this was about as much as she could stand. She did remember him.

Rosenburg.

CHAPTER 36

"Wint! Wint! Wint!" Elizabeth shouted, running down the courthouse hall in her red stilettos. *Running two days in a row. What am I, an Olympian?* she thought. "Forget it!" she screamed as she kicked off one of her shoes and stooped down to pick it up. She threw her arm back, but knew she couldn't hit him. She looked to the closest person beside her, a stocky female in her fifties. "Excuse me, ma'am, you look like the type of gal who used to throw a football with one of the boys," she said as the woman snarled at the backhanded compliment.

"I didn't say you were manly, just you looked it," Elizabeth sighed to herself. She looked to her other side and found a slim man in his forties. "Excuse me, can you throw this shoe at that officer storming down the hall?"

"And get me arrested?" he scoffed.

"What is up with you people?" she yelled. "Fine!" She started running with her arm raised behind her like throwing a javelin. She threw her arm and her body weight forward, releasing the shoe. It flew through the air like a cardinal. She stopped and watched amazed at her own accomplishment. Sadly, her trajectory was off. By a few dozen yards.

She watched as Wint's head kept bobbing down the hallway. She knew she only had one option to stop him. She inhaled a deep breath and screamed at the top of her lungs, "Bomb!"

Roars of fearful, panic-stricken people caused Wint's head to whiplash back to see the commotion. People were running away from Elizabeth as Wint heroically ran towards harm's way.

Elizabeth stood waving her hands to get Wint's attention as a group of men tried to sedate her. "Sorry, false alarm! I don't have a bomb!" she screamed.

Wint arrived after his sprint up the hallway and asked the gentlemen to release her. "I should arrest you for that."

"Wint, wait a second," Elizabeth stopped as she started talking to one of the men who was holding her down. "Can you be a doll and go fetch my other red shoe? It's down there by the water fountain."

"I will not," he scolded as he stormed away from her.

"Where is the chivalry these days?" she asked Wint as he watched her expressionless. "Wint, what happened in there?"

"I…I…" he stuttered, unable to fully comprehend himself. "I don't know who that woman is," he said as he started walking away.

"Wint!" she shouted as she started hobbling beside him wearing only one stiletto. "Jenny forced her. That's the only explanation."

"No," Wint said as he continued to march down the hall. "Jenny didn't force her to draw divorce papers."

"Wint," Elizabeth said desperately. "She might have drawn up the papers, but she didn't go through with it. You've got to believe me, that wasn't Veronica in there. She's changed in the last few months."

He stopped walking and looked Elizabeth in the eyes. "The best liars can convince anyone they have changed." He started to walk towards the exit again. "She's one of the best there is."

Elizabeth tried to stop him from leaving, but it was no use. Wint wouldn't listen to her, and she couldn't blame him. His wife just roasted him on the stand like he was a criminal himself. She twisted their failing marriage as a reason for police corruption. She poked enough holes in the prosecution's defense to have reasonable doubt for the jury.

She poked one hole in particular. Stabbing Wint in the back, piercing his heart in the process.

Elizabeth grabbed her cell phone and immediately called Solo.

CHAPTER 37

"Solo, it's bad, really bad. You've got to go rescue him," Elizabeth said before I could even say hello.

"Rescue who?" I asked, confused as I rode the subway towards the courthouse. "Who's in trouble?"

"Wint. I'm worried, Solo. It was bad in there." Elizabeth proceeded to tell me the events of the morning. I sat on the subway train saddened. My heart was breaking for my best friend. I didn't think this day could get any worse, but apparently, I was wrong. It seemed life had a funny way of showing how ignorant we were.

"Wint, come on, man, pick up! Pick up!" I said as I quickly called him from the subway train. I was still a few stops away, and my reception was cutting in and out.

"This is Officer Winston Cooper, leave a message," his voicemail chimed with a friendly voice.

"Wint, bud, give me a call! Come on, man, call me back!" I said with urgency. In all the years of our friendship, Wint had always been the one to show his emotions and tell his friends and family how much he cared for them. I, on the other hand, would playfully reply with a jab. He knew I didn't say words like that to just anyone. Well, today, he didn't need to know it, he needed to hear it. "I love you, brother. Please give me a call. I need you today as much as you might need me."

I swiped my phone to end the call, and my heart started to break even more as I recalled what Elizabeth had told me about what Verny had said to Wint.

My blood was boiling with rage at her lack of character to parade Wint through all that pain, just for the purpose of winning a case. A case she knew she needed to lose.

What's up VERNY? Breaking Wint at home isn't enough fun for you so you have to do it in public now too? I texted to Veronica. At this moment, I didn't feel like being the polite Solo she had known the last few months as our relationship became more cordial and friendly. I didn't feel like being the good guy since she wasn't playing nice at the moment either.

I didn't know what she was going to hate more, me calling her out or me calling her Verny. Even though my heart was a little colder than normal this morning, this text at least caused my heart to pump a little more blood into my veins.

Who cares about milk? Vengeance does a body good sometimes too.

CHAPTER 38

The court room was buzzing livelier than a honeycomb of worker bees. The question was, who was the queen? Was it the stunning prosecution of Jill Stapleton, the smart, capable, independent rising star of the district attorney's office? Or was it the defense just minutes ago led by the insatiable, cunning prowess of Veronica Hyde-Cooper? Or was it the puppet master of this grand charade, Jennifer "Jenika" Ascot?

Jenny and Miloslav "Milo" Alexeev whispered most of the hour as Veronica sat numb. Just moments ago she'd believed she was in control of her own fate. Now, she realized it was just an illusion in the masquerade Ms. Ascot was hosting.

Unbeknownst to Veronica, Jenny and Milo had a long history. Their families had been tangled in a web of murder and cover-up long before Jenny was ever born.

It was over two decades ago when Jenny first formally met Milo, even though he had been a part of her life before her birth. Milo gained the reputation as a scummy lawyer. He played dirty, and his clients were filthy and usually tied to the Russian mob with the usual crimes. He did anything to get his clients an innocent verdict. Anything.

He had only received a few guilty verdicts in his lifetime. Each one came with some form of justice devised from his own head to the person responsible for the loss in court. It was nothing to issue a hit for a witness, a prosecutor, or a family member of the accuser. No one was safe if his client was not freed.

One was Jenny's father, Dimitri Lechkov, found guilty of the death of his wife, Anne Samples Lechkov. The mother of Jenny and Alexei was murdered in her home with two bullets to her head. Milo had been a longtime friend of Dimitri, and Dimitri actually named his firstborn son after his dear friend, so Alexeev became Alexei. He had always felt guilt for not absolving Dimitri of a prison sentence and had spent many restless nights wondering how he could have tried the case differently.

When he saw the reports of Jenny Ascot or Jenika Lechkov being tried for murder, he knew this was his way of redemption. A way to right the wrong caused many years ago when his beloved friend was sentenced to prison and then murdered like a common criminal behind bars by an opposing gang member.

Milo was known in the Russian circles as Young Yagoda. Genrikh Yagoda was appointed under Joseph Stalin as the director of the NKVD, the Soviet's intelligence agency, in the 1930s and organized the first Moscow Show Trial. Milo had quickly risen in his status in the Russian mob, just as Yagoda quickly rose in ranks. Both had assisted in executions. Milo had never been around to witness the gruesome deaths. He had just orchestrated them.

Milo took the first seat of the defense table with Jenny sitting between him and Veronica. Veronica only heard broken pieces of what Milo was saying, but what she heard she couldn't unhear.

"You will be free, Jenika, trust me, or there will be blood. I promised the same to your father, and I upheld my promise."

Veronica's stomach slightly heaved. She was sitting at the defense table with one of the cruelest attorneys on the Eastern coast. He rubbed elbows with murderers and rapists on holidays. He called executioners and kidnappers brothers. He was tight in the inner circle of the Russian mob, and some said he was its leader. Whenever he snapped his fingers, he had someone to take care of the problem. He did this not only for his friends, but for anyone who could pay the small fee.

He leaned over the table and stared at Veronica. "Your father trained you well, Veronica. Tell him I said hello. We go way back, remember?"

CHAPTER 39

He sat on the toilet with one phone on each of his thighs. He had a tech savvy iPhone on one leg and the disposable burner phone on the other.

He logged into the District Department of Transportation database, hacking through the mainframe to get the information he needed -- a GPS map with locations of the working cameras for tonight. He sent the encrypted map to a chain of self-forwarding emails that would ultimately end on his burner phone.

Suddenly, he saw the glorious image of a new text message. He opened the text and saw an attached file. Clicking on the attachment, his cheap phone started the decryption process. He watched with hungering breath as the percentage of the decryption process slowly started to grow.

He sat there, hearing a few guys enter and leave the restroom. A couple left without washing their hands. He wanted to start looking at people's shoes and figuring out who to avoid eating with during the monthly birthday celebrations, but he had more important things to worry about than dysentery.

The percentage neared the halfway mark as he felt his burner phone grow warmer against his leg. He didn't think converting and downloading the map would take that much energy and battery, but with the size of the Washington D.C. metro area and the weakness of gas station disposable cell phones, he was starting to get nervous.

As the percentage on the phone neared eighty, he was getting both anxious and nervous. He was almost there with all the streets that should not be passed tonight, but his phone was also about to burn through his pants. He quickly picked up the phone and held it in his hands, but the touch of the hot plastic against his bare skin caused him to jerk.

The iPhone on his other leg started to fall, flipping through the air. He didn't know what was worse, the thought of his screen breaking or his phone landing this close to the men's toilet. The phone slammed against the off-white sticky tile floor. Frowning, he reached down, knowing the five second rule was a made-up philosophy parents told their kids. It only took a split second for germs to attach onto a surface.

Picking up the phone with just his thumb and index finger, he winced as if in pain. He was relieved the screen on the tiny computer didn't break, but he desperately wanted to run to the sink to wash both his phone and his hands.

He held the phone as if his fingers were tweezers with his arm straight ahead. He didn't want to get his face close to the contamination. He almost forgot about the other phone, when suddenly it quietly chimed. He was afraid to look; he didn't know if that meant the file was completed or denied.

He exhaled in relief as the word *Complete* lit across the tiny screen. His map was set.

He forwarded the encrypted map to an app on his iPhone and suddenly, there was his lovely city with his own freedom trail lined with a yellow neon light. He didn't mind being called Dorothy tonight. He had his cast set: the scarecrow, tin man, and cowardly lion. He didn't care who played which roles. Nametags weren't needed. The route was what he needed more than anything.

All that mattered was this was going to be his yellow brick road tonight. The destination wouldn't be Oz. He didn't care about returning back to Kansas or meeting a wizard. All he knew was he was off to kill a witch tonight.

A wicked witch of his past.

CHAPTER 40

Assistant District Attorney Jill Stapleton seemed unfazed by the grinding Officer Cooper endured earlier. She'd had Cooper state the facts of the case. All of the hoopla Veronica was drudging up was nothing unforeseen. Except for the last bit of information about the divorce. Cooper didn't know about his wife's intention to get a divorce. But that had no relevance in the case, and the jury should be smart enough to see past all the smoke and mirrors the defense was putting up.

"We call Dr. Raul Santiago as our next witness," Jill announced as the handsome 42-year-old chief medical examiner for Washington, D.C. approached the stand in a slim fitting tan suit, a neatly pressed white Stafford shirt, and a perfectly balanced red bow tie. His dazzling white smile shined against his mocha-colored skin. This was the confidence Jill needed. Dr. Santiago was as faithful as the rising sun with his examinations and findings.

They did the normal introductions of name, occupation, education, and work history. He started giving detailed accounts that aligned perfectly with Officer Cooper's evidence. Dr. Santiago was as polished as they came. He spoke directly to the jury, making sure he made eye contact with each one. He clicked through his computer presentation of each of the deaths and the composition of the chloroform that matched the exact composition found in the oxygen tank.

Santiago detailed the deaths of each victim: seven from carbon monoxide poisoning; the park ranger, Mitchell Ebley, who was bludgeoned to death with a hammer; and Betty Appleton, who was murdered in the hospital after escaping the lethal dose of carbon monoxide.

"Do you agree all of these deaths are connected?" Jill asked.

"Yes, it appears with the crime scene evidence the police obtained and the causes of death, these deaths were connected."

"And just to clarify, the chloroform found in the oxygen tank on the night Ms. Ascot was arrested matches the traces of chloroform on the victims that were abducted and later murdered?"

"Yes, that is correct. Chloroform can be made rather simply with just three ingredients: bleach, acetone, and ice. The process is a little more complicated, but anyone with a general knowledge of chemistry can make this without any problems. When I compared the composition of chloroform on the victims to that in the oxygen tank, the test results confirmed it was a 99.4% match. The same person who made the chloroform to kill these individuals was the same one who made the chloroform in the tank found with Ms. Ascot."

"Thank you, Dr. Santiago," Jill smiled as she went back to her seat. Angus passed Jill a note on his jury observations, and she optimistically smiled with his hypothesis.

Milo stood up, towering at almost six feet six inches and stared for a moment at Dr. Santiago before continuing.

"Dr. Santiago, you say the same person made each of the compositions of the chloroform, correct?" Milo asked in his heavy accent.

"Yes, that is correct."

"Can you tell which chemistry student concocted this potion?" he asked with a cynical gaze.

"No, all I can affirm--" he started to say as Milo stopped him.

"So you don't know who made the chloroform? You can't say my client, Ms. Ascot, made the chloroform. All you can say is there was chloroform in the oxygen container that matched the traces on the victims."

"Yes, that is correct."

"And once again, was there any DNA evidence on any of the victims that links my client to their deaths?"

Dr. Santiago smiled cordially at the question and remained calm. "No." He knew the shorter the answers, the harder it would be for the defense to trip him up.

"So, just as Mrs. Hyde-Cooper stated earlier, you have no proof our client is guilty of this crime. For all we know, Mrs. Hyde-Cooper here could have made the chloroform herself."

"There is no evidence for that fact," Dr. Santiago answered confidently.

"Just as there is no evidence that ties these crimes to my client, Ms. Ascot. There were no traces of the ingredients for the chloroform found in my client's apartment. There were no traces of chloroform found on her hands when she was arrested."

"Objection, your honor!" Jill shouted. "Where is the question?"

"Yes, Mr. Alexeev, you know the rules," Judge Ogdon said, siding with the prosecution.

"Many apologizes, your honor." He returned back to his seat and nodded to the judge. "No further questions, your honor."

Jill got back up and wanted to hammer into the jurors that the chloroform found on the victims matched 99.4% to that in the oxygen tank. It was undeniable that the same person created it.

"I do not know who made the chloroform, but what I do know based upon my history as a medical examiner, at least two people used it when they abducted and murdered these innocent civilians," Dr. Santiago ended. "At least two people killed these nine individuals. And based upon logistics and semantics, one of the two people was undoubtedly Ms. Jennifer Ascot."

CHAPTER 41

Elizabeth held her phone in her lonely hand, hoping to hear back from someone, anyone. Silence. Agonizing silence. She looked up from the gallery and saw Veronica sitting statuesque, as if made of rock. Not of marble, hard and sturdy, able to be sculpted and chiseled, but of sand. One strong tidal wave would wash her out to sea.

Come on, Wint, Elizabeth texted, but she already knew he wouldn't respond. He hadn't responded to the other dozen texts she had sent.

Any news? she texted to Solo, but just like Wint, he was unresponsive. A haunting fear flashed like terrifying lightning. *What if he knows?* she thought. *He has dreams. What if he dreamed me finding out I could have saved his wife's life six years ago?*

Suddenly, a new text arrived. *I can't get ahold of him. I'm trying to track him down. I'll let you know what I find out.* She read Solo's text and warmth started to spread to her fingers. She started to type a message. She wanted to let him know what she was feeling, but she wondered if something like that should come across in a text.

Thanks for letting me know, Lizzy, Solo texted back. Lizzy was a name he had started calling her a few months back when they were in the trenches together. Following a possible mugger down a darkened alley before midnight wasn't anything new. They could write a book with the dreams they'd had, but who would believe them?

She had never been called Lizzy with such brotherly affection before. She sat staring at the text and could hear voices from her childhood when bullies or numbskulls would call her Lizzy Wizzy when she spilled her juice in her lap in the third grade. She'd hated the name Lizzy from that day forward. Yet, when Solo said it, she didn't want to sucker punch him like a kid on a tire swing. She didn't want to kick him where it would hurt him the most.

Instead, she wanted to hug him. She knew his heart was breaking for Chelsea, and now his heart was probably breaking for his best pal. She looked down at the text she had written and slowly started to backspace until nothing remained.

Thinking of you, Solo, is what she had typed along with a list of the dreams she'd had the night before.

She wasn't ready to unburden herself just yet.

She looked up and saw Jill Stapleton getting ready to call her next witness as Veronica stretched her neck. She craned her head around and their eyes connected.

Elizabeth's hands went frigid as her phone slipped through her icy fingers. She had never seen her sister look so terrified. Veronica was the brave one. The one who faced every obstacle with a *come and get me* look. But now, she looked like a defeated animal. Her large eyes stared into Elizabeth's soul like a pair from a defenseless animal being led to slaughter.

"You got this," Elizabeth mouthed to her strong, older sister. "You got this."

Veronica looked at her emotionless. She didn't smile. She didn't nod. She didn't reciprocate in any way. All she did was blink and turn her head back around to look at the judge.

Veronica may have thought her sister was giving her some words of encouragement, but really, Elizabeth was trying to convince herself, "You got this."

When you see fear in your fearless sister's eyes. It's bad.

CHAPTER 42

"Hey, man, where are you?" Wint finally responded to my countless texts. I had tried contacting everyone we had in common. No one knew. No one.

"I've been looking for you!" I quickly called back. "Could you not have answered any of my texts? Wint, what happened?"

"Where are you?" Wint asked once again, not answering anything I had asked.

"I'm walking around downtown. I was heading to the station to see if you were there."

"Well, I'm not there. I'm at your front door," he answered coldly. "Can I stay with you for a while?"

"Anytime, man. Anytime," I said as I stopped walking and leaned against a storefront window.

"That's good, because I've already dropped off my stuff and now I'm heading to work," Wint said grimly. "You need to find a better place to hide your key. You live in an apartment building that's practically in the ghetto," he laughed.

I loved hearing his laugh right now. I needed to hear it. "I'm no detective," I kidded. "I see people on police shows all the time hide their keys behind the heating units in the hallways."

"Exactly. Everyone else watches those shows too," he barked. "I left your key on the counter. I didn't want anyone stealing my stuff on your couch."

I watched the people walk past me with a sandwich in one hand and their cell phone in the other. Could they not see my devastation? Could they not see my world was on shaking ground? Nope. I smirked when I saw a guy drip a few drops of mustard on his navy tie. *Serves you right.*

"Wint, spill it. What are you thinking?"

"I'm going to be late to work," he honestly replied as he revved his engine and spun his tires out of the parking lot.

"Really?" I asked annoyed. "Work is all you are thinking about? What do you think about what happened this morning?"

"I don't want to talk about it right now, Solo. Just give me time."

"You need to talk about it," I said, pounding my fist onto the glass, and causing the cashier inside to shake her head madly at me. I waved and apologized, but I was still upset. Holding in all the feelings wasn't going to do any good. It would only cause it to fester even more.

"It's not your life! Don't tell me what I need to do," he said before hanging up.

I looked down at my phone showing my call had ended. "Well, you little," I grunted as I quickly called him back.

"This is Officer Winston Cooper, leave a message," was all I heard.

"You want a message? I'll give you a message," I said, but I knew he didn't need another enemy right now. He needed his friend who would stick beside him through thick and thin. "Whenever you're ready, you know where I'll be."

CHAPTER 43

It never gets easy phoning in an anonymous tip to the police. I know they probably get a lot of wackos calling in for their fifteen minutes of possible fame, telling all their Facebook friends they were the ones that helped catch the Westside cat burglar. They probably wait with anticipation watching the nightly news for just the possibility of hearing their voice recording.

After these last six months, I had gotten tired of watching the news. If something didn't go as planned and a crisis wasn't diverted, it was just another reminder I didn't save everyone I could have for the day.

I called in a tip about the drug deal at Guy Mason Recreation Center in the early afternoon and gave all the details about being near the baseball field. Chuck would be in a white Cadillac Escalade selling his white powder while observing his boys playing on the nearby diamond. The memory of his boys sitting in the backseat tugged at my heartstrings. I didn't want Chuck to be another felon with a rap sheet I helped catch. I didn't want the dad of the two boys to waste his days behind bars at such a crucial time in his sons' lives. I didn't want to get him arrested. I wanted to get him help.

I made my way to the park by means of a few subway trains and bus routes. It was a lovely day, and I wished I had the heart to try to enjoy it, but today wasn't the day to lie in a grassy field and recall moments of catching the last popup fly in my little league championship game. Although, that memory was a lie. I had actually dropped the ball, causing my team to lose. I definitely didn't want to let that memory linger any more than necessary.

I plopped down on a wooden green park bench and waited until I saw Chuck and his boys arrive in their white SUV. One would think I would be a professional at approaching people, swaying them to not make a bad decision. One would think wrong. No matter how many times I had done this, I got very little appreciation. I usually got called a few choice words and warned as a clinched fist was just a few inches from my bent nose.

I prayed for a sign of what I needed to do. I waited, staring up at the clouds, thinking maybe God would show Himself. Maybe He would part the clouds and a hand would fly down from the sky and point me where I needed to go.

Nope. It didn't work that way. Faith wasn't about proof. If we had proof, why would we need faith? My mind wandered in that philosophical loop until I bravely stood up and walked away from the park bench and my thought process. Slowly, various cars with young boys with baseball gloves and bats started arriving. I stood out like a sore thumb, a middle-aged single guy walking around a parking lot alone. I felt like I needed to tell them I wasn't a child predator. I was just a guy trying to save another guy from making a big mistake.

"Bubby," a little girl softly yelled. I looked behind me and saw a cute little redhead, about three years old, lying in the grass where she tripped and fell.

"Chels, get up!" her older brother shouted, not turning back to help, but picking up speed to catch up with his other teammates.

"Mommy," Chels moaned to her mother behind her as she slowly stood up.

"You got it, Chelsea Belle. You got it," the mother said as she grabbed her daughter's hand. The two started walking hand in hand, following the line of outfielders.

"Really," I said, looking over at the parking lot where a white SUV came to a stop and two small boys jumped out of the backseat and ran past me to catch up to their friends. "Message received."

I walked in the direction of Chuck's nice ride and felt a warmth I hadn't felt all day. I didn't believe in ghosts or loved ones coming back from the dead or psychics conjuring someone from the past. But I did believe in other things that were out of this world and beyond the realm of my finite understanding. It was as if God was reminding me of a time when Chelsea was walking beside me, telling me, "You know what you got to do. You got it."

"I know, honey. I know," I whispered to myself.

I reached Chuck's SUV and stopped to tie my shoe. I needed a moment to collect my jumbled thoughts and emotions. I touched a rock on the ground, needing to feel something tangible, even though that warmth seemed as real to me as the rock I was touching. I stood up, took a deep breath, and stepped up to his window.

"Excuse me, are you Chuck?" I asked tapping on the window. "Do you have a minute?"

CHAPTER 44

"What's it to you?" Chuck asked through his glass window. I thought he would have rolled it down, but he had another idea. He didn't feel like getting chummy.

I quickly felt like I wasn't going to get chummy with him either. "Well," I said, stopping and looking around to make sure I couldn't be heard. "I know what you're here for, and…" I said as his eyes slowly scanned the parking lot to see if anyone was watching.

"What I'm here for is to watch my boys play," he said angrily. "I'm not into what you're looking for."

"No. No, I'm not looking for that," I said, quickly shaking my head.

"How do you know my name?" he snapped back, unbuckling his seat and opening the door. He got out of his SUV and stood a good five inches taller than me. I felt like a dwarf next to this giant.

I didn't feel like answering his question. Even if I did, he wouldn't believe me. "You don't have to do this anymore," I sympathetically said, looking into his eyes and hoping I was striking a nerve. He looked over his shoulder at the field where his boys were playing.

"Get in the car," he menacingly said through clenched teeth.

"I'm okay out here." I backed away and bumped into the sedan behind me.

"I said, get in," he forcefully whispered as he reached his arm to his side, showing the handle of his gun.

"Okay, I'll get in," I said cheerfully while feeling foolish. "This is a nice car," I remarked getting into the back seat. "My friends looked at one like this but decided on a BMW instead." I turned into a chatty Cathy of annoyance. "Leather seats. This is nice. And are these back seats heated? Get out, man!"

"Will you shut up!" he barked after he got into the back seat and shut the door. "Just shut your mouth!"

I sat frozen and quickly ran down all the research I had done in case I ever got in this type of situation. Being in a locked car with a guy with a gun isn't a good scenario. *Be calm, stay calm. Don't make any sudden moves. Follow his orders. Gain his trust.*

And if that fails, kick and run!

"Who sent you?" he asked, pointing the barrel of his gun between my eyes.

"What?" I asked confused.

"Was it Logan? Did Logan send you?"

"I don't know who Logan is," I answered as calmly as I could. *Why do I get myself in these situations? Stupid Solo, trying to save the world. Some people just don't want to be saved!*

"Give me a name!" he yelled, ramming the gun closer to my head, almost whacking me with the metal.

"No one sent me!" I said. "I just know what you came here to do, and I just wanted to tell you…you don't have to do it."

"What, kill you?" he said with a smile.

That's not what I expected him to say. I gulped, even though my mouth was dry. *Help me, God. Help me, God. Help me, God.* "Come on, Chuck. You don't have to do this. Your kids are over there and they will be coming back soon."

"Have you been spying on my kids, you sick pervert?" His voice rose with rage.

"No, I'm not a pervert," I replied thinking I would have to kick and run soon. "My name is Solo."

"Solo?" he laughed, still aiming the gun at my forehead. "What kind a name is that?"

"Biblical?" I shrugged my shoulders with a squeamish laugh. My sense of humor wasn't going to save me, but yet it shot out of me like it could.

"Shove it!" he barked. "If you don't tell me who sent you, I'll shoot you now. As you know, my seats are leather. Your blood can be wiped down in time to take my boys home for supper."

"Chuck, I know you're a drug dealer with two small boys, but you don't have to do this. You can stop. You can be the man you were meant to be. You can leave this way of life behind and be the best dad in the world. Come on, Chuck. You don't have to live like this," I said in one long breath. I closed my eyes wondering if he was going to shoot me dead or think about what I had just said.

Suddenly I heard a tap on the window. The stupid college age kid in my dream just showed up to get his fix. "You got the goods, Chuck?" he said, opening the door to the backseat. "Oh, are you in the middle of something?" he dumbly asked.

Couldn't he see through the glass window I had a gun to my head? I sat in shock as he stood with the door open staring at Chuck like he was at McDonald's wanting to place a takeout order.

Stupid dope fiend.

CHAPTER 45

"Get in and shut the door!" Chuck yelled, pointing the gun away from me and now at the college kid.

"I'll leave you two," I winced as I tried to get out of the car, but he grabbed my shoulder and forced me back into my seat.

"No, you both are going to stay here for a little while," Chuck hissed staring coldly into my eyes. "Now, get in the vehicle and shut the door!" he commanded like we were his two boys who got into trouble. The college kid slowly obliged.

"I have to be somewhere in an hour, so will we be done by then?" the college kid naively asked.

I stared at his complete stupidity and let out a disgusted breath. "Really?" I asked shaking my head at the poor state of our educational system. "How long have you been using?"

"Uh," he answered, trying to remember before Chuck snapped.

"If you both don't shut up I will make you," he barked moving his gun like a game of deadly ping pong between the two of us.

"I borrowed this shirt from my friend, so I've got to give it back to him later," the college kid foolishly commented as Chuck stared at him confusedly.

I rolled my eyes and uttered, "Really?" again.

"What? He did and I already told him I would drop it off to him later," he remarked, oblivious to my bewilderment.

"That's the least of your worries," Chuck said shaking the gun in his face.

"You better be careful or you're going to shoot someone," the college kid said sincerely.

"Oh, dear God," I moaned at the kid's lack of understanding.

"What?" the college kid asked, cocking his head at me like a confused dog and then at Chuck. "What?"

"That's the point of me having this gun, is to shoot with it," Chuck said. "You're making me want to rid this world of you, and we just met a few minutes ago. How do the people who see you each day deal with you?"

"Oh, you know," the college kid smiled shyly, still not understanding what was going on. I watched as Chuck pointed his gun at the college kid and looked around, surveying the scene. I knew if I was going to do something, now was the chance.

Chuck's hand was inches in front of my face and I could only think of one thing to do.

Bite him. So I did.

Like a rabid dog.

CHAPTER 46

I bit down on Chuck's thumb muscle on his palm, digging deep into his skin until I felt a drop a blood run down my chin.

"GEEE OWWW!" I screamed with my teeth clinched on his hand.

Chuck was screaming in pain, hitting my head with his free hand, but since we were in the backseat, he couldn't swing his fist hard enough for me to let go.

"What?" the dumb college kid asked.

I kept biting down on Chuck's hand, but I admitted I would be slightly relieved if Chuck's gun went off, injuring the kid. It wasn't like he was going to suffer from not finishing his college education any time soon.

"GEEE OWWW!" I shouted once again, grabbing Chuck's free hand with my two hands and bending his fingers back.

The college kid still didn't get the picture.

I quickly unclenched my jaw and Chuck's hand became free, dropping the gun on the back seat floor. "Get out!" I screamed, pushing the college kid toward the window.

He opened the door and Chuck reached down to grab the gun. I scooted away closer to the door and rammed my knee back into Chuck's chin. He groaned in pain, but he still continued to reach for the gun. I knew I had to do it. It was the only thing I knew to do that would freeze him. I raised my knee to my chest and kicked forward into his groin.

I connected with the region no man ever wants to be kicked in. Especially from another grown man.

His face went red as he fell onto the back seat floor. I jumped out of the SUV and slammed the door closed. I watched the college kid walk away like he was strolling through the park on a Sunday instead of running for his life.

"Bob and weave, bob and weave, bob and weave," I kept repeating to myself as I zigzagged my body around the parking lot as fast as I could. I looked back to see what Chuck was doing. That's when I collided with a moving car's front bumper, throwing me back onto the hard concrete. My head slammed against the asphalt as I laid dizzy and wounded.

"Solo!" a male's voice shouted, getting out of the car. "Go get him!"

I looked up and noticed a man standing over me, but I couldn't see anything from his silhouette before I blacked out.

CHAPTER 47

The courtroom air was feeling stale as Assistant District Attorney Jill Stapleton called her next witness. "Abner Abernathy, will you tell the court what your occupation is?"

She hoped this witness was going to be better than the last one, Dr. Angela Lars, a psychologist and the state's expert witness. She had stated, "Ms. Ascot was clearly in sound mind during the last year. There are no findings of psychological issues that needed to be raised as a defense for the crimes Ms. Ascot is accused of." She was an expert with her knowledge and work experience, but not in dealing with Ms. Ascot's new attorney. Mr. Alexeev twisted all of her findings and theories into mere hodgepodge, a blob of opinions that resembled a bowl of porridge more than solid facts.

"You are aware Ms. Ascot was seeing a psychiatrist. Then when her brother entered back into her life, she stopped her regular visits. She was fearful of her brother. Did you speak to her psychiatrist or are you merely stating your findings after a two-hour interview with my client? An interview blatantly one-sided with your belief of her guilt," Milo had hissed in disdain.

"I...uh..." Dr. Lars had stammered at the beginning when answering all of Milo's questions.

Jill Stapleton rolled her eyes at the lack of confidence Dr. Lars had showed and knew her testimony was going to go down in the history books as one of the worst ever. She needed to get this case back on track.

"I am the Washington D.C. Police Department IT specialist," Abner answered in an oversized suit that looked like he borrowed it from his father. His neon green Coke-bottle glasses magnified his beady eyes, as if highlighting his nervous twitch for Mr. Alexeev to spot a mile away. After he answered Jill's standard questions on qualifications and work history, the good stuff began.

He showed the videos Wint had showed earlier of the various video footage they had received from the garages, subway stations, and street cameras. The grainy black and white videos showed a male and female abducting unsuspecting strangers, moments before their death.

"Mr. Abernathy, can you tell me about your sophisticated, high-tech computer program?" Jill asked as she watched some of the jurors lean in with anticipation.

"Yes, we use a program called Digitex that magnifies and clarifies images that may not be the best quality in their original state until you can see a detailed image. It is like taking a photo that has aged years and making it brand new. I like to think of it as computerized archeology. I wipe away the unfinished image, layer by layer, until a clear image appears."

"Can anyone use this software?" she asked. "I mean, is it easy to use, or do you have to be a specialist?"

"This software is highly sophisticated and requires a great deal of expertise," he asked confidently.

"And you are an expert, correct?"

"I don't want to brag, but I would say I am an expert in this software."

"Will you please show us the images of the killers before and after you used Digitex?" Jill asked as if she hadn't been shown the images a hundred times before.

"Yes. Here are the images we have created using Digitex." He displayed the photographs on the enlarged computer screen for the judge and jurors to see the near perfect match to Alexei and Jenny in a wig and medical mask.

"Do these images resemble anyone?" Jill asked, waiting for the gauntlet to drop.

"Yes, these pictures match with a 98.7% accuracy to Alexei Lechkov and 99.1% accuracy to Jennifer Ascot," he smiled to the jury and Jill.

"How can you prove these photographs are authentic and not doctored?" she asked, just like she had done before.

He pointed at the upper right hand corner of the blown up image where there was an encrypted graphic code. "This data matrix code systematically proves the authenticity of each picture. You can scan this code and it will tell you if anyone manipulated the image." He scanned the code and a neon green check mark was displayed over the photographs. "That means this image is a genuine, unaltered photograph."

"Can anyone forge a photograph and have it pass this honesty test?" she asked.

"No," he answered assuredly. "No one."

"Thank you, Mr. Abernathy, for your expertise in identifying these killers," Jill said as she turned to Judge Ogdon. "Your honor."

"Your witness," Judge Ogdon said to Mr. Alexeev.

Mr. Alexeev stayed seated for a few seconds looking at the images on the computer screen that looked strikingly similar to his client, as if looking at a Rembrandt portrait with all the details smooth and elegant. "Mr. Abernathy," Mr. Alexeev said as he stood, taking the courtroom hostage with his undeniable presence, "did you see the image of the suspects before you created this image?"

CHAPTER 48

"I don't see why that matters," Mr. Abernathy answered, quickly looking at Jill with uncertain eyes.

"Well, I hired an expert with Digitex myself, and the images he provided me from the same technique you mentioned are not even close," Mr. Alexeev said in a deep, slow, Russian tone. "Your honor, I would like to give you Exhibit 12. It's remarkable how different the two appear." He pulled out the photographs of a male and female. "Hmm," he said, staring at the images he pulled out of his briefcase. "Can you tell me who these people look like?"

Mr. Alexeev raised the pictures up for the jury to see. Then he quickly showed Judge Ogdon the photographs. Judge Ogdon squinted his eyes and looked at the defense table and Mr. Abernathy in the witness stand. Mr. Alexeev then turned around to show the two images to the defense and prosecution tables. Lastly, he showed the two images to Mr. Abernathy.

Jill Stapleton's mouth dropped and she quickly jumped up from her chair. "Your honor, these images had to be manipulated."

Mr. Alexeev shook his head in disapproval. "Tsk tsk, Ms. Stapleton. Your witness just stated that images cannot be doctored with this program. Didn't you allow Mr. Abernathy to show the images he produced using the Digitex software? I am just showing the images my specialists produced, your honor."

Judge Ogdon agreed with Mr. Alexeev, allowing him to continue his questioning.

"I never said you can't doctor the images. But if they are doctored, it will not pass the authenticity test."

"Oh dear me," Mr. Alexeev answered confusedly. "So, you are telling me these images are not true?" He fumbled his words around and tried to take back the image, but Mr. Abernathy saw the look of dread on Milo's face and quickly scanned the matrix code with his phone.

"We will find out in a second how falsified these images are," Mr. Abernathy smiled as he watched his phone.

"Your honor," Milo calmly said, but stopped as he watched Mr. Abernathy's face crumble. "Will you please tell the court, Mr. Abernathy, what your, what did you call it, Ms. Stapleton, your honesty test, is showing? I like the sound of that, honesty test."

"Th—This can't be right," Mr. Abernathy stammered.

"Oh, but you just said no one can doctor a photo using Digitex, didn't you?"

Mr. Abernathy sat frigid, unable to look up from his phone.

"I didn't hear you answer my question, Mr. Abernathy. What can't be right?"

Mr. Abernathy didn't look up. He wanted to hide, but there was nowhere to go.

"Your honor, please have Mr. Abernathy answer my question," Milo said with a scathing smile.

"Mr. Abernathy, you swore to tell the truth and you must," Judge Ogdon commanded.

Mr. Abernathy slowly looked up. "Your image is coming back as 100% authentic."

"Isn't that interesting?" Milo had a tone of whimsy. "So, my question is, if you just said no one can misrepresent a photograph, which one is the true image? Your photo or my photo?"

"I know my photograph is true!" Mr. Abernathy shouted. "I didn't rig this photo."

"So, are you saying my expert rigged his? I didn't think that was possible with your sophisticated software."

"He must have! The only way your photo could look like that is by manipulating the image to what you want it to look like."

"So, Mr. Abernathy, I return to my original question. Did you see photographs of Mr. Alexei Lechkov and Ms. Jennifer Ascot before you finalized your pictures?" he asked, walking across the hard floor, his shoes tapping against the wood, adding to the tension. He grabbed the handrails of the witness box, leaning down until he was at eye level with Mr. Abernathy.

Mr. Abernathy looked over at Jill who laid her pen down on her notepad and folded her arms. She knew what he was about to say and it made her cringe.

"Mr. Abernathy, you must answer the question," Judge Ogdon demanded.

"Yes, but--" he answered, but Mr. Alexeev wouldn't let him finish his statement.

"There are no 'buts', Mr. Abernathy. You claimed your software did this image, but didn't you take some liberties on defining the images shown in your precise and beautiful recreations?" Mr. Alexeev asked, standing beside the large computer screen, scraping his fingers across the head of Jenny Ascot's picture, as if trying to brush the loose hairs out of her eyes.

"Yes, but--" Mr. Abernathy answered as he once again was shushed by Mr. Alexeev to only answer the questions asked. Nothing more.

"I am amazed how your software created those images," Mr. Alexeev said, pointing at the computer screen, "but my specialist created these images in my hands. Can you explain how this happened?"

"Not without speaking to your specialist I cannot, but it appears he received Ms. Stapleton's and my photographs and shaped the image to resemble our faces," Mr. Abernathy stated confidently, nodding his head at Jill and the jury as if he scored a point for the prosecution.

"So, the software you used, Digitex, can be, would you say, manipulated to get the finished product you want?" Mr. Alexeev asked in bewilderment. He had trapped Mr. Abernathy, and the scared, wounded animal knew he was in a corner.

Mr. Alexeev had his claws sharpened and ready.

He turned and walked back to his chair as he stopped and froze for a second. "Oh, I almost forgot," he said melodramatically, slowly turning around. "Wasn't Alexei Lechkov even picked up and questioned a few days before the police shot and killed him and arrested my client for this grizzly crimes? One would think if they had the supposed criminal after seeing some of the video footage they would have connected the dots then. Not wait until you completed your fictional masterpiece."

"Objection, your honor!" Ms. Stapleton shouted, but before she could say anything else Mr. Abernathy interjected.

"It's not fictional!" Mr. Abernathy yelled, clutching onto the guardrails for steadiness.

Mr. Alexeev held his two images in each of his hands and raised them up for the entire courtroom to see. "Anyone can make anyone look guilty with this type of computer program. I don't know why the police never questioned Ms. Jill Stapleton or Mr. Abner Abernathy, because based on my specialist, their images matched his photographs 99.8%. That's a little higher than the images Mr. Abernathy concocted."

"I didn't concoct anything," he stammered, looking at the judge and then whipping his head around to the jury. "I didn't. I didn't make these images up. I'm not a liar," he said forcefully.

"Mr. Abernathy, I never said anything like that," Mr. Alexeev said solemnly. "I was just stating how two people can come up with two different images using the same technique. Guilty conscience?"

"Your honor," Jill Stapleton stood up, but Mr. Alexeev had already made his point.

"You don't have to answer the last question, Mr. Abernathy. I think we all know the answer."

"Your honor!" Jill Stapleton shot up from her chair, but it was too little, too late. Mr. Alexeev had dismantled her tangible proof.

CHAPTER 49

"Shots fired! Read me? Shots fired at the Guy Mason Recreation Center! We need back up! One person down!" Wint shouted as I found myself regaining consciousness slumped over behind his police cruiser. "You okay, man?" Wint asked with wide-eyed concern.

One person down, quickly echoed in my head as a burst of adrenaline shot through me like ten espressos. "Where? Where?" I started babbling rubbing my torso for the bullet wound.

"Where what?" Wint said, hunkering down beside me while raising his gun over his trunk.

"Where am I shot? Where am I shot? I don't feel anything, Wint," I whispered in fear. I didn't see any blood and knew he must have gotten me from behind. I reached my hand up to feel behind my head and felt a wetness. My stomach heaved as I saw the redness of blood on my hand. "Oh, no!" I yelled knowing a bullet to the head was deadly if not treated immediately. I clutched the back of my head to stop the bleeding if I could, or at least lessen it.

"You're not shot, man. You're going to be okay," he said not looking away from his target, firing another bullet that shattered glass.

"But you said…" I responded as I suddenly looked to my left and saw Dakota rocking someone in her lap, applying pressure to the small body.

"Look what you made me do!" a man screamed at the top of his lungs. "Look what you made me do!" he repeated once again as a few more rounds of bullets pierced the other side of the police cruiser. "Ty! I'm sorry, son, I'm sorry!"

"Just drop your weapon, sir!" Wint shouted from behind his barricade. I looked around the parking lot and saw other kids and parents huddled behind vehicles. A few were running away in the grassy outfield to flee the scene to safety.

"Wint!" Dakota screamed behind the Chevy Tahoe, "Are they coming?" Fear was in her eyes as she looked away from our position and quickly looked down encouragingly at the small boy. "Ty, you're going to be okay. Just stay with me, Ty. Okay? Just stay with me. The ambulances are on their way, and you are going to be okay. It's just a small cut. Nothing major, Ty. Okay? Just stay with me, Ty. Just stay with me. Ty, stay with me. Ty, come on, keep your eyes on me. Ty, you can do it. Ty! Ty! Ty!" she started saying louder and louder and she applied more and more pressure to his small chest.

"His name is Chuck," I said watching the sad scene a row away.

Wint darted his eyes at me and then back at the shooter. "Chuck, just put your weapon down. Your son needs you!"

"Ty, I'm sorry, son. I didn't mean…" he started, but then he fired another bullet towards us, and I felt a few pieces of glass fall beside my thigh.

"Chuck! Just surrender and you can be with your son! I promise! Just surrender and you can be with your son!"

"Daddy!" another little boy shouted sitting behind a Toyota Rav4, with a woman wrapping her long arms around his skinny body. She was his protection. She wasn't going to let him run into the middle of the gun fire like she just saw his brother do. "I want to go home!"

"Yes, Chuck, just drop your gun and we can get everyone home!" Wint shouted while he listened intently for his radio telling him an ambulance and police were on the way.

"Not everyone," Chuck selfishly cried as he fired another bullet over my head, breaking the driver's side window of the car two spaces away.

"Chuck! Chuck! Stop this! No one else needs to get hurt!" Wint yelled as he prayed for a sign the ambulance was near. He still couldn't hear any sirens.

"My son is dead and I shot him! I don't deserve to be alive!" Chuck groaned in agony as he punched the side of his Escalade. "I don't deserve to be alive either," he moaned as one more gun shot went off.

"Chuck!" Wint shouted as he inched up to get a better view of the shooter. "Chuck!" He got up and ran around the car and saw a limp body lying beside the beat-up Escalade, its blood starting to spill around the body like the car was leaking gas.

"Daddy? Daddy?" his other son said as the woman clutched his body into hers, not allowing the small child to look. She held him tightly and started asking him what his name was and other questions to get his attention on her and not on the situation.

"Trevor," he answered as he heard the screaming sirens echo though the parking lot.

The ambulance quickly stopped and two EMTs jumped out and started administering CPR to Ty, but by the look in their eyes, Dakota knew he was too late for saving. One of the other EMTs ran to check Chuck's vitals, but it was no use when they saw him wide-eyed with a bullet hole through the back of his head. They jumped into the ambulance, gunning the engine to try to save this poor, child's life.

Wint walked up to Dakota who had finally stood up and assessed the situation. She didn't let the child's death leave her incapacitated; she still had a job to do. "Anyone else hurt?" she yelled, scanning the area as she watched heads of adults and children rise from behind vehicles, trees, trash cans, and anywhere else they could find to hide.

"Solo, are you okay?" Wint came up and asked, checking the back of my head. "The bleeding has stopped, but you still might need to get it checked out."

"Yeah," I moaned. I was relieved I was alive, but the thought of a medical bill just for them to tell me I was okay made me a little sick.

"Solo, you know I don't ask too many questions," Wint said as he stopped and looked me in the eyes as he helped me to my feet. He had a look of confusion, but then a wave of relief washed over him.

I waited for him to ask, but he didn't. His look was enough. I just didn't know what to say.

"Dakota, go to his other son, and I'll start blocking off the crime scene," Wint said as he watched a few patrol cruisers skid into the parking lot with their red and blue lights flashing.

I walked away, nursing my bruised head as the memories of the moments before the gun fire erupted. A sickening feeling launched at me like a missile and I had a target at my heart.

I caused this mess!

Ty and Chuck were dead because of me!

CHAPTER 50

My anger for Veronica hadn't dwindled from the morning, it just evolved. I didn't want to check on her well-being, but I did care about the trial. "How'd it go today?" I asked from a park bench. I had left the crime scene and found a nearby spot to chill and regroup a few blocks away.

"Not good," Elizabeth said as she sat in her car in the parking garage near the courthouse. "Not good at all. I tried to talk to Veronica, but she couldn't talk."

"I don't care about Verny right now," I said rudely and to be perfectly frank, I didn't care. "Not after what she did to my boy."

"Your boy? I would do anything for Wint," she said affectionately. "Solo, she was forced to do that!" Elizabeth shouted quickly defending Verny like a little sister would.

"Really?" I asked unbelieving. "Verny has been a cruel and vindictive woman her entire life. I don't see how she could be so innocent now."

"If she's playing me, she better watch out, but I've never seen her play the fragile type before. That's not in her wheelhouse of emotions."

"Ice can be both hard and fragile, Elizabeth," I shot back with tenacity. "Veronica is the Queen of Ice."

"She is a cold one, I can't deny that," she agreed. "She tried to dismantle my trust when I was seventeen because I wore a shade of blue eyeliner that didn't match my shoes. She told my father he couldn't trust 'a crude thrift shop vagabond' with his money. She was trying to erase my name for a freaking pair of Jimmy Choos! She's ravaged sometimes."

"So, you agree with me now?" I asked, hoping she finally saw the light, even though it was one made of Swarovski crystal.

144

"You missed my point," she said, banging her palm on the steering wheel. "She has the strength of titanium that would cause men of steel or gold to bend and break like sticks. I'll give it to you, she is ruthless. But weak? Weak isn't in her caliber."

"I'm not buying it. Wint's moved out--" I started to say as she barged in.

"Moved out? No, Solo, you have to stop him. You have to. You just have to."

"I tried, but he wouldn't listen to me, and I really don't blame him. I'm not the best one for advice, especially about Verny," I leaned back and watched a couple in their middle twenties holding hands across the street. They were smiling and laughing without a care in the world. When I imagined Wint and Veronica, I couldn't say the same. "He can crash on my couch as long as he wants."

"We need to meet tonight. This isn't Veronica. This isn't. I know Veronica. I know how twisted and unscrupulous she can be, which at times empowers me, but she's the one being twisted. She's being wrung out to dry. I'm not used to seeing her look all disheveled and aloof."

"I could use supper soon. Want to meet then?"

"Sure, I was going to meet Jeremiah, but he doesn't mind being a third wheel," she laughed.

"I thought I would be the third wheel," I rebutted.

"Oh Jeremiah is oblivious to that type of social stigma. You would think a guy with a doctorate in anthropology would have a better understanding of social settings, but he's clueless. He tells me all the time he butts himself into conversations with two other people. He doesn't say 'butts in' but I'm pretty sure that's what he does. 'Elizabeth,'" she started in her Jeremiah impersonation, "'I overheard this couple talking about Russian art and how this artist is classically trained in this art form' and blah, blah, blah. He goes on and on and then he would say, 'I had to correct them the style of art they stated wasn't an actual process until after the artist's death, so they were wrong. Isn't that just hilarious? They were speaking of post modernism when it was actually cubism. Comical, isn't it?'"

"He's a one of a kind," I smiled.

"I tried to tell him people aren't always right when they talk to people and not to eavesdrop on other people's conversations. It's not polite."

"What did he say when you said that?"

She coughed to start her Jeremiah impersonation once again, "'What's not polite about correcting someone who is wrong? If someone was driving down a one-way road, would you not try to get their attention before they had a wreck, possibly killing someone, Elizabeth?'"

"He does have a method for his thinking," I said, watching the happy couple turn the corner still walking hand in hand.

"Method? I call it madness. But whatever his mode, it needs to stop. It's embarrassing going to dinner with him when he taps the shoulder of the patrons next to us to correct them on the proper fork to eat with," she stopped. "Third wheel."

"Gotta love him," I laughed. "Text me the details and I'll meet you. Maybe I'll get to witness this creature of habit in his natural environment."

"Oh, Solo, he may be a third wheel, but you're just as bad in some respects," she said as she ended the call before I could say anything.

Just as bad? What have I done? I thought as I put my phone away. I needed a few more minutes to reflect on what had happened so far. Elizabeth had tried to sway me, but I still couldn't fall victim to Verny's ploys. I was still on team Wint.

For now.

CHAPTER 51

"You were amazing today," Jenny beamed at Mr. Alexeev in her holding cell as Veronica sat unflinchingly on a metal chair in the corner. "Wasn't he, Veronica?" Jenny asked, snapping her attention to Veronica, dramatically changing her mood from joyful to vengeful.

"You did very well, Mr. Alexeev," Veronica stated politely.

"Yes, I do think it went rather well, Jenika," he smiled smugly at Veronica, showing each of his porcelain veneers paid for with mobster money.

"Since he's doing such a good job, I feel my services aren't needed," Veronica said, standing up to take some authority in the room.

"No, no, no, Mrs. Thing," Jenny reared up from her seat like a viper about to attack a field mouse. "I will tell you when your services are up. And we still need you," she said menacingly. Jenny started looking at her fingernails; the neutral color paint was chipping at the ends. "Do you have a nail file?"

"Uh, I don't think so," Veronica answered, not looking in her purse.

"What, do you think I will try to kill you in front of my godfather?" she hissed, as he glanced at Veronica from across the room.

"Dear, dear Mrs. Hyde-Cooper, why are you so disconnected? You have a duty to defend your client with utmost will and cause," Mr. Alexeev softly said, almost in a hum as if starting a Russian lullaby sung to the Romanov's children before their untimely execution.

"Mr. Alexeev, you seem to know this case better than I do, and you seem to be defending Ms. Ascot better than I could ever dream," Veronica stated in a matter-of-fact tone.

"Really?" Jenny laughed. "I have seen you defend guilty scumbags as if your life depended on it because of the hefty fees they were paying the firm. But for me…" she laughed again hysterically. "For me, a mere employee who signed the clause of representation, I get third rate service. I thought you of all people would have given it your best."

Veronica took her seat again, looking at the door like it was her only way out, but no matter how quickly she could bolt from this room, she would still have to show up again tomorrow.

"Jenika," Mr. Alexeev cooed compassionately. "Don't be so harsh to Mrs. Hyde-Cooper. Her father and I go way back," he said turning his attention directly to Veronica. "Way back," he echoed with a terrifying wink.

The wink stole Veronica's breath. It seemed like she was being tag-teamed in this psychological game. She didn't know what was worse, knowing she was on the defense team for a woman who wanted her dead and was blackmailing her, or partnering with a man who held the proof to the hidden scandal of her past.

It was a scandal that involved a murder for her father.

It was a murder ordered by Mr. Alexeev.

It was a hit Veronica had unknowingly dropped off the cash payment for. Veronica closed her eyes and started to relive the horrific past.

CHAPTER 52

Why, oh, why did I look? Veronica often questioned herself with punishing remorse as she flashed back to that awful day. But Mr. Alexeev wasn't going to let her off that easily those many years ago. No, he purposely opened the briefcase and thumbed through the cash in her presence. She wouldn't have thought anything by it, but the words he said were prophecies that stung too close to home. "Tell your father she will be taken care of tomorrow."

Veronica had looked up at Mr. Alexeev's eyes and wondered if he witnessed the murder the police claimed was a suicide. When she heard about the death of Mia Rosenburg, she knew it wasn't a suicide. She knew her father had his mistress killed. She knew Mia would never hold her unborn baby. No, Luther Hyde was still married and had to silence Mia Rosenburg. When she had refused an abortion, he knew there was only one way out.

"Veronica, I need you to deliver a legal contract to someone tonight. It's very important you get it to him tonight," her father had said like a stoic.

"I'm finishing a brief," she remembered saying as if it was yesterday when she glanced down at her watch that signaled it was almost 9 p.m.

"I don't ask much from you, Veronica," he said with a demeaning tone. "Now."

He dropped the briefcase on her desk, almost smashing her fingers and then turned and walked away.

She still remembered the moment she dropped off the briefcase, thinking it was just a legal document anyone could have dropped off. That's why they had runners to deliver the documents, but no, he wanted Veronica. He wanted her in the mix. He wanted her to know what he was capable of doing.

They never had a true father-daughter bond. She was just an outcome to get his nagging wife off his back about her need for children.

Jenny was right. Her father didn't love her. He only used her for his schemes.

Always.

CHAPTER 53

"Why did you have to hurt me so badly?" he whispered to himself behind the steering wheel in his black Ford Fusion. "Why?"

He watched as his target, Piper, left her Honda CR-V in the parking lot behind Stu's, a local bar frequented by college and young professional singles in hopes of hooking up for a good time. Stu's wasn't a sports bar, but more of a merlot drinking watering hole for pseudo-intellectuals, so-called thespians, and wannabe-philosophical junkies. This bar didn't have poetry night on Thursdays because that would be beneath them.

He breathed deeply, thinking he caught a whiff of her perfume he used to inhale during fourth period geometry. He could still remember the emotions she conjured up that junior year of high school. The lightheartedness of walking hand-in-hand down the bustling hallways, passing by navy blue lockers with flimsy combination locks. She would smile, tossing her blonde hair for everyone to notice. He had been the king of the jungle with this lioness by his side, but sadly, his title was quickly relinquished.

Looking down at his hand in his lap, he recalled the moment she let go of his in the hallway -- the first time they walked side-by-side without a part of their skin touching the other. He could see the signs now, but at the time, he was still deliriously in love. The free hand just gave him more chances to high-five or thumbs-up his friends lining the lockers. Before he knew it, one of those so-called friends had stolen his girl.

His retaliation tonight wasn't just toward Piper. No, he had another bird flying freely in the air he was taking aim at. His Brutus was unaware of his position in the crosshairs, but one day he would become enlightened. One day he would reap what he had sown. One day he would swallow the pill of his pride.

Not tonight, but soon.

Very soon.

CHAPTER 54

"Are you sure about this?" I asked Elizabeth as we met at the hostess stand of Marti's, an older establishment where Democrats and Republicans would secretly meet when one started to lean toward the other party's positions.

Elizabeth rolled her eyes at Solo's question. "He's on cloud nine thinking you're going to have dinner with us."

"And I didn't even bring him flowers," I kidded.

"The closest cloud I've ever gotten to with Jeremiah is cloud seven and three-quarters when I wore my Hermione costume for Halloween two years ago," she said passively. "Um, ma'am, we've been waiting for our table for a few minutes and no one has even approached us," Elizabeth barked belittlingly. "It's only six. Has the retirement home come for dinner here tonight? That would be the only acceptable excuse for causing this lag."

The hostess started fumbling around her stand, looking for an open table that could seat three. "And, since we had to wait, I would like one not in the middle of the chaos, preferably away from the kitchen and restrooms as well."

The hostess looked up with a petrified smile, trying her best to locate a quick, adequate spot.

"Elizabeth!" I snapped like I was reprimanding a little girl before turning to the hostess. "I'm sorry for my friend's rudeness. Our third guest isn't even here yet," I stated staring at Elizabeth's rolling eyes and mimicking tongue as the hostess looked up at me with warm, kind eyes.

"I apologize for the delay," the teenaged hostess said appreciatively as she smiled up at me. "I think we have a spot that just became available. Let me check to see if it's ready."

She hurried away as Elizabeth leaned over and whispered in my ear, "Maybe you can tutor her in algebra and she can repay you by going dow--" she started to say as I quickly stopped her unflattering remark.

"Elizabeth, not everyone uses sex as currency," I answered chivalrously.

"Oh, Solo, you're the only one who still uses traveler's checks on vacation. Live a little," she laughed seeing Jeremiah's reflection in the glass coming up behind them. "Jeremiah will agree with me," she said as he stepped into the conversation.

"Agree with you on what?" he asked as he shook my hand with a warm greeting.

"That women--" I started as Elizabeth quickly interjected digging inside her purse, as if looking for something.

"And men," she snidely said with an elbow to my side, "use sex to get what they want."

"Very much so," Jeremiah agreed.

"Told you," Elizabeth snickered like a school girl being told she was correct.

"To be honest, I said, 'not everyone uses sex as currency.'"

"I still have to agree with Elizabeth that we all use sex as currency," Jeremiah replied like a professor in his tone. "Try to find a civilization today or in the past that hasn't used their sexuality as a means to further their own agenda. The good and the bad use it alike. They may have differing methods, but they each have their own style. You will not be able to find a group or tribe that agrees with your statement."

"I understand what you are saying, but I don't think I use sex that way," I quickly rebutted as I stared, waiting for them to surrender their case.

"What did you just do here, Solomon? You twinkled your eyes to that teenybopper to get your way," she said bluntly. "She quickly turned to you and did what you wanted."

"No, I did no such thing. I was just being polite to undo your rude shortcomings," I said as I smiled.

"See," she laughed. "You did it just then. You charmingly smile to help prove your point you are a good guy, but some women would see that as you playing them."

"But I'm not," I defended, standing in shock looking at Elizabeth and then at Jeremiah. "Come on, man, tell her she's wrong."

"You are a handsome, strapping man, who unknowingly flirts a lot," Jeremiah said, sinking back slightly as Elizabeth roared in an outburst of laughter.

"Oh, my, that just made my day," she said breathing as if she just ran a marathon. "That was too good, Jeremiah. If only I'd recorded that," she said as she pulled out her phone. "Well, what do you know, I did." She quickly went back ten seconds on her voice recorder app and replayed the last bit of the conversation, mainly Jeremiah's part. "Man, who unknowingly flirts a lot, flirts a lot, flirts a lot," she giggled as she replayed those last few words a dozen times.

"We get it," I said as I shook my head, not agreeing with their assessment. "You may think I use it as a currency, but I'm broke," I replied with a laugh as I pulled out my front pockets revealing only lint balls.

"Oh, Solomon," Elizabeth said in a patronizing way. "You don't know the wealth you could hold," she said with a wink as she and Jeremiah walked toward the hostess showing the three of us to our seats. I stood in contemplation as a thought popped into my head.

"But you know I'm not holding it, so that proves my point."

155

"Come on," Jeremiah said, waving me to the table. "We can agree to disagree, but I'll let you know a secret," he said as we all sat down. "You're wrong."

"Anyways," I responded as a thought hit me. "Do you always record our conversations?"

Elizabeth smiled cunningly.

"Well, do you?" I asked again.

"Only when I know you are going to be wrong," she winked.

"And how do you know that?" I asked, a little too quickly from her dumbfounded look.

"Anyways," she said playfully as she started a new topic with Jeremiah.

CHAPTER 55

Veronica pulled into her garage and sat in her car for a few minutes. She watched as the garage door slid down, secluding her from the rest of the world. She was safe. She was alone. She was allowed to crumble. She clung onto her steering wheel, her manicured nails digging into the fine crafted leather as she sobbed uncontrollably. She held onto the wheel as if it were the only thing keeping her from collapsing into the passenger seat.

Her eyes gushed puddles of tears that fell onto her lonely lap. She didn't feel like talking to anyone. Who would she talk to? She didn't have anyone she could confide in anymore. The one person she used to tell her secrets to was Jenny. Now, she dreaded ever allowing herself to open up to that treacherous vile of a human.

She knew she needed to get out of the car, but she couldn't. She couldn't move. She sat paralyzed. The mind games Jenny and Mr. Alexeev were playing were too much for her. She thought she had the mental willpower of a Navy SEAL, but she'd learned in the last few months the drive that empowered her was losing fuel. She didn't have the inner gumption to fight till her last breath anymore. She was beginning to feel what the rest of the world felt. She was going to have to relinquish her crown forged with steel and find one more suitably fashioned with dandelions. She was beginning to feel like a defenseless child picking daisies in a meadow instead of one of the top defense attorneys of the greater Washington D.C. area.

"You can do it," she told herself as she removed her hands from the steering wheel, unbuckled her safety belt, and opened the car door. She didn't reach for her briefcase. She didn't need the added weight. She was going to have a hard enough time walking through the garage to the house. She got out of the car and stood for a few seconds, leaning on the side of the car, her eyes red and her nose running. She looked at her reflection in the car window and shuttered at her image. It wasn't of a strong-willed woman; it was of a weak school girl with no one to turn to.

Shuffling her feet, she made her way to her house. She opened the door, finding it completely dark and unwelcoming. She missed the nights when Winston was at home making her supper. She missed walking into the kitchen and smacking his butt as he stood behind the stove stirring a pot of pasta. She loved him. She really did. But she knew she had messed up. She walked through the kitchen as cold as her heart. No amount of flame would be able to warm her insides.

She wasn't hungry. She just wanted to relax with a good bubble bath. She walked into her bedroom and froze when she flipped on the lights. Winston's closets were open, but they were bare on the inside. His dresser drawers were open, but nothing was in them except the decorative paper lining the bottom.

She started to weep once again. She knew she had messed up, but she didn't realize he would go this far. She laid on her bed for what seemed like hours. She had cried all she could cry; her eyes were dry.

She walked into her bathroom to start her bath and saw the writing on the mirror in red lipstick. Her legs went weak once again. She wanted to keep going to marriage counseling and she thought it was working. She was learning to show him affection, and Wint was learning to understand her mannerisms. They were growing closer together. That was until this morning. She grabbed a bottle of perfume on the counter and threw it at the mirror, shattering the written image. She watched as the red lettering fell like broken confetti. Yet she still remembered what it said.

I'll sign your papers now.

CHAPTER 56

"Sorry to leave you guys, but Whitney got back home earlier today, so I'm heading out," Grant said with a manly smile.

"Go on and have a good time with your wife," Jordan jabbed, "you ol' dog you."

"Try and get to bed soon," Collin chimed in, the rest of the guys a little shocked by his risqué notion. "What?" Collin asked, his naivety getting the better of him. "I meant, because we have an employee meeting tomorrow morning to go over the changes in the coming months," he noted conservatively. "Get your minds out of the gutter, boys."

"On that note," Grant said as he waved goodbye and headed out to see his beloved wife after dropping off the names and phone numbers of the various women he had gotten for Stewart.

"He's a beast," Jordan boasted staring amazed at the number of contacts Grant dropped on the table.

Grant walked two blocks to catch the local metro train and headed home. He loved his wife. He had fallen madly in love with her his sophomore year of college and he had never stopped loving her. The guys never would admit it, but they were jealous of his life. He was the good looking one in their group, but he wasn't cocky about it. There was no need to be cocky; he already got the woman of his dreams.

He rode the subway train, texting Whitney like they were in college again. His fingers still got excited when he saw a text was from her. He hoped their passion would never fade and didn't have any fears of that happening any time soon.

Where are you? she asked with a sad emoji face.

I'm almost home, he texted back quickly with a heart emoji. He wanted to bring her home some flowers, but it was too late. All the

159

florist shops had already closed around their home. *I've missed you*, he texted.

Missed you too, stud, she texted back as his smile widened.

He exited the train and walked the three blocks to his home, stopping periodically at the crosswalks to text his loving wife and look up at the sky. He couldn't see the stars living in the city. The city lights drowned out the glowing heavenly freckles. He'd been on a few vacations that allowed him to see the heavenly lights in all their glory, but only a few. He was amazed as a kid on his trip to Yellowstone when he would lie in his sleeping bag and see what seemed like a million stars overhead. But now, in the city, he was lucky to catch a few of the brightest lights.

After his last crosswalk he swaggered down the street, saying hello to a few neighbors who were taking their dogs out for the last time before bed. He punched in his code for his security system and the cameras instantly recognized his face. The deadbolts unlocked allowing him to enter his safety confines.

"Whitney, I'm home!" he shouted from the entryway as he dropped his keys and wallet on the foyer table.

"I'm upstairs, waiting," she said seductively.

"Coming," he said, sprinting up the stairs and undoing his belt. "I've missed you so much."

"What have you done the last few days?" she asked, nibbling on his ear as she untucked his shirt.

"Nothing much," he lied.

CHAPTER 57

"What's wrong, Solomon?" Jeremiah asked as the three of us sat around finishing our dessert, which I had barely touched.

"You have barely eaten anything all night," Elizabeth commented as she sipped her cappuccino. "Still dwelling on the fact you're like us?"

"Oh, no," I said solemnly. "I've just had a rough day."

"Yes," Jeremiah agreed. "It has been one of much mental anguish with Winston and Veronica."

I glanced up at Elizabeth, and she knew there was something else weighing on my mind tonight. "What if you did something with good intentions, but it caused more problems?"

"You just move on," Elizabeth said coolly.

Jeremiah looked at her coldly with squinting eyes.

"Well, that's how I deal with it," Elizabeth quipped.

"Most of the world isn't like you," Jeremiah scathed. "Fortunately."

"Well," Elizabeth sarcastically huffed. "At least I sleep with a clean conscience," she said staring at Jeremiah with a playful smile.

She then looked at me and her smile faded. It was like a look of guilt washed over her. I brushed past her expression and carried on with my question. "Really. I don't mean something small, but I mean a huge problem has arisen all because I stuck my fat nose where I thought it belonged, but my intrusion made it much worse."

"Solo, Winston and Veronica's issues are not your fault," Jeremiah compassionately said. "They have more issues beneath their surface than what happened today. You opening your home to your friend isn't going to cause any more of a problem than you telling him no. He would have found another couch to sleep on."

I listened to Jeremiah with grateful ears, knowing he didn't understand that a little boy and his father were dead tonight because of me. All because of me. And there was one sad little boy without a brother or dad tonight. All because of me.

Jeremiah excused himself from the table after his compassion-filled speech, and I was finally able to expel my pain.

"I went down to the park to stop a drug deal today, Elizabeth, and before I knew it…" I started to say, but I couldn't finish. I looked down at my plate of caramel cheesecake then darted my eyes around the restaurant.

"Before you knew it, what?" Elizabeth asked with a tender whisper. "Solo, before you knew it, what?"

She reached over and placed her hand over mine. The touch of her skin shocked the tears out of my eyes. I looked up into hers, and a few tears spilled over. I shook my head and tried to stop my wet eyes, but they wouldn't cease.

"They…" I got out before my air was stolen. I tried to speak again, but all I could get out was the same first word.

"Breathe, Solo, just take a deep breath," she warmly recited. "It's not your fault, Solo. It's not your fault. You were trying to help someone. You were doing a selfless good deed, Solo. It's not your fault."

Her words washed over me like a warm blanket, but I couldn't allow the warmth to stay. I didn't feel worthy of the compassionate, judgment-free words.

"They died because of me!" I stammered, pulling my hands away from hers. "They died because of me!" I shouted once again, quickly fumbling for my wallet to find a twenty to leave on the table.

"Solo," she said, "you didn't cause it. You didn't cause it, Solo."

"I've got to go," I said quickly, throwing the money on the table and walking away.

I sped out of the restaurant and darted down the first alley I could find. I slinked behind a garbage can and curled up with my knees to my chest and bawled. I cried for the anniversary of Chelsea's death. I cried for the idea of my best friend leaving his wife. I cried for the notion I caused two people to die today.

"God, I need your help right now," was all I could say through the sobbing.

My darkest fears and doubts suddenly crept up as I pleaded to God again. I was afraid I didn't deserve to be heard. I doubted there was anyone out there to listen to me. "God, if you're real, I need you right now."

"Help me!" a woman screamed. "Help me!"

CHAPTER 58

"Help me!" the terrified muffled voice echoed through the darkened alleyway of dungy trash bins scattered beside graffiti-covered walls.

"Get off her!" I yelled, picking myself off the ground and running in the direction of two pairs of tangled legs on the ground. He must have heard me, because the almost-rapist quickly jumped to his feet and fled the scene darting between oncoming traffic to get across the street and run toward freedom.

I quickly stopped chasing after the hooded figure once I saw the bright lights outside the alley and the thug running at a breakneck pace. I went back to the scared woman, who was still huddled on the ground with her skirt above her waist.

"You okay?" I asked, slowly stooping down so my eyes were at her level. I kept eye contact. I didn't want her to feel any more betrayed. She looked at me in disbelief.

"I…uh…I was just…" she started as she looked around the alley, clearly confused with what just happened.

"What's your name?" I asked, helping her to focus on herself once again. Her shimmering black hair contrasted her caramel-colored skin as her hazel eyes radiated distrust.

"Fiona," she quietly said as she lowered her floral skirt and buttoned her red blouse. "My name is Fiona."

"Do you know the guy who was just here?" I asked, keeping a safe distance so she wouldn't feel cornered once again.

"No," she quickly said.

"We need to contact the police."

"No," she stated defensively. "What are they going to do about this?"

"Find him!" I said like she was my little sister. "He doesn't deserve to be on the street."

I helped her up to her feet, and the fragile little girl suddenly morphed into a calloused young woman. "Most men wouldn't be on the street then," she confidently huffed.

"What do you mean by that?"

"Exactly how it sounded," she said as she started to walk down the alley toward the lights from the traffic.

"Fiona. Fiona," I said walking two steps behind her, but she didn't stop. "Fiona!"

"What? Want a reward for saving me?" she turned around with a jaded look in her eyes. It was a look that sent a chill to my core. I thought I was saving her. She was the one who screamed out for help; yet, when it boiled down to the nitty-gritty, she didn't think she needed any help. No one had ever saved her before tonight, and by the look in her eyes, no one would help her in the nights to come. She could fend for herself.

"If you need anything, ask for Officer Cooper," I said as I stood back in the shadows of the alley. "He's a good cop."

"They're all the same," she said with a roll of her eyes. She turned on her heels and started her march home. She was obviously used to watching her own back.

I watched as she walked all alone down the crowded sidewalk. She walked with her shoulders hunkered down by the weight of the careless world in which she lived. She kept her head down as if to keep from making eye contact with any new strangers.

I continued to stand in the shadows, leaning against the brick wall under dripping gutter eaves. The droplets of water were just the refreshment I needed.

"I hear you, God," I smiled as I watched Fiona continue to walk her lonely path. "I hear you."

It was then she casually turned her head to look behind as if to make sure she was still being watched from a safe distance. I'm not positive if she saw me watching in the shadows, but I'm pretty sure she did. Her posture rose with some unjaded confidence, as if she discovered for the first time tonight a little good in the world. Sadly, it took a near horrific episode to see a little ray of hope. Usually, the light shines brightest in the darkest of times.

Be safe, Fiona.

CHAPTER 59

Elizabeth sat annoyed in the driver's seat of her vehicle, but she wasn't sure if she was more annoyed at herself or at Solo. She had called him to see if he would be willing to drive around town looking for the shooter tonight, but he declined.

"Elizabeth, we did that last night and it was useless."

"But tonight could be different," she responded, a little bewildered at her own sense of optimism when she usually wore the crown of pessimism proudly, as if it was a badge of honor from years of being Veronica's little sister.

"You have nothing, Elizabeth. Nothing."

She quickly ended the call before Solo could say anything else. She wanted to be angry with him. She almost convinced herself she had the right to smack his smug face, but reality hit her with a frigid wave of guilt like the wind of a northeaster. Not more than twenty hours ago she had the sickening realization she could have stopped Solo's misery – if she had only done something to save his wife from that bullet.

She stared out her window, not looking at anything, but visualizing the many possible ways she could have saved Chelsea's life. She could have called the cops, tackled her to the ground, screamed across the street to drop. It would have been easy. She would still be alive.

She shook the thoughts away, not liking the feeling of accepting blame. She'd lived a privileged lifestyle. She was taught from an early age she could always blame someone weaker for her failings. They wouldn't be brave enough to defend themselves, so it was just survival of the fittest, but she preferred to think survival of the *finessest*. God knew she would never be able to do a pull-up, unless there was a pair of Jimmy Choo shoes on the top rack calling her name, but she had a way with her ingrained Hyde air to get whatever she pleased.

She shook off her guilt like it was a clearance rack knock-off Kate Spade purse. Looking into her rearview mirror she made a vow, "It wasn't your fault! You know what you can do and you will do it!"

She turned the ignition and revved the engine. She didn't know where she was going, but she knew with her solid instincts she would find what she was looking for.

She pulled out a tube of lipstick from her original Kate Spade clutch purse sitting in her passenger seat and applied a generous portion onto her puckering lips.

"This shade has never let me down yet," she said blowing a kiss to her reflection. "And it's not going to start tonight."

CHAPTER 60

All the guys left Stu's and parted ways, each heading a different direction, some to a bus or metro stop, and one back to the hidden parked car. Stewart walked with a bigger wallet in his back pocket, not from dollar bills, but from the names and numbers the rest of the guys scored for him through the night.

They had ended their night a little earlier than the night before, so he thought he would recline the driver's seat for a little while. He sat his alarm on his phone for one hour, knowing that would give him plenty of time to watch Piper leave her shift at Stu's and begin his journey.

He reached into the glove compartment and found the baseball cap and fake mustache. With the light from the nearby street light he strategically placed the mustache perfectly. "Hey, handsome," he winked in the vanity mirror, mocking the tone he would often hear his backstabbing friend say in high school after gym class as he would check himself out in the mirror while combing his hair. "You're not so handsome anymore," he laughed.

It almost disgusted him to put on the Baltimore Orioles cap, but after readjusting the tightness he quickly put it on. This time, he had to flip up the vanity mirror so he couldn't see his reflection under that orange hat. The thought of being seen wearing it almost made his stomach curl, but he knew it was what *he* would have worn.

He found the pair of sunglasses in the cup holder and put them on. As he reclined back into the seat, he recalled one of the lines from an 80s song and smiled at how fitting Corey Hart's words were for this night.

He smiled at the thought of watching her weave through the traffic, but he hoped there would be very little weaving in and out of vehicles. His plan was to find a desolate stop and watch her breathe just like the song said. Then he would also watch her stop breathing.

Closing his eyes, he recalled just two hours earlier when he'd ordered a drink from her.

"I'll take a beer with a lime," he said.

"Nice one, man," Piper said with a smile.

Nice one, man? he thought with a little humility punch to his gut. But he hadn't flinched at her response. He could have, but he didn't.

How dare she not remember me, he thought as he waited for his drink.

"Here you go, buddy," Piper had said sliding the mug across the wood, moving to wait on the next customer. "What'll you take, bud?"

He glanced down at his phone and only five minutes had passed since he set his alarm. It was going to be a long hour of waiting.

As each minute passed, he got wider awake.

His heart was pumping with the thrill of causing his ex-girlfriend, who didn't even remember his face, to breathe her final breath.

His smile widened as he looked down at his phone and opened the map app he had installed showing the possible route for the night. He almost started to become a giddy school boy as he looked in the passenger seat and saw his buddy for the night.

"You did very well last night so don't fail me tonight," he said looking at the shiny gun. "I want to introduce you to an old friend of mine. But don't worry about giving her your name. Apparently, she won't remember it.

Piper, Piper, Piper. You'll never know what you could have had.

CHAPTER 61

Dakota sat in the police squad room, slightly dazed from Ty dying in her lap. She had tried to wash the blood off of her uniform for thirty minutes, but there were blotches on her lap and chest from where she cuddled the dying child. Her face showed the remorse she was feeling, and everyone could see it.

"Cheer up," Detective Young jabbed as he walked by. "It wasn't like it was your own kid that died."

"Are you for real?" Officer Cooper said in shock at the distaste of Young's words.

"What? It's true though," Young said, snapping back with a look that told Cooper he was his superior and must be respected.

Dakota looked up at Young, disgusted. Disgusted at his words, but also disgusted at herself for her past of clinging onto the hope he was the knight in shining armor she wished him to be. Her eyes were opened six months ago, and every time he spoke, her stomach turned a little more for once finding him appealing.

"Come on," Cooper said to Dakota. "Our shift has ended and Young's has started. I would hate to disrupt his paperwork," he said as he helped Dakota to her feet.

They passed through the swinging doors of the squad room and walked down the brightly lit yet eerily quiet hallway to exit the building. Cooper walked beside like a big brother watching out for his younger sister.

"It will get easier," he said as their shoes resounded through the hall. "It may not feel like it will, but it will."

She stopped and turned to look at him. "I feel like I should be saying the same thing to you right now."

Her heartfelt words were true. He was hurting as well. He may not be showing it, but his world had been flipped this morning. He woke up this morning knowing it would be strange giving his testimony to his wife. But he had never envisioned her blindsiding him in the courtroom to defend a woman she knew was guilty.

Dakota continued to speak, but he wasn't listening. He had zoned out and was reliving the dreaded morning. The words she said, the pain he felt, the tyranny she bestowed so easily. He had even wished her good luck this morning with a warm kiss.

"Wint?" Dakota said waving her hand in front of his face.

He rapidly blinked and woke up from the frightening memory. He shook his head, hoping the memory was just a figment of his imagination, but by the look on her face he knew that was wishful thinking.

"We will get through this," she said. "Tomorrow is a new day."

He choked up an appreciative smile, which was fake, but she couldn't tell. He had learned to master the fake smile after years of formal dinner parties with Veronica's family and friends.

"Yes, tomorrow will be a better day," he lied.

They started walking down the hall as he casually looked to Dakota. She looked broken but strong. He knew tomorrow would be a better day for her. He looked inward at himself and wondered the same.

Tomorrow wouldn't be any better for him. It was going to take a lot of tomorrows to get through this.

CHAPTER 62

My depressing apartment seemed a little livelier with Wint's belongings strewn in the middle of the living room. The image would have conjured happy feelings if a loved one was coming to visit for the weekend, but as I sat on the couch looking at his suitcases, happy wasn't what I was I was feeling.

I looked down at the text message I sent to Elizabeth shortly after she hung up on me. No response, which was expected after dealing with her emotional highs and lows in the last six months. I couldn't say the learning process hadn't been without any hiccups. A few of them almost resulted into full-blown regurgitations by our stubborn prides.

Elizabeth, I know you're getting my messages. Your freakin' car reads them to you, I texted, knowing a female computerized voice would read the message emotionlessly.

Sitting the phone down, I ping-ponged back to Wint. Between the two of them, I didn't have much time to wallow in my own self pity of Chelsea's murder, Ty and Chuck's deaths, and Fiona's lack of appreciation. Maybe it was God's way of showing me everyone had days like this. It rained on the just and the unjust. I wasn't trying to say Wint and Elizabeth were unworthy humans, at least not Wint.

I looked down at my hands in my lap and noticed I had basically rubbed my ring finger dry. I had a nervous tendency of feeling for the hard golden band that used to be wrapped around my finger like I was to Chelsea. After today's drama, I needed the strength and confidence she exuded. Feeling for the wedding band was a warm reminder she was still a part of me, even though my friends and family almost cut off my finger to get it off. It took some time, but I was finally able to have some closure, but it didn't mean I didn't miss her each day.

My phone chimed informing me of a new message. *Feeling guilty for standing me up?* Elizabeth texted back.

I shook my head at how she was always up for a fight, but I wasn't feeling a fight tonight. I was feeling the need for the touch of an olive branch. *If it was any other night, I would be out there with you. You know that.*

I waited for the text to be sent, read, and responded to. I watched my phone light up with an incoming call from Elizabeth.

"Just let me rant at you for a second, okay?" she yelled. "You know how important this is for me! You know I'm the one getting the dreams, and I have no clue how I'm supposed to save this stupid girl tonight. I feel like God has some kind of twisted sense of humor tonight giving me only snippets in my dreams as if He's playing me like some kind of windup toy. 'Let's pull her string and watch her go crazy!'"

"Anything else?" I calmly asked.

"As a matter of fact there is! Why is the creepy stalker always a man? He gets paid more than a woman. He doesn't have to endure childbirth. He can pee standing up, because you don't want to get me started on public restrooms. I'm surprised I don't have any more UTIs from constantly holding it in until I get home. You don't know how easy you have it, Solo."

"You're right. We men are pigs. Anything else?"

"Why can't this serial killer go after old, grandma types? It really freaks me out when they go after people my age. These girls have a full life to live, and well, some eighty-year-olds are just wasting space."

"Elizabeth! That's harsh," I said with a chuckle. There is one thing I loved about Elizabeth – her ruthless honesty in her stream of consciousness thought process.

"It's true!" she roared back with hysterical laughter. "I'm driving around some of these lonely streets looking for a gunman, and for all I know, he could be looking for me. What if me looking for him has somehow twisted my dream and I'm going to be the next victim?"

I sat in thought for a minute. "If a car pulls up beside you at a light, run it."

"Solo! I'm serious! A little while ago I was surging with rage to find this psycho, but now that I'm out here, I feel like a target is on my back. And I've already run two red lights tonight when some car pulled up beside me. I checked my review mirror and I think one of them was a Girl Scouts van. I still don't understand why a man was driving it, but it clearly said Girl Scouts on the front. Really? Girl Scouts! You men are now trying to take over the women organizations of the world too! Come on dude, stick to your misogynous boys club. I'm cool with that!"

"Elizabeth, calm down. If it's freaking you out that much, go home. And are you sure it said Girl Scouts and not Girl Scouting? I think there's a strip joint called that."

"Gross!" she laughed. "Why do they have a van? Do they have mobile stripper poles in the back for bachelor parties?" She stopped to consider that. "You know, that's not a bad idea. Could be an interesting venture. Siri, remind me to look into mobile strip clubs later."

"Elizabeth, you don't need to start up an adult entertainment business. What would Jeremiah say?" I asked smiling.

"He would just tell me, 'Elizabeth, you know that is the world's oldest profession. Look at the civilizations of so what and this and that.' I think he would be proud of me for wanting to learn some history."

"The history of making some bills at other women's expense," I agreed able to hear Jeremiah in her voice.

"I'll be a nice madam," Elizabeth said in a calmer tone. "Are women strip club owners called madams or just the brothel owners?"

"You would shoot anyone who called you madam."

"Yeah. Sounds old."

"Now go home. We can do this tomorrow night. Maybe you will get another dream."

"But what if this is the last kill?" she asked solemnly.

"Then he's done and we can move on to other things," I said sincerely.

I listened for her response, but all I could hear was her breathing. "Elizabeth, you all right?"

"Yeah. Just thinking," she said, sounding annoyed. "You are probably right, which makes me hate it even more."

"Don't you know I'm always right?"

"Except earlier tonight when you weren't," she buzzed back. "Are you doing better from dinner?" she asked, her tone changing from blistering to compassionate.

"Better is a word I may use tomorrow. But for right now, I am just doing."

"Well, you know you are not alone, Solomon," she said motherly.

"I know," I answered as I heard a knock on my front door.

"Come in," I yelled as I watched Wint uneasily enter the room.

"Elizabeth, Wint's here so I will let you go. And you go home."

"Sure. I'll call Verny. Night, darling," she said as she ended the call.

"If I didn't know you any better, I would think there was a thing between you two," Wint kidded as he took off his boots.

I quickly stood up from the couch and went to my friend and hugged him.

No words were said.

There would be plenty of words tonight.

CHAPTER 63

After I fixed Wint a quick turkey sandwich, we started from the beginning.

"What happened?" I asked sitting on one end of the couch with Wint on the other.

"Man, she was different today," he unemotionally said, as if in a trance.

I had to bite my tongue because it was not the time to tell him that's how she'd treated me for years. "What do you mean, different?"

He stopped his zombie-like gaze and looked directly in my eyes. "It was like she just changed. As if she was done playing married and it was time in her appointment book to end it and move on to her next goal in life."

"Do you think she wants to get Jenny off?" I asked shocked. "That can't be right."

"She sure acted like it today when she was busting my chops," he said getting up to get another glass of tea.

I sat confused. No matter the grudge I had with Verny, this seemed unfathomable.

He sat down with his full glass of iced tea already half drunk. "You know what gets me the most?"

I shook my head no.

"That she waited until I was on the stand to tell me she had written our divorce papers," he said with astonishment. "Good Lord, couldn't she had told me during one of our counseling sessions? I would have taken it better there. But to have that dropped at my feet in front of a room full of people. I'm pretty sure I heard Jenny snicker when Veronica said it. It's like she had this planned."

"That's a tough one, man."

"And you know what really gets me?"

I once again shook my head no.

"Wondering if she has been playing me this whole time. Do you think she and Jenny were in on this together, and this was just a strategy they had planned?"

"No," I said quickly. "Couldn't be. I would say Verny, I mean, Veronica, is capable of a lot of things, but murder wouldn't be one of them."

"I don't know, Solo. Our marriage started to break open during the killing spree last October. She went and stayed the night at Jenny's place the night before they were caught. What if they were planning their grand finale? Jenny told me as I was cuffing her that Veronica was writing the divorce papers, and I didn't believe her."

I couldn't believe what I was hearing. It showed how wounded Wint was to come up with such a farfetched tale to comfort his fragile heart.

"But she called you to warn you something was going to happen at the train station. I told her to…" I stopped and realized that over the last six months we had never talked about how I knew what was going to happen.

"Yeah, she said you told her to call me, but that still doesn't make sense to me how you knew. Unless you overheard Jenny say something," he said unconvincingly.

"The point is not how I knew," I quickly said darting away from that topic. "The point is she called you to save you. If she was in cahoots with Jenny, she wouldn't have called you. She would've ignored what I said."

I watched as the wheels in his brain started spinning, either to connect the dots or to concoct another excuse. "So, what if she wrote up divorce papers the night before? Heaven knows I've told you to write them."

"You probably have them hidden somewhere in the living room right now," he laughed. "Always ready to hand them to me when I said okay."

"Anyways," I said once again changing topics, "when it mattered, she had your back."

We sat in silence for a few minutes until he responded.

"But did she really?"

Wednesday
CHAPTER 64

The phone chimed him awake from his meditative state fifteen minutes earlier. He was all set and ready. He scanned the interior of the car and found everything was in place. He double-checked the gun's chamber to make sure it was full of bullets, even though he had already checked it twice earlier in the evening. He hoped to only use one bullet with a perfect kill, but better to be safe than sorry. It didn't need to be pretty. He wasn't going to mount her head on the wall or anything.

He turned on some music on his phone, and Chris Isaak's "Wicked Game" was the first song played on his shuffle. He smiled at the timing as he watched Piper's silhouette walk out of Stu's to her parked car.

He started singing along with Chris Isaak as Piper came closer into view. Turning his ignition his voice spiked on the chorus high melody. He sung the haunting words as he moved the car from park to drive on the gear shift. He repeated the chorus as he started to follow her down the road.

He began to smile as the song became the soundtrack for the night. He felt as if Chris wrote the song just for him by how the lyrics aligned perfectly with this monumental night. He clicked his phone to keep repeating the song as he drove before he opened his map app with the various routes he could drive tonight.

He quit saying the words but continued to hum the haunting melody as he followed the Honda CR-V a few car lengths ahead. He looked in his rearview mirror and noticed there weren't any vehicles behind him. He smiled at how fortunate the night was turning. Glancing down at his phone's map, he saw was following the correct course. He was going through all the intersections that weren't using the surveillance cameras tonight.

He slowly picked up speed, tired of playing the careful tortoise. He was ready to portray the speedy hare. He was ready to hunt down his game like a hound dog.

Piper's SUV came to a stop at a four-way light as he casually slid in beside her. He didn't look over at her, but hit the infotainment screen on his dashboard. With his right hand he gripped the handle of his gun. He wiggled the barrel through the hidden keyhole, and suddenly the image of Piper appeared on the screen.

He recalled a moment in high school when he saw her singing proudly in the driver's seat of her parked Pontiac, oblivious that he was watching. He had honked his horn and startled her, causing them both to burst out in laughter. Now, many years later, they were in the same predicament. She was singing and he was watching.

Except there was something else he wanted to burst out of her than her laughter.

He started to sing as the song was halfway through the second play. The light turned green and they both proceeded down the road. He continued to check the traffic at each intersection, and it was a peaceful night. There were no cars to be seen, except the ones that were parked. The sidewalks were free of late-night walkers, and even the homeless seemed to have hidden away as well.

He looked down at his phone and knew she would be turning soon. He slowed down allowing her to pass as he glided his car behind hers. Just like clockwork, she turned right.

So did he.

He started to grip his steering wheel a little tighter as he noticed a few stoplights ahead.

He sung as he quietly hoped the green light would change to red.

It didn't. They each proceeded through the intersection, but he still had a few more lights ahead.

They started approaching the next light, but it, too, stayed green.

He sung as his heart started to beat faster. He only had a few more lights before his easy chance was going to be gone.

Suddenly, the light two blocks head changed from yellow to red. A smile formed on his face as their cars started to once again meet at the same stoplight.

He looked down and noticed he had never removed his right hand from the gun. He stopped next to her car and aimed the gun at the side of her head. He watched the infotainment screen until it was aimed perfectly. He sang the poetic words as he fired the gun.

Her singing instantly stopped while his continued.

The light turned to green and he was quickly out of sight.

He softly sung as he followed his predetermined escape route on his phone's map. Within thirty seconds, he was four blocks away without anyone even noticing him.

It was just him and Chris.

CHAPTER 65

"Wint, you can't be serious!" I said, almost starting to shout. I even shocked myself as the thoughts in my head were defending Verny. "Veronica was totally, undeniably wrong with how she acted today in court. I'm on your side, man, but you've got to see that it's ludicrous to believe she and Jenny are up to this together."

Wint was silent, almost sulking on the couch. I knew he was hurt. I knew he was wounded beyond measure. But to grasp at invisible straws in hopes of grabbing one was beyond me.

"Wint," I said as he continued to stare at the blank television screen. He was mentally tuning me out. "Wint, I know you hear me."

He continued to stare into space. It wasn't bad enough his wife flipped his world like a pancake, but now his best friend was not being the friend he wanted.

"Wint," I said again, "You know at the end of the day, I'll always have your back. You know that, right?"

He slowly turned his head to look at me. He opened his mouth, but then stopped. He paused and looked around the room as if the words would be found written on the wall. Words that would prove his point. Words that would side with him. Words he could stuff down my throat. They weren't. He silently got up from the couch and slammed the bathroom door behind him.

I knew it was going to be a long night, and I wondered if Elizabeth was having much success talking to Veronica. I quickly grabbed my phone and texted her. *How's Veronica doing????*

I quickly watched the three flashing dots signaling Elizabeth was typing. *She didn't answer. Must be asleep. Wint doing ok?*

I looked at my phone and then at the closed bathroom door. *Peachy*, I texted with a thumbs down. *Just peachy!!!*

Gotcha! she quickly responded. *You boys have a great night*, she texted with a laughing emoji. *This gal's gotta get her beauty sleep.*

I tossed the phone on the couch and waited a few minutes before barging into the bathroom.

"Solo!" he shouted sitting on the toilet seat lid. "Knock first!"

"My walls are thin here, so I knew you weren't doing anything in here except forcing me away."

"I could have been," he growled.

"It's not like I haven't seen it before," I laughed.

"Just get out and leave me alone," he sulked.

"No," I calmly said, leaning against the doorframe.

"Come on, just leave me alone," he said again.

"Not gonna happen," I replied looking down at my watch. "I have all night, no place to be, and this is my only bathroom. I don't live in a castle like you."

Wint looked down at his feet as a smile started to break through his tough exterior.

"You're out of toilet paper," Wint casually said as he stood up.

"It's behind you," I said, pointing at the stack of old magazines.

"You've got to be kidding me," he said, his eyes widening in disbelief.

"Yeah," I said digging into the bathroom cabinet for a couple of rolls. "I only use the cologne ads for special occasions."

"You're something else, Solo," he grinned as he came towards me for a hug, but psyched me out instead and smacked my skull.

I wasn't expecting it, so my head bounced off the wooden door frame. "What'd you do that for?" I asked, rubbing the side of my head.

"For not knocking," he laughed. "Your mom wouldn't be happy, and I have just the nerve to text her."

"Are you going to tell her you hit me too?"

"You deserved it," he laughed as we headed back to the couch. "She would agree."

"Yeah, but you also hit me with your car today, and I never retaliated," I said still nursing my wounded head that had been hit twice within twelve hours.

"Why were you at the park today? And how did you know the shooter's name?" he asked.

I looked at him speechless.

Suddenly, his CB radio started to scream an alert. "We have a Code 3, a 10-54 and an 11-25 on the corner of 16th and Constitution Avenue."

"On my way," a man's voice said before the dispatch operator came back on.

"Ambulance is on its way," the operator said routinely.

"What was that about?" I asked as Wint lowered the volume on the radio.

"Appears to be a 187," said the muffled dispatch.

"Sounds like someone was murdered in the middle of the street," Wint answered. "Sadly, it's nothing new."

I shook my head and realized Elizabeth's dream probably came true. He had killed again. I grabbed my phone from the couch and typed a message to Elizabeth.

"You know I'll do anything for you," I said holding the phone in my hand.

"I know," he nodded. "I know you will."

"I'll always have your back."

"I know," he solemnly grinned.

"You can say anything to me, any time. I'll be there for you."

"I know," Wint echoed.

"And when you start to talk crazy, you know I won't let you slide. Friends don't let friends ruin their lives like that."

185

"I know."

"But whatever decision you make, you don't have to go through it alone," I said sincerely. "Whatever decision."

"You're not going to tear up on me, are you?" Wint kidded as he got up to get another drink.

"I've cried enough today, man. No more tears from me," I said truthfully.

Wint froze in the kitchen as he started to pour another glass of tea. The words hit him hard, and he realized he wasn't being the best friend right now either. I watched as his head turned to the calendar on the refrigerator door with today's date circled.

"Oh man, I'm sorry. I totally forgot about what day today was for you. How are you doing?" he asked, beating himself up for not asking sooner.

"Well," I started. "It was yesterday since it's past midnight." I had to pour a little more salt in his wound as I watched him flinch in regret. "It's okay. It really is okay. It happened years ago."

"She was a good one, Solo," he said with a smile. "She was a real good one."

"Yes, yes she was," I choked out as I felt my eyes start to water. I shook my head to stop. I wasn't going to cry today. "You had a tough day. I had a tough day. We both suffered some. But I've learned tomorrow will be a better day."

"You mean today," Wint said with a grin. "It's got to be compared to yesterday."

My phone vibrated in my hand with a text from Elizabeth. *Knew it! Maybe tomorrow will be better.*

Just what I was telling Wint, I texted back.

"Elizabeth says hello," I lied as Wint looked at me with a puzzled expression.

"I don't understand you, Solo," he laughed shaking his head. "I don't understand you at all."

"I don't get myself half the time," I chuckled as we both got comfortable on the couch. It seemed like it was going to be a long night. Maybe not for talking, but just for being there for one another.

"You know I'll always be there for you too," Wint said as I turned the television on with the remote.

"I know," I smiled as I flipped through a few channels. "You've been there in my past, and I know you'll always be there in my future." I started to laugh hysterically.

"What?" he said, confused. "What's so funny?"

"It's like you are some kind of toe fungus or herpes or something."

"Wow," he said amazed. "Never knew athletes' feet could be so glamorous to be compared to me."

"Or is it the other way around? Never thought you could be so grotesque to be compared to an STD?"

"Well, there is no cream you can use to get rid of me, bud. I'm here for the long haul."

"Me either, Wint. Me either."

CHAPTER 66

Detective Young arrived on the crime scene and got a feeling this seemed strangely familiar to the homicide from last night. The Honda CR-V with a broken driver's side window was parked with the front right tire on top of the curb edging close to the sidewalk. There, sitting motionless, was another dead woman with a gunshot wound to her head. Just as last night.

"Did anyone see anything?" Detective Young asked the first patrollers who arrived on the scene as he looked around at the residential apartments and townhouses that were housed over the closed bakery and cellular phone store on each corner. The red and blue lights ricocheted off the buildings like a dance club a few blocks away.

"No one," Officer Denton said.

"What about the traffic cameras?" Young asked, motioning overhead at the surveillance cameras mounted to catch reckless drivers.

"Aren't on," Officer Denton answered. "I just called transportation to get the feed, and they said this camera hasn't been used in some time."

"Why have these cameras all over the place if they aren't going to use them? Stupid!" Young ranted as Denton nodded in agreement.

"I never understand government policies. But look who we work for," Denton smiled and walked away to see if he could help anyone else. He had heard the talk about Young, and he didn't want to be anywhere near his scope of influence.

Young stepped aside to the sidewalk aligned with cherry blossom trees that had bloomed two weeks earlier. He inhaled the sweet aroma of the petals that were strewn along the ground while inwardly despising the flocks of tourists that came each spring to see the beauty of these trees. He pulled out his phone and attentively found Captain

Bradley Johnson in his contact list. "Yes, Captain, it appears we have a problem," Young calmly spoke as he kicked a few of the petals to clear an area on the sidewalk for him to stand. He and Captain Bradley hadn't been on the best of terms over the last few months. Bradley was the one who spearheaded the position change for Young and even requested his removal from the police force. Somehow, Young managed to squeak by with just a blemish on his record from the elbows he and his family had rubbed through the years.

"Problem?" Bradley coughed, clearly enjoying a night of sound sleep. "What's so urgent that it couldn't have waited, Young?"

"Sir, the shooting that happened last night with the woman in her car. Well, it happened again tonight."

"Okay, so why are you calling me?"

"Because it looks like we have a killer on the loose," Young gulped.

"Are you sure these incidents are connected? Have you gotten anything that would prove this?" Bradley barked, knowing Young had jumped the gun too many times in his past.

"No, not exactly sir, but the shooting happened in a similar location as last night."

"Shootings like this happen often in D.C., Young. Don't jump to conclusions without getting all the facts," Bradley lectured. The same lecture he had been preaching to Young since day one.

"But--" Young tried to speak, but was quickly shot down.

"When you are certain these two crimes are connected, that's when you can call someone of higher rank, but not me. When they agree with you, then you call someone else of higher rank. If they agree with you, then you can call me. Until then, don't!" Bradley spit out before hanging up.

"But…" Young stammered, knowing he was fighting an uphill battle. Quickly, he turned and shouted to the police officers standing by. "Do you have any other information? Anything at all?"

Officer Tilly approached the raging detective. "No, we just arrived here ten minutes before you, and we just had time to confirm with dispatch what we discovered and secured the crime scene."

"When's the medical examiner's office coming?" Young asked agitatedly. "Does anyone know that?"

They looked around confused. "You mean, that guy over there?" Tilly asked, pointing over at the chief medical examiner who was inspecting the dead body.

"Why didn't you say Dr. Santiago was here?" Young turned flush with anger.

"I didn't know I had to announce everyone who got here to you, Young," Tilly said, smiling sarcastically.

"Next time you better remember," Young stomped off. "And it's Detective Young."

Tilly made a gesture when Young had his back to him. "Yes, sir, Detective Young."

"So, Dr. Santiago, is this murder connected with the murder from last night?" Young quickly asked as Dr. Santiago stood up from the corpse.

"Officer--" Dr. Santiago started.

"I'm a detective. Detective Young."

Dr. Santiago always remembered a face and name, but he also had a wicked sense of humor, especially when it came to arrogant people. "Oh, sorry, Detective Young," he grinned charmingly with his handsome smile that would cause any woman to overlook Young's frat boy good looks. "And which murder are you speaking of? I have a room full of bodies to get back to."

"The woman who was shot last night," Young answered. "It looks like these murders could be connected."

"Until I do ballistics and some other tests, I can't definitively say this homicide is associated with another," Dr. Santiago answered. He wanted to wipe the smug expression off Young's face, but he, too, had a duty to serve the people of D.C. "But at first sight, I would agree your assessment is reasonable, but not yet fact. The gunshot wound of this victim is strikingly similar to that of Sabrina Latener."

Young looked shocked at Dr. Santiago's memory of the previous night's victim when he had trouble remembering his name, even though he had worked with Dr. Santiago for years.

"I will get this victim back to my office. After my analysis, I will decide if there is a connection or not. As soon as I find out, I will let you know, Officer Hung," Dr. Santiago said as he took off his latex gloves and motioned for his assistants to get the body back to his office.

"It's Detective Young," Young softly and dejectedly said to himself when Dr. Santiago was out of earshot. "It's Detective Young."

CHAPTER 67

"What are you doing all up and dressed?" I asked Wint when I saw him in the living room in his police uniform as I strolled through in a pair of boxers and gray t-shirt. We had sat on the couch until 3 a.m. discussing stupid stuff like we did in our dorm room in college. Occasionally, he would bring up Veronica, just like in college as well.

"The chief called me this morning. He wants me on the shooting from last night," Wint yawned before taking a bite of his breakfast banana. "Why are you up? Got class today?"

I looked at him and lied. "Yep." Actually I was about to get ready to head to the courthouse to meet up with Elizabeth. I took a few bites of an apple as he headed out the door and I headed to the shower.

Wint was on the case for the shooter, I thought as the water woke my body up from the four hours of sleep. I felt confident my friend was fully capable of finding the clues and capturing this murderer before he caused any more havoc. I stood under the jets of water as I recounted the dreams I had the night before. None of them involved a shooter, so maybe he was going to take the night off. I crossed my fingers Elizabeth and I would have a fairly easy day of services. The two dreams I had weren't earth-shattering, a simple telephone call to a local high school to inform a U.S. history teacher of a cheating scam involving seven students and comforting an elderly woman grieving on the subway this afternoon. They may not be newsworthy events, but to the people experiencing them, it was monumental.

I dried off and put on a pair of khakis and a blue polo shirt and headed out the door. As I headed into downtown on the subway, I called Mr. Rickland. He was surprised by my call at first, but after I explained to him his students had somehow found the test answers, he felt confident that creating a new test wasn't a bad idea.

"How did you ever find this out?" Mr. Rickland asked.

I didn't answer but ended the call. He didn't need to know how I got my information. He wouldn't have believed me anyway. I got a few glances from other pedestrians on the subway who overheard my phone call. A couple nodded favorably while a few others shook their heads disapprovingly. I couldn't help but judge, but the ones who looked at me with disgust didn't appear to be having the best life. Maybe if they hadn't cheated in school they would be in a better spot in life.

Suddenly, a twinge of guilt slapped me in my face. Who was I to judge by appearances? From the outside looking into my life, living in a run-down neighborhood, some would think the same of me. How quickly we judge before knowing all the facts. Sadly, if I was being tried, I would be found guilty most of the time with my sideways glances and eavesdropping ears. No matter how hard I tried, I still failed daily.

I texted Elizabeth my dreams for the night, telling her one had already been resolved. She soon sent me a long text detailing her dream in excruciating detail. Once again, like many nights before, she only had one dream. Sadly, as I read I knew some poor girl would most likely be killed tonight by being shot in the head at point blank range while she sat at a stoplight. I read the text and my heart sank as I read the woman's name. It was a name I had recently heard, and I wondered what the odds were of hearing this name again. Washington D.C. was a large metropolitan city, with millions of people living in this geographical area, so there were bound to be multiple people with a common first name. But truly how many?

How many Fionas were there?

Was she the same Fiona I saved last night?

Another question surged forward. Would I be able to save her again?

CHAPTER 68

"Can you believe it, Solo? Can you freakin' believe it? I have a name! Fiona!" Elizabeth shouted as they met on the front steps of the courthouse.

"I saved a Fiona last night," I timidly replied. "Do you think that's just a coincidence?"

"Coincidence, Solo? Really?" she gawked. "We've been doing this for six months and I can't tell coincidence from…from…" she stopped. "What's the opposite of coincidence?"

I shook my head, not knowing either.

"Well, whatever it is, I don't know anything anymore," she said. "We've got to save her!"

"Slow down," I reiterated. "We have to figure this out and figure it out fast."

Her smile broadened. It turned from playful to cunning.

"What?" I asked, looking around tentatively.

"I didn't tell you because I was so excited."

"Didn't tell me what?"

"It's good. It's really good," she grinned, dangling the carrot a little higher.

"Elizabeth, spill it."

"Where's the fun with that?" she playfully jabbed.

"Fine," I said leaving the conversation to walk up the cement steps to enter the courthouse.

"Oh, no boy, we are not going in there today," she announced with an attitude.

"Don't you want to see the defense's side?" I asked, confused because it had been Elizabeth's idea to meet in front of the courthouse.

"Don't you want to know what I know?" she asked.

"I want to know your name," said a handsome twenty-six year old young professional who walked up beside her in his well-tailored suit, holding a cup of coffee with a messenger bag strapped across his chest.

"If I wanted a man with a backpack I would go to a high school," she said shooing the hunk away.

"Your loss," he uttered dismissively.

"My loss?" she shouted, scaring a few nearby pigeons away. "I'm not the one who asked for my name. I already know it! Seems like you're the only one walking away empty-handed."

I walked back down the steps until we were close enough to whisper. "You do know he had a coffee in his hand, so technically, he wasn't empty-handed."

"That's not the point, Solo. But, yeah, I noticed that a second too late." She stopped and recollected her thoughts. "But he was probably too stunned by his rejection to put that together. Where was I? Oh, yeah. I think I know where it's going to happen tonight," she beamed radiantly. It was a sight I hadn't seen in her eyes all week. After yesterday's meltdowns, I needed some bright rays of optimism.

"Where?"

"Well, that part we are going to have to figure out," she said casually as she turned and started walking down the steps.

"Elizabeth, I thought you said you knew where it was going to happen."

"I said, 'I think I know,'" she corrected. "'I think I know.'"

"Well, where do you think it's going to happen?"

"By Sips and --," she smiled.

"Sips?" I asked wide-eyed. Sips was a locally owned coffee house establishment that had surged in the previous two years with a new location about every month. "There must be a few dozen Sips in D.C."

"Yes, but--"

"No buts. There are a lot of places to narrow down before tonight," I huffed.

"Yes, but--" she started once again.

"There is probably a Sips in every neighborhood now," I said, dismissing her claim for knowing where the hit would take place tonight.

"Yes, but--" she winced agitatedly.

"Look, there's a Sips," I pointed across the street. "And if you turn down the block, there's a Sips down there too."

She stopped and turned around. "Will you shut it?" she erupted. "You didn't let me finish before you started Soloing yourself."

"Soloing?" I said astonished. "What is Soloing?"

"It's when you do what you do."

"And what do I do?"

"Oh, honey, if you don't know by now, I don't want to wake you from your delusion."

I smiled at her tact or lack thereof. "Fine, I'm listening."

"Thank you," she said as she continued to walk down the sidewalk.

"Well, are you going to tell me?" I asked as I trotted beside her.

She looked over at me and winced. "I'm not feeling it now."

"You're not feeling it?" I laughed. "A minute ago you went ballistic because I wouldn't let you finish."

"What can I say, the Supreme Court says I have the right to choose."

"Really? That's your stance, your right to choose?" I said, rolling my eyes, which happened often when I was with Elizabeth.

"Fine, but I'm not relenting because you're telling me to."

"Whatever you need to believe, but it's a man's world," I quipped.

"If you say that to me one more time, I'll take you to a vet and get you snipped," she hissed. "Because I know a woman who will do it for me," she said nonchalantly as she pulled out her sunglasses from her purse. "Believe me, she owes me a favor."

"As you were saying," I said as I tucked that new bit of information into my memory bank.

"It's going to happen near Sips and a gym," she smiled courageously behind her bee eyeglasses.

"That may narrow--" I started to say as she quickly interjected.

"Did I mention both Sips and the gym are on the corner?"

"Oh, no you didn't," I said. "You kind of left that bit of information off."

"Well, if you would've just let me talk and not kept interrupting me, you would have," she said strutting down the street in her high heels as she pulled out her car keys.

"Where are we going?" I asked.

"I'm feeling like a coffee," she said clicking her remote starter on her keychain starting her BMW a few cars away. "Wanna grab a drink from a couple of Sips?"

CHAPTER 69

Veronica sat down at the defense table more fragile than she had ever sat behind it before. She usually held a commanding stature that displayed her confidence and strategic mind. Now she felt like a wounded bird, or even the shattered egg shell it just escaped. But unlike the free bird, she felt caged to the secrets Jenny and Mr. Alexeev held. They held that knowledge with the same hands that held the key, dangling it wildly for Veronica to see.

Jenny and Mr. Alexeev sat professionally staring ahead at the judge, which caused a chill to creep up Veronica's spine. She was used to them grinning and scheming at her expense, but now they were aloof, distant. As if ignoring her presence. Yesterday she wished they would have cut her loose. But today, today she felt the jadedness and it was frightening. She knew this was the day Mr. Alexeev would shine, and they let Veronica sit in the dark. She didn't know the agenda for today. She was just to sit pretty and let Mr. Alexeev do this devilish dance. A dance he'd been perfecting for forty years.

"The defense calls Detective Smith Young," Mr. Alexeev announced.

Veronica's heart stopped. She knew that name from Winston's tirades, and she knew Detective Young was a loose cannon. He wasn't one to defend Winston's name. No, he was going to smear it even worse.

Detective Young walked confidently up to the stand like a model on the catwalk. He turned, allowing his blond locks to flip, catching a couple pairs of eyes from the two attractive women on the jury.

"Detective Young, you encountered a similar situation during the killing spree of the Carbon Monoxide Killers as Officer Winston Cooper where you thought you apprehended the criminals, only to be corrected. Is that a fair assessment?" Mr. Alexeev asked politely, standing behind the defense table beside his client.

"Yes, that's correct," Detective Young answered.

"Can you describe the couple?" Mr. Alexeev asked.

"It was an older man and a young woman. The older man looked frail and sick with a mask over his face. The young woman was helping the man to the car, also wearing a mask."

"Were they with any one else?" Mr. Alexeev prodded, leading Detective Young down the rabbit hole.

"Yes, there was another couple, a man and a woman."

"So, at first sight, you thought these were the killers?"

"Yes, they fit the description. I was on a stakeout with two fellow officers, Officer Knightly and Officer White. Officer Knightly was up along the subway platform and informed me there were two suspects approaching the parking lot. I noticed the perpetrators and saw they were getting in a vehicle with a healthy-looking couple. They fit the description, and they were in the location we were watching. They matched, so I approached the suspects and apprehended them."

"What? You didn't shoot them first?"

"Objection," Jill Stapleton said, annoyed by Mr. Alexeev's playful use of words.

"Apologies, your honor," Mr. Alexeev said, waving off the last question. "Let me rephrase. Is it customary to shoot a suspect before obtaining proof of their guilt or innocence?"

"Absolutely not," Detective Young said. "We are trained to only shoot in life and death scenarios. Police officers who shoot too quickly give the rest of the police officers a bad name."

Veronica's blood started pumping with boiling rage, a fire Jenny quickly realized. Jenny patted Veronica's knee sternly, leaning over to whisper in Veronica's ear, "Calm down, dear. Your husband, I mean, future ex-husband, killed my brother, so I think you don't have a reason to be upset."

"So, in your opinion, Detective Young, did Officer Cooper follow protocol?"

"In my assessment of the scene, I believe he jumped the gun. Pardon my pun," he answered with a snicker.

"Your honor, objection!" Jill Stapleton said jumping up. "This is in bad taste."

"I agree, Ms. Stapleton," Judge Ogdon assured. "Detective Young, please hold your distasteful remarks aside."

"Sorry, your honor," Detective Young said, lowering his head in regret.

However, Mr. Alexeev smiled even more broadly. "Detective Young, you outrank Officer Cooper, correct?"

"Yes, yes, I do."

"And you believe Officer Cooper did not follow protocol?"

"No, no, he didn't."

Mr. Alexeev stepped away from the defense table and moved closer to the jury stand. "Detective Young, you actually questioned the defendant's brother a day before his untimely death, correct?"

"Yes, yes, I did."

"And did you believe him to be one of these killers?"

"No, we took him in for questioning because he said he saw who the killers were. He couldn't describe them, except to say it was a man and a woman."

"So, you were sitting face to face with the supposed killer, and you didn't think he was someone capable of killing nine people?"

"No," Young answered shortly. "He didn't come off that way to me."

"So, in a matter of twenty-four hours, this young man went from a polite young man to a sadistic killer in Officer Cooper's eyes?"

"It appears that way," Young answered once again shortly.

"So, Detective Young, this is going to be a hard question, but you have to answer it honestly. Do you believe Officer Cooper killed one of the Carbon Monoxide Killers?"

Detective Young loved the attention he was getting. He couldn't remember the last time he'd had so many pairs of eyes on him and heard his name *Detective Young* said so many times. He looked over at Veronica, Officer Cooper's wife, and grinned. "I don't see why he killed Jennifer Ascot's estranged brother."

The courtroom gasped as Veronica's heart sank. She knew Young wasn't helping her. But he sure was helping Jenny.

"So, you believe Alexei Lechkov was innocent?" Mr. Alexeev asked solemnly.

"With the evidence I have seen, I don't know if I could indict him."

"What evidence are you speaking of?" Mr. Alexeev asked.

"None. We don't have any telephone records. We don't have any receipts or banking documents. They have an alibi for a Halloween party the night of his death. I don't see any corroborating evidence pointing to either of them except being at the wrong place at the wrong time."

"Thank you, Detective Young," Mr. Alexeev announced. "I just wish there were more police officers like you on the police force. Maybe there would be less hate between civilians and cops if people talked before shooting."

Veronica sat stunned. She looked over at Jenny's unshackled hands and wondered how many more days she would be wearing handcuffs when she left this courtroom. It seemed like in a few days she would be leaving the courtroom with a different type of bracelet around her wrist. It wouldn't be silver. Mr. Alexeev had already promised her a diamond tennis bracelet, paid with money from the civil suit they would file a few weeks after she was freed.

Veronica couldn't do anything but stare coldly at Detective Young. She was even tuning out the prosecution's questioning, and she knew if she wasn't listening to Ms. Stapleton, some of jurors probably weren't either.

CHAPTER 70

Mr. Alexeev called Jennifer Ascot's psychiatrist, Dr. Jules Krishner to the stand. The fifty-two-year-old Dr. Krishner sat in the witness stand in a neat black skirt, polka dot blouse, and Harry Potter-styled black-rimmed glasses that went sleekly with her pixie cut black hairstyle. She stated her credentials routinely, almost bringing the jury to a state of boredom with all her degrees and scholastic achievements.

"Dr. Krishner," Mr. Alexeev started, "how would you describe Jennifer Ascot?"

"Ms. Ascot has been a patient of mine for about two years, and during that time I would describe her as a likeable, dependent, intelligent, hardworking young woman."

"So were you surprised when she was arrested for these crimes?" Mr. Alexeev asked, teetering on his heels.

"Yes. I couldn't believe it," Dr. Krishner answered flatly without a hint of emotion in her voice.

"So, you counseled the defendant for two years and you never saw this type of outrage in her psyche?"

"No."

"Do you believe she is capable of this type of crime?" Mr. Alexeev asked as Jill Stapleton shot up.

"Objection, your honor," Jill said.

"On what grounds, Ms. Stapleton?" Judge Ogdon questioned, looking intently at the young lawyer.

"Matter of opinion," Jill confidently answered.

"Your honor," Mr. Alexeev intruded. "My witness isn't just giving her opinion, but her scientific hypothesis after years of therapy analysis." He stopped and eyed Ms. Stapleton like she was one of his granddaughters. "I'm not asking a computer technician on her mental state, but a licensed and highly revered psychiatrist."

"Overruled. Answer the question, Dr. Krishner," Judge Ogdon said.

A twinge of a smile landed on Mr. Alexeev's face as Ms. Stapleton's eyes rolled in annoyance.

"I can't definitively say if she is capable of these crimes, because studies have shown anyone is capable of anything in certain circumstances. But in my past experience with Ms. Ascot, I never saw any warning signs."

"So, are you saying, given a scenario, I am capable of killing someone?" Mr. Alexeev said.

"If the studies are correct, yes, even you are capable."

"What about juror number six, is he capable of killing someone?" Mr. Alexeev said.

"Objection, what is the point of this questioning?" Jill Stapleton stammered.

"Yes, Mr. Alexeev, I believe you made your point. If you don't make a new point soon, I will have to side with Ms. Stapleton," Judge Ogdon remarked.

"Yes, your honor, I am getting to my point," Mr. Alexeev smiled undisturbed. "Dr. Krishner, did you read over the assessment Dr. Angela Lars, the prosecution's psychiatrist, wrote about Ms. Ascot?"

"Yes," she answered firmly.

"And what is your assessment of the written report?"

"I hate to take apart a fellow psychiatrist's findings, but even the best person in our field cannot fully diagnosis someone in as little as two hours."

"So, are you saying if you were a member of the jury you wouldn't listen to Dr. Lars' assessment?"

"No, I wouldn't say that," she answered.

Mr. Alexeev looked shocked by her answer, "Oh, really, why?"

"A juror should listen to each statement said behind this bench, but each statement should be weighed. They should listen to Dr. Lars' findings, but her findings should not be given as much weight as two years of therapy."

"Interesting," Mr. Alexeev said soothingly. "So insightful. I hope the jury is listening to that."

CHAPTER 71

Jill Stapleton approached Dr. Krishner and tried her best to dismantle some of the key points she said, but no matter how hard she tried, there was very little luck.

"Dr. Krishner, when was the last time you met with Ms. Ascot before she was accused of these crimes?"

"The last time I met with her was last autumn."

"When you say last autumn, do you mean six months ago or eighteen months ago?"

"Eighteen months ago."

Jill hoped her last few minutes of rebuttal would be remembered by the jury, since these were the only questions that really mattered.

"So, you didn't meet with Ms. Ascot after she supposedly reconnected with her long lost brother."

"I cannot say because I don't know when her brother entered back into her life."

"Well, Dr. Krishner, did you know Ms. Ascot had a brother? In your two years of analysis did Ms. Ascot ever mention her brother once?"

"I cannot recall," Dr. Krishner answered unfazed.

"Can you really not recall, or is that your way of saying no?" Jill asked, getting some traction.

"No, I really don't recall. I take notes during my session, but I don't write everything down," Dr. Krishner answered with a little more tension in her tone.

"So, why did Ms. Ascot quit coming to see you?"

"I don't know," she answered without care.

"Your patient of two years just up and quit coming to you, and you didn't reach out to her to find out why?"

"I have a receptionist who handles my schedule, and it is none of her business why patients cancel or don't reschedule," she answered coolly.

"Interesting," Jill Stapleton said, mocking Mr. Alexeev. "So, it seems like even though you have two years of experience with Ms. Ascot, she is no more important to you than another billable hour. I'm not sure we should rely upon your analysis of Ms. Ascot either."

"Objection," Mr. Alexeev said.

"No further questions," Jill said, sauntering off, feeling a little more confident than yesterday. Just a little more.

CHAPTER 72

"So, your plan for the morning is going to each of the Sips and seeing if the place looks like what you saw in your dream?" I asked as I sat in the passenger seat searching through Facebook.

"Do you have a better plan?" she asked, flipping off a teenage driver running a red light. "What are you doing over there?"

"I'm trying to find the Fiona I saved last night," I said, but I was amazed by how many Fionas were in the Washington D.C. area.

"Gotta love social network's lack of privacy," she laughed.

"Well, I'm just thinking if we can find the Fiona you saw in your dream then maybe we can narrow down the Sips search. Maybe figure out if she works or lives near one."

"I like my idea better," she snidely commented. "I at least know what I saw in my dream."

"Fine, what did you see in your dream?" I asked facetiously. "Tell me, what makes this Sips different than another one?"

She whipped her head over in my direction, giving me a look that didn't need any words. "Well, for starters, there were pots of purple flowers beside the door."

"Good observation," I said. "But you know that Sips' logo is purple. Purple flowers may be at a lot of the locations."

"Yes, I know that!" she snapped. "Why are you being such a negative Nancy this morning?"

I continued to look through the Fionas I was finding on Facebook, but none of them looked like the woman I saved last night. "I'm not being negative," I returned. "I'm just trying to be pragmatic."

"Well, it just seems like since I'm having the dreams and you're not, you don't really care about saving this girl," she said ruthlessly.

"Are you serious?" I shot back. "Do you think I'm jealous?"

"Over the last few months, any time you had an important dream we did everything there was to figure it out. Now, I'm having a life and death dream, and you didn't even come out with me last night to save the girl's life."

"Elizabeth, you know that's not true," I said, trying to blow off her comment by finding Fiona.

"Think about it. Last month when we saved the doctor on the golf course from the killer flying ball, your dream. Or when we tracked down the swimming coach who had a seizure during practice to keep her from drowning, your dream. Or when we--" she started, but I couldn't stand to listen to her say one more thing.

"I always thought we were a team. I'm not better than you and you're not better than me."

"Well, sometimes I feel like your sidekick," she lashed out.

"Sidekick? We're not Batman and Robin."

"Good thing, because I don't want to envision you in tights," she laughed.

"Whatever. I work out."

"Not enough, fluffy."

"Fluffy? Now that's hurtful." I smiled, looking away from my phone and down at my stomach. True, it wasn't as tight as it was a few years ago, but I was far from fluffy.

"Oh, that's right, Mr. Solo is also Mr. Vain," she smiled as she slowed her car and swerved to a stop.

"That sounds more like a villain's name than a good guy."

"Who said you were one of the good guys?" she smiled.

Sarcastically smirking at her dig, I felt the car stop. "Why are we stopping?" I asked, fruitlessly skimming through the photos on Facebook.

She looked over at me and then pointed outside my passenger side window. "Getting a cup of java. Want anything?"

I glanced up from my phone and noticed we were at the first Sips of the morning. "You buying?"

"When do I not buy, Solo?" she smiled as she unbuckled her seatbelt. "Here's your twenty from last night," she said pulling out the bill from her purse.

"You know I don't use you for your money. I can pay for my own," I said with a lion cub roar of masculinity.

"Yes, I know, Solo. Your little weddings and birthday photos pay exceedingly well as indicated by your roach-infested bachelor pad."

"I'll have you know it was fumigated last year."

"You need to move," she laughed. "Who puts on an advertisement for renters, *Newly Fumigated?* Wow. Now, that's classy."

"I like my place," I grinned.

"Roaches come back. They always come back," she moaned.

"See, I fit in with them. Even when you are rude to me, I always come back," I laughed.

"If you start to hide when someone flips on a light switch..." she drug on.

"Aren't we here to check out this place and not bash my living arrangements?"

"Oh, hon, I can do both. I'm a woman. I multitask."

"That you do," I said getting out of the car and noticing no pots of purple flowers by the door. "No flowers," I said as I turned to get back into the car while she proceeded to the door. "Why are you going in?"

"If I'm going to be driving around all day with you, I need two cups of coffee to chill my nerves," she huffed. "Want your lady tea?"

"Make it a raspberry tea. I'm feeling freaky today," I smiled as I opened the door for her so her hands wouldn't have to touch the filthy door handle.

"Oh Solo, if raspberry tea gets you freaky, I want to take you for a tequila shot on Friday and see what that makes you do. Let's just call it my own little science experiment."

"What would Jeremiah say?"

"Jeremiah might be proud of my quest for science, but he would probably just be home reading in bed. He's more boring than you are."

"I'm in good company then," I smiled as we walked into Sips and I inhaled the robust smell of coffee beans.

When she ordered and got the coffees and tea, we headed out for the next Sips location. I took a sip and noticed writing on my cup that usually would be my name, but it said Virginia instead.

"How did the barista get Virginia out of Solomon or Elizabeth?" I asked.

She almost coughed up her coffee as we left the shop.

"What's so funny?" I asked.

She got into her car almost on the brink of crying tears. "When they asked for names, I gave her yours."

"But how is my name Virginia?"

She continued to laugh as a few tears rolled down her cheeks. "Well, I guess they thought I said Virginia."

I stared at my cup for a few seconds, looking at Virginia intently, when suddenly a light bulb moment went on over my head. "Virgin? Virgin? Really, Elizabeth. You know I was married," I shot back.

"Yeah, but you didn't have any kids, so there isn't any proof of a sex life, Virginia."

CHAPTER 73

He sat at his cubicle with eyes wide open. He hadn't slept a wink all night, still basking in the thought of ending Piper's existence. He knew he would be able to sleep soundly another night. The nightmares of her jilting him in the hallway would be long gone now. He knew he needed to wipe away his smug expression and headed to the bathroom to splash some refreshing water on his face. As he exited, he saw his band of brothers each walking down the hall, getting to their cubicles for another day of work.

"So, Stu, any news?" Grant asked concerning the various numbers he had called recently.

"Nothing yet," Stewart said sadly. "But I've only called about six of them."

"Six?" Collin said chuckling at Stewart's expense. After the looks Jordan and Grant were giving him, he quickly changed his attitude. "Six years ago today my nephew Rico was born," he tried his best to cover up his mistake. "That boy always makes me laugh when I think about him."

"You don't have a nephew named Rico, Collin," Stewart corrected solemnly. "You have a niece and only one of them."

"Um, I've got a busy day, so I better start right on it," Collin said, skidding away to his cubicle down the hall.

"Why do we keep him around?" Jordan kidded, but by the looks on Grant's and Stewart's faces, it was a reasonable question. "I guess that's one for the ages."

"Guess so," Grant agreed.

The three of them parted ways and headed to the daily grind of keeping the good people of D.C. in good graces in the realm of the Department of Transportation.

The murderer found his computer and quickly logged in. He checked his emails, but nothing of great importance was flagged. So he leaned back in his chair and replayed the events of the night.

The glorious night when Piper left this world.

His smug smile was going to be hard to hide. Maybe tomorrow he would worry about removing it.

CHAPTER 74

Veronica wanted to bang her head on the defense table as she watched Milo swirl doubt around in the jury's mind like he was making a mixed drink. She listened intently, and she, too, started to question the reliability of everything Jill Stapleton's prosecution testimonies said just a day before. She knew if her mind was spinning wildly, the jurors' were about to fall off their rollercoaster.

She couldn't believe how he twisted the testimony of his information technology specialist, Jonah Carney. Jonah was the individual who created the masterpiece images on Digitex of Jill Stapleton and Abner Abernathy that Milo used the day before to sacrifice Abner mercilessly on the stand. "So, did you modify the images of Jill Stapleton and Abner Abernathy?" Mr. Alexeev asked.

"Well, yeah," Jonah blatantly answered. "Anyone with just a little knowledge of the system knows how to manipulate the images."

"So, you are telling me you made the images of Jill Stapleton and Abner Abernathy by manipulating the data processes."

"In laymen's terms, yes," Jonah smiled. "Anyone can do it."

"Yesterday, Mr. Abernathy gave us two images of Alexei Lechkov and Jennifer Ascot," Mr. Alexeev said, pulling out the images from his briefcase. "Can you tell me that these were not altered?"

Jonah looked at the image and then at Jennifer Ascot, then back at the image in his hand, then at the blurry image before the Digitex system being used. "It is impossible to get this image out of this blurry image without any knowledge of what he was trying to uncover."

"Impossible? Really?" Mr. Alexeev gasped. "But Mr. Abernathy said he didn't manipulate the image."

"He may not have *manipulated* the image, but he took creative liberties in finalizing these images."

Jill Stapleton tried her best to get Jonah tongue-tied or confused, or even a little off guard, but the more she tried, the more she looked frazzled. She knew she was not showing the jury the confidence she had two days ago. She knew the jury would sadly remember this unflattering moment in the deliberations, and the memory of her blazing opening statement would escape them like a fleeting bout of dementia. She soon resigned her questioning and Milo greeted his next witness.

He found the first homeless individual, Billy Thorngood, known as Skeet, whom Jenny had given the hotel room card and cell phones to. He couldn't pick out Jenny from Lady Freedom painted on the wall. He was a stunning defense witness. Milo didn't have to prep the witness or even offer him a bribe. He asked only a few questions and then gave the witness over to Jill Stapleton. He hoped with the few questions he asked Jill would see that as a ray of hope to dig deep into her questions.

She fell into his trap.

"So, tell me Mr. Thorngood, how long have you been homeless?"

"I, uh, I don't know," he answered confused.

"You don't know?" she asked bewildered. "How do you not know?"

"I don't have a watch to tell me what day it is, ma'am," he answered defensively.

"Do you remember when you became homeless?" she asked, knowing that the line of questioning seemed disparagingly rude a second too late.

"No," he answered coldly. "I don't like to think of the day I was kicked out of my home."

Milo was squirming silently in his seat. He hadn't thought seeing this questioning would be so entertaining, but he was wrong. He was being more entertained than anything ever showcased at the Kennedy Center.

Jill tried her best to clean up her mess, but she eventually hobbled away like an injured animal. She wondered who the jury thought was more broken, her or Mr. Thorngood.

She wasn't ready to find out.

Mr. Alexeev stood up, erased his gleeful smile, and called his next witness. "The defense calls Luther Hyde."

"You're calling my father?" Veronica whispered to Milo, shaking in her seat. "What does he have to do with this case?"

"Wait. And. See. Dear," Jenny said menacingly. "Wait and see."

CHAPTER 75

"Officer Cooper, walk with me," Chief Johnson commanded as Wint and Officer Peterson sat in the squad room going over the evidence collected so far in the shooting from the previous night.

Chief Johnson had a rough exterior, and the officers under him knew not to mess around or they would be reaping the consequences. "I see something in you," Chief Johnson said as they walked down the hall away from the normal commotion.

"Thank you, sir. Thank you," Cooper replied without breaking a smile. He knew Chief Johnson was pure work and no play.

"I still don't understand why you didn't accept the promotion I offered you, but I need you to not settle for a patrol cop. You are better than that, so that's why I have you working this case. You got me?"

"Yes sir, I understand."

"I need you to want this," Chief Johnson urged. "It's a cruel world out there, and we need cops like you."

"I want it, sir, I really do, but I have my reasons for denying the promotion right now," Cooper answered.

"Don't let Officer Peterson hold you back," he instructed firmly. "You don't have to be her partner. I can get another officer to train her."

"I just feel I need to be with her at first since I was the one who suggested it."

"You are a good guy, Cooper, but don't let your good guy ways leave you empty-handed. You hear me?"

"Yes sir, I hear you."

"Well, go get your partner and we'll head to the M.E.'s office. I think Santiago has some information for us on the corpse," Chief

Johnson said as Cooper walked back to the squad room to find Officer Peterson looking over the crime photos.

"I don't know about this, Cooper," Peterson said waveringly. "I don't know if I'm ready for this type of case just yet."

"You're not," Cooper said unsympathetically, "but it will be okay. I didn't think I was ready the first time either. The important thing is to take it in, watch what is being done, listen to what is being said, take notes, and remember everything."

"That's all?" Peterson said with a struggling smile.

"Oh, and only speak to me. You don't want to make a fool of yourself."

"Thanks," she said sarcastically.

"We're partners," Cooper said. "I'm not going to let you look dumb," he said with a slight chuckle. "Let's hope I don't look dumb for the both of us."

"I have my fingers crossed," she grinned.

They continued to walk down the hall where they were away from everyone else. "I haven't asked today, but how are you doing?" Peterson asked sincerely.

"Let's focus on what we are about to see, okay?" Cooper said sternly. He didn't want his outside circumstances to have any effect on his next few hours. His personal life didn't matter when he was in uniform. When he was in uniform, work came first.

CHAPTER 76

"So far, we have crossed off three Sips on the list and found one it could possibly be," I said, still scrolling through the various social media apps I could find to secure a picture of the Fiona I helped last night. I kept thinking it couldn't be a coincidence. It just couldn't.

"Pretty good odds, I think," Elizabeth said as she put in the next address on her phone in a section of town north of Georgetown. "And it looks like there are only three more Sips we have to go to that have a gym near it. So, fingers crossed, none of them will look like the one in my dream."

"My fingers and legs are already crossed," I said, twitching my toes to get my thoughts off anything related to water.

"Does my little buddy have to go pee-pee?" she laughed.

"Just drive," I said angrily. "Just drive."

"It would be horrible if I had to slam on my brakes," she said as she gently pressed on her brake for no reason other than because she was Elizabeth.

"It would be horrible if I went right here on your seat too, so do whatever you want."

"You wouldn't dare," she said, eyeing me suspiciously.

"If you brake like that two more times you won't have to dare me."

"Why didn't you just go in the last Sips?" she asked systemically.

"They were cleaning the restroom and had it shut down," I whined as I kept my attention on my phone. "So, the next place is how many blocks away?"

"We will be there in about ten minutes depending on traffic," she said making sure to glide in slowly at the next traffic light. "So, no luck on finding your dream woman?"

"I'm not scoping out pics for a date," I scoffed.

"I would be," she laughed.

"That's where you and I are different."

"There'd better be more than that one difference between us, Solo. As God is my witness, I'd kill myself if we were alike in every other way."

I glanced up from my phone and didn't know whether to be hurt or agree. If I was like Elizabeth I might be looking at my razor each morning with a different light of appreciation.

My phone vibrated. *We need to meet for tea this afternoon*, Jeremiah texted.

"Your boyfriend just texted me for a date," I laughed.

"When?"

"This afternoon sometime," I smiled as I texted back saying, *Sure. When and where?*

"Solo, you can't meet with him today," she ranted. "We have to figure this out and get our plan for tonight."

"We've been together all morning. I think you can do without me for an hour," I grinned as I got a time from Jeremiah. "He said 3."

"Solo, I'm serious. Just tell him no. It's life or death!" she said breathlessly.

I put down my phone and looked over at her; she looked petrified. Her voice didn't quiver with anger, but it shook with concern. A concern I had never seen before.

I knew I needed to be a good friend to her.

"Fine, I'll text him and see if tomorrow morning will work instead. I'll tell him I'm busy," I said compassionately. "Even though I already just said I would, but I'll look ignorant for you."

"You look ignorant most days without me," she smiled.

"Done," I said as Jeremiah quickly replied with 8:30 a.m. and let me know Dr. Eugene Wright would be joining us. Dr. Wright was a theology professor I met last fall during one of his lectures, and he had become a common acquaintance for tea and coffee. It was an interesting threesome: an atheist anthropology professor with a PhD, a theology professor with a PhD, and a mundane photographer and theology student with only an IOU for his next month's rent.

"Thanks, dear," Elizabeth said as she came to a stop.

"Are we there?" I asked, clinching my legs tighter together as I looked up and noticed we were stuck in a mid-day traffic jam. "I don't know if I can hold it much longer."

"Well, you are going to have to, there are no trees for you to use," she snapped.

"Yeah, but there are many other restaurants around." I looked to my left and right and found a few places I thought would have restrooms. "I'll meet you at Sips," I quickly said as I unbuckled my seat and jumped out the door.

Elizabeth started to say something, but I had already slammed the door. I had one thing on my mind and it was emptying my bladder. I walked awkwardly to the first restaurant I saw and was pleased to find a men's restroom near the front door.

"Thank you, Jesus!"

CHAPTER 77

"Mr. Luther Hyde, you are the managing partner at Manfield & Hyde?" Mr. Alexeev asked as he walked away from the defense table and found a commanding spot near the jury.

"That's correct," Mr. Hyde answered with a charming smile. He was the face of what a managing partner looked like. He had the stylish slicked-back gray head of hair, a fashionable pair of Gucci glasses that would be advertised in the GQ magazine by a slightly younger looking model, and an exquisite gray three-button suit with a stormy blue tie. He looked like the husband all middle-aged women wanted and the father all young adults wished they had.

"Can you tell me about Ms. Jennifer Ascot?"

"She is a very loyal associate with Manfield & Hyde. She has always met or exceeded expectations on her quarterly evaluations. She exemplifies a hard work ethic and understanding of the law. She is a very beneficial member of the firm, and I wish more associates were like her."

"That's some very high praise for someone accused of nine deaths," Mr. Alexeev commented.

"In my eyes, Ms. Jennifer Ascot is innocent until proven guilty, and I will gladly welcome her back to her position once she has been found not guilty," he said, looking directly at the defense table. But instead of looking at Jennifer Ascot, he shot his look at Veronica. "We are a family at Manfield & Hyde, and when one member of the family is in trouble, we help him or her."

"That's very kind, Mr. Hyde," Milo said sincerely. He walked around the jury stand. "How many hours did Jennifer Ascot put in during a normal work week?"

"Our associates usually work at least sixty hours a week," he answered looking at Milo and then at various members of the jury.

"We strive to serve our clients well, and not everyone is up for this type of workload, but Jennifer Ascot never complained about any of her cases," he said, turning his scathing attention to Veronica. "Not once."

"For someone to commit these horrific crimes, they must have been very planned out and rehearsed. In your opinion, could she have committed these crimes and worked sixty hours a week?" Milo asked.

"Objection, your honor," Jill Stapleton announced. "Matter of opinion isn't a viable defense."

"Let me rephrase, your honor," Milo kindly said. "Would you have time, Mr. Hyde, to plan, choreograph, and rehearse such a lofty ambitious scheme to kill nine people on different nights of the week, in one week after working sixty hours?"

Jill Stapleton shook her head annoyed, but Milo did rephrase the question. She had hoped he would have just removed the question.

"No, I don't know how one person could do all that in one week and keep up the grueling work schedule we adhere to at Manfield & Hyde." He smiled, almost laughing at the audacity of such a week. "If I had done this, I would need a week or even a day off," he commented.

"And did Jennifer Ascot ask for any time off during, before, or after this week in October when these crimes were committed?" Milo questioned.

"No, she was at the office each day on time and even stayed late some nights to make her minimum required hours for the week," Luther answered.

"No further questions, your honor," Milo said as he walked back to the defense table.

Jill Stapleton didn't have very many questions to ask, but she knew she needed to redeem herself from the last few witnesses. "Mr. Hyde, you said associates in your firm work a large number of hours. Do some of them work from home for some of these hours?"

"Yes, we allow our associates to work from home if they like," he answered.

"So, could people lie about their billable hours?" Jill questioned, knowing it was human tendency to stretch the truth in tough situations.

"I believe they could, but--," but she didn't allow him to finish.

"So, how do you know for sure Ms. Ascot worked these long, tiring hours? She could have lied and said she was working from home, but was really planning these crimes with her brother. It would be easy to overbill some clients a few hours here and there to reach her weekly quota."

Luther looked over at Milo and then the jury and then finally to Jill Stapleton. "Yes, we have some people who may take advantage of our flexibility, but Ms. Ascot wasn't one of them."

"But how do you know for sure? Do you have some type of sophisticated security system watching all your employees' work progress?" she said with a laugh.

"Actually, yes," he said with a smirk. The smirk caught Jill off guard. "As you know, most laptops come with webcam capabilities, so each computer and laptop is programmed with specialized webcams to record each of our associates as they work. They are required to use this type of security as a way to deter fraudulent billings to our clients – to our trusted clients. Once our associates log onto their computer, the billing program takes snippets of the screen as added proof of the work process. This way, if someone isn't actually working, the program will estimate amount of time lost and decrease the billable hours by the lost time. So we do have a very, very sophisticated program, because next to our associates, our clients are also our family. So when I say Jennifer Ascot worked over sixty hours a week, I know beyond a shadow of doubt she worked over sixty hours a week."

Milo looked over at Jennifer Ascot and leaned into her ear. He whispered something, but Veronica couldn't hear what he said.

She didn't want to know what he said.

CHAPTER 78

"Purple flowers," I said, walking up to Sips finding Elizabeth looking around the exterior of the building.

"This place looks really, really familiar," she said, looking at the light brown brick on the building.

"This places looks the same as the other Sips," I sadly said. "Purple flowers, the same white lettering on the window, the same gym across the street. I don't see any differences."

Elizabeth closed her eyes on the sidewalk causing pedestrians to stare as they maneuvered around her. She was expressionless. I hoped she was going to see something in her memory, but she started to frown.

"Not the place?" I said.

She didn't respond. She walked away and examined the brick again. Then the fire hydrant. Then the pots of African violets.

"What?" I asked. "What are you thinking?"

"I'm thinking," she said and then stopped. "I'm thinking," she started again and then stopped. "I'm thinking, I'm thinking I don't know."

She stormed across the street, not looking both ways before she crossed.

"Hey!" someone shouted as they honked their horn, slamming on their brakes before nearly hitting her.

"Go hey yourself," she yelled back.

I ran across the clear street and caught up with her. "What's wrong with you? He could've hit you."

"She's going to die tonight," she stammered. "She's going to die because I can't tell if it's this place or the last place, and we still have a few more places to see. What if the next three places each have purple flowers and look just like this place?"

"Elizabeth," I said calmly, "it's not even noon yet. We have time to figure out parts of this puzzle. We've done it before."

She looked through me to see Sips across the street. She closed her eyes once again, leaning against the glass of the gym window and started to breathe deeply.

My stomach rumbled which caused her to hit me.

"Will you just shut up for a second?" she ignited.

"You can ignore the traffic and the jackhammering from up the street, but my growling stomach is too much for you to concentrate? Give me a break," I said as I stomped away, starting to talk to myself. "All I've had all day is a half-eaten piece of fruit and an unsweetened tea." *How could she forget to ask them for some sugar? Just because she drinks disgusting drinks doesn't mean the rest of the world has to.*

I took a deep breath. I needed to lower my blood pressure because it looked like we were going to have a long day ahead of us. I focused my eyes on a tulip in the flower shop window. I inhaled a deep breath and exhaled. I didn't feel any better. I knew I was going to need a few more deep breaths to feel even a little less stressed.

I inhaled again, still concentrating on the tulip. Then I exhaled.

I closed my eyes for ten seconds, continuing my breathing, and I started to feel a part of the tension around my shoulders ease. I found my focal point, the tulip, and took a deep breath once again.

That's when I saw it.

In the glass's reflection I saw a woman wearing a floral skirt with a red blouse. After my moment of deep breathing and trying to relax, my heart rate started to increase once again. I turned to watch the woman walk down the street. Something in my gut wanted me to follow.

I continued to watch her from about ten feet behind. I didn't know where I was going, but something was urging me to follow. She crossed the street as the crosswalk sign blinked, warning me to stop, but I couldn't. I had to follow.

I kept walking until she stopped and turned into a restaurant. My heart was pounding harder, nearing pain with each beat. I opened the door and walked into the restaurant and saw four women wearing the same outfit.

"Hola, welcome to Miguel's," one of the women said as I walked in. She smiled warmly with her red blouse and floral skirt. "How many?"

"How many what?" I asked dumbfounded.

She looked at me and then around the restaurant. "How many seats do you need?"

"Oh, uh," I stuttered. "None." I quickly walked out the door and left, walking back to the gym.

"This is the place," I said to Elizabeth still with her eyes closed, standing like a stoned hippie.

"How? How do you know?" she said confusedly, squinting her eyes as if seeing daylight for the first time.

"Just follow me."

CHAPTER 79

We went back to Miguel's, a fairly new Mexican restaurant that opened less than a year ago, and got a bite to eat.

"Are you going to ask her?" Elizabeth asked as she sipped her margarita.

"I'm trying to figure out how to ask it," I asked.

She looked at me astonished as she scooped a chip full of salsa. "What are you trying to figure out? 'Hola, senorita, is there a Fiona that works here?' What is so hard about that?"

"One, that sounds suspicious to me to just ask if someone works here. Two, how do we figure out what her last name is? Three, if the waitress does give us that information…" I stopped and thought for a second.

"There is nothing else you need, moron. We get her last name and we can track her down and see if she's the one we need to save," Elizabeth interjected with a snap of her fingers. "It's as easy as that."

"If it's so easy, you do it," I barked back over the mariachi music that blared over the scratchy speakers.

"Fine, why do you men have such a problem asking for help?" she laughed as she slurped her alcohol through a plastic straw.

"Because," I said matter-of-factly.

"Very wise, Solo. So wise you are."

The waitress came back with our plates of chimichangas and chicken and cheese quesadilla that smelled heavenly. "Be sly," I whispered.

Elizabeth winked at me and took a sip of water to clear her throat. "My friend here wants to know Fiona's last name," she said. "He was too scared to ask her name and number last night."

The waitress turned to me and smiled broadly, looking at me with a hint of humorous judgment. "Fiona?" she said in a thick Puerto

Rican accent. "Why should I just give her name out like that? He wasn't brave enough to ask it last night, and now he's getting his friend to ask me for it? Sad."

"I know, pathetic," Elizabeth joined in. "I told him women like a man to, you know, take charge, but he needs a little help."

"I don't need a little help," I said, scolding Elizabeth.

"Come on little man, tell her off," the waitress egged on.

I looked up at the waitress nervously, as now I had two pairs of judgmental beady eyes looking at me suspiciously. "I met Fiona last night, but I didn't get the chance to ask her name and number. I think her shift ended before I could," I lied, remembering I saved her shortly after my dinner with Jeremiah and Elizabeth.

The waitress looked over at Elizabeth and tilting her head as if asking, *Should I believe this fool?*

"He's telling the truth, senorita," Elizabeth said playing along. "That's the reason we came here for lunch because he was hoping to see her again and get her digits."

"Umhmm," the waitress said unconvinced. "Let me go check something," she said before walking away.

"Really? Pathetic? You think I'm pathetic?" I asked digging into my chimichanga. I didn't know what hurt more, Elizabeth thinking it or actually saying it. I knew she kidded me about things like this, but to say it out loud to someone else just hurt.

"I was just playing with the waitress to get her name," Elizabeth said. "You were the one who told me to do it."

"Uh huh," I said, taking a bite of my beans and rice, letting her excuse brush down my back.

"Didn't you say for me to get it?" Elizabeth fired back, stabbing her quesadilla with her fork, ripping apart the tortilla like a lion shredding an antelope.

"Yes," I answered without looking up, taking another bite of my rice.

"You can't be mad at me for that!" Elizabeth laughed. "You wouldn't have gotten the nerve as quickly as I did."

I didn't respond. I cut into my chimichanga and tasted the spicy deep fried chicken shell.

"Go on, pout," she said, taking a bite of her food. "But I'm going to get us results, and that's all I care about."

"I know," I said quickly. "That's all you ever care about."

The words must have gotten to Elizabeth because she didn't comment. In most settings she would have torn into me about my sensitivity or my fragile sense of humor, but she didn't say a word. The only sounds she made were the fork and knife scraping the bottom of her plate.

"Fiona did leave work before closing last night," the waitress said. "I'm not going to give you her name or number, but I will let you know she works tonight 'til closing time."

"What time is that?" I asked, wiping my chin from the drop of cheese that slipped down my fork.

"We close at eleven," the waitress commented. "Need any refills?"

"I'm good," I said politely.

"I could use another water," Elizabeth commented.

"Be right back," the waitress said as she walked away.

We finished our lunch in silence as I got my wallet out to pay. "You know I got this," Elizabeth said grabbing her purse and pulling out her American Express card.

"Let this pathetic man pay for his own meal, please. I do have a little dignity," I said getting up with my bill, throwing a few dollars on the table for my tip.

I walked up to the cashier as Elizabeth followed behind, mouthing, but I wasn't listening. Something once again caught my eye.

It was photos of birthday celebrations of people wearing sombreros and whipped cream on their face. In the middle of some of the photos was the Fiona I saved last night.

"Solomon, you know I don't like to apologize, so you're going to have to get over this," Elizabeth said disgruntled.

I heard her words, but I ignored them. I was too mesmerized with the various photos of Fiona. She looked happy in each one.

"What?" Elizabeth asked as she looked over at the glass case of celebratory pictures.

I lifted up my hand and pointed at a picture of a joyous midnight black haired woman with mocha skin.

"That's her," Elizabeth said, her eyes widening. She leaned closer to the picture as I followed. "That's the woman in my dream."

I smiled, breathed a sigh of relief, and quickly said a silent prayer of thanksgiving. It was as if the last fifteen awkward minutes between me and Elizabeth drifted away to be a forgotten memory.

"That's the woman I saved last night. That's Fiona."

"You did it, Solo," Elizabeth said quietly in my ear.

I knew that was the closest thing to an apology I was going to get from Elizabeth today.

"No," I said leaning up away from the pictures. "We did it."

CHAPTER 80

Judge Ogdon called a recess for lunch, allowing Milo and Jenny to strategize their afternoon.

"I'm not sure if you need to go up on the stand," Milo said as he walked around the small holding cell, humming a Russian folksong with a childlike smile.

Veronica sat in the corner, as if in trouble, like she had the entire week. The few words she spoke were usually because she was forced to do so.

"What do you think?" Milo asked Veronica, causing her to stir a little in her chair.

"What do I think?" Veronica asked, confused why they were asking her opinion since they hadn't all week.

"Yes, do you think Jenika should testify?" he cooed softly, stopping his melody and fixating his eyes directly at Veronica.

"I…uh…" she stuttered fearfully, which caused Jenny to smile wickedly. Veronica didn't like the feeling of being their puppet. Given any other case she would be confident, cunning, ruthless, and systematic. This week she was nothing but a melted blob of what she used to be. But the smile on Jenny's face caused a surge of emotion. Veronica wanted to smack the smug grin off her face, and Jenny's cheek getting caught on her ring would make it even more pleasant. "I don't think she should testify."

"Why did you come to that conclusion?" Milo asked quizzically.

"Yeah, why?" Jenny barked angrily.

"Because, Ms. Ascot, you have very little experience with a murder trial. It's easy to get tripped up. You may have worked a few years at the district attorney's office, but that was a few years ago. In the last year you have mainly worked on family disputes. And you very rarely stated your case in front of a judge, let alone a jury."

Milo listened, rubbing his diamond pointed chin and taking in all the words Veronica was saying. "Well, with that viewpoint, and it is a good point of view," he stopped and nodded his head encouragingly, "I think ultimately it is your decision, Jenika. But Veronica does make some valid points."

"The only point I heard from Veronica is my lack of experience," Jenny hissed agitatedly.

"So, you agree with her then," Milo responded, once again slowly marching around the cell as if a soldier guarding the Kremlin.

"I didn't say I agree with her, Milo," Jenny growled. "I want to show her what experience I do have," she menacingly said, looking in the corner where Veronica sat. "I want to show her I'm just as smart as she is." She stopped and smiled. "Maybe smarter," she said with a wink.

"It's your life," Veronica commented shrugging her shoulders.

Jenny grinned wickedly turning her attention to her godfather, Milo. "It's not just my life on the line," she said confidently turning her head to look Veronica in the eyes. "It's not just my life on the line."

"Is that a threat?" Veronica asked, standing up from her cold metal chair. Her weak legs weren't weak anymore. Her fragile exterior had become calloused to Jenny's verbal attacks. Her mind was breaking free from the icy cage Milo had locked her in. It was time to stand her ground. It was time to be courageous. It was time to take back her life.

Jenny didn't answer but casually shrugged her shoulders with an undetermined expression. Milo finally stopped walking around and sat down at the table and nibbled on his bowl of potato soup.

Veronica pulled out her phone and texted the love of her life whom she had damaged the day before. *I love you, Winston. I hope we can talk tonight, because I have something I need to tell you. I was scared before, but not anymore. I need you. I need you more than anything else. You are my everything.*

She sent the message and hoped he would read it. All she could do now was hope.

CHAPTER 81

"So, what did you find, Raul?" Chief Johnson asked as they walked into Dr. Raul Santiago's medical examiner's office where dead bodies were covered with white sheets throughout the room.

Peterson and Cooper followed behind, pulling out their notepads, ready to take notes on all the information Dr. Santiago was about to tell. Cooper glanced over at Peterson and realized he forgot to give her some smelling ointment to put on.

"Here," he said, dabbing his fingers with the concoction and lathering his upper lip. She followed and generously applied some of the sweet relief.

"Well, Piper Michaelson, age 27, was murdered in a very similar way as Sabrina Latener was two nights ago. I examined the bullets of both deaths, and they seemed to have been fired from the same gun, an AR-15 semi-automatic rifle."

"Raul, that isn't what I wanted to hear," Chief Johnson sighed as he looked over at Cooper.

"I didn't want to see it myself," Raul agreed, as he quickly showed them a magnified image of each bullet, showing them the proof of the etch marks of the bullets that matched one another. "It looks like there is a killer on the loose."

Chief Johnson shook his head in frustration as he recalled the telephone call the night before from Detective Young. Johnson wasn't ready to let Young know he was correct in his preliminary suspicions. Johnson knew it was a lucky guess on Young's part, but Johnson also knew Young was going to state it was not a guess.

"Anything else you got that can help us?" Johnson asked.

"Not yet," Raul answered passively. "I have someone examining their stomach contents to see if there are any similarities in possible locations, but I'm waiting to get Michaelson's results."

"As soon as you get something, let us know," Johnson said before turning to Cooper. "Do you have any questions?"

"None right now, sir," Cooper answered, turning his head to Peterson who shook her head no as well.

"Thanks as always, Raul," Johnson said before leaving with Cooper and Peterson as Raul lowered his facemask to get back to work.

"Go back to the squad room and get the evidence for the Latener murder and compare the two scenes, Cooper," Johnson said before stomping away. "Oh, and keep me informed," he shouted as he continued to walk away.

"We have a killer on the loose?" Peterson groaned. "Why couldn't it just have been a domestic issue with an off-the-rocker husband or boyfriend?"

"If only," Cooper replied with a nod of his head.

CHAPTER 82

The courtroom was eerily quiet as Jennifer Ascot sat in the witness stand taking her oath, an oath that didn't matter in a murderer's eyes. Jill Stapleton looked befuddled when Milo Alexeev called Ms. Ascot to the stand. Jill and Angus started scribbling notes and questions as soon as Jenny rose from her seat.

Veronica put her phone away, but Winston had never responded. Her cell phone showed he hadn't even read her message. She looked around the courtroom, hoping to see a friendly face, but none were found. She was alone once again.

"Ms. Ascot, can you tell us the events of the night when your brother, Alexei Lechkov, was murdered by Officer Cooper?"

"Your honor," Jill Stapleton said at the word 'murdered'. The judge agreed and Milo changed the wording to a less heart-stopping one.

"My brother and I were on our way to his friend, Suzanne Pinkerton's, Halloween party around Alexandria, Virginia. He came up with the bold costume of the Carbon Monoxide Killers, and since we had just reconnected a few months earlier, I wanted to please him. I was trying to be the compromising older sister," she said warmly. "In hindsight, it wasn't the best choice, and I regret it each day. I should have stood up to my little brother and told him it was in bad taste, but I grew up as an only child, and I was just trying to bond with him."

She scanned over at the jury and looked solemnly at an older lady, "I should've known better. I should have, and I don't go a day without being reminded of the mess I'm in because I didn't tell him no."

"So, you were on the subway train…" Milo said, lassoing his client back to the scene of Alexei's death.

"Yes, we met downtown and rode into Huntington Station, and from there we were going to take a cab to the party a few miles away.

238

He was so excited," she gushed, spinning the lie further. "He grew up in the foster care system, so he never had a good Halloween as a kid. Well, we exited the train and that's when Officer Cooper started yelling at us. I was shocked because I had even forgotten I was in costume. I was trying to talk to Officer Cooper, because I actually knew him, but he wouldn't listen to me. I guess my medical face mask muffled my speech because he kept warning us.

"I don't know what happened, but my brother freaked out. I think he thought I was in trouble, and he jumped to protect me, but Officer Cooper thought he was jumping at him. That's when Officer Cooper shot him," she said sincerely. She didn't shed any tears, but her voice quivered periodically for dramatic effect.

"So, you saw Officer Cooper shoot and kill your brother? How did you feel?" Milo asked compassionately.

"I was surprised. I don't remember anything else because my world I was just getting back was taken from me. I really don't remember anything else," she said sadly, shaking her head in frustration.

"You don't remember anything at all after that?"

"No," she moaned. "I wish I could remember it, but I want the city to know I don't have any anger toward Officer Cooper. He was just doing his job. Yes, we looked suspicious, and I have to live with that bad decision, but I didn't kill anyone," she cried. "I would never hurt anyone. Never."

Veronica watched the theatrics and wondered if the jury was believing the charade. Veronica had to turn her head away from the jury stand after seeing an older woman wipe away a tear. If she watched much longer, she was going to be sick.

CHAPTER 83

Milo ended his questioning as Jenny looked like a wronged woman during the Salem witch trials. All she needed was the puritan garb, and she could have been a spitting image of Sarah Good. Her hands were folded neatly in her lap, and her eyes were droopy with a sympathetic gaze as her fragile breathing heaved a few deep breaths at pinnacle moments in her fabled tale.

The courtroom was silent. The jurors looked astonished, the stands were hushed, and even the court reporters had laid down their pens and paper. They were all being hooked by the grand lie told by the best fisherman, Jenny Ascot.

Jill Stapleton felt the weight of the entire judicial system on her shoulders after their duo performance. She knew with every fiber in her being Jenny was guilty of these sadistic crimes, but convincing a jury was another matter. She looked down at the chicken scratch on her notepad, familiarizing herself with her quickly written questions and slowly rose from her seat. She inhaled deeply. She let the circus of tension circle her being. Most people would push the pressure away, but not her. She lived for it.

She exhaled a calm breath and started her production. It may not be as glamorous as the last, but it would be memorable.

"Ms. Ascot, you said you didn't kill anyone, but did your brother?" Jill asked suspiciously, walking toward the witness box, gaining strength with each commanding stride.

"No," she calmly answered.

"So, why was chloroform found in his oxygen tank?"

"I don't know," she replied smoothly. "He was killed before I could ask him."

"That's some coincidence your brother had a matching form of chloroform in his Halloween costume props as was found in the victims. Do you know how to make chloroform?"

"I do not," she answered.

"Well, don't you remember the other day, Dr. Santiago told us how simple it is to manufacture chloroform? It's only a mixture of a few chemicals. Or do you not remember that either, just like you don't remember the night of your arrest?"

Jenny looked over at Milo, shaking her head for him not to object to Jill's round of questioning. "Yes, I remember his testimony, but just because I know what chemicals are needed to make chloroform doesn't signify I know how to make chloroform."

"Well, it's really easy. I actually looked it up last night and watched a quick video on YouTube on how to make the deadly combination."

"If you are so knowledgeable on chloroform, maybe Jonah Carney's photographs are the correct ones, and you and Abner are the killers," Jenny slid in wickedly.

"Your honor," Jill exclaimed, "I didn't ask a question."

Milo slowly stood, "Yes, your honor, I didn't hear a question posed by Ms. Stapleton either. Strike that comment." He smiled knowing even though Judge Ogdon would command the jury to not take the last comment into account in their verdict, the jury couldn't erase what they'd just heard.

"My apologies," Jenny said sincerely to Judge Ogdon and the jury. "I do know better."

Jill walked back to her table to reexamine her questions. "You got this," Angus whispered forcefully, like a team captain on the lacrosse field. She needed that boost since the last round of banter jolted her rhythm. She looked at her scribbles and smiled, looking up at Jenny.

"Ms. Ascot, when did you reconnect with your brother?"

"It was a little over a year ago," she answered.

"Your brother had a troubled past, correct?"

"Yes, he bounced around in the foster care system until he was kicked out at eighteen," she answered attentively, looking at a few members of the jury.

"He had quite an extensive rap sheet," Jill commented. "Were you aware of all of his previous indiscretions?"

"All of them?"

"Yes, all of them."

"I knew of a few things my brother did before we reconnected, but I wouldn't say it was extensive," Jenny answered feebly.

"Were you aware he was caught making meth?" Jill crept in, waiting to pounce.

"Making meth?" Jenny choked up. "I, uh…I didn't…I didn't know," she stammered, looking over at her defense table for support as a lone tear started to trickle down her cheek.

"Are you saying you were not aware your brother could make this drug? If he could make meth, he could easily have made chloroform."

"No, I didn't know," she answered weakly.

"Interesting, because he appeared in court around the time you two reconnected. Guess who the public defender was on that case. You!" Jill said, slamming her fist on the table, as if showcasing an exclamation mark on her game of chess. Check.

Jenny cocked her head toward Milo, who winked at her. "My brother wasn't being tried for the making of meth when I was his public defender. He was caught with a small amount of marijuana, which the judge dismissed due to faulty police work. If my brother ever made meth, it was before I was in his life, and I didn't intrude on his shady life before me. Are there any police reports on my brother in the last year?"

242

"Three years ago," Jill quickly said, pulling out a paper from her folder. "He was sentenced for the production of meth in the state of New York."

"I was not aware of that," Jenny said, lowering her head. "My poor brother lived a hard, hard life. I knew he did some things in his past, but he would never share them all with me. He was trying to get his life back. He was actually working a job at a local coffee shop to make an honorable living," she said with heart-wrenching emotion that would have caused even the coldest of hearts to melt. "I was trying to get him to a good place."

Jill wanted to sink into a hole. She knew to never ask a question she didn't have a known answer for, but she thought she could trick her. She thought wrong.

"If you loved your brother so much and wanted him to be in a good place, then why didn't any of your friends know about him?"

"He wanted it that way," she answered. "He didn't want people to look at him like a reject. He wanted to get his life straight so people wouldn't think he was just in my life to use me."

"But he did use you. How much money did you give him in the last year?"

"None," she said, thinking, *You've got nothing on me, girl.* "He would never accept any of my money."

"That's interesting," Jill said, pulling a year's worth of bank statements from her folder and flipping one open to read. "Why are there so many ATM withdrawals every week? $400 on June 4th, $500 on June 12th, $350 on June 20th, and so on and so on. That's quite a lot of money to be pulling out every week."

"Ever heard of Dave Ramsey?" Jenny laughed playfully. "He is a radio financial advisor who recommends paying everything with cash. That's why I have so many ATM withdrawals." She looked at Jill and thought, *I have an answer for every question you ask. Answers are easy when everything is a lie.*

"So you pay everything with cash? Then why do you also have some debit card transactions and checks on your bank statement?"

"I don't practice what I preach all the time. My landlord requires a check, as do various bills I pay. I write a check for all my charitable giving such as the Humane Society and Big Brothers Big Sisters so I can deduct it on my taxes. The IRS frowns upon cash donations because it's not easily traceable." Jenny also started to laugh as she regaled about her charitable giving. *What killer gives to the United Way or Wounded Soldier? None that I know.*

Jenny looked over at Milo who looked into his little Jenika's eyes with newfound appreciation and adoration.

Jill stood at the prosecution table, almost trembling. She hadn't made one point that could sway the jurors to a guilty verdict. She had done more harm than good. She had one more line of questioning to cling to.

"Your father was found guilty of killing your mother twenty years ago. Could your brother have had some rage at retired age individuals, or individuals who could have adopted him twenty years ago so he wasn't put into such a bad life? Could your brother have killed these retired travelers as an act of revenge for not adopting him twenty years ago?"

Jenny stopped and swallowed. "I never thought of that," she said softly. "He did mention to me a couple of times about how lucky I was being adopted while he got abused by strangers. But he never acted out his rage when I was around him. He was always loving to me." She stopped and dropped her head. "Poor Alexei, I should have been a better sister to you."

She raised her head with an inviting fragility to look around the courtroom. "But when I was adopted, my parents took me to counselors and they slowly started to erase my memories of my life before being adopted. The first time I met Alexei, I thought he looked familiar, but I didn't remember him. I am such a bad sister. I lived such a spoiled life," she sobbed. "There are kids out there living on the street, and here I am living in a plush apartment. It's not fair I got a good life, and he got nothing. It's just not fair. I don't even want to think Alexei killed anyone, but…" she stopped.

"But what, Ms. Ascot?"

"But…" she started and shook her head.

"You are under oath, Ms. Ascot."

Jenny looked up at Judge Ogdon, then Jill, slowly turning her head to Milo and then lastly to the jury. "But if my brother did kill all these people to get revenge for what happened twenty years ago, who's the woman in those videos? She's still out there."

"We know who the woman in the video is," Jill said flatly. "It's you, Ms. Ascot. You are the woman in the video."

Jenny shook her head frantically, looking at Jill with puppy dog eyes and then turning her attention to the jury. "But I didn't, I swear I didn't. If my brother was the one who did this…" she stopped and started to sob. "Alexei, why?"

Jill looked down at her notepad and noticed all the points she wanted to make were left blank. She had unknowingly put more holes and doubts in the jurors' heads than a mechanic's favorite worn-out shirt.

She relented the floor and sat back down.

She had failed.

Miserably.

Even Angus couldn't look at Jill with optimism. He saw the writing on the jurors' faces.

245

CHAPTER 84

"So, what's your plan now?" I asked Elizabeth as we sat on a park bench in the warm springtime sunlight in Book Hill Park, three blocks from Miguel's.

"Save Fiona," she said dumbfounded as she gave me a quizzical look of sarcasm. "What do you mean, 'what's your plan now'?"

"Exactly how it sounds, what's your plan? How are we going to save Fiona without looking like a bunch of crazy folks? We can't go to her work and eat chips and salsa all night and then leave a mysterious message right when they are about to close: 'Watch out, someone's going to try to kill you tonight. But no worries, we are going to stop them.'"

"When have we ever done that?" she gawked.

"When have we been in this situation before?" I asked point blankly.

She stopped and sulked in silence for a few minutes, watching the passing cars puttering down the busy street as if doing so would produce a solution. The only flashes she saw were blinking turn lights.

"Fine. You got any ideas on what to do?" she resigned, fixing her attention towards me and away from the four-lane road.

"I always have ideas," I smiled charmingly, leaning my back into the hard wooden bench, closing my eyes, and letting the sun's rays bathe over my pale face.

"Fine. You got any *good* ideas?" she asked again, reclining to relax for a little bit herself.

"There you go with specifics," I snarled without opening my eyes.

We sat in companionable silence on the park bench for half an hour. There were moments in our relationship I would pay Elizabeth all the money in my bank account to shut her up, and I know she thought the same about me. She even paid me a hundred dollars a few months ago to walk away from one of our conversations during a snowstorm that left a few people deserted without a working vehicle. She was tired of hearing me talk about something I didn't remember, and she actually gave me a wad of cash to get out of her car with a foot of snow on the ground so she could go pick up the stranded family in some peace and quiet. It was cold walking those few blocks back to an open coffee shop, but I warmed myself up with three glasses of tea, on her.

"I think I may have something," she said, opening her right eye so she could see me sitting beside her.

"What is it?" I asked, opening my left eye to look at her.

"I'm getting there. Give me a little more time, but I think I'll have it," she said closing her eye once again to play through the upcoming events in her head.

"Well, you have about ten hours until showtime, so I guess you have time to sift through all the ins and outs."

"There is no sifting needing," she remarked as she raised up her hand. "Gold finds me. I don't go looking for it."

"Huh?" I asked, raising up and looking over at her.

"You know, sifting. Like sifting for gold," she said. "I thought as a middle class civilian you would get that reference."

"Oh, I get people sifting for gold, but I just don't get your entitled persona," I scoffed passively. "I've seen you get those diamond ring-wearing hands dirty for no other reason than to save a beggar on the street."

"I had a moment of weakness," she smiled. "I gave myself a shot of a million dollar bottle of whiskey when I got home that night to let the alcohol kill the traces of poverty that might have infected me."

"Million dollar bottle of whiskey?" I laughed. "Liar."

"I know, the whole whiskey collection cost a little less than a mil," she said casually. "I was just talking with theatrics."

"Did you say mil or meal?"

"Oh, Solo," she laughed. "I think you know what I said."

"How can you enjoy a shot of whiskey that cost more than the average person makes in a week?"

"With Amedei Porcelana's chocolate, it's easy to forget the cost of the whiskey," she cooed, relishing the decadence of the expensive Tuscan sweet.

"I have no idea what that is," I replied leaning my head back once again.

"I know," she smiled.

"Strange how we spend so much time together, yet…" I stopped.

"Yet what?" she asked in her meditated state.

"Nothing."

"No. Yet what?" she asked again, rising.

I didn't open my eyes, but I could feel hers looking over at me. "It's nothing."

"If it's nothing, tell me."

"Fine. It's strange how we spend so much time together, yet if we both didn't have this *gift*, we would never have become friends."

She reclined back into the park bench without saying a word.

I waited a few minutes, expecting her to say something, but she never did. "Well, aren't you going to say something?"

"Why?" she asked unfazed. "It's true."

CHAPTER 85

"I'm not seeing anything, Cooper," Officer Peterson said as she looked over the crime photos of the last two murders. She analyzed the shards of glass of the victims' cars and the placement of the bullets, but besides that, there was nothing. "It just looks like a drive-by shooting."

Officer Cooper came over to the desk they were working at and stood on the opposite side, looking at the photographs upside down.

"You can move the pictures," Peterson said as she started to flip them around so he could see the images right-side up.

"No," he said stopping her and placing the images upside down. "Sometimes you can't see something because it's too obvious." He lowered his head looking at each of the pictures from a new perspective. "If you move your vantage point, sometimes you will see something new."

"I've looked at the pictures from every direction," she said standing up. "I'm going to get some coffee."

Walking around, Cooper continued to stare at the crime scene. He didn't see anything jumping out that would warrant a clue or a hint of who the killer was either.

There were no distinguishable track marks, nothing that would point them in a direction of the whereabouts of the killer, definitely not any DNA or forensic data. The only thing that would help them was some video footage or an eyewitness.

"And they have checked the sounding stores for surveillance footage from their security cameras?"

"Yes, the only camera that picked something up showed a blurry image of a dark vehicle around that time. IT was looking into clarifying the image, but they couldn't even tell if it was a car, truck, or SUV.

They just know the killer wasn't on a motorcycle," Peterson answered thoroughly. "Why does the city put up bogus surveillance cameras?"

"To deter traffic violations," Cooper said, not taking his eyes off the pictures.

"Seems like they should have actual cameras picking up the footage and not some knockoff pretend cameras to scare people into not speeding," she continued. "If the cameras were working, this case would be solved by now."

"Maybe not," Cooper said rubbing his dry eyes. "Some of these surveillance cameras only start recording if there is a violation. If the killer didn't speed through the intersection or run a red light, these cameras still might not have caught anything. I'm not sure how the cameras around the city work."

"Stupid," Peterson muttered. "I pay these taxes to keep me safe, and all I see are news headlines about a new dog park. I'm sorry, dogs don't need a park for themselves until all these streetlights have working cameras on them," she said as rage filled her eyes. "I bet those stupid dog parks have working cameras to make sure no one vandalizes their area."

"Not a dog person?" Cooper grinned as he took a step back for a new perspective.

"Actually, I love dogs," Peterson smiled. "I just hate stupid decisions. It's not the dogs' fault our politicians are ignorant. It's our fault for voting them in and allowing them to pass these laws to limit working cameras to certain nights. It's just stupid."

Cooper walked around the desk and grabbed Peterson's cup of coffee. "I think you've had enough of this for a while. Maybe you should try decaf."

"I will cut you if you take away my drug of choice."

He calmly set the coffee back down on the desk and walked away.

"Since you're up," Peterson said leaning back in her chair and taking a gulp of her coffee, "I could use a refill."

CHAPTER 86

The warm afternoon sunlight was desperately needed, especially with the upcoming night we would be having. I left Elizabeth to sink deeper into the Vitamin D nourishment while I called Wint. As the phone rang, I prayed he would pick up. I wanted him to know I was thinking of him. I knew he could hear it in a voicemail message, but I wanted a dialogue with my friend. I wanted to know how he was.

"Hey Solo, I can't talk right now," Wint answered in a hushed muffled tone.

"That's fine man, I just wanted you to know I'm thinking of you, brother," I quickly shot back.

"Thanks," he said, but nothing else. He didn't end the phone call, but he didn't sound like he wanted to continue it either.

"I found something, Cooper," a muffled woman said. "The same number called both the victims around the time they were killed."

I waited a few seconds, hearing the commotion in the background of fellow police officers talking about car wrecks, restraining orders, and child protection orders. "Are you okay?" I finally asked, breaking through the silence.

"Find out who called them. Give me a minute," he said.

"That's fine. No rush," I said, strolling through the park, kicking tree branches that had fallen from their new springtime growth.

"No, not you," he came back on the line clearer than before. "I was talking to Dakota."

"Oh, tough case?" I asked, hoping tonight there would be a little less death on the streets and maybe a criminal caught.

"It's not the case," he said in a defeated tone. "I got a text from Veronica earlier. My brain was telling me to not read it and delete it, but something else was telling me to read it."

"And?" I asked like in a cliffhanger moment.

"And I finally read it a few minutes ago," he said. "No joke, I read it just before you called. Did you know she texted me?"

"Did I know?"

"Yes, did you put her up to this?" he asked painfully.

"No, I haven't talked to her at all today," I answered, kicking the same stupid stick on the sidewalk.

"Well, did you see her at the courthouse?"

"We didn't go in today," I said. "We were going to, but something else came up."

I could feel the aggravation in his words. I felt them too. I wanted to despise Veronica for the damage she did yesterday, but something in my gut was telling me the same thing as Wint.

"I don't know what to think," Wint finally said. "I am so ticked off at her that I got a good divorce attorney's contact this morning, but then she sent me that text."

"What did it say?"

"She needs me," he said.

"She needs you?" I said shocked. "Needs you how? To use you or something?"

"I, I don't think so," he said slowly, as if hearing the words the first time himself. "Either something's wrong or she's just toying with me."

"You know my feelings on Veronica," I said with a matter of fact tone. "I have never hid anything major about her, even though I know you probably wish I did sometimes."

"And?" he commented, waiting for my famous last words.

"And I don't know what to tell you, man," I said with a heavy heart. "I know that isn't what you want to hear, but you need to watch yourself. What's the expression about fooling someone once or twice?"

"I know, I know," he said in a defeated tone. "Am I a fool?"

I didn't know what to say. Why did I get myself in these situations? Why did I feel the need to call my friend to see how he was doing and then expect him to not reach out for any advice? If he had asked me this same question six months ago before his birthday, I would have said, "Yes! You are a stupid fool who is thinking with the wrong part of your body!" But now, now, I felt as foolish. I was seeing Veronica through a different lens. I was trying to remove all my feelings from past years of drudgery and tainted memories. I knew two Veronicas, the ghost of my pre-dreaming days and the being of my post-dreaming days.

But what she did yesterday morning drug up the haunting images from my past moments with her – the cold, heartless Veronica that would rather insult me to my face than offer a kind word. That Veronica destroyed a little bit of Wint yesterday.

But which Veronica was real?

"If you're a fool, Wint, I am too then."

CHAPTER 87

"You were brilliant, Jenika," Milo softly said, hugging her tenderly as Veronica watched from the corner of Jenny's holding cell. "The way you railroaded all of her questions into innocent naivety and then used your brother as the ultimate scapegoat…" He stopped and held her face in his hands as if looking at a delicate rose. "You amazed me. Your father would have been proud. Your brother too."

Jenny's eyes started to sparkle with the start of a few tears, but she held them back. She wanted Milo to see her strength. She wanted her godfather to see her as an independent woman. She wanted him to see her not as a little girl, but as one who could replace him in his society in the future. "I hope so."

Veronica couldn't sit silent anymore. She was wrestling with too many demons and she wanted to squash them with the sound of her own voice. "Closing arguments are tomorrow, Milo. Are you ready?"

"Why should I be ready?" he looked confusedly. "Jenika wants you to do it, Ms. Hyde."

"Me?" Veronica gasped. She had sat speechless in the courtroom since Milo was added as head counsel, and she assumed Jenny would have him give the closing.

"Yes, you, darlin'," Jenny said cunningly. "Do you have a problem with that?"

"Well…I just thought…" Veronica started, but got interrupted.

"I don't need you to think," Jenny said snappishly. "We are doing the thinking here, dear. You just say what we want you to say."

"And what is that?" Veronica asked condescendingly.

"Your script should be here any minute," Milo interjected as he offered Jenny a seat at the table where he was seated.

"Script?" Veronica commented mystified.

"Yes, Ms. Hyde," Milo kindly replied. "It should be here momentarily."

Veronica continued to sit in the cold corner as Milo and Jenny whispered into each other's ears, keeping their words hidden. Veronica reached into her purse to check her messages. She had nine messages, but none from Winston. Her heart sank with the knowledge Winston was ignoring her. She couldn't blame him, but she desperately wanted to read his encouraging words.

The silence was broken by a tapping on the door before it slowly creaked open.

"Luther, so kind of you to do this for me," Jenny said, standing up to shake his hand as he entered the room.

"Yes, I know you haven't actually been in a courtroom setting in some time, but I recalled moments of utter astonishment in your closings thirty years ago, and I urged Jenika to allow you to do the closing," Milo said kindly.

"It has been some time since I wrote a closing argument, but I think this should seal the deal," Luther said, shaking Milo's hand and handing him the manila folder.

"It better," Jenny said wickedly, then smiling gingerly. "I have no doubt in your abilities after Milo requested this."

"Here's your script," Milo said handing Veronica the folder Luther just handed him. "We shall see if the Hydes are up to this challenge."

"She isn't a Hyde," Luther said coldly. "At least you'll have the words of a Hyde. I can't guarantee the presentation will be up to my standards."

Veronica felt the daggers from her father's words cut deeper than anything he had ever said to her – practically denouncing his relationship with his oldest daughter to a pair of pathological criminals.

She didn't know if she could feel any lower than she did yesterday, but those crushing words of disapproval wrecked her. But right then and there, she vowed they wouldn't anymore.

"I will never be at your standards, Luther," Veronica said, using the last bits of her strength to stand to look the three of them in their eyes. "My standards surpassed yours years ago," she said with a powerful gaze. "Years ago."

She had never stood up to her father, but she was no longer going to take his slanderous, backhanded comments with a childish smile. She was stronger than that. She felt the uneasiness in her legs fade as a newfound strength quickly spread throughout her body. No more knocking knees. No more sunken shoulders. No more tangled knots in her stomach. His words were true. She wasn't a Hyde. She was a Cooper. She just hoped it wasn't too late to persuade Winston of that.

She looked into her father's eyes as he rolled them.

She didn't care. She didn't need his recognition anymore. She didn't need him. She wondered why it took her so long to stand up to him. Too many years had been wasted, but no more. She had stood up to him.

It felt good.

CHAPTER 88

"Fiona Maria Sanchez," he said under his breath as he left the Department of Transportation building for the evening. He had a few things to do before meeting up with the rest of the guys for a late dinner at Miguel's.

He hopped onto the metro train heading toward the garage that housed his Ford Fusion. The car had been driven much more than usual this week, and he wanted to fill it up with gasoline and give her a quick washing before the evening started. He couldn't remember the last time the vehicle was driven this many times in one week, but he wanted the car to look nice for Fiona. She always liked the color black, if his memory was correct. *It was.*

He drove the car through a car wash. Water bathed the car as a thin layer of soap washed over its length. Jets of water sprayed over the vehicle in every direction and cascaded over the glass as the tides collided with the soap, forming a thick layer of bubbles over the entire exterior. He watched as the bubbles overtook the glass, darkening the interior. The blackness soothed his mind as the sound of the water hitting the roof relaxed his mind to memories locked in his inner psyche.

Fiona was the girl that never gave him the time of day in high school. She never gave any guy a second thought. That's what intrigued him about her. He recalled the countless times when he'd asked her out for a movie, a dinner, a concert, or even to study, but she had always declined. Always.

He wasn't used to always being turned down so much by the same person. It seemed like during his senior year of high school he'd asked her out a couple of times each week. He thought eventually she would be worn down by his relentless begging. He tried befriending her friends, sitting at her lunch table when she was alone, helping her with literature homework, and he even joined the Cultural Diversity Club to gain her attention. The only thing it gained was a line on his college admissions application.

After they graduated high school, he tried one more time to win her over, but she was brutally honest.

"When are you going to learn?" she shouted on the platform of the subway station as the words echoed throughout the entire underground cavern. "I've said no to you every time! Are you that stupid?"

"But…I…" he'd stammered, never seeing her rage. He'd always seen her playfully dismissing him. But this was a new side of her. A side he didn't like.

"Where's your gang?" she'd groaned. "Did they finally leave you too?"

"They would never do that," he'd said.

"You shouldn't be so trusting," she had said sadly. "There is no one you can trust. No one." Those were the last words he'd heard her say before she'd stepped onto the red line train.

As it turned out, her words were true.

The soapsuds disappeared and the water stopped. The darkness vanished with a ray of sun shining through the clear glass. He exited the car wash and got out to examine technology's handiwork. He was impressed with the cleanliness, marveling at the image of his reflection on the car hood. He grinned a smile that had never charmed Fiona, but it enticed the ladies now.

Tonight, Fiona, there is no one you can trust. No one.

CHAPTER 89

Officer Cooper drove to the possible suspect's home while prepping Dakota on protocols, standard procedures, questioning, and the general lowdown for first-timers.

"Geez, I got it," she said with a kidding tone. "You're talking to me as if I've never done this before." She stopped talking and finished scribbling her notes, which was every word Cooper said. "Which I haven't," she admitted with a nervous laugh.

"We all have first times," he said encouragingly. "So take a deep breath, act smart because you never know, and watch your surroundings."

"Gotcha," she said. "Any other words of wisdom?"

"Don't get us killed is a good one." He smiled as he made a left turn through a quiet street to their possible perpetrator. "So, what's the background on this guy again?'

"Let me get it," she said pulling up the information on her laptop. "Okay, here we go. Stewart Weatherby, 26, works for the D.C. Transportation Department. He moved here in 2008 from England."

"Twenty-six?" Cooper asked. "How old are the victims?"

"Around that age," Dakota answered as she opened up their files on her laptop. "Yes, twenty-five and twenty-six."

"Do you know which high school he attended?"

"Let me search," she said, quickly typing in the command in her search field. "Looks like Woodrow Wilson High School," she said.

"Where did Sabrina Latener go to school?" he asked, trying to find a common thread.

"Didn't see that coming," she said in shock. "Woodrow Wilson."

"What about Piper Michaelson?"

"Already started looking," Dakota added as she opened up her file. She stopped and looked over at Cooper amazed. "How'd you know?"

"I didn't," he answered. "Just luck."

"I wouldn't have put that together," she remarked as she re-examined each of the files to look for more similarities. "Never."

"I was just guessing," Cooper replied passively. "Sometimes it works, but most of the time, it doesn't. I was just trying to look at the case from as many directions as possible."

"So, could be an old lover's spat? A dumped boyfriend getting revenge? Scary," she shivered.

"What?"

"I would hate to have all my exes coming after me," she said as she turned the mood from solemn to lighthearted. "Not that there would be that many. And most of the time, I was the jilted one in the relationship."

"You?" Cooper let out in surprise. "Dumped?"

"Always," she shrugged. "Now look at me, a newbie cop, still single, barely making it week by week with rent and student loan payments, wearing a manly uniform and carrying a gun. If I keep going on this tangent I may be the next Stewart Weatherby."

"You wouldn't dare," Cooper smiled as he slowed his cruiser down approaching Stewart's townhouse.

"There are days when I think of not even loading my gun because I'm fearful of taking it out on the next guy I see."

Cooper's eyes widened in alarm. "You're always to have it ready and available," he spit out like an older brother looking out for his little sister.

"I know," she remarked with an exhausted expression on her face. "I said there are days I *think* about it. But I never actually do it."

"Okay, you scared me for a second," Cooper said, taking a relieved breath as he stopped his cruiser.

"My thoughts usually scare me longer than just a second," she casually replied. "Ready to get him?"

CHAPTER 90

The atmosphere was alluringly serene in Elizabeth's two-story townhouse nestled on a quiet street of the Bloomingdale neighborhood. I looked out her back living room window and saw the tombstones and statues of Prospect Hill Cemetery just beyond her fence. The carved crosses and cement angels looked stunning in the springtime sun, yet a chill of eeriness crept into my soul. Even though I knew the purpose of a cemetery, it hit me that Fiona could be one of the gravesites in the coming week.

"Are you asleep?" I asked as Elizabeth reclined on her chaise lounge with a satin eye mask infused with lavender and chamomile.

"Not if you keep walking around like a buffalo," she murmured without removing her eyewear. "With every step you take I hear my great grandmother's china rattle in the dining room cabinet."

"Sorry," I said as I quietly tiptoed across the dark oak wood floor, shuffling the decorative pillows until I found a seat on her leather couch.

"If you chip a measly saucer with your pounding, you'll be more than sorry," she drowsily responded. "It's going to be a long night, so get some rest."

I put my shoeless feet on her couch and fluffed three of her matching feathered pillows. I leaned back and stared at the flawlessly plastered ceiling with crown moldings along the edges. Elizabeth's home was starkly different than my drab ghetto bachelor pad apartment. Just looking at her ceiling reminded me I had at least two cracks on each of my rooms' ceilings. Granted, I only had five rooms in my apartment, but each one had a spreading gash that made me often wonder if my upstairs neighbor wasn't causing them with the latest in home aerobics DVDs.

"You have a nice place, Elizabeth. I have to give you credit for that," I kindly said, trying to close my eyes, but it seemed like I had springs keeping them apart.

She didn't respond, but I couldn't blame her. She'd had a stressful week dreaming nightly of the killer's agenda to knock off another defenseless woman. I looked over at her; it appeared she had finally succumbed to a blissful rest as her left arm looked like dead weight, barely on the lounge.

My eyes darted around the room. Even though we had been together almost every day for the last six months, this was the first time I had stepped inside her home. She thought it would be best to get a quick nap in before the excitement of the evening. We had a rough timeline planned out, but we each knew that given the delicate matter of a life or death moment, we needed to be in top form.

I said a quick prayer for Fiona's sake.

Before I knew it, the springs on my eyelids disappeared. I passed out on her couch with my legs sprawled like a dog on its back with its tongue sticking out. I drifted off into a dreamless sleep.

The first time in many weeks.

CHAPTER 91

"Stewart Weatherby?" Officer Cooper asked as he showed the person who answered the door his badge as Officer Peterson stood behind, observing the interaction.

"Yes, I'm Stewart," he answered confused and shocked as he opened the door to two police officers.

"Do you mind coming down to the station with us for some questions concerning an investigation of two deaths?" Cooper asked as he put away his badge and secretly assured himself his gun was in his holster.

"Two deaths?" he gasped. "Who died?"

"We can discuss that matter at the station, sir. Will you follow us?" Cooper recited like he had done many times before.

"I didn't kill anybody," Stewart stammered as he turned around in his foyer to grab his cell phone and keys off the table. "Do I need to call an attorney?" he rambled as his voice lightly trembled.

"You can if you feel that is needed, but we just have some questions on an ongoing investigation."

"Well, I didn't kill anyone, so I guess it's not needed," Stewart replied as he walked outside and locked his front door. "I don't have a car to follow you," he said.

Peterson looked at Cooper giving him a look that read *liar*.

"No problem, you can get in the back seat," Cooper said as the three of them walked down the path to the street. "This is only a formality, but I have to say this," Cooper started as he stated Stewart his rights.

"Was that necessary?" Stewart asked as he ducked his head to get into the back of the police cruiser.

"Yes, it's a formality we say to everyone we question," Peterson responded as she closed his door and got into the front passenger seat.

Stewart sat in the backseat, awestruck as a child on Christmas day. "I have never actually been in a police car before," Stewart said mesmerized. "But it actually looks like what I was expecting," he added as the wonder left him like it was December 26th.

"Just another car with a metal barricade between the front and back seats," Cooper said as he started the engine and headed towards their station.

"So," Stewart said grabbing his phone from his pocket and starting to text, "who died?"

CHAPTER 92

Grant was the first one of the group to enter Miguel's as he asked the hostess for a table of four. He glanced down at his phone and noticed he had a new text message from Stewart.

Not sure if I'm going to make it tonight, but save me a seat anyway. The cops want to question me about some deaths. Strange. I'll try to get there before the third round of drinks.

I can't stay long tonight, Grant texted back, *but I bet Collin or Jordan will be here till they close.*

He put down his phone as the waitress brought some menus and baskets of tortilla chips and mild salsa. He ordered a water with lemon as he started to skim over the menu typical of every Mexican restaurant. He debated over trying something new, but knew that wasn't his forte. He was content with his chicken bean burrito.

"Hear about Stewart?" Collin asked as he plopped down in his chair, quickly gobbling up a few chips before Grant could answer.

"Yeah," he answered, watching Collin feast like a starving sixteen year old. "Sounds like a formality or something."

Collin looked around the restaurant and hunkered down to lower his voice. "Did it say anything about deaths?"

"It was a group message, Collin," Grant laughed as he finally succumbed to the pressure of chowing down on some chips and salsa. "We all got the same message."

"That's right," Collin said with a clueless expression and a dribble of salsa on his chin.

"You got something on your chin," Jordan said throwing Collin a napkin as he sat down next to Grant. "So, it looks like we won't be helping Stewart pick up some ladies tonight."

"I think he has enough numbers for a while," Grant said, rolling up his long sleeves and trying to get the waitress's attention. "I can't stay too long tonight, men, so I need to eat and dash."

"How come?" Collin joshed. "Wifey need you do some chores before bed? I thought you took care of the plumbing last night."

"Crude," Jordan said disapprovingly.

"What?" Collin asked, acting shocked. "You know he did."

"That's not the point," Jordan defended.

"You two are just getting lame in your old age," Collin remarked, stuffing another chip into his mouth.

"You're three weeks older than me, chum," Grant said, smiling as he lightly smacked Collin on his cheek. "And if you eat too many of those chips, you'll die before me too."

"You're younger than me?" Collin gasped.

"Did you already have a drink before you got here?" Jordan asked bewildered. "You know Grant is younger than you. You always bring it up how you're the oldest in the group."

"Number-wise," Collin corrected. "I'm the oldest number-wise. And number-wise only."

"Sorry to break your heart, dear, but age is a number," Grant said with sympathy.

"Not for me," he responded looking Grant dead into his lucid eyes. "I don't feel my age, so that's all that matters to me."

"You may not feel your age, but it's still your age," Grant winked. "Old man."

CHAPTER 93

"So, do you know Sabrina Latener and Piper Michaelson?" Officer Cooper asked as they sat in an interrogation room. Stewart sat across from Cooper and Peterson at ease. The frightened look he had when they first introduced themselves had subsided to a more casual appearance.

"That's who you two are investigating?" Stewart asked. "Names sound familiar, but I'm not sure."

Peterson cocked her eyes at Cooper and whispered in his ear. "Pin this guy to the floor."

"You called Sabrina Latener Monday evening around the time of her death. Then you called Piper Michaelson Tuesday evening around the time of *her* death. Can you explain that?" Cooper asked with a commanding and aggressive tone.

"I went out with friends Monday and Tuesday evening to pick up women," Stewart calmly answered. "I got these women's numbers, and I called them."

"So, why did you pretend to not know them a second ago?" Cooper attacked.

"I only knew their first names," Stewart echoed back. "Most people don't give their full names at bars when you pick them up. Women have to be careful these days. And I called a few other women those nights too."

Peterson watched unfazed by Stewart's reasonable answers.

"So, you never met either of these women before you met them in the bar?" Cooper interrogated kindly, as if trying to eliminate Stewart as a suspect.

"No, not that I'm aware," Stewart answered. "I didn't kill those girls," he sighed. "I have a security camera system at my home. You can check that to see I was there after I came home from the bars."

"Would it surprise you to know Sabrina Latener and Piper Michaelson were classmates with you at Woodrow Wilson?" Cooper grilled unremorsefully.

"That was ten years ago," Stewart laughed. "I wasn't in the popular clique in school, so I don't keep in much contact with people I went to school with."

"What time did you leave the bar Monday and Tuesday nights?" Cooper asked flipping open the victims' files.

"I would say around 11," Stewart answered as he pulled out his phone.

"What are you doing?" Peterson asked, eyeing him suspiciously.

"I'm pulling up my home security footage from Monday night to show you when I arrived home. Gotta love technology," he answered with his thick British accent, looking up at her snidely. He found the video and slid his phone across the table. The black and white video showed Stewart walking into his house as he had said.

"We will need to verify this footage is reliable," Cooper remarked as he leaned beside Peterson to watch the video. "You understand, right?"

"Sure, I understand," Stewart said agreeably as he exhaled. "I know videos can be tampered with, so do what you need to do with my phone. But that video hasn't been altered," he stopped and chuckled to himself. "Good thing I kept my clothes on most of the night. Hopefully you don't have to watch the entire night's video."

"Why not?" Peterson asked.

"I usually get up for a drink in the middle of the night," he blushed. He noticed Peterson and Cooper didn't catch his drift from their faceless expression. "And I sleep in the buff."

"Oh, yes. Thank you for your candor," Cooper said with a smile as he stood up with the phone. "This will speed up the process for you."

"Oh joy," Stewart remarked as he leaned back and stared through the two-sided mirror. "Are there other people watching us like they do on TV?"

"Sometimes," Peterson answered as she, too, stood up to follow Cooper out of the room. "We'll be right back."

The door closed and they went into the adjacent room so they could watch Stewart for a few minutes behind the two-sided glass. "Do you believe him?" Peterson asked doubtfully.

"I do," Cooper sighed.

"Stupid Brit," Peterson moaned. "I do too."

The two scanned through the video for the night, looking at different cameras throughout the house and noticed what he said was true. They turned up the volume and watched as Stewart called Sabrina while sitting on the couch.

"He did call her and leave a message," Peterson said deflated. "He didn't lie to us."

"Nope," Cooper agreed. "There are some good guys out there."

"Can I see that?" Peterson asked as she grabbed the phone and started scanning the video for later in the evening. "Just checking to see if he ever left again for the night."

"I was about to do that," Cooper nodded.

Peterson fast-forwarded through the night until the moment Stewart woke up and walked to the kitchen.

"You don't have to let it play, you can keep fast forwarding it to see if he returns to bed," Cooper sighed. "And Sabrina was already killed by, what time does that say on the camera?"

"It shows 3:24 on the camera and on the wall clock," she answered.

"So, just fast-forward through that and get through the rest of the night," Cooper said, smirking as he realized what she was doing. "Are you seriously watching that video to see a naked man? You have the Internet, don't you?"

"Just say I'm researching for a possible relationship," Peterson grinned as she watched the video, bringing the phone up closer to her face so she could see everything.

"You thought he was a killer three minutes ago, and now you're checking him out for a possible date on Friday night?" Cooper laughed, grabbing the phone from her hand.

"I wasn't done with the night," she groaned.

"I'll finish it," he said fast-forwarding through the rest of the night as Stewart tossed and turned in his bed. "I'm ashamed of you," Cooper jokingly scolded.

"If it makes you feel better, the video image was too dark to see any details," she jabbed. "He just looked like a pasty white ghost roaming the halls for a glass of milk."

"I'll let you tell him that," Cooper remarked. "As you ask for his phone number."

"Why ask?" she laughed. "I already sent his contact to my phone."

"You didn't!" Cooper gasped with his mouth gaping open. "That's a violation, tampering with evidence."

"Jeez, Cooper. I was just messing with you."

CHAPTER 94

"Peaceful night, isn't it?" I said with my right arm out the passenger window, letting it rise and fall against the wind like I did when I was a kid when I dreamed of becoming a pilot. Some dreams fall by the wayside of life when the world screams conformity louder than true calling. Even if I had followed that nine year old's dream, it wasn't my true calling.

"Eerie, don't you think?" Elizabeth said in between humming along with the radio. "To think that in a couple of hours from now there is going to be a sadistic, planned-out killer driving the downtown streets."

"A couple of hours?" I looked at her inquisitively. "You know he's out there right now."

She closed her eyes as she came to a stoplight and lightly shook her head. She watched intently at the red light, as if in the optometrist's office following the light. "I don't like to think about that."

"But it's true," I commented as I went back to looking out the rolled-down window and catching a whiff of mouth-watering garlic from a nearby Italian restaurant. I watched couples walk hand in hand down the brick sidewalks to their evening dinner plans wondering if that man could be the possible killer. Anyone could be the killer.

"So is the fact or myth -- whatever you believe -- that you swallow twenty spiders in your sleep. There are things that happen around us that I am content with being oblivious about."

I glanced over at her catching her profile and I noticed her hard exterior she tried to maintain was slightly diminishing. It wouldn't have been noticeable to the untrained eye, but her shoulders were sunken a little more than normal with her hands resting on the steering wheel. It looked as if the years of seeking that unattainable high standard of elitism was softening with shades of a caring heart.

Then she spoke. "And don't say you're not."

Twisting my head to look out the window again, I played on both sides of the net. There were days I would dive into the realm of seeking out all the problems and chaos we caused with hopes of finding a resolution, while there were other days where I limboed under the net and found solace in the fact that I was only one person in this humongous world, and there were plenty of piles of sand to stick my head into.

"Are you still there?" she said snidely, raising the volume on her stereo to drown out my answer.

"Yeah, I'm here," I finally mumbled.

"Making sure, because I don't need you going spastic on me later during your meltdown."

"When have I melted down?" I asked, wiggling around in my seat to give her my undivided attention.

"There've been moments," she said, shrugging her shoulders casually.

"A meltdown?" I scoffed. "Really? A meltdown?"

"Well, maybe not a meltdown," she said, taking back her words. "Maybe more of a thawing out."

"And what does that mean?"

She continued to drive through the sunless streets as the moon slowly began to rise into the darkening sky.

"You can't say that and not explain it," I laughed, trying to remind myself that Elizabeth loved to play mind games and get under my skin.

"Fine," she huffed. "There have been times when if things didn't go as you planned, you got a little out of whack for a while."

"Out of whack?"

"You know, not yourself," she said casually as if the words weren't hurtful, just like she was ordering a coffee through a drive-thru.

"And how is 'myself'?" I asked condescendingly.

"See, this is what I don't like to get into. These are conversations that are best unsaid," she stopped. "Thought, but not said."

"You can't stop the conversation just because it's uncomfortable for you. Life is uncomfortable," I said defensively. "If there's something I do you don't think is right, you have to tell me."

"Solo, it's not like that at all. I was just shooting the breeze with you," she remarked, paying closer attention to the road than she had been a few minutes before.

"Well," I said in an annoyed tone, "it's hard for me to forget things you say when you say you're just shooting the breeze when I know that's not the case."

"Let's just drop it," she said in a motherly tone, as if I was her teenage son being dropped off at soccer practice.

"Fine. By. Me."

CHAPTER 95

The aroma of the lavender vanilla bubbles soothed her more than the three glasses of red wine she had drunk with her caesar salad. Every time Veronica read the closing argument script her father wrote for Jenny's case, she needed a gulp of wine to drown out the distaste.

Her blood pressure rose each time she read the elaborate lies her father had penned. "Model citizen" or "ideal daughter" or "warm-hearted employee" – those descriptions of Jenny may have been used seven months ago through the masquerade she exquisitely portrayed, but now the words seemed more like "deranged citizen" or "hedonistic daughter" or "cold-blooded employee."

She ran the warm bathwater and texted Wint once again, but he still hadn't responded to her earlier texts. Her heart was crushed, but somewhere in the midst of the fragments she had a touch of hope. She knew if Wint would listen to her, she could prove her love to him. She knew if Wint would look at her, she could show him her true heart. She knew if Wint would sit down beside her, she could reveal the secrets she'd been hiding. And she knew if she could get Wint to lie beside her, she would be sleeping more peacefully than she had ever slept before.

The trouble was getting Wint to give her that inkling of a chance, a chance she wouldn't have given to him a few days earlier. That thought sickened her as she stepped into the tub. She rested her head on her bath pillow and inhaled the sweetness of the vanilla and the calming lavender.

Thoughts swirled around her head as if battling in a game of queen of the hill. A negative thought of self defeat and condemnation quickly reigned and reached for the flag but was quickly sideswiped with a positive affirmation that she was a work in progress of continual growth of character and integrity.

Sinking lower in her bath, she let the water rise just below her nose and rested her eyes on the surface. Every breath she exhaled caused a ripple moving the bubbles. She watched as the mountain of bubbles slowly moved with each fragile breath, intrigued as the foamy tides drifted further away from her vision. The sight plunged deep into her core.

She grabbed her cell phone with her soapy hand and quickly called the love of her life. It went to his voicemail. "Winston," she said breathlessly, as if calling him for the first time in college with a family of monarch butterflies getting ready for their annual migration, "I've been a horrible wife. You have all the right to divorce me. I've lied to you. I've kept secrets from you. I've belittled you to your face. I've been the detriment of your entire existence." She stopped as a tear fell down her cheek, falling into her bath water.

"I know my history doesn't have any merit for asking for a second chance, but," she stopped once again and took a deep breath, "but I will make it my lifetime ambition to prove my love for you, Winston. I don't care about anything else in life anymore. My work isn't my life. My career isn't my love. My promotion isn't my definition."

She stopped once again, wiping the tears out of her eyes as her nose started to run. "What I'm trying to say, Winston, is I now see. I now see the man you are, and it's the man I want to be with for the rest of my life. You are my life. You are my love. You are what defines me. So, I'm just pleading for you to hear me out. Please, Winston. Please forgive me."

She ended her phone call and let her tears fall freely. She didn't care about the case. All she cared about was proving to her husband that her love was true.

"Do you mean that?" a muffled voice said through the door.

"Someone there?" Veronica shouted through her blurry eyes and sobs. She didn't hear the words, just a noise.

"I asked, 'Do you mean that?'" the voice asked again, this time with utmost clarity.

Veronica crumbled in the tub. She didn't know she could feel so broken and vulnerable. Her breath was stolen at the sound of Wint's voice through the door. She tried to talk, but all the air was stolen from her lungs. She gasped, trying to spit out one word, but it wouldn't come.

He lightly tapped on the door and turned the knob to enter. He stood in the doorframe looking handsome in his police uniform. "Did you mean what you said in your message?" he asked from the bedroom. He didn't step into the bathroom but stood safely at a distance. Staying guarded.

Veronica released all the heart-wrenching tears that were unbeknownst to her, as if hidden somewhere in the locked confines of her soul. She mouthed, "Yes, Winston," but she couldn't audibly say it. Her voice wasn't strong enough to pronounce the simple, heartfelt words. She nodded her head emphatically as she continued to sob in her lukewarm bathwater. She couldn't see him anymore as her eyes clinched shut in remorse and regret for what she had put him through in their marriage. She started to shake uncontrollably, heaving rivers of tears until she felt a touch.

His touch on her shoulder.

"I love--," she tried to say, but he wouldn't let her finish.

"Shhhh," he whispered in her ear as he bent down, kneeling beside the bathtub. He wrapped his strong arms around her naked body and felt her weakness and fragility. "Just shhhhhh," he repeated as he wiped her eyes. "I've got you."

With those words, she broke a little more. She freed her tears that gushed from her along with the hidden stories of her past. She didn't want to hide any more secrets from him.

She finally felt free in the arms of a hero.

CHAPTER 96

Elizabeth and I waited in silence at the corner of Sips and Dead Lift Gym. She sat at the darkened café table checking her text messages and Twitter feed as I leaned against the glass window of Sips ten feet away. I looked across the street at the deserted gym and down the street; not a running vehicle in sight. I checked my watch: 10:34 p.m.

I wanted to ask her if she was ready, but I wasn't ready to talk. We had had moments like this, the tension fueled by possible outcomes. It also didn't help we had been side by side since early this morning. Even as we napped this afternoon, we were still within breathing distance of one another.

I didn't want to apologize, but I knew I was the one who always had to start it.

"You okay?" I asked casually. "Are you ready?" This was my form of an apology. I wasn't feeling the need to technically say the word 'sorry', since I hadn't said anything I was sorry about.

"Just thinking," she said without looking away from her phone. After a few seconds she placed her phone back into her purse and gave me her undivided attention. It was the first time she had looked at me in two hours.

"It's going to be okay," I said encouragingly. "We've done things like this before."

"Never with a killer on the loose," she laughed.

"Killer, shmiller," I remarked like it was no big deal. "This is going to be just like any other dream. We save the girl, stop the guy, and give the cops the info to catch this psycho."

"Sure, easy breezy," Elizabeth said as she nodded with a lying approving grin. "This is going to be a piece of cake." She glanced over at the purple flowers and smiled. "It's funny, the things you remember in dreams."

"I know," I said, pushing myself off the glass and walking towards an empty seat at her table. "Do you ever wonder if everyone gets dreams like this, but they don't remember them when they wake up?"

She cocked her head in my direction and thought for a few seconds. "I have never thought that."

"They say you have many dreams each night, but you don't remember them," I commented as I sat down. "I read somewhere you could have as many as a hundred dreams a night because your dreams typically last only one or two minutes, but then I also read you only have five or so."

"That's a big difference," she said with an astonished tone. "You would think science could narrow it down."

"How?" I laughed. "They can't read your mind and see what you are dreaming to realize a dream has ended and a new one has begun."

"I don't know, brain scans or something," she said in her typical Elizabeth rant. "But they should be able to narrow it down."

"But how?" I laughed once again at the catch-22 we were finding ourselves in.

"You just like to push my buttons, don't you?" she laughed, looking inside Sips, almost salivating at the espresso machine that sat lonely inside.

"Maybe," I smiled back. "How could you think about getting a coffee this late at night?"

She looked at me and shrugged her shoulders. "I'm sitting outside a coffee shop at this Godforsaken hour waiting for a killer to drive by and try to kill a woman I don't know, so my nerves are just a little on edge."

"Doesn't coffee rattle your nerves more than calm them?" I asked condescendingly.

"And who are you, Dr. Oz?" she quipped back as she dug into her purse, pulling out a package of expensive chocolate-covered coffee beans.

"But it's true, ain't it?"

"Ain't isn't a word, Einstein," she mocked. "You can ramble on about dreams and scientific studies and the chemicals of caffeine, but you can't speak proper English?"

"I pick and choose my topics of interest," I smiled. "English ain't one of them."

"God help us all," she billowed as she rolled her eyes jokingly. "God help us all."

"Amen!" I quickly slid in.

"Best prayer I've prayed in some time," she winked.

"Gotta start somewhere," I commented as I checked my watch glowing in neon blue. "What time do you think this is going to happen?"

"Not sure," she said sadly. "Could happen in two minutes or two hours."

"So, it's just like the dreams, can't you narrow it down a little?" I mocked facetiously.

"Why don't you go stand over there," she said, pointing across the street by Dead Lift Gym.

"So, you think it's about time?" I smiled, standing up and stretching my aging legs.

"No, I just want you to be across the street," she said casually as she picked up her phone once again, ignoring my presence.

"Well, back at ya," I remarked as I strolled to the crosswalk. "Distance makes the heart grow fonder."

"I don't think that's what Sextus was implying when he wrote those words. And my heart doesn't need to get any fonder of you."

"And why not?" I yelled from the middle of street.

She ignored my question. I knew she heard it because I saw her smirk. It could have been something funny she read on her phone, but I believe it was because of me, and not from what Mindy Kaling posted on Twitter. Of course, she would never tell me.

CHAPTER 97

After dinner at Miguel's, he only got one drink from the bar. He didn't want to be intoxicated for the upcoming fun, but he needed a drink to calm his nerves. The thought of putting a bullet in Fiona's head was the rush that any adrenaline junkie would crave.

He parted his dinner company and walked the quiet street to his hidden vehicle, parked three blocks away in a used car lot. He didn't think anyone would notice his car among the masses of other vehicles. It was the perfect place to blend in.

Sitting in his car, he got out the usual gear. The Orioles baseball cap snuggly fit on his head, but the mustache was losing its adhesiveness, so he reapplied a thin strip of double-sided tape. Looking in the visor's mirror, he strategically placed the mustache on just as his nemesis grew it. He wasn't ready to put on the sunglasses but placed them in his lap to remember for later. Lastly, he checked his trusty friend in the passenger seat.

He caressed the metal, feeling the coldness it exuded. The gun had a force stronger than any magnet. No matter how much he tried to ignore his comrade, his gaze returned to the deadly weapon. It demanded his undivided attention. His heart pumped with angry ambition. His thoughts ran rampant in the devil's playground of deadly revenge. He was fueled and ready for the night.

The keys hung motionless in the ignition. He felt the desire to turn on the beast of the engine and start their evasive rendezvous. He glanced down at his watch and knew the time was coming closer to the chase. He turned the keys and soft pop music filled the quiet car. Wanting to hear a different type of music, he turned off the radio and listened to the car purr. Even though the car had aged, its sound still relaxed him. He felt his shoulders sink and his breathing get a little deeper. Fearful of falling into a sleepy state of euphoria, he reached over on his phone and found a random heavy metal classic to head bang to.

This was his prelude.

The time had come when Fiona would be getting off her shift. He switched from park to drive and escaped from the lot of unwanted vehicles. He drove to Miguel's and glanced into the restaurant, finding Fiona waving farewell to her coworkers. He knew her car was parked a block away, so he quickly circled the block, returning back to the debarkation for the evening.

He waited for this perfect evening to hunt Fiona because he knew she drove to work on Mondays, Wednesdays, and Fridays, and her roommate drove the vehicle on Tuesdays and Thursdays. This Wednesday shouldn't be known as hump day, but bump day, because he was about to bump her off the earth.

Her silver Nissan Altima brake lights lit up, signaling to him half a block away that it was go time. She proceeded up the road and came to a stoplight. He edged beside and positioned his gun barrel through the chiseled key hole. He wasn't ready to kill her yet, but he knew, based upon his map, he had a short journey. Shorter than the ones in the previous nights.

The infotainment screen lit up, showing a red light shining into her backseat. Maneuvering the gun, he watched with a dry mouth as the red light, visible only to him, shined on the side of her left temple.

The red street light changed to green and she gingerly drove down the road. He looked in his rearview mirror and noticed an empty street. Ahead, luckily no cars were heading towards them. He kept his right index finger on the trigger and waited for the next light to turn red so he could prepare for the kill shot.

The street lamps were fading from the brightly lit section of the neighborhood behind to a more residential area ahead. The next red light quickly changed to green, causing his heart to skip a beat. The next light needed to be red. It had to be red. If not, he didn't know what he would do. Something drastic maybe.

He glanced over at Fiona who sat stone-faced as she drove. She wasn't singing or talking on the phone. It was as if she was the last woman on earth without any emotional attachment. He wondered if anyone would care if she was gone because how close could that piece of rock get to another living, breathing human?

His heart leapt with enthusiasm as he saw the light ahead changing from green to yellow. He knew by the time they were at the light, it would be red.

He did another check of the surroundings. No cars. He started braking and came up beside Fiona and positioned the gun. He took a deep breath and aimed the gun. The red laser light pierced the side of her skull.

"Solo!" a woman screamed. "It's them! Fiona! Watch out! He's going to shoot you!"

He was rattled; he didn't expect this.

"Stop!" a man shouted as he ran up to the car window, slamming a brick into the driver's side window.

He definitely didn't expect this. He looked over at the man who was shouting uncontrollably as his finger flinched on the trigger.

He fired.

CHAPTER 98

"Solo!" Elizabeth screamed from across the street. "It's them!"

My adrenaline kicked into turbo charge. I knew the killer heard Elizabeth, because her voice wasn't one that could easily be ignored. I grabbed the hardest thing I could find. I wasn't sure why, but I thought a brick in hand was better than nothing. I started to run up to the car, ignoring the crosswalk lights because I knew no car was going to be coming down the street if her dream was correct.

"Fiona!" Elizabeth screamed as she, too, jumped out of her chair to run up to the car. "Watch out! He's going to shoot you!"

"What?" Fiona screamed as she cracked her passenger side window to hear a little better.

I clinched the brick in my hand but didn't know what to do with it. Then all I could think was break the glass. I ran with all my force and threw all my body weight into the killer's glass window, shattering it.

"Go! Go! Go!" Elizabeth screamed to Fiona, who slammed on her gas pedal.

I tried to keep my balance, but the force knocked me to the ground. I clung onto the brick as I heard a gun shot go off and the sound of glass shattering.

The killer's car sped away. My body was numb, but all I could do was wonder if Fiona was okay.

I jumped up and noticed Fiona's car had turned right at the light. She was alive.

It was Elizabeth lying on the ground that stuck a knife to my heart.

"Elizabeth!"

CHAPTER 99

"Elizabeth!" I screamed, running over to her lying body.

"I'm fine, I'm fine!" she screamed as she raised herself up off the ground. "I fell to the ground to be safe."

"Smart!" I yelled as I ran over to her to help her up.

"Don't worry about me!" Elizabeth barked. "Go get him!" she roared throwing her car keys in my direction. "Now, Solo!"

I ran to her nearby parked car and gunned the gas. I still saw his car moving four blocks ahead. I prayed. Oh, I prayed. "God, please help me not get killed! Oh, Jesus, help me not get killed! Oh, God, I don't want to get killed tonight!"

I watched my speedometer quickly pass seventy miles per hour, and I wasn't letting up. His taillights were getting larger so I knew I was gaining on him. The numbers on the speedometer continued to rise as if it was summertime, eighty-seven miles per hour. "Please Jesus, don't let me get hit! Elizabeth will kill me if the wreck doesn't!"

The black vehicle was getting closer, and then he quickly turned left. I ran a red light and then turned left after him. My wheels skidded. I definitely left marks on the road, but I wasn't worried about that. I saw his taillights one block ahead when a thought entered my brain.

What if he shoots me from up there? I mean, desperate people do desperate things and aiming a gun behind you going sixty miles per hour is pretty crazy.

I didn't care about the consequences; I needed to catch this guy. I pressed the gas to the floor once again watching the speedometer easily fly by the speed limit. I was a few car lengths behind him when I could vaguely read a few of the numbers and letters on the license plate.

"FN" I read out loud as the first two letters. "Come on, eyes!"

My eyes started to read the numbers as he quickly squealed his tires and turned right.

I followed, but since I wasn't expecting it, I didn't do it as smoothly as he. I once again got on his tail, pressing the gas pedal as hard as I could. I started to read the numbers "1513."

I continued to repeat the license plate number "FN1513. FN1513." I looked at the back of the car and noticed it was a black Ford Fusion. I wasn't sure what else I could do, so I reached for my phone in my pocket to call the cops.

It wasn't there. "Really?" I screamed out.

Suddenly, a chill came over me like I had never had before. As if I was being warned. The light ahead of me was red, and I considered running it, but something in my inner conscience was telling me to stop.

I slammed on my brakes and skidded fifteen feet as a police car came blazing through the intersection.

"Thank you, Jesus," I said, knowing if I had run the red light, I would have been t-boned by another speeding car.

I unclenched my nails that were dug into Elizabeth's steering wheel and looked up to see a deserted road.

I had lost him.

CHAPTER 100

He looked behind him and noticed the speeding car following him was gone.

"Where'd you go, man?" he asked softly with his fragile breath.

He still didn't feel safe. He glanced down at the GPS map on his phone and turned left since the surveillance camera ahead was working this evening. He felt lucky he'd missed all the cameras.

At every intersection he wondered if the man behind him was going to pop up again. "How'd they know?" he asked himself, but he didn't have an answer. He had been so careful.

He ran another red light, still trying to flee the scene, when a thought resonated. "What if he stopped because he got my license plate number?"

The thoughts kept coming. "If he got my license plate number, that means they will trace it and get Simon's vehicle instead." Even though he was relieved they would come after him, he knew his fun would end tonight. He knew once the cops pinned Simon for these crimes, the killing spree would have to come to a close for some time.

He glanced down at the GPS and found a working camera nearby. "Let's give them proof," he said as he quickly turned left and then made a right. He slowed his car down as he approached the upcoming traffic light which was still green. He wanted a red light. He wanted a traffic violation for the first time in his life.

Scanning the street, he made sure no cars were around in this deserted section of town. It wasn't even midnight yet, but this area looked like a retirement village with closed shops and flickering street lamps. He glanced in the rearview mirror and noticed he looked just like Simon.

His heart slowed to a light beating as the green light changed to yellow and then to red. Coming to the light, most people would have braked, but he actually pressed the gas pedal a little harder. He wanted to have the surveillance cameras get a nice picture of Simon driving his getaway car.

"Here goes nothing," he said to the red traffic light. "This is for you, Simon."

He wanted it to look realistic, so as soon as he went through the light, he slammed on his brakes and angrily slammed his fists onto the steering wheel. He wanted the surveillance camera to see his "uh oh" moment of going through a working camera. He wanted the cops to read the license plate with picture perfect clarity. He wanted them to see him speeding off and heading home at breakneck speed.

A speed any criminal would drive if they were fearful of getting caught.

"Criminals can be so stupid sometimes," he said, chuckling to himself.

He routed his car to Simon's house, driving through all the intersections with surveillance cameras, as if playing a game of connect the dots. He didn't want the cops to have any doubt Simon was the killer.

He didn't want the cops to have any reason to look for another suspect.

Stopping at a red light, he closed the GPS on his phone and opened his last message from Stewart and reread it.

I'm just now leaving the police station. It's been a weird night, so I'm just going to head home. See u guys tmrw.

Glad you're free, he texted only to Stewart in a new message.

He looked down at the gun in the passenger seat. "Time to get rid of you, old friend. I'm taking you back home."

CHAPTER 101

"You didn't get him, did you?" Elizabeth asked solemnly as I walked up to the crime scene now bustling with cops. The quiet corner an hour ago was now the busiest intersection in all of Washington D.C.

"I got his license plate number though," I said with a wink. "That should do it." Elizabeth wasn't one for affection, and neither was I, but after this long day, we both opened our arms for a long hug. "I almost had a wreck in your car."

"Glad it was almost," she teased as she let go of the embrace. "Where are my keys?"

"I thought you gave me the car," I kidded as I handed her the keys noticing the lack of personal heirlooms: no monogrammed glittering key chains, no souvenirs from a memorable trip.

"The only thing I would give you is my two cents," she snapped back.

"Your two cents over the last few months has accumulated to $42.76."

"Wow, I never knew the amount of my wealth of knowledge," she remarked as she walked away to get a cop. "Well, are you going to follow me?" she barked. I wasn't sure if she was talking to me, and by the look on the cop's face, he had the same question, but we both met halfway.

"Solo, I mean, Solomon here has some information on the car that tried to shoot the girl."

She said *tried*. In all the excitement, I had never asked if Fiona was okay. I assumed she was, but I never actually asked.

"I have a license plate number," I said as I recited the number to the cop who quickly jotted it down and read the number into his microphone for dispatch.

"Thank you," he said coldly which surprised me. I thought he would be beaming, knowing the criminal would be caught soon, but he acted like it was no big deal.

"You understand, you got the guy with that license plate number," I said condescendingly. "I made sure to get close enough to get it right."

"Yes," he smiled facetiously. "I understand how the system works here," he said before turning away to stand around with the other police officers.

As he walked away, Elizabeth said a few choice words for his demeanor, and given any other time, I would have reacted. But her words were true. He was as she called him.

"So, have you already given your statement?" I asked, looking around at the scene knowing if we hadn't been here tonight, the cops would be working a totally different investigation.

"Yeah," she said shrugging her shoulders. "They didn't seem really interested since no one died. And that ticked me off. So I let them have it."

"I bet you did," I said as we turned to head back to her car.

"Wint showed up a few minutes ago," she said wide-eyed. "That was interesting."

"How come?" I asked, even though I thought I already knew.

"He looked at me like," she stopped and tried to process her thoughts.

"Like what in the world are you doing here?" I chimed in leaving the loud commotion behind and walking closer to a quieter locale a couple blocks away.

"Well, I was going to say something different, but yes, that was the look," she replied as she dug into her purse pulling out a phone. "You dropped this."

"I realized that when I was going to call the cops as I was driving."

"Call the cops while driving?" she gasped. "I didn't know I was walking with a known felon."

"That's not a felony," I laughed. "And I didn't do it. You had my phone."

"Good thing," she smiled. "I'm not sure jail would be good for you. You would probably end up being someone's bit--" she stopped and rephrased. "Someone's friend."

"Oh, my, did you just censor yourself from cussing?" I said, gloating with an enthusiastic grin. "Have I taught you that much?"

"Don't pat yourself on the back too much, wiseass."

"There's the Elizabeth I know and love."

"Yep," she mocked. "Here I am."

CHAPTER 102

Fiona sped home as if her life depended on it, and per the shouting woman on the street and the bullet lodged somewhere in her backseat, her life did depend on it. She dialed her mom while she drove, crying and frantic, but it went straight to voicemail.

"Pick up, Mom!" she screamed, but she ended the call before leaving a message. She knew her mother wouldn't notice the missed call or voicemail until the morning anyway.

She thought of anyone else to call, but her list of friends was dismal. She debated calling her roommate, but they weren't really friends. They just both needed a roommate, and Suzi had replied to the ad Fiona posted at the local coffee shop. There was no emotional connection, just financial reasons keeping them together.

While she placed her phone in the drink holder of the console since she had no one to call, she realized her life hadn't always been this jaded. There was a time when she had smiled. There were moments she would laugh out loud. There were distant memories when she had felt safe and innocent. It had all changed one weekend during the summer of her sophomore year of high school.

She didn't like to think about that incident – the incident she swore wouldn't define her. She had been naïve to believe a popular boy in school would like her for her, but all he'd wanted was something she wasn't ready to give. He'd taken it anyway, despite her pleading, telling him no, screaming, and crying for him to stop. But he had one thing on his mind. One thing only.

She had told her father, but he had only looked at her with shame. "Fiona, what did you do to lead him on?"

"But Papa…" she remembered the words as if they were yesterday. The tears came back as if they were stored in canisters for moments like this. "I didn't. I promise you, I didn't."

"Well, it's your word against his and we don't have the money to get a big time lawyer," he'd said with a downcast look, as if all that had happened was a fender bender and he was telling her to flee the scene.

"But Papa, he raped me," she'd cried as her mother consoled her on the living room couch. "He…he…" she'd tried to continue, but her mother hushed her.

Her mother had whispered in her daughter's ear, "Stay strong my little Fiona, stay strong."

Her mother had defied her husband and taken her daughter to the cops. They'd asked the questions, collected the DNA, and scrutinized Fiona like she was a dumped girlfriend acting in revenge. During the entire time, her mother had held her hand.

Fiona finally made it safely to her apartment building and ran inside in case the shooter had followed her. She quickly locked her apartment door and fell to her knees, leaning against the back of the door for support. She looked down at her empty hands and wished her mother was beside her once again, holding her tight, whispering encouraging words of justice, healing, and protection.

Ten years ago, her rapist was never tried. He'd walked the hallways of her school as if nothing ever happened. He'd even been smug enough to blow her a kiss when their paths met.

The police didn't help then.

Would they help her now?

She picked up her phone and dialed. "Hello, this is Fiona Sanchez. I think someone tried to kill me tonight."

Thursday
CHAPTER 103

Elizabeth was nice enough to drive me home, even after we had spent the entire day together. We reminisced about the events and how the cops should be able to pick up the killer any moment.

"I'm still shaking," she said with uncontained happiness. "I am literally shaking," she said, raising her hand inches in front of my face to see her hand tremble.

"I see," I said as I smacked her hand away. I was always conscience of Elizabeth having her hand in my face. It usually ended in me getting slapped.

"We did it," she beamed. "We actually did! There were moments today I thought, 'Nah, this isn't going to work.' But it did!"

"Proud of you," I said softly, looking over at her as if she was my little sister retelling the game-winning hit of her softball tournament. "Very proud."

"I couldn't have done it without you," she gushed. "You figured out the connection between Fiona and the Mexican restaurant. We make a pretty good team sometimes."

"That we do," I said as I closed my eyes to relax for a bit.

"And teammates aren't supposed to have secrets, right?" she said a little shaky in her tone.

"Good teams don't," I replied, catching a hint she needed to talk. "I have my eyes closed, but I'm listening. Go on."

"You are an amazing guy, Solo, really. I have never met anyone like you," she started. "You are kind and smart and funny in your weird, cheesy, nerdy, Jesus way, and you would do anything for anyone, which astounds me most days. And you're not cocky."

She stopped and took a breath. "I need to tell you something," she said slowly. "I don't know how to tell you, but I feel you need to know. I hope you listen to me," she started to ramble.

"Elizabeth, I like you too, but," I started because I wanted to stop this conversation before it went any further. "But like a friend. That's all. I hope you can understand that."

"Yeah," she remarked with an obvious tone.

"I thought you were about to bare your heart and soul to me and tell me you loved me."

"Solo, we would never make it," she said hurtfully. "I mean, that sounded bad, but I don't have any romantic feelings for you."

"Man, you really know how to drop a guy from 'you're an amazing, good looking, guy.'"

"I never said good looking," she smiled. "Maybe I should take back the cocky comment."

"Anyways," I added for her to go back to what she was originally saying.

"I need to tell you something, and I don't know really how to tell you," she said. She drove for a few seconds and came to a red light. She turned her body in my direction. "I need you to look at me when I say this."

"Fine," I said, opening my eyes and looking over at her. I was startled by her body posture while she put the car in park. "You know the light is going to turn green any second."

"It's past midnight; they will go around me," she said systematically. "Okay, you know I have been having these dreams for years, since I was a little girl, and I did nothing about them."

"Yeah, you told me."

"And how I would just make a list and check them off once the dreams happened," she added.

"Yeah, your dream journals."

297

"Well, there are many dreams I wish I had done something about. I wish I had met you when I started having these dreams so I wouldn't have this guilt on my shoulders of my -- I don't know what you call it -- selfish past."

The light turned green, and we continued to sit as Elizabeth spoke from the depths of her heart. "We all have regrets, Elizabeth. It's not the mistakes we made in our past that make us but how we move on from those mistakes."

"Oh, Solo, I have made some fu--, I mean, some really bad mistakes," she confided. "Things that make me question how I can live with myself."

"Elizabeth, you have to forgive yourself," I compassionately said, looking deep into her eyes, hoping my words absolved her of any guilt on her hands.

"Oh, Solo, I'm not sure you mean that," she sighed. "It sounds good in theory, but it's really hard."

"If I didn't mean it, I wouldn't have said it," I remarked, watching the green light fade to a steady red light.

She closed her eyes and took a deep breath. "I was looking through my journals the other night, and one dream stood out. A dream I had a few years ago."

"Okay," I said, not seeing the relevance yet.

"It's a dream that wrecked someone I love, but at the time I didn't know them."

"Elizabeth, has the person moved on?"

"Actually, yes, they have," she answered confidently.

"Then, you should too. What's in the past is the past, and I think they would tell you the same thing."

"Solomon," she said looking deep into my eyes.

Right when she said my name, I knew. I knew what she was about to tell me. I turned my head and stared out the window, looking at all the other places I could be other than sitting in this car right now.

"I'm sorry, Solomon, I am so, so sorry, but," she started to cry, but I still couldn't look at her. All I saw was my reflection in the window and noticed I was crying too. "I didn't know you then. I was just a stupid girl writing down my dreams. But I dreamed about Chelsea. I dreamed of her murder."

I closed my eyes as tears escaped through my eyelashes. Each drop felt like it weighed a hundred pounds, and with each tear, I got a little weaker.

"Say something," she pleaded. "Please Solomon, please forgive me."

I couldn't listen to her words anymore. I had to get away.

That's when I opened the car door and escaped the confines. I ran down the sidewalk, quickly darting into a lonely alley, bawling my eyes out as if Chelsea was dying in my arms once again. I heard Elizabeth screaming my name as I ran, but I didn't look back. I never said a word.

I was done with Elizabeth.

CHAPTER 104

Two police officers approached a darkened duplex on a worn-down street on the southeastern side of Washington, D.C. in the Washington Highlands neighborhood. Most of the streetlights didn't work, so they held their flashlight with one hand and their gun with the other. They couldn't be too cautious in this section of the city where crime was as common as lemonade stands in the summer. They peeped through the garage's glass window and found a black vehicle parked in the darkness. They couldn't tell the make and model, but they could definitely tell it was black.

They walked around the perimeter of the house, investigating possible exits as they waited for another set of officers to help with their pending arrest.

"It looks too quiet," Officer Shoulders whispered to Officer Oglesby. They each had been on the force a couple of years, and their blood was pumping with excitement at the thought of catching a killer on the loose. He had only killed two girls and attempted to kill a third, but it already seemed like a pattern was emerging with the shooting tonight. "What if he's not here?"

"His car is in the garage," Officer Oglesby answered as they circled back to the front of the house. "So unless he stashed the car here and ran, he's got to be here."

They stood in the house's shadow in between the bushes as they watched a car's headlights spotlight their location. Two other police officers joined them in the shadows.

"What have you got?" Detective Young asked in a superior tone as he gripped the handle of his pistol tighter.

"A black car is in the garage and it is quiet inside," Officer Oglesby answered in a gruff, husky tone.

"Good enough for me," Detective Young replied as he walked up to the rickety porch that had a few wooden beams missing on the ceiling. The boards under his feet creaked and whined with each step, as if signaling to the killer an unwelcomed guest had arrived.

Detective Young banged on the front door as he commanded Oglesby and Shoulders to watch the back of the house in case of a possible escape. "Simon Tenney? D.C.P.D."

They each watched as the darkened house ignited with light inside from a singular bulb. Soon, the house became brighter when another light was turned on and then another until they heard the deadbolt and chain on the door unlock.

"Simon Tenney?" Detective Young asked once again.

"Yes," the sleepy man answered, rubbing his eyes awake to find two gun-toting police officers on his front porch. He didn't care about his appearance in a pair of Christmas colored boxers with a wife beater tank top.

"I am Detective Young with the D.C.P.D., and we have some questions for you," he said sternly as Simon's eyes started to close then bolted open.

"Now?" Simon asked. "It's the middle of the night. Can't this wait until the morning?" he yawned, scratching his bed head hair.

"Yes, now," Young barked. "Do you drive a black Ford Fusion with license plate numbers FN1513?"

"I think that's the license plate number for my car, but I'm not positive," he answered unconfidently. "Why?"

"Where were you this evening between ten and midnight?" Young asked, holding his gun close to his side, ready for whatever might happen.

"I was here," Simon answered drowsily in between another big yawn.

"Is there anyone who can corroborate that account?"

"No," he answered shortly. "Just me."

"Do you mind opening your garage for us to look at your vehicle?" Young asked politely, which was a new tactic he had been trying to learn.

"Open my garage? Why do you care about my car so much? What is all this about?" Simon started asking, finally waking up to this strange line of questioning. "Do you think I did something tonight?"

"We just want to see your vehicle, sir," Young said with a fake smile.

It was a smile Simon saw through.

"Unless you have a warrant, you can get off my property!" he said, raising his voice into a stern volume unlike the sleepy one he was using a minute earlier.

"We have a warrant on the way, Mr. Tenney, but I was hoping it wouldn't come to that. The sooner we can look at your vehicle, the sooner we can leave and let you get back to bed," Young persuaded, but it wasn't any good.

"No warrant, no garage," Simon said as he slammed the door in the officers' faces.

"When's the warrant going to get here?" Young asked Whistler agitatedly as they walked down the porch steps.

"I don't know," Whistler answered. "You were supposed to call in for a warrant."

Young stopped in his tracks and looked at Whistler and then back at the porch with the closed front door. "Yeah, I know. It should be coming," he said walking down the driveway back to his cruiser. "Well, you stay here and keep watch as I check on the warrant. He's not going anywhere," Young said shrugging his shoulders as if he did nothing wrong.

Whistler hated working with Young, but it seemed like in the last few months Young cycled through everyone on third shift, and he couldn't find anyone that could measure up to his standards, so he said. It was more like no one cared for Young long enough to partner with him.

Young stepped away from Whistler who stood guard on the front porch. He got inside his police cruiser and closed the door. "Hello, Chief, this is Detective Young. We need a warrant."

CHAPTER 105

Officer Cooper and Officer Peterson quickly tracked down the home address of Fiona Sanchez and went to her apartment. They found her crumbled behind her door, crying and frightened from the events of the evening. Peterson was sisterly, making Fiona a cup of tea after she scurried in the cabinets for a single tea bag, which was hidden behind a box of saltine crackers and a half eaten jar of peanut butter.

"Fiona, I know this is a hard situation for you," Cooper said as he stayed a cautious distance away on the couch to allow Fiona to feel a little more at ease. "But can you tell me about tonight?" He scanned the living room and saw very few trinkets or family photographs on the wall. The beige paint screamed loner loud and clear with no sign of hospitality or welcoming doormats.

"What about it?" she asked timidly as she gingerly sipped her hot tea with a spoonful of honey.

"Did anything seem out of the ordinary today or this evening?" Cooper answered patiently, looking at Peterson to take the lead of this questioning session. Fiona shook her head no slowly.

Peterson stared shocked at Cooper's unsaid words and fumbled her first sentence before regaining composure. "Have you had anyone following you lately? Say, an old boyfriend, an old friend, a frequent customer at the restaurant that caused an uneasy feeling?"

"No," she answered quickly and strongly, as if the tears on her face a few minutes ago vanished like amnesia. "Not that I can think of."

"That's good," Peterson said with a smile. "When you were leaving your work, were you followed? Maybe by a co-worker who could have seen something you didn't see?"

"No, a few of the people were still shutting down and mopping the floor, but I had finished my jobs so I left," she said as she looked over at Cooper suspiciously. "So, any clue who did this, or does it matter since I'm not dead?"

"It definitely matters," Cooper replied, scooting closer on the couch so he could reach out and touch Fiona's hand. "We are going to catch this guy, but we just need your help."

Fiona huffed pessimistically as she set down her tea and curled her legs up onto the couch. "You probably say that to everyone but with little success," she returned snidely.

"Officer Cooper is a top rate police officer, Fiona. He is smart and good at his job, but he is also honest and caring," Peterson snapped. "We didn't have to come to you since you didn't give the dispatch your address, but we came to check on you and try to find the guy who did this. If we didn't care about you, we could have ignored you."

"Fine," Fiona said gruffly as she folded her arms and wiggled her neck around to release some of the tension behind her shoulder blades.

"I can't guarantee we will catch the guy, Fiona," Cooper said looking directly into her eyes, "but you can rest assured we are going to try."

Fiona uncrossed her legs and got up from the couch, grabbing her teacup from the table and placing it in the kitchen sink. She needed to walk around like a free animal, not sitting on the couch between two police officers like a chained lion. With each step she recalled the moment when she went to the police station last time under her own terms. Yet last time it didn't end up like she wanted. She was left wounded, and her attacker was left a free man.

"Well, that's better than what I got the last time," Fiona snarled as she returned back to the couch.

"Last time?" Peterson asked confused. "What happened last time?"

Fiona didn't know why she opened the secrets of her past up to these strangers as she was telling them the story of when she was in high school. With each sentence, she kept telling herself, *Just stop talking, Fiona. They didn't help you then, and they aren't going to help you now.*

Yet, something else was telling her to spill her guts. Maybe she wanted the feeling of remorse on the cops' faces for not catching her rapist. Maybe she wanted to see the defeated looks in their eyes when she told the horrific events of that summer night. Maybe she wanted them to see her not as a broken little girl, but as a strong woman who had been through worse than a random bullet to the back of her car.

"Why didn't the cops do anything? Could they not find the rapist?" Peterson quickly asked, sitting on the end of her seat as she listened to the drama unfold.

"Oh, they said it was consensual, because what teenage girl wouldn't want to be made into a woman by the prince of Woodrow Wilson High School?"

"Prince of Woodrow Wilson High School?" Peterson asked, glancing over at Cooper who caught the significance of that place.

"Yes," she said sternly.

"Who was the prince?" Cooper asked, leaning closer into the discussion as if Fiona was going to whisper the name.

She didn't. She said it loud and proud, and with that name, Cooper and Peterson both shook their heads in disgust.

"Simon Tenney," Fiona said angrily. "Simon Tenney."

"Fiona," Cooper said as he stood up from the couch. "Do you mind coming down to the station with us? We have some more questions and things we want to show you, and we think you may have helped solve this case."

"Sure," she said standing up as well. "It's not like I'm going to be going to sleep anytime soon." Suddenly she remembered the other night when a stranger rescued her. "Did you say your name was Officer Cooper?"

"Yes," Cooper nodded. "Why?"

"Someone mentioned you to me the other night," she said leaving the room to get her belongings. "Just strange."

Cooper looked at Peterson who shrugged her shoulders, confused as well. "Who?" Cooper asked as she returned.

"I don't know, just some guy who saved me the other night when I was attacked."

"Can you describe this guy to me?" Cooper asked.

"Wait a minute, you were attacked the other night as well?" Peterson jumped in like a mother hen.

CHAPTER 106

I ignored the vibrating phone in my pocket for the twelfth time as I walked the quiet streets under the cloudy sky. It was probably just Elizabeth again, and I didn't want to talk to her. I passed a couple of bars and considered walking in and drowning my sorrows with a stiff drink, but I knew drinks only hid the pain. They didn't eliminate it.

Looking in the shady establishment with neon lights advertising every beer company, I saw the smiling faces from jokes the bartender was telling. I watched a few people sitting silently, nursing their scotch alone in a darkened corner. I wished there was a middle ground in the bar to stand, but the only spot was an empty dance floor. A cold, lonely slab of hardwood varnished with scuff marks and sweat.

If I had a bottle cap, I would have flipped it and let my feet follow its fate, but since I didn't have one, I continued walking the lonely sidewalk. I knew in either place there would be the common thread of loneliness. At least this way, I would wake up without a hangover.

Thirteen. I felt the phone vibrate, but ignored it once again. I was tired of feeling her regret in my pocket. As if a few words and tears would forgive the selfishness she harbored. I was angry she had spent the last two days by my side knowing she was hiding a secret from me. I was fine with never looking into her uncompassionate eyes again. I was content with never hearing her voice.

That thought brought comfort. To eliminate the source of the pain. To delete all the unheard messages. To trash all the unread texts. To forget her existence.

I pulled out my phone and quickly deleted any trace of Elizabeth on it.

Goodbye, eight voicemails.

Adios, five text messages.

Ciao, Elizabeth Hyde's contact.

I blocked her number. Elizabeth was now just a distant memory of someone I once thought I knew.

The key word was *thought*.

I found a local park two blocks away from the rundown bar and walked through the deserted trees and bushes. I felt a calmness knowing Elizabeth would never be able to reach me again. Some people would say my outburst was elementary, but for the first time in an hour I smiled.

Even as I was being mugged, I felt at peace. I happily gave the heroin addict my cell phone. Now Elizabeth wouldn't be bothering him either until he could find a local pawnshop to sell it to.

CHAPTER 107

"Is anyone going to tell me what this is all about?" Simon Tenney billowed in outrage as he paced around the interrogation room, pounding his fist on the wall at every turn.

Detective Young watched the pacing animal behind the safe confines of the glass window. He popped a few Skittles into his mouth as if watching the latest movie at the theater.

"Aren't you going to question him?" Officer Cooper asked Detective Young as he and Officer Peterson walked into the room. Cooper wanted to smack the back of Detective Young's head, as if getting onto a rowdy teenager, but counted to three to hold back his anger.

"I tried, but he won't say anything," Young said as Cooper looked though the glass and witnessed Simon shouting belligerently.

"He looks like he's talking to me," Cooper shot back as Peterson stood silently by the wall. "Are you deaf, Young?"

"You can't talk to me like that," Young shouted, jumping up from his chair and throwing his package of Skittles onto the desk. The rainbow-colored candies spilled from the bag, rolling freely onto the tiled floor.

"What are you going to do about it?" Cooper asked with a smirk. "Tell on me?"

Young looked at Cooper and then at Peterson, with whom he used to flirt last autumn. "When you get tired of patrolling with him, come see me, and I'll show you real police work."

"Why don't you show me now by questioning Mr. Tenney, Detective?" Peterson smiled cunningly. "That is, if you can."

Young clinched his fist and his mouth, trying hard to control the words he wanted to say and punches he wanted to throw. He glanced at Tenney still pacing on the other side of the glass, but muttered something unrecognizable under his breath as he quickly exited the room. Cooper and Peterson waited for Young to stampede into the interrogation room, but after thirty seconds they realized Young was just fleeing the scene – a scene that would show cracks in his skills.

"So, you know what to do?" Cooper asked.

Peterson took a slight breath and nodded her head. "I think so."

"Let's go."

CHAPTER 108

"Simon Tenney," Cooper started as he and Peterson entered the brightly-lit interrogation room. He calmly sat down at the table with a notepad of questions and a file of the victims' information.

"Yeah," Tenney shot back gruffly as he stopped pacing the small, white-walled room, staring menacingly at Cooper.

"Why don't you sit?" Cooper asked politely, clicking his ink pen to start taking notes.

Tenney looked down scathingly at Cooper and huffed, annoyed at the entire situation.

"Sit!" Peterson shouted as she arose from the table and commanded the room. "You might've been able to scare women in your past, but I see through your charade of masculinity."

"What are you talking about?" Tenney stopped and looked Peterson square in her eyes, placing his hands on the table and leaning down to her eye level.

"You're not so tough without your gun, are you?" Peterson ravished. "So you better sit down and answer our questions."

"Gun?" Tenney asked shocked. "What's all this about?"

"There have been a few shootings this week, and your car fits the description of the car that has been involved in these drive-bys," Cooper rationally said as he pulled the seat back for Peterson to sit.

Tenney scrunched his face in confusion, "Well, it wasn't me."

"You went to Woodrow Wilson High School, didn't you?" Peterson chimed in menacingly.

"Yeah, what's it to you?" Tenney answered agitatedly.

"Do you remember Sabrina Latener?" Cooper asked looking down at his notes.

"I don't know," he answered unconvincingly.

"What about Piper Michaelson?" Peterson jumped in, pointing her finger inches from his face.

"I don't know," he once again answered, but this time more aloof than before.

"Seems like you're hiding something, Simon," Peterson remarked. "We already know you went to school with these women, so just be blunt."

"Fine," he answered leaning back in his chair. "So, I went to school with them."

"Did you have anything against either of these women?" Cooper asked, staring at his notepad without giving Tenney any eye contact.

"Against any of them?" Tenney asked bewildered. "I haven't seen them in ten years. What would I have against them?"

"I don't know," Cooper replied. "So, you haven't kept in contact with them?"

"No."

"Well, Ms. Latener and Ms. Michaelson were murdered this week," Peterson said flatly.

"Pity," he said sarcastically looking into Peterson's eyes coldly.

"Two women were killed this week and all you can say is 'pity?'" Peterson erupted.

"Fine," he said sympathetically and then cruelly smiled. "It's sad they are gone because they were both fine."

"You are one sick--" Peterson started before Cooper stopped her.

"Officer Peterson," Cooper scolded as she stormed out of the room slamming the door as she left. "My apologies, Mr. Tenney."

Tenney shrugged his shoulders as if not caring and began to yawn. "How much longer?"

"I just have a few more questions," Cooper answered as he flipped over his page and scanned through his questions. "Where were you Monday evening between ten p.m. and two a.m.?"

"Home, in bed," Tenney answered as he looked down at his watch and noticed it was well past his bedtime.

"Can anyone vouch for you on that?" Cooper asked, scribbling his notes.

Tenney shook his head no and folded his arms in front of his once defined chest. Now the only definition was due to the rolls of fat.

"What about last night during the same time?"

"Same," he answered. "At home."

"Once again, can anyone verify your whereabouts?" Cooper asked, looking up from his notepad and giving the man across the table a friendly gaze.

"Nope."

"What about tonight?" Cooper asked.

"Well, you guys should know," he chuckled. "The cops came to my house during that time and brought me here."

"And once again, can anyone concur?"

"No!" he shouted. "I go to bed around ten, and I live alone. Do you have anything else? Because no matter how you ask the question, that's going to be my answer."

Peterson entered back into the room with a look in her eyes that shined brighter than a flame. "What about Fiona Sanchez?"

"What about her?" he smiled. "Did she die too?"

"She was shot at tonight," Cooper answered.

"Too bad," Tenney said without remorse. "She was fine as well."

CHAPTER 109

I hopped over the ticket machine at the subway station and walked towards the waiting area in the lonely station. I had hopes of getting home in the next hour, but I knew the route would include a few metro line changes. Instinctively, I reached for my phone as I stood along the tiled wall only to realize the mugging wasn't a dream. It actually happened.

A numb feeling had covered me like a wool blanket. I could recall the events of the night, but they seemed like memories from years ago, not something that happened within the last hour. I felt sick to my stomach, yet I also felt empty. I didn't have any fear of throwing up. I didn't have any fear of anything. I had already been robbed of my emotional stability and of my cash. I didn't know which mugging hurt worse.

Yes, I did. The lies Elizabeth had kept hidden from me cost more than the money in my wallet. Anger was swirling with depression as I realized she'd waited until the perfect moment to drop her bombshell. She had strategically waited until she could unleash her burden with the least amount of ramifications for her cowardly life. She had waited until we were basking in the glow of saving a life. She'd thought her lack of action could be forgiven with a simple apology.

She had thought wrong. I was furious. A word could not undo the years of pain I had trudged through. An utterance of choked remorse couldn't untangle the knots that had been anchored in my stomach at the thought of sitting at the kitchen table alone for another supper. A coldhearted apology didn't deserve a second thought.

I had been a fool to think Elizabeth's DNA wasn't intertwined with the Hydes' facets of self-centeredness. I'd been a clown to her snide remarks in the last six months, a muse for her bullying entertainment.

No more.

No more would I fall victim to Elizabeth's scheming.

No more would I allow myself to be just another back with roadkill tire marks.

No more would I allow myself to be gutted even though I did it to myself. I had opened myself to her fraudulent character.

But no more.

As the train entered the tunnel, a bright light shined through the darkness, and the station was filled with a loud mechanical braking. I witnessed the train, but I didn't see the light. I didn't hear the sound. I didn't feel the breeze. I was still numb.

Slowly, I left the confines of my wall and entered the deserted train car. I'd found my safe place.

I knew I had been hurt too many times from people I thought I could trust, people I let into my honest inner regions of my tormented self.

But no more.

I was done with that. As I looked out the window and saw the concrete walls spray painted with graffiti soar by, I knew. I knew it would be safer traveling through life like this train.

Alone.

CHAPTER 110

"Well, she was shot and fled the scene, and as she was dying, she said she recognized the killer," Peterson said as she stood by the door. "She said it was you."

"That lying whore!" Tenney erupted.

"Come on, tell me how you really feel!" Peterson shouted back. "Tell me about this whore!"

"You women are all the same," Tenney said under his breath, looking across the table for Cooper to nod in agreement.

"Excuse me?" Peterson asked defensively. "What do you mean by that?"

"Just what I said," Tenney angrily answered. "You think you're so innocent, but you're not. You're all the same."

Cooper opened a tattered-edged manila folder and pulled out a few handwritten documents stained with age through the years. He was flipping through the papers and pictures as Peterson snatched them in angst, almost crinkling them in her clinched hands.

"Simon, DNA has come a long way in the last ten years."

"So?" Tenney said with a tone of annoyance.

"So, Fiona Sanchez stated you raped her ten years ago and got off scot free," she stated superiorly.

"She wanted it," Tenney grinned boyishly. "She wanted me."

"And why would she want you?" Peterson laughed. "I was looking at your yearbook and you didn't look like someone girls would flock to."

Tenney looked up at Peterson with flames in his eyes. It was one thing to bring up the past, but it was another to dismantle his masculine history of getting any girl he wanted. "You wish."

"I wish what?" Peterson snapped back. "To be a notch on your belt? You're a piece of work."

"I have standards," he laughed. "I wouldn't have given you a second glance in high school," he said, closing his eyes, "or even now."

Cooper watched the tension in the room, and he was impressed with the bait Peterson was dangling in front of Tenney's face. And he was biting.

"Back to Ms. Sanchez," Cooper said, trying to play it coy.

"I'm not finished," Peterson ranted.

"Little girl, you better listen to your boss," Tenney said snidely.

"You may think you're a big man, but you're nothing but a sad, pathetic, has-been, still living in the past when you thought you were something. But you weren't. The only way you got what you wanted was because you forced it," Peterson said cruelly.

Tenney opened his eyes and stared at the woman across the table. "They begged for it."

"The only begging you heard was to stop!" Peterson shouted.

"They wanted it!" he shouted back. "They all wanted it."

"They all wanted it?" Peterson snapped. "How many women did you rape?"

"They only got what they asked for."

"Did Fiona ask for this?" Cooper asked, pulling out photos of an innocent high school girl with bruising along her neck and wrists.

"She wanted it rough," he smiled. "They all liked it rough."

"Peterson, can you give us men a moment alone?" Cooper commanded condescendingly.

Peterson huffed at the testosterone-fueled boys' club. She looked at Cooper frustrated and shocked at the misogynistic attitude. She flipped her hair and stomped out of the room.

"Now that she's gone to fix her makeup or something like that we can talk," Cooper said. "I understand, Simon. Sometimes you have to take charge. Show a woman you're the man. Show her who has the power. Don't all women want a man like that?"

"The straight ones do," Tenney laughed.

"In college there was a girl who I asked out a few times, and she kept turning me down. Then I *showed* her, and she didn't even know what hit her," Cooper smiled, reminiscing a lie.

"That's all it is," Tenney nodded. "Sometimes they don't know what they want, so you have to show them."

"And if they fight it, well, that's just more fun," Cooper laughed. "It's our duty as men to teach them what they need. And to show them what we want, so next time they'll know."

"And next time they won't fight because they know how good it is," Tenney grinned.

"Exactly," Cooper nodded in agreement. "I mean, at first she didn't want it, but by the end, by the end I knew she saw it my way. She knew she wanted it and stopped fighting."

"They always stop when you hit the right spot," Tenney smiled wickedly. "It's like they finally realize I was right and this was more fun than they expected."

Cooper nodded his head and leaned down to a whisper. "When I showed Alesha what I was made of, she soon saw it my way."

"The same with Fiona," he said. "At first she was like, 'Stop, stop,' but by the end, I could tell she wanted it. She was just nervous since it was her first time. Virgins are always scared at first, but you've got to keep going to show them it's not going to kill them."

"And it didn't kill them," Cooper winked. "It's just a passage of womanhood."

"And I led the way for a herd of them," Tenney cockily said, puffing his chest out.

"A herd?" Cooper said, gasping in admiration. "You're lying."

"If only," Tenney smiled. "I don't remember all of them, maybe a dozen, but the three women you said tonight, well, I welcomed each of them to being a woman."

"Get out!" Cooper said with amazement. "You dog."

"They just needed to be shown," Tenney beamed. "And I showed a lot of them."

Cooper calmly looked up at the video camera in the corner of the room and changed his demeanor. "So, you're telling me you forced Fiona Sanchez to have sex with you?"

"Hey, now," Tenney stammered. "You were just agreeing with me that we men have to do it to help them. It's like our duty."

"Yeah, but I was lying," Cooper said standing up. "There's no Alesha. And unlike you, I was never accused of being a rapist."

Tenney looked up confidently. "Fine, you got me," he said. "But it was ten years ago. The statute of limitations is up."

"You know, I didn't think you would know about statute of limitations," Cooper said with a defeated look.

"I know more than people give me credit for," Tenney winked. "And I still remember the sound of Fiona's voice as she begged for me to stop. But just like them all, she eventually stopped."

"Yes, many states have a statute of limitations for rape cases at ten years," Cooper said with a stern look as Tenney interrupted.

"Sad, isn't it?" Tenney frowned sadistically.

"Yes, it is sad," Cooper said shaking his head. "Because these crimes are horrible." Cooper stopped and picked up the notepad and folders on the table and then turned to leave the interrogation room. "But I know something that's even more sad. At least for you."

"What?" Tenney said playfully.

"In D.C., rape cases stay open for twenty years, not ten," Cooper said as he placed his hand on the door knob. "Did you get all that Peterson?"

"Loud and clear," Peterson said as she walked through the door looking down at Tenney's guilty eyes. "We have it all on video."

"I think I need my attorney."

"It's too late for that," Peterson winked. "Do you want to show me what kind of man you are?" she asked facetiously. "Because I think I already know. A rapist and a murderer."

"Need a pillow while you wait?" Cooper asked with a smile. "I don't see many attorneys coming in at this hour of night for scum like you."

CHAPTER 111

Sleepless nights were the worst: the tossing and turning, the steeplechase of sheep counting, the gnawing of unanswered questions, and the images of regret seen on the back of her eyelids. Elizabeth wasn't enjoying her plush mattress for the second time this week.

She tried texting and calling Solomon a few more times once she got home, but he didn't respond. She pondered driving over to his place, but the memory of him running out of her car was too painful to relive in person. She wasn't ready to visually confront her regrets. She was physically drained by the emotional and physical hurling she had done. She had to stop three times on her way home for fear of throwing up on the steering wheel.

She grabbed her phone and noticed no new messages. She scrolled down her text messages to Solo and found they were still all unread. He was ignoring her. She didn't know whether to be furious or sad. She was filled with rage at his unforgiving attitude since he was actually comforting her during her apology. But she was also distraught with a depressing low of the turmoil she unknowingly caused.

She wanted to reach out to someone, and the name that ran ahead of the pack of friends and family was her sister. *You up?* she texted to Veronica. *How are you doing tonight?*

She waited for the message to be received, but as she watched the phone screen remain unchanged, she knew a text at 3:29 a.m. was asking a little too much for her sister. Elizabeth knew Veronica was going to have a challenging day in a few hours. She wondered if Veronica would even send her a text back before she headed to court.

"This is ridiculous," Elizabeth said, rolling out of bed. She quickly put on a pair of yoga pants and a gray hoodie and headed outside for a quiet walk.

In most places in D.C. she would feel unsafe walking alone this time at night, but she knew her street was one of the safest places to be. She used to hate the feeling of living in a gated community as a kid, living the privileged lifestyle where her parents socialized with politicians and Nobel Prize winners. But now, it had its benefits. She didn't have to watch her back for sexual predators or teenage delinquents. She was able to walk in peace.

Well, she was able to walk in safety. Her mind was racing too much to gain a moment of peace. She walked past the homes and townhouses, each shining a light on their front porch with a sign in the yard warning the home was covered with a security service. She turned left when she came to the end of her street and felt her phone vibrate.

"I hope I didn't wake you," Elizabeth said as she continued to walk the well-lit street.

"I was up but had my phone charging," Veronica warmly said, which shocked Elizabeth. "What's wrong?"

"I don't know, Veronica," Elizabeth said with a frown. "I just don't know anymore." She knew she couldn't tell Veronica all the details; risking her secrets to her sister wasn't something Elizabeth was willing to do. But just hearing a friendly voice allowed her to relax, even if it was Verny.

At least a little.

CHAPTER 112

I think I slept a measly thirty-nine minutes throughout the night. I got home around 3:30 a.m., and sleep still wasn't my primary focus. I rolled out of bed at 6:13 and walked groggily into the living room that still had fragments of broken vases and coffee cups on the floor from where they were thrown at the walls.

I still had some rage left in me.

After the numbness of being mugged wore off somewhere over the Potomac River, I quickly replaced it with pure fury. I exploded when I got home, picking up and throwing anything I could get my hands on. Pictures on the wall were now photographs with broken frames scattered on the couch. I almost completely fell from sanity when I picked up my television set and dreamed of hurling it from my second story floor. Reality quickly sank in when I realized I was hugging my longest lasting relationship. So I set it down. If I had thrown it off and watched it crash into smithereens I would have eventually spent money on a new television because sometimes binge watching a comedy with a tub of ice cream was better than a therapy session. That's when I decided I had enough and needed to go to bed.

I scanned the aftermath of hurricane Solomon and knew I had two choices. Start picking up the debris or leave it for another day.

Another day it was.

I grabbed a banana from the counter and inhaled the fruity goodness. As I chugged a glass of milk, a smile appeared on my face.

This was the first night in six months I didn't have a dream.

No damsels in distress.

No thugs robbing a convenience store.

No juvenile delinquents causing a ruckus at the Korean War Memorial.

No snotty-nose kids falling on their heads from a tree their parents told them not to climb.

For the first time in six months, I had a day to myself. And since I didn't have a phone, no one would be able to contact me from my superhero saving sabbatical.

It was as if God had the criminal mug me for a reason – to slow down and refocus. This would be the day to get my life back in order, to reorganize my plan in life and figure out a few things I had put on the back burner.

This was going to be the first day of the rest of my life.

That was, until I sat down on the couch and found the remote control under a mound of stuffing from a ripped up pillow.

Cheers was beckoning instead, at least until I met Jeremiah for coffee.

A life change could be put off until tomorrow.

CHAPTER 113

Attorney Frank Chumbler reached the interrogation room and met with his client, Simon Tenney, at 8:03 a.m. Frank looked well-rested and dressed in his beige polyester suit his father had handed down to him on his deathbed, whereas Simon resembled a frazzled poodle recently struck by lightning.

Cooper and Peterson walked into the interrogation room with two cups of refreshing coffee and a smile.

Frank spoke first. "My client didn't mean what he was saying last night. You woke him up, brought him here, and interrogated him through most of the night. He was clearly sleep-deprived and not speaking with a clear head."

"He seemed pretty lucid to me," Peterson chimed in. "Bragging about all the escapades he had in high school."

Tenney started to wiggle in his seat since his attorney had told him to not say a word. Tenney wasn't used to remaining silent.

"We have the interrogation recorded, and no jury will find him innocent on the rape charge once they see his smug smile describing how he was just teaching the girls how to be a woman," Cooper stated calmly. "No one would."

"He tricked--" Tenney started to say, but Frank shook his head to hush his client.

"I can easily convince a jury you connived your way into manipulating my client," Frank said egotistically, "like all cops do."

"We have Fiona Sanchez's reports stating she was raped by your client, and then we have your client confessing," Cooper said, shrugging his shoulders. "Seems open and shut to me."

"Well, those documents are ten years old, and the police officers at the time thought Fiona was lying," Frank smiled. "So it may be a little confusing for the jury to get a correct picture of the supposed crime when the cops originally didn't think there was one. And now, almost ten years later, they believe these unfounded claims." Frank leaned back in his chair and folded his arms, as if saying, *Sounds open and shut to me*. "Oh, and it's a pity your victim was murdered last night. And per my client, he didn't kill her. It's going to be hard to get her to testify since she's dead."

Peterson and Cooper looked at one another and smiled. "Ms. Sanchez was shot at last night, but…" Peterson said and stopped and looked to Cooper to finish.

"But she wasn't shot," Cooper concluded. He watched as Frank's mouth opened. "And she definitely is still alive. She's actually in the other room writing her statement and all the accounts of her rape. She's making sure to leave nothing out since we believe her, and your client confessed."

"You lied!" Tenney shouted, standing up, ready to punch Cooper in the jaw, but Frank slowly got up and grabbed his client and forced him to sit down.

"Your rape charge is nothing compared to the two murders we are going to get you with next," Peterson said as she took a sip of her coffee. "Just waiting on ballistics from the gun they found in your garage."

"Gun? What gun?" Tenney screamed.

"As I was saying," Peterson began, "the gun the police found in your garage matches the bullets found in the victims. They haven't run the ballistics test, but the make of your gun matches the bullets. And we should get the test results back soon."

"I don't keep a gun in my garage!" he shouted. "I keep them locked in my house."

"Will you please just stop talking?" Frank commanded his client. "Just let me handle this."

"Not last night, I guess," Peterson smiled. "Guess you forgot to clean up your mess because there was still some residue in the gun showing it had been recently fired."

"My client was at home last night during the shooting," Frank rebutted, hoping his client's claims were true.

"It wasn't me," he began to answer more calmly. "I didn't shoot anyone."

"But Ms. Sanchez identified you as the shooter," Cooper stated, looking over at Peterson and then at Tenney.

"I didn't shoot Fiona!" he yelled. "I haven't seen her since high school! She's out to get me! She's just saying that to get back at me!"

"Why would she say that?" Cooper asked. "Why would she say it was you?"

Tenney leaned over to his attorney and whispered in his ear. Frank listened and took in every word he was saying and gave his advice in a whisper back into Tenney's ear.

"Are you sure about that?" Frank asked, but knew it was ultimately his client's decision.

Tenney nodded his head yes and started talking. "Fine, I raped Fiona," he said as he rolled his eyes at the word rape as if it wasn't a real crime. "But I didn't try to kill her. I didn't kill anyone."

Cooper reached into his folder and pulled out a picture from a traffic surveillance camera. "This picture looks a lot like your car, and isn't that your license plate number?"

Tenney looked down at the picture shoved across the table. "That's my car, but I wasn't driving it last night. Someone must have broken into my garage and stolen my car."

Reaching into the folder again, Cooper pulled out two photographs showing the driver of the car. One was blown up to see the baseball cap, sunglasses, and mustache. The same mustache he had.

Tenney looked down at the image and sat silent. He looked over at his attorney who put on his glasses and examined the photograph and then the side profile of his client. He took off his glasses and thought for a moment and then leaned over and whispered into his client's ear.

"Can we have a few minutes?" Frank asked, looking over at a frightened Simon Tenney.

"Sure," Peterson said as she stood up and walked out first.

"We'll come back in and check on you in a few minutes," Cooper said. He started to walk away as Chief Johnson walked into the interrogation room with handcuffs in hand.

"Will you please stand and put your hands behind your back?" Chief Johnson asked.

"What? What's this about?" Tenney stammered as he slowly stood up, looking over at Frank for guidance who only returned his confused look.

"Yes, what is going on here, Chief Johnson?" Frank asked confidently.

"Simon Tenney, you are under arrest for the murders of Sabrina Latener and Piper Michaelson and the attempted murder of Fiona Sanchez," Chief Johnson recited.

"And the rape of Fiona Sanchez," Peterson interjected.

"Yes, and the rape of Fiona Sanchez," Chief Johnson corrected.

"But I didn't…" Tenney said, trembling beside the metal table, clutching onto the chair as he stood. "This is a big mistake."

"Ballistics say otherwise," Chief Johnson said unfazed. "We just got the report back, and it was a perfect match to your gun."

"But…" Tenney started as Chief Johnson shackled his hands with the heavy metal cuffs. He was bound just like he had forced two other girls his senior year of high school. Fiona Sanchez wasn't the only one.

Just as he admitted, he had led a herd to womanhood.

CHAPTER 114

I sat amazed listening to Dr. Eugene Wright and Jeremiah speaking on different sides of the chasm. They spoke cordially, yet frankly, posing deep questions, ready to pounce with only a smile and an appreciative nod with each other's opinions and thoughts.

"Well," I finally spoke up. "I heard a new take on the subject," I started as I heard Jeremiah chuckle to himself and watched Eugene shake his head with a beaming smile.

"Really? A new take on the subject? Do you really believe that, Solomon?" Dr. Wright asked, as if I was seated in his advisory office, ready to be scorned for my naivety. Jeremiah's light chuckle started to increase until he lost full control of his politeness.

"What? What am I missing?" I asked, looking at both gentlemen with wonder and confusion.

"You think this new theory is really a new theory?" Eugene asked with conviction as he pointed his twisting finger towards my face.

"Go ahead, Eugene," Jeremiah said, smiling as he regained some dignified composure. "Preach your sermon."

"Don't mind if I do," he said sitting up a little straighter in his chair. "Do you believe when it says in Ecclesiastes that 'there is nothing new under the sun'?"

"I believe at that time there were probably no new findings," I said earnestly. I looked at Jeremiah for some reinforcement, but he folded his arms, as if taking a step back from the conversation.

"So, when wise King Solomon wrote those words, he was implying only in his time. Not in the times to come?" Eugene asked condescendingly.

"Well, how do you explain the technology we have?" I asked, looking down at Eugene's iPhone on the table.

"This little gadget isn't new," Eugene said picking up his mini computer, "It's merely improved."

"Okay, but I don't care about the version you have, what about the original iPhone? That was brand new," I said, thinking I was making a valid point. But by the way Jeremiah snickered, I knew I had just skimmed the surface.

"This iPhone is merely an assistant. It does what I want it to do. It makes my calls, keeps my appointments, entertains me when I need entertaining, and sings to me when I need relaxing. It answers every question I can ask. It's a glamorized assistant. How long have assistants been around?" He stopped as he looked away from me. "Jeremiah?"

"A very long time," Jeremiah softly sulked melodramatically with rolling eyes that quickly twinkled with a smile.

"Exactly. The very first assistant was mentioned early in Genesis. I don't mean to sound sexist because we can conceivably say Adam was assisting God, but God formed Eve to assist Adam. She may not have buttons to push to command her to do something, but when asked politely and with respect, as all assistants deserve to be treated, they will do as they are needed."

"That's an interesting concept, but I don't see how nothing is ever new," I said with a twinge of doubt.

"Try to think of something, and I will prove to you it wasn't a new concept or idea," Eugene pressed, winking at Jeremiah.

"Okay," I sat for a few seconds and noticed Jeremiah's cup of tea. "Okay, what about a cup? Someone had to come up with that idea first."

"When God formed lakes for the water to collect, is that not like a cup? It has a bottom and sides. It can spill over the edges onto its shore. To me, that's what a cup is."

"I've tried for years, Solomon, to debunk him on this. I have yet to find anything he can't explain within his realm of faith."

331

"So, you agree with him?" I asked, shocked an atheist would believe this as fact.

"I can agree with him up to a point," Jeremiah said as he placed his elbows on the table. "It's in the rudimentary beginnings we differ. He believes someone in the cosmos caused all the firsts, while I believe all the firsts were founded on their own."

I looked at both men, eyeing each other like two fencers with their foils in hand, ready to strike. The more I thought, the more I started to see Eugene had a lot of truth in his statement. All the medical advancements weren't new, but improved. When going to the root of our findings, the ingredients for all the medicines had been here since the dawning of time. The Wright brothers took their examples from watching birds in flight. Shipbuilders got their inspirations from looking at fallen leaves on the pond. Even my cup of water showed proof that someone's first reflection wasn't first seen in a mirror, but probably in a peaceful lake.

"It's okay," Eugene said as I sat in deep thought, looking around the room for any sign of new convention. "I've tried for years and I have yet to find anything resembling anything new."

"I'll pay today," Jeremiah said as he stood up, clasped Eugene's shoulder, and walked away with our bill in his hand.

"It just saddens me," I said, looking up at Jeremiah and then over at Eugene.

"I know," he said as he, too, looked over at Jeremiah. "He sees what we see, but yet he doesn't want to see what we see." He stopped and leaned over and whispered in my ear, "In my darkest hours, I sometimes have considered praying to God I be wrong – that a man of his genuine kindness and loyalty be granted access into heaven. But then as I am about to speak, I am filled with such regret, and I dare not say those words."

"But why?" I said.

He looked at me with compassionate eyes that filled with tears. "Because if I ask to be wrong to my Lord, then I am spitting in the face of Christ and the sacrifice he suffered for my reckless humanity. I cannot, nor will I ever, utter those words in deepest prayer, because when I pray to my Lord, it is one of awe and adoration. I would rather die than denounce Christ. I've caused him too much pain already. A backhand isn't one Jesus deserves, even if I am saying the words with love for my kindred brother."

I listened not only to his words but at the tone gushing from his heart. I could hear the burden of a lifetime of witnessing that had been placed on his back, a cross he had carried willingly for forty years in hopes of seeing his friend come to the light.

"But you know, Solomon, it's in those moments I pray for a new way to show Jeremiah."

"A new way?" I smiled with a playful grin.

"Touché," he smiled. "I believe we may not always see our prayers answered with our own two eyes, but I believe I am seeing one of them now."

I turned slowly around, glancing around the coffee shop that resembled any other coffee shop in the D.C. area. I didn't comprehend what he was meaning, and he could tell.

"It's you, Solomon."

"Me?" I replied shocked. "I haven't done anything. I've probably caused more doubts to creep into his head solidifying his disbelief."

"I highly doubt that," Eugene said taking a sip of his black coffee. "Your questioning shows that even one of faith can have doubts and still have faith. Someone of faith who says they never doubt is someone he can never relate to. You don't have to believe it, Solomon," he said, "but I have to. It's the only thing getting me through these dark moments now – knowing."

"Knowing what?" I asked.

"You'll know," he said as he stood up to give his friend, Jeremiah, a warm hug, whispering something in his ear before departing out the door.

Jeremiah returned to the table with a heaviness on his shoulders. "Still mulling over his theory?"

"We've moved past that," I said as I looked out the window, watching Eugene walk to his car parked on the other side of the street.

"It's hard to believe," Jeremiah said as he, too, glanced out the window to watch his friend walk away.

"What?" I asked.

"He didn't tell you?" Jeremiah said surprisingly. "That's why I walked away because he wanted to tell you."

"Tell me what?"

"Dear me, why does he put me in these positions every time?" Jeremiah awkwardly smiled. "Every time he does."

"What?"

"Well, he made it seem like he told you."

"Told me what, Jeremiah? I am so confused right now. We just talked about prayer when you walked away," I said, which wasn't technically a lie.

He looked out the window watching his friend's car fade into the distance. "He's got an inoperable brain tumor."

"What does that mean?" I said shocked. "I mean, I know what that means, but what's his prognosis?"

"I don't know," he shrugged. "He wouldn't tell me. I was hoping he was going to tell you."

"He didn't tell me, but I don't think the prognosis is a good one," I said as I lowered my head in sadness. I looked across the table and noticed Jeremiah bowing his head as well. Maybe it wasn't in prayer, but it's been said even a faithless man will cry out for God in desperate times.

334

This was a desperate time.

I thought coffee with Jeremiah and Eugene would be a nice way to forget about my problems. It only added to them.

CHAPTER 115

Veronica rolled into the courtroom with a ball of emotions, but she was determined not to become unraveled. She had rehearsed the scripted closing remarks so much she no longer wanted to gag at the defamatory and blatant lies. She was but an actress reciting a Shakespearian monologue she told herself while looking in the mirror putting on her lipstick. She didn't have to believe it. She didn't have to enjoy it. She didn't even have to hope for it to work.

It was just a job. She was just like a prostitute, selling herself to please her client, Jenny Ascot. That thought sickened her, but in the last few years working for her father, she had been placed in this compromising position too many times.

She had been tinkering with an idea – an idea that would dramatically shift her life. She didn't know if she could follow through with her ambitious plan, but she knew she was getting closer to biting the bullet and taking the ramifications like a woman. She wasn't bulletproof, but she could handle the healing process if she had someone beside her during the agonizing aftermath. After her brief conversation with Winston last night, she felt one step closer to opening herself more than she had been willing a week ago.

Jenny might have thought this case was going to break me, Veronica said to herself as walked down the center aisle to the defense table. *She might have wished she could witness my downfall, but it only made me see the truth. I'm ready for the avalanche that's going to come. I'm ready for the rip current that will try to drag me out to drift. I'm ready for the tsunami to crash into me. I'm fine with being broken, because I was never truly whole.*

She smiled to Milo who was already at the table. "You look confident this morning, Mrs. Hyde-Cooper."

"Call me, Mrs. Cooper," Veronica corrected professionally. "As of last night, I'm dropping Hyde from my name."

"You can drop a name, Mrs. Cooper, but you can never erase the identity," Milo smoothly whispered in a grandfatherly tone.

"Maybe not," she said nonchalantly, "but my identity needs a makeover." She opened up her briefcase and pulled out the script. "I'm ready to move on from this patch in my life. Where's Jenny?"

"The guards should be bringing her in," he answered as two guards escorted the sane-looking Jenny into the courtroom. "There she is now."

"Good morning, Milo," she softly spoke as the guards walked away. "Are you ready to give the closing?"

"I'm--" Veronica started speaking as Jenny shot her a stern disapproving look.

"I wasn't speaking to you," Jenny hissed. "I was speaking to Milo."

"Yes, Jenika," he smiled wickedly as he turned to look at Veronica. "I'm more than ready."

"You didn't really think I was going to place my final chance of freedom in your hands, Veronica," Jenny playfully laughed as she sat down in the middle chair between Milo and Veronica.

Veronica sat befuddled and in shock. She had spent six of the last twelve hours reciting the grotesque closing remarks until she was fully confident. Once again, this was another game Jenny was playing.

"I just wanted you to memorize all the kind words your father wrote about me. What a great employee I was. What a loyal friend I was. What a compassionate citizen I was. What a loving daughter I was," she stopped and let the words sink into Veronica's inner thoughts. "You know, he would have never written such a glowing closing for you, dear."

"Jenika, lower your voice," Milo said, hushing Jenny's audible tirade.

"Why?" she smiled. "The jury's not in yet, and they can't say anything," she commented to the crowd two rows behind her.

"Just taking precautions," Milo said encouragingly.

"Thank you, Milo," she said softly as she patted his leathery hand and turned her head toward Veronica. "If your father wrote a life or death closing for you, can you imagine what he would put?"

Jenny stared deeply into Veronica's eyes, allowing their souls to connect and swirl into a messy mixture.

"Let me ease your mind," Jenny said, leaning down to her ear. "He wouldn't," she said patting Veronica's smooth, delicate hands. "He wouldn't have wasted his time on a closing for you. You were just a mistake. He probably wishes he had the gall to murder your mother like he did *Rosenburg*. You wouldn't be here. I wouldn't be here. His life would have been so much better if you had been aborted like he wished."

"Jenika," Milo said, gaining her attention as Judge Ogdon walked into the courtroom.

"All rise," the bailiff announced.

Veronica stood beside Jenny and kept repeating to herself, *I'm fine with being broken because I was never truly whole. I'm fine with being broken because I was never truly whole. I'm fine with being broken because I was never truly whole. I'm fine with being broken.*

CHAPTER 116

Please call me, Elizabeth texted Solo from the courtroom stands, about to listen to the prosecution's closing statements for Jenny Ascot. She looked down at her phone and scanned through all her recent texts to Solo. None of them showed they had been read. Shaking her head, she knew she had burned the bridge with him. She knew it was going to take a miracle to get him back into her life. She felt funny, but she was at her last straw.

She bowed her head and stammered through a heartfelt prayer. She prayed for forgiveness. She prayed for healing. She prayed for a second chance; well, with Solomon, she prayed for third, fourth, and fifth chances. She wasn't an emotional type, but as she whispered these words a single tear rolled down her perfectly sloped nose until it fell off the tip, landing onto the palm on her hand.

"Stupid Solo," she smiled as she wiped her eyes. "Only one other man, other than my father, has ever made me cry. You're my second."

She continued to sit silently, hoping God would answer in a mysterious way. She started thinking of ways He could resolve this blunder. Erasing her words from Solomon's memory was just one of the many ideas.

"Amen," she said ending her prayer as she watched Jill Stapleton rise from her table.

She watched Jill approach the jury and begin her closing statements, which caused her to bow her head once again.

"One more thing, God. I know I should love and forgive people, but some people make it very hard to do. Very. Why you even allow some of these people breath is beyond me. I know I'm not perfect, but forgiving Jenny is something I can't do. I'm not sure I could ever stand by and do nothing if she's found innocent. So, if you can make an exception on Jenny and find her not only guilty, but let her fry, well, I would be eternally grateful. Amen."

CHAPTER 117

Jill Stapleton stated the same information she had exhibited for the last few days. She recited verbatim the findings from the medical examiner on the chloroform found in the oxygen tank. She hammered into the jurors' minds the police testimonies of their certainty Jennifer Ascot was the surviving killer. She showed the video of the silent confrontation between Officer Cooper and Ms. Ascot and how she was trying to escape from Huntington Station. She quickly summarized all the evidence in a memorable fashion so when the jurors went to deliberate they could easily remember her final remarks.

"The defense is going to try to poke holes in the facts. They are going to try to tell you there isn't enough proof to convict Ms. Ascot on these murders. They are going to try to form some kind of doubt in your mind to get their client a not guilty verdict. They will do this if you allow them.

"The defense team over there," she stopped and pointed over at the defense table, "they get paid to get their client a not guilty verdict. I, on the other hand, don't get anything but the satisfaction of doing my job. If the police weren't certain of Ms. Ascot's guilt, they wouldn't have arrested her. If I felt we didn't have enough evidence to find her guilty, I would've asked the judge for a few more weeks to get all the incriminating proof. If I didn't think she was guilty, I wouldn't have stepped up to this case.

"I have lived and breathed this case for the last six months. I don't have a personal vendetta against Ms. Ascot. If I didn't think she was guilty, I would have spoken up a long time ago and told the police something didn't add up. I never spoke up because she's guilty. All the evidence points in her direction. Beyond a shadow of doubt she is a manipulative, sadistic, scrupulous murderer who doesn't deserve another moment of freedom. If you do one thing right, find her guilty."

Jill walked back to her seat, and Milo rose dramatically and started his soliloquy.

"Ms. Stapleton is correct; we as defense attorneys get paid for serving our clients, but just like her, I have nothing to gain from getting Ms. Ascot an acquittal. I will sleep peacefully tonight whether she gets a guilty or not guilty verdict. It's interesting Ms. Stapleton dragged on so much to warn you of my closing. The only reason she did this was because ultimately, she knows beyond a shadow of doubt, her supposed evidence is easily explainable as you have heard us prove." He stopped and walked slowly to the jury stand. He took a breath and then started his rehearsed closing remarks.

Veronica listened for her father's words, but as Milo spoke, it was nothing like she had rehearsed. Milo had a totally different closing already planned. She glanced over at Jenny who sat statuesque. She sat with perfect posture and aloof. No smiles or frowns. Her hair and makeup were flawless. She looked innocent.

Milo started to debunk all the evidence one by one. By the end of his closing statements, everyone in the courtroom wondered if Jenny was innocent or guilty. It was going to be a coin toss.

Milo came back to his seat and Jenny lovingly patted his hand for a job well done. Jenny turned to Veronica and smiled. "He did a great job, didn't he?"

Veronica nodded her head in agreement. That was one thing she couldn't deny. Milo did an amazing job.

Was it all truthful? No.

But in his life, honesty wasn't a character strength. It was a flaw.

He wasn't called Young Yagoda for his smile.

CHAPTER 118

"It's good to see you free this morning," Grant said as he smiled down at Stewart sitting in his cubical.

"Free?" a woman in the next cubical asked as she walked around to find the gathering of four handsome men. Roberta was married with two toddlers, but she couldn't resist her daily glances of eye candy around the office.

"It was a big misunderstanding," Stewart groaned. "The police came to my home yesterday evening for questioning about a couple of murders," he said dramatically. "I was nervous at first."

"Nervous?" Grant spoke up. "Collin would have pissed his pants."

"Whatever," Collin chimed in with masculine flaring. "I would have been cool and collected. More than Jordan."

"Why bring me into this?" Jordan asked shocked.

"We couldn't leave you out," Grant laughed.

"On a murder accusation, I'm fine with being forgotten," Jordan said casually. "Call me Mr. Wallflower."

"Mr. Wallflower?" Stewart said, busting out in laughter.

"What?" Jordan asked confused.

"Who says things like that?" Stewart said, chuckling to himself as a few of the guys joined in.

"Apparently, Jordan does," Collin slid in. "Do you want to say anything else or are you wanting to sink back into the corner and hide?"

Jordan didn't respond but slinked down to the hall to his cubical.

"We're only kidding, Jordan!" Grant shouted. "Why'd you do that?"

"What?" Collin asked shocked. "He knows I was kidding."

Roberta watched the young rippling muscles through their polo shirts and ignored the conversation. She was mentally undressing Grant, hoping to catch a peek of a few strands of his midnight black chest hair escaping his unbuttoned placket.

"Would you have thought that?" Stewart asked, looking up at Roberta, who was mesmerized with the way Grant's blue shirt clung to his torso.

"What? Huh?" she stammered, waking up from her daydream.

"Did you think he was too tough on Jordan?" Stewart asked again.

"I don't know," she laughed playfully. "You know, boys will be boys," she said, taking one final look at Grant's flat stomach before returning to her desk to take a drink of water to quench her thirst.

"Fine," Collin smirked. "I'll go talk to him later."

The four of them went to each of their cubicles and started their day.

One of them, however, was still reeling from the night before and how close he had come to getting caught. His mind finally eased when he went to the Hill Rag's website for up-to-date news and saw what he was wanting to find.

The top story on the website: "Local Man Arrested for Killing Spree," caused goosebumps to spread all over his body. He clicked on the link and started reading.

"Over the last three days there has been a killer on the loose shooting at women at stoplights in the city. Simon Tenney was arrested for the murders of Sabrina Latener and Piper Michaelson, and the attempted murder of a third woman."

Part two of the plan was finished. Now to move to part three.

CHAPTER 119

"How are you feeling?" Cooper asked Peterson as they walked down the hall to leave work for a nice restful day off.

"Shocked," Peterson answered surprisingly. "I am just shocked."

"About what?" Cooper questioned with a yawn.

"It's over now," she replied genuinely. "I mean, it just seemed too simple."

"It doesn't always happen like this," Cooper corrected.

"Oh, I know," she agreed. "I just mean, he was so planned with no evidence found on the first two crimes and then last night, it was like he lost it."

"We got lucky he missed Fiona," Cooper pointed out. "I think when he watched her drive away, he panicked. When you panic you don't think rationally and you are in survival mode. He became frantic and tried to escape. When you are frantic, mistakes are bound to happen. Mistakes are godsends."

Peterson listened intently, but wheels were still spinning in her head. She was trying to see it from Cooper's perspective, but something still didn't align. She couldn't put her finger on it, but something seemed out of place.

"He admitted to raping Fiona," Cooper said, stopping in the hallway. "You did that! Without you pressing his buttons, we might not have gotten that out of him. He probably raped Sabrina and Piper too, but since they never said anything, we will never know."

"Yeah," Peterson nodded in slow agreement. "You're probably right. Maybe I'm just sleep-deprived."

"Sleep-deprived?" he laughed. "You drank a whole pot of coffee yourself."

"I don't recall you saying no when I offered to fill your cup."

They started walking down the hallway when the silence was broken once again.

"I didn't tell you, but I spoke with Veronica last night," Cooper spoke softly, staring ahead at the door up the hall.

"About what?" Peterson gushed.

"We had a good talk," he answered.

Dakota stopped and looked at Cooper. "You have to tell me more than just having a good talk, Wint." She pressed into him like a little sister finding out Santa Claus was really their parents.

"It's not going to be an easy road," he said as he stopped and leaned against the wall. "But at least it's a road."

"Yeah."

He smiled. "It's a road we will start to walk together. No more her walking her direction and me walking mine."

"Can you handle that?" she asked rationally. "I mean, not to sound negative, but is this really what you want to do?"

He thought for a moment. He let her words sink into his soul. He hadn't thought much about his decision after he and Veronica spoke, but in his heart of hearts he knew. He slowly nodded his head. "I want to try."

A few cops passed by them and stared as they were leaning against the wall, but they didn't care. Many police thought there was a thing between Dakota and Cooper. They were both attractive and personable; she spoke positively about him, and he was constantly encouraging her. Their relationship may appear romantic from the outside, but they each knew their place in each other's lives. There wasn't room for romance in their partnering friendship.

"That reminds me, I need to head to Solo's place," Cooper said as he pulled out his phone to give him a call.

"Are you moving back home?" Dakota asked.

"I don't know," Cooper honestly said. "A part of me wants to, and then a part of me wants to play it safe. What do you think?"

"You'll know," she said. "You two will know when it's right."

CHAPTER 120

"So how long do you think it's going to be?" Elizabeth asked as she sipped her latte at a Sips around the courthouse.

"I don't know," Veronica moaned as she stirred her black coffee. "One side wants a quick verdict and then another part of me wants this trial to never end," she said sadly. "I'm afraid, Elizabeth."

"Afraid?" Elizabeth said with a mouthful of blueberry danish.

"You don't know what Jenny is capable of," Veronica said softly, pinching off a piece of Elizabeth's danish.

"Do you want me to buy you one?" Elizabeth asked jokingly as she slid her pastry across the table to her sister. "I think I know her true colors."

Veronica delicately dug into the sweet treat, licking her fingers to remove any evidence of her loss of self control. "I don't even know her true colors."

"She's psycho. What more do you need to know?" Elizabeth ranted as she stood up to get a refill of their coffees. "There's no understanding crazies."

"But…" Veronica cautiously said as Elizabeth winked at the good looking college-aged barista who was pouring coffee into their mugs. Sips was surprisingly empty, so they freely spoke among the rumbling espresso machine.

"But what?" Elizabeth remarked snappishly as she came back to the table. She looked at Veronica and her fearful expression spoke louder than the cappuccino machine. "Spill it."

Veronica only shook her head. She wasn't ready to expel all the dirty laundry of the Hyde name. She didn't want her little sister to know the secrets of the family Jenny was vindictively holding over her head. She'd been naïve to believe she could trust Jenny with her skeletons. She felt foolish to have been so girly as to share so much information over a drunken stupor of margaritas after a long day at work. She felt compromised, as if someone stole pictures of her in a delicate situation.

"Well," Elizabeth said shrugging her shoulders as she added a few packets of sweetener, "when you're ready to talk, I'm here."

"Thanks, E," Veronica warmly smiled as she inhaled the freshly roasted coffee beans. "I wish life could be as good as a good cup of coffee."

"Yes, but without the calories," Elizabeth laughed. "But I would let him pour me a cup of coffee any day of the week," she smiled wickedly at the handsome blond behind the counter. "This may be my new go-to for my caffeine fix."

"Caffeine fix?" Veronica grinned unconvinced.

"With biceps like those," Elizabeth stopped and turned her attention once again to the barista handling the coffee pots like dumbbells. "Yum."

"You're too much," Veronica laughed. She needed a good laugh. This week had been one with too many tears and not enough laughter. She needed a moment of not thinking about Jenny. She needed this trial to be over with a guilty verdict.

"We're all not blessed with an all-American husband," Elizabeth smiled. "He's yummy too. When he takes his shirt off." She stopped and wiped her forehead to cool herself down.

"That's my husband, your brother-in-law, you twit," Veronica roared, throwing her used napkin into Elizabeth's face.

"So, I'm proud of you and your trophy husband. You don't always make me proud, but when you brought him by the first time, I was impressed with your taste. Didn't take you for a model-jock type. I thought you would settle down with another bore like your high school fling, Niles or Jiles or Miles. Even his name wasn't memorable."

"Huh?" Veronica stopped and flashed back into her memory. "What was his name?"

"Anyway, are you doing lots of making up?" Elizabeth asked childishly as if they were having a sleepover.

"Don't you have somewhere to be today?" Veronica asked, changing the subject. "Like salivating over Tarzan over there."

"I'll be his Jane any day," Elizabeth said as she growled seductively. "If he swings by my place."

"Elizabeth!" Veronica roared with laughter. "What about Jeremiah?"

"Oh, Jeremiah and I are good," Elizabeth said, sinking back into her normal persona and not a sex-starved cougar. "We are good," she said as she took another sip of her coffee, "but there's nothing wrong with looking," she winked playfully. "And if I just accidentally brush past Mr. Tarzan over there and feel his firm backside, well, that would just be an accident."

"You're awful," Veronica kidded. "Just awful."

"Yeah, but it's easier to ask for forgiveness," she stopped and thought for a second, "than living a life without knowing what his butt feels like." Elizabeth stood up with her empty cup in hand. "I'll let you know what it feels like."

Elizabeth walked over and casually pretended to bump into the barista.

"Oops," she said apologetically and then strutted back to the table.

"So, was it worth it?" Veronica asked, shaking her head disapprovingly.

"Oh yeah," Elizabeth grinned. "Well worth it. Need a refill?"

"No!"

CHAPTER 121

"Wint," I said walking into my living room finding him sitting on my couch beside the broken pictures.

"What happened?" he asked, staring down at the floor with fragmented coffee cups and plates.

"Long story," I said in a defeated voice as I shook my head.

"Man, you've got to talk," he said encouragingly. "What's been going on?"

I wasn't ready to talk. I didn't know when I would be ready or if I would ever be willing to open myself up again. I only revealed myself to Elizabeth because she was in a similar predicament and I needed some guidance. The next person I would tell my secret to may be the crazy guy on the subway who whispers to the mouse in his pocket. He wouldn't tell anyone, and if he did, who would believe him?

"Well, I'm here for you when you are ready," he said as he stood up and stepped over the broken glass to head to the kitchen. "Just like you are always there for me when I need you."

I nodded, but I didn't feel it. It seemed like I was the one who was always needing reassurance and a kind word. It was rare for Wint to call me for help, but I felt like I'd worn out my welcome mat. Yet Wint was the friend we all wished we could be, faithful to the end without any strings attached.

"Did you get my message?" he asked as he poured himself a glass of juice.

I shook my head. "Sorry," I apologized. "I just got some tough news."

"What?" he asked, bringing two glasses of juice with him and handing me one.

"Found out another friend has cancer."

"Who?" he asked compassionately, taking a swig of juice.

"No one you know. Just a professor from school," I said, nursing my juice like it was a gin and tonic.

"Seems like everyone knows someone with cancer," he said as he leaned back on the couch. We sat in silence for a few minutes and stared up at the ceiling before he spoke again. "Veronica and I talked last night," he said casually, still looking up at the ceiling.

"You did?" I asked shocked, almost spilling my juice onto my worn-out carpet. "So?"

"It's going to take time, but I think we will get there," he said optimistically.

Wint was always optimistic. In school he was the team captain who rallied his team to victories. On the force he was the morale police who always watched out for the underdog. In his relationships he was the one who always gave a second chance. Even to me.

After Chelsea died, I pushed everyone away. Slowly people started following my orders of leaving me alone. Everyone but Wint. He never listened. He knew being alone wasn't the best thing for me. He had a keen awareness on things like that.

"You can stay here as long as you need," I finally said. "I mean, while you are working things out with Verny. Or if you need a place to unwind. You always have a spot here."

"Thanks," he said, looking away from the ceiling and giving me a friendly smile. "Means a lot." He sipped his juice and closed his eyes for a brief moment. I, too, took the chance to close my eyes.

"So, you're really not going to tell me what happened here last night?"

"I got mugged last night and I was angry," I said nonchalantly. Technically I didn't lie.

"Mugged?" he shot up from the couch. "Why didn't you call?"

"As I said, I got mugged," I said slowly, as if speaking to someone in a foreign language.

The words hit him and he understood. "Did you go to the cops? Did you tell them what the guy--" he stopped. "It was a guy, right? I mean, there's nothing wrong with getting mugged by a girl because they are just as ruthless, but..."

"Yes, it was a guy," I snickered, not thinking of a mugging as a sexist occasion, "but I didn't go to the cops."

Wint looked at me shocked.

"They wouldn't have done anything, and by the time I had made it to the station, the mugger probably would have already pawned the phone for a quick buck." I shook my head. "It really is okay. It's actually been nice not having the phone attached to my hip like a third wheel."

"You still don't have one?" he asked shocked. "Solo, you need to get a phone. What if someone needs you?"

"No one needs me," I said passively as I stood up and drank the rest of my juice, taking the empty cup back to the kitchen.

"Don't say that," Wint quickly defended. "I needed you this morning."

"And you made it fine without me."

"That's not the point," he remarked. "Promise me you'll get yourself a phone."

"I'll get one someday," I said, rolling my eyes as if my father was commanding me to mow the grass or have a prostate exam.

"Solo," he laughed. "Go get you a phone."

I smiled at him. "I'll eventually get one."

"Why do you do that?" he asked clearly irritated.

"Just to rile you."

"You do a good job at it."

I walked back into the living room and sat down in the recliner and propped my feet back. "I'm exhausted."

"Me too," he said, scooting the broken picture frames onto the floor so he could spread out on the couch. "I'm going to take a short nap."

"Sounds like a plan, man."

We were both falling asleep when he asked one more question. "Why were you and Elizabeth at the shooting last night?"

I didn't answer. I pretended to be asleep. I wasn't ready to give an honest answer, but I wasn't willing to tell a tale yet either. So ignoring the question was my way out.

CHAPTER 122

"I didn't do it," Simon Tenney continued to mutter to his attorney. "You've got to believe me."

"I don't have to believe you," Frank smugly said from the other side of the bars.

"But you have to get me out of here," Simon begged as he looked down the hall at the tattooed-covered men in the other holding cells. "I don't belong here."

Frank started looking through Simon's rap sheet and the evidence the police used in arresting him for the murders of Sabrina Latener and Piper Michaelson. "The gun used in the girls' deaths was found in your garage," Frank said like a stoic. "And it's a gun you purchased a year ago, per the ATF."

"Let me see it!" Simon shouted, reaching through the steel bars for the picture of the gun. Simon looked at the photo, squinting his eyes to see the tiniest detail. "That gun was stolen from me months ago."

"If it was stolen, why was it found in your garage?"

"I don't know!" he shouted louder.

"You've got to quiet down, Mr. Tenney," Frank calmly said, speaking to his new client like he was a disturbed child. He spoke to a lot of his clients with this tone and demeanor. "Now, think. Do you remember where you were the last three nights?" he asked, thinking he could have an insanity plea.

"I was at home! How many times do I have to tell you all that?"

"But are you sure you were at home?" Frank gingerly asked once again in a soothing voice.

"I'm not crazy," Simon snarled. "I know I was at home, and I know I didn't leave my house to kill anyone. If I was going to kill anyone it would be my ex-wife. Not them."

Frank looked down at the statement the police gave him and found nothing abnormal or obscure.

"Someone must have stolen my gun, killed the girls, and then brought the gun back to my place last night while I was sleeping."

Frank looked up at his client with an unbelieving look. "Who would do that to you? Do you have any enemies?"

"Basically anyone I have ever met," he chuckled to himself.

"Well, that's not going to do any good," Frank replied as he stuffed the information back into the folder, clinching it under his armpit.

"Why are you putting that up? Aren't you going to do something to get me out?" Simon asked terrified.

"I have to go back to the office and work on a few things. I'll try to come by tomorrow," Mr. Tenney waved as he walked freely down the hallway between two rows of jail cells. He needed to go back to the office to create a retainer and representation agreement. He wasn't going to do any more work without getting Simon's signature and a large down payment for the upcoming services. Based upon the police report, a not guilty verdict was most likely impossible, but he would do his best to keep him off death row.

That is, if the check cleared.

CHAPTER 123

"The accountant called," Whitney Harper said on the phone as she packed for her next flight to Madrid.

"Oh yeah, I've been meaning to call him about our taxes," Grant agreed as he walked down the street to pick up a sandwich on his lunch break. "When do you leave?"

"Flight leaves at four," she answered as she grabbed her toiletry bag and threw it in her carry-on luggage.

"And you'll be back on Tuesday for three days?" he asked, deciding which food truck to let satisfy his taste buds today.

"Wednesday," she huffed as she zipped up her luggage and carried it down the stairs. "Chris asked me to take his flight on Tuesday for some reason. I wasn't really listening to him yap on about his dog or niece; someone's having surgery."

"Always the kind one, you are," Grant smiled as he picked out the Indian truck from the masses.

"I'll text you before I leave. Love ya," she said and then ended the call before he could say anything else.

He ordered a vegetarian chutney burrito to keep his waistline in tact. As he took his first bite, he knew April 15th wasn't too far away, and he needed to call his CPA about his questions.

"Hey, Don," Grant said quickly swallowing his first bite. "Whit said you called. What'd you need?"

"Let me bring up your file," he said, typing away at his computer. "Okay, here we go. I am working on your partnership tax return, and I had a few questions to finish it."

"Shoot."

"Did you earn any income in your business?"

"Nada," Grant said, taking another fast bite between questions.

"Any unusual expenses or anything new to deduct?" Don asked robotically.

"Nope," Grant answered. "The only expenses were those related to the car."

"Yeah, you already gave me those," Don answered. "I think I should be able to finish the return and get you your tax return this afternoon or tomorrow."

"Thanks man," Grant warmly said. "Oh, one thing for this year. The car got stolen, so you can scrap it on the books. The cops weren't much help, so who knows where it's at now."

"The Ford Fusion was the only asset the partnership had, and you've never had any income in this business. Do you want me to do a final return, or do you want me to keep it open another year?"

"Yeah, just keep it open," Grant smiled wickedly. "We'll use the business for something else next year."

"I don't understand having a Nevada partnership for just a car since you live in D.C., especially when you didn't earn any money, but who am I to judge? As long as you pay me my fee, I'll do whatever you want."

"Music to my ears, Don," Grant grinned. "Always nice chatting with you this time of year. How's the weather in Seattle?"

"Same as any other day," Don groaned. "Gray and misting."

"Well, it's gorgeous here," Grant teased as he looked around at the blooming flowers in the park nearby. "Until next year."

"I'll send you the forms as soon as I'm done."

"I appreciate it. Bye," Grant said, ending their phone call as he took another bite of his burrito. Things were lining up nicely. He wasn't too pleased the revenge murders were ending so soon, but he was bubbling inside to pin it to one of his ex best friends, Simon Tenney.

He finished his burrito and threw away the wrapper in a nearby trashcan. A fleeting thought wafted through his brain, and he caught hold of it before it vanished from his mind. *I need to get rid of the car before Whit comes back. I can do it this weekend. Then I can start planning the next round of killings. There are still many more names needing to be eliminated. And in high school, there were plenty of other bullies to tie the murders to.*

He walked with a new skip in his step. He may not have everything planned out, but it was a start to a beautiful brainstorm. It was going to get stormy in D.C.

CHAPTER 124

Elizabeth and Veronica parted ways when Veronica felt it was her duty to go and sit with Milo and Jenny. As she walked back to Jenny's holding cell, knots tightened in her core from stress. She would prefer her stomach firming up from crunches and Pilates, not from the thought of sitting in a room with Milo and Jenny.

"Kind of you to join us, dear," Jenny said with a snarky tone. "I mean, we were only best friends for a decade."

Veronica held her tongue. The Jenny she was looking at right now wasn't the Jenny she shared an apartment with in college. The thought that she'd shared a two-bedroom apartment with a future sadistic serial killer was sometimes too much for her handle. When that thought came into her mind, she usually thought of something else. The latest fashion trends in *Vogue* were usually the first thing that killed the threatening thoughts.

"Mrs. Hyde," Milo said grandfatherly. "Pardon me, Mrs. Cooper, would you mind to get me a black coffee? I don't want to leave little Jenika at this moment." He menacingly stared at Veronica like a cobra watching a lonely field mouse.

"Sure," she said, forcing a smile. She left the room and stood by the door to eavesdrop.

"Jenika, you may need her in the future," Milo said with a calming tone. "Don't push the Hyde family away. We can use them later on."

"Milo, you don't need them," she said disparagingly.

"But we do," he sighed. "Luther is a powerful man."

"What can he do?" Jenny laughed.

"You don't need to know, Jenika," Milo said standing up to pace around the room. "Just play nice to the girl. Your fun with her is over," he said cruelly.

"But Milo," Jenny said defensively.

"If your father only saw how you've been acting around her, he would be disgraced."

"I'm sorry, Milo," Jenny said, cowering in fear.

Veronica didn't know how she should feel after hearing that. Frightened? Distraught? Concerned? Confused? She was paddling her thoughts like playing ping-pong, slapping the thoughts around as a new one just reappeared. Yet, as she walked down the hall to get the cup of coffee, she was walking with a little more confidence.

There was a pep in her step, an unfamiliar feeling.

She didn't care about Jenny's feelings towards her. She couldn't care less about her father's reputation. She wasn't going to lose any sleep tonight on Milo's coercive remarks.

A faint smile skated onto her face at the memory of Jenny's frightened tone. She only wished she had recorded it so she could listen to it before she fell asleep each night.

She was going to replay Jenny's fragility in her head the next few weeks to help her dream a little more peacefully.

Veronica tapped on the door and proceeded to enter with a fresh cup of black coffee. "I didn't know if you wanted any sugar, so I brought a few things."

"I just take it black," he answered flatly.

"Oh, come on," Veronica smiled. "Live a little. Try the French vanilla."

Milo looked at her suspiciously and shook his head no while Jenny ignored the entire conversation. She huddled herself in the corner and stared at a chip in the wall's plaster.

"I prefer some flavor," Veronica continued to speak annoyingly. "Do you want some, Jenny? I'm not sure there are many flavors in prison, so you'd better get it while you can."

Jenny quickly snapped her head in Veronica's direction and gave her a look that would have scared Lucifer himself.

361

Veronica only smiled back. She felt strangely protected with Milo around. She didn't know if she should trust him, but something in her gut told her Jenny was more scared of Milo than anyone else.

Earlier in the week that thought would have rattled Veronica to her inner core. Now, it barely caused a ripple.

CHAPTER 125

Elizabeth scrolled through the notes of her dreams on her phone and felt a twinge of sadness. For the last six months, she had woken up to a text or a phone call from Solo, or they would meet for breakfast somewhere to discuss the day's agenda. Some days the breakfast lasted till lunch if neither had any plans.

But today she was alone.

She crossed off the first dream on the list, helping an elderly woman with a flat tire. She had no clue how to change a flat and had no intentions of learning. Her manicurist was on vacation until next week, so she didn't want to risk breaking a nail. She called a wrecker and told them to charge it to her credit card but not to tell the woman. Dream number one fulfilled.

Getting into her car, she put in the approximate address in her GPS and let Siri lead the way. She made her way towards Mount Olivet Cemetery to help another unsuspecting soul.

She arrived at the Roman Catholic cemetery and reread her synopsis of the next dream: man dies of a heart attack beside a large woman statue. She parked her car and headed into the cemetery. She had driven past the gravesite many times, but she had never paid much attention. Graves were for the dead, and she was fully alive. She lost her breath when she saw the size of the cemetery and the number of concrete statues.

"Really?" she muttered to herself, annoyed this possibly easy dream was going to be a search and rescue. She didn't want to run in her new Christian Louboutin pointy toe pumps but knew time was of the essence. She carefully slid her size seven foot out of each black high heel shoe and laid them delicately behind Esther MacGill's tombstone. "Every woman likes a nice pair of high heels," she said.

363

"But they better still be here, Esther, when I get done with Father Kingston."

She scanned the horizon for any sign of the beloved priest walking the grounds, but all she saw were concrete hiding places. She took off jogging down a paved path, looking back and forth on both sides as she ran, hoping to see a kneeling priest saying the Lord's Prayer, or any other prayer Catholics said while walking through a graveyard.

She wondered if it was respectable to shout among the dead, but she was already running past graves of the saints, so why stop at one distasteful move?

"Hello!" she shouted. "Father Kingston, are you here?"

She listened, holding her breath so she could hear something other than her heaving.

After a few seconds of silence, she gasped for air. Her cardio-fearing lungs were begging for a place to stop and rest, but if she didn't find Father Kingston soon, his lungs would be begging for air as well.

"Father Kingston!" she screamed at the top of her lungs, but once again, no one responded. She glanced down at a tombstone as she was jogging by and thought of asking Mr. and Mrs. Livingston if they could tell her where the priest was hiding. In her morbid sense of humor, she smirked at the distastefulness. "Thanks for your help," she ranted as she made it to a fork in the path.

"Really?" she stomped in frustration. "Father Kingston!" she yelled again as she took a left. "Come out, come out, wherever you are!" She kept running, seeing more statues up ahead. Too many statues.

Her head was spinning around the graveyard as her Apple watch started vibrating. She had more important things to do than take the call. "Father Kingston!" she screamed once again and suddenly stopped.

"Hel…" she faintly heard in the distance, but she couldn't tell which direction the fragile sound was coming from. She just knew she was getting closer.

"I'm coming, Father!" she yelled as she closed her eyes and strained to listen to the slightest sound.

"Help," he moaned once again, a little clearer, as if behind her.

She turned back where she had just run and turned left down a narrow row of nicely maintained landscaped ground. She was running, but she still didn't know if she was running in the right direction.

"Father, I'm coming!" she yelled, but this time, there was no response.

She hit her watch and commanded it to call 9-1-1. She immediately told the operator to get an ambulance to her fast. She had hopes of getting to the priest before he went down, but it seemed like now she was too late.

"Father, the paramedics are coming!" she shouted as she continued to run aimlessly. She turned her head and something caught her eye. It looked like a moving shadow.

Running toward the image between two large statues, she realized it wasn't a shadow.

"Father!" she said hopefully as he was lying face down on the ground, his head inches from a sharp corner of a tombstone. Rolling him onto his back, she checked his pulse. Nothing.

"Come on, Father," she pleaded as she started doing chest compressions. "Come on, breathe man, breathe!"

She counted her compressions and then opened his mouth. Leaning down she placed her rosy red lips on his thick black skin and breathed into his lifeless body.

"You can do it, Father," she said audibly as she started doing compressions again. "One, two, three," she started counting out loud as she once again reached the magic number and leaned down to give another blow.

"Please, Father, the world needs you," she pleaded as she heard a siren cut through the silence. "They're here!"

Suddenly, she realized she didn't tell the operator where they were in the cemetery. She kept doing compressions but looked up to the entrance of the graveyard. She couldn't see anything two rows ahead, and she knew if she couldn't see them, they definitely couldn't see her. She jumped up, but couldn't see anyone. She looked down and wondered if it was better to be seen or doing compressions.

Compressions.

"Sorry, Father," she said. "But this is the only way."

She unbuttoned her blouse and quickly took it off and threw it up on the angelic statue beside her. She went back to do compressions in her bra.

"I'm back here!" she shouted. "I'm back here beside the statue with the blouse on it!" She continued to shout and then stopped when it was time to blow into Father Kingston.

"Hello!" she screamed. "Back here behind the statues! Back here! One! Two! Three! Four!" she continued to scream as she counted, hoping the paramedics would hear her voice and see her waving blouse. She now thought the whole blouse thing was idiotic, but at the time, it was the only thing she thought of.

"Where are you?" she heard a man shout.

She raised up from blowing into Father Kingston and started shouting. "I'm here! Beside the statue with the blouse on the left! Four! Five! Six! Seven! Eight! Nine! Ten!"

She stopped yelling when she saw a paramedic running toward her. He wasn't concerned she was shirtless. He was only concerned with the man lying on the ground.

He quickly cut the priest's shirt and placed the defibrillator pads on his chest and flipped the switch. He started compressions as two other paramedics arrived with a gurney.

"He's breathing!" he shouted as he continued to do compressions to keep the momentum going. "Twelve! Thirteen! Fourteen!"

Standing up, she got her blouse from the blushing angel and put her arms through the holes.

"You might have saved him," one of the other paramedics said as she was buttoning up her blouse. "Who knows if anyone would have found him?" he asked as they quickly got the priest on the gurney and rushed him to their ambulance.

"All in a day's work," she said to herself as she walked barefoot through the grass.

She found her shoes where she left them. "Thanks, Esther."

When she got back into her car, she noticed she had one new voicemail.

"Elizabeth, the jury's back. They have a verdict," is all Veronica said in a frantic tone.

Elizabeth gunned her car to get to the courthouse. She didn't know what to think. Was it good they were that quick? Maybe after all the evidence they each knew Jenny was guilty. Who could think she wasn't?

That question scared her.

CHAPTER 126

"Wint!" Elizabeth screamed, forgetting she didn't have to scream anymore. "Sorry. Veronica called," she started.

"I know, she called me too," he answered. "I'm leaving Solo's now and heading to the courthouse."

"Is Solo with you?" Elizabeth asked concerned. "Is he okay?"

"Yes. He just woke up, so he hasn't said much. We'll be there in about twenty minutes," Wint said, speeding through traffic, wishing he had his police cruiser to turn the lights and siren on to cut back about five to ten minutes.

"Okay, did Veronica say anything else?" Elizabeth asked, hoping Wint could say something to ease her mind.

"Only that this could be a really good sign or a really bad sign," he said pessimistically. "I don't have a good feeling."

"I'm glad I'm not the only one," Elizabeth said before ending her call, but she didn't know if the bad feeling was because of the verdict or seeing Solo.

Elizabeth didn't want to sit in silence. "Hi, Dad," she said cheerfully, trying to convince herself everything was going to be okay.

"Do you need something?" Luther asked coldly.

"Veronica called and the jury is back," she said tenderly.

"And?" he asked agitatedly.

"I didn't know if you were going to go to support her," she said timidly as if she was a four-year-old girl again.

"I have other matters to tend to," he answered flatly. "Anything else?"

"No," Elizabeth replied with a chill. "That was all."

She was about to tell her father goodbye, but he had already hung up. She had never had a good relationship with her father, but she tried to keep the conflict at a minimum. She often envied Veronica for following in her father's footsteps whereas she'd followed her socialite mother. Growing up, she'd often wondered why her father loved Veronica more than her, but when she hit the middle school years, that ambition of catching her father's heart died. She joined the debate club with the sole intention of having her father's blessing, but he never attended any of her matches. After that, she was content with being the forgotten one. The only connection she had with her father was his monthly payment to her trust fund.

Veronica said many times Elizabeth was the favorite. That was why Veronica followed in her father's legal career, to gain some attention she thought Elizabeth had.

Sadly, each sister wished they were more like the other to gain the love and affection of their father. They had never said such to one another, because if they had, they would have realized their father didn't love either of them like the other had originally thought.

Luther only loved himself. No one else.

Human relationships were just carnal means to a momentary satisfaction. Love only showed weakness. Love was for the unfortunate in his eyes.

CHAPTER 127

Wint and I walked up the courthouse steps in silence. Thoughts were flowing through my head like runners in a relay race. Each new thought passed its baton to another intriguing or frightening realization. We passed through the security checkpoints and headed toward the courtroom to discover Jenny's fate.

"It's going to be okay," I finally said as I opened the door for Wint. He slightly smiled, but it was forced. I could tell he didn't believe it. I didn't believe it either.

"No matter the verdict, it's not going to be okay," Wint whispered to me as we found a few seats available near the back of the courtroom. "If she's found guilty, they will have appeals Veronica will have to handle. Appeals will bring a possible new court case. So, a guilty verdict won't be the end of this," he grimaced painfully. "I'm not sure Veronica can do this again."

I listened to him, but what I really wanted to say was, "I'm not sure either of you can do this again." But I didn't say it. I just sat beside him and nodded in agreement.

"And if she's found not guilty," Wint said rolling his eyes. "Well, God help us all."

"Just need to find the lesser of two evils," I said downcast.

"And which one is that?"

I thought for a moment which one was the better option, but I couldn't decide. I didn't want to say what I thought, because if someone overheard me they could accuse me of plotting a murder. That would have been the best option for all of us.

We watched as Veronica walked slowly to the defense table, almost limping as if brutally attacked an hour ago. I guess realizing the end was in sight felt like getting kicked in the stomach with the way our judicial system worked.

She turned around and did her tell of her classic three succession movements ending in a slow blink.

"You'll get through this," I softly said to Wint, who didn't take his eyes off of his wife. "You will."

He didn't respond, but as Veronica turned around and watched, the jury entered the courtroom. Wint turned and looked me in the eyes. He didn't say anything, but his eyes spoke the uncertainty circling us all.

"How's she doing?" Elizabeth asked, squeezing in beside Wint.

"Not good," he said in a hushed tone.

I didn't acknowledge her. I kept my eyes on the jury to get a read from them, but I didn't have the discerning ability to read people's faces. Elizabeth and Wint continued to talk, but I tuned out the conversation. Elizabeth was just a blur.

I had watched court shows on television, but this was the second time I was going to see the conclusion – the reading of the verdict. The first had been the judgment of Chelsea's murder. The judge followed the standard time-consuming formalities. I sat staring into space, almost nodding off until something caught my attention.

The foreperson read the verdict. A hush filled half the room and commotion the other side. It felt like a tornado was about to form from the frigid cold and the abrasive heat colliding in this small room.

Veronica grinned to the courtroom. The judge commanded each of the jurors to state their verdict. One by one they all agreed. In a matter of a few minutes, the weight of the world had shifted.

I kept hearing the verdict over and over, but my ears couldn't believe it. I didn't know why I couldn't believe since I had dreamed it just an hour ago.

And just like all my other dreams, this one came true.

"Not guilty."

371

I watched as Milo hugged Jenny, both beaming with relief. But their smiles were genuine. Jenny pulled Veronica in for a hug and whispered something in her ear.

Veronica's smile was forced. She had to play the part of a caring defense attorney congratulating her innocent client.

Veronica turned around and scanned the room. She found the three of us sitting together, huddled in shock and defeat. She continued to smile, but once again, I saw the sign she was about to crumble.

I saw her smile with a slight nod and a long blink.

All I thought was, *What did Jenny just say?*

CHAPTER 128

The three of us sat in silence, too shocked to speak. The crowd in the courtroom slowly started to trickle away as we waited for Veronica in the second to last row. Jill Stapleton and Angus Staufferson looked aggravated, but they each professionally shook hands with the defense council before fleeing the scene to go work on their next case. Or to get a stiff drink at a nearby bar.

Wint jumped up, following Jill out the door and leaving Elizabeth to sit beside me without any barrier or buffer. I could tell she was looking at me, but I didn't give her the satisfaction of turning my head. She started to say something, but I couldn't take it. I didn't even want to remotely hear her voice, so I followed Wint out of the courtroom eavesdropping on the last bit of his conversation.

"Milo is a manipulative piece of work," Jill stated angrily, but in a controlled tone. "No wonder the jury believed the lies he was feeding them. They tasted as sweet as cotton candy. Who wouldn't have gobbled them up?"

"It's just not right," Wint said as he patted her shoulder. "But it will eventually come back to her."

"Doubt it," Jill said not agreeing with Wint's idealism. "She's free without a penalty for her actions. The only hope we have is she'll be stupid enough to do it again and mess up."

"I wish there was something more we could've done," Wint said as Jill agreed before they parted ways.

"You okay?" I asked Wint as we were about to reenter the courtroom.

"I will be," he said confidently. "And Veronica will get there. She rebounds faster than anyone I know."

"Faster doesn't mean better," I said as I opened the door to come face to face with Jenny Ascot and Milo as they were leaving.

"I forgive you, Winston," she mouthed silently as she passed by us.

I felt the fury like it was a match just struck in Wint's eyes. I could tell he wanted to snap back, but I stood between the two of them and pushed him into the courtroom.

Jenny stopped and turned back and tapped me on my shoulder. "You and I would never have worked, you know that, right?" she said casually, as if the court case never happened. I didn't respond, but proceeded to follow Wint back into the courtroom. "Because you're in love with Winston. I guess I'll just move on," she snickered as the door closed behind me.

We walked back into the courtroom and found Elizabeth standing beside Veronica in the back of the room.

"What did Jenny say to you?" Wint demanded.

"Huh?" Veronica asked confused and not clear-headed.

"After the verdict, Jenny hugged and said something to you," Wint explained. "What did she say?"

Veronica looked at each of us with a terrified look in her eyes. "She said, 'See you at work, sis.'"

"That cold-hearted, bit--" Elizabeth started to say before Veronica stopped her.

"She said something else that wouldn't mean anything to you, but it was a threat," Veronica said as she started to walk towards the door to leave this room and the haunting feeling of the atmosphere.

"She threatened you?" Wint asked furiously.

Veronica nodded and went in for a hug. Wint wrapped his strong arms around her small torso. She wished she could let all the cares and worries sink into his stronghold, but she couldn't let it all go.

"We'll get through this," Wint said tenderly, looking into Veronica's eyes to let her know he was sticking beside her for better or worse.

"Together we will," Veronica nodded as she finished her embrace and held his hand. She liked the feeling of having her man beside her during their trying time.

"Come on," Elizabeth said, "let's get out of here."

"You two go on; we will be right there," Veronica said. I started walking away, but I could still hear Veronica's faint whisper to Wint as I proceeded through the door, watching it close.

"She also said, 'Don't forget I own you, sis. Rosenburg.'"

CHAPTER 129

I didn't feel like being around Elizabeth, so I parted company as the three of them went to Wint's house.

Elizabeth tried to say something to me as we were walking out of the courthouse, but I didn't listen. I ignored her completely. She was just a figment of someone I used to know.

I hopped onto the closest metro subway and headed back towards the rundown section on the outskirts of the D.C. area where I lived. I reached into my pocket to pull out my phone to kill time on the train ride, forgetting I still hadn't purchased a new phone. Being disconnected was nice in some moments, but in others, it seemed like the train ride was going to be a complete waste of time since I couldn't do anything but reread the various advertisements of the production of *Wicked* at Benjamin Banneker Academic High School in three weekends or the telephone number for a substance abuse helpline. After this week, I felt I may need to have a substance to abuse for a while to help numb the memories.

"Yo, you got a phone I can use?" a teenaged thug asked as I stared up at the ceiling.

"No," I said, shaking my head and shrugging my shoulders.

"Dude, I just need to text my mom. My phone died," he said gruffly.

"Dude," I snapped back, "I got my phone stolen yesterday when I was mugged, so back off."

"Okay, man, I was just asking," he said defensively as he started walking down the aisle to go to the next train car.

"No, you had a tone when you asked, man," I shot back, but he ignored me as he entered the next train car.

I knew I shouldn't have gone off on the kid, but he rubbed me wrong with his attitude. I wanted to continue to tell him off, but I was sitting alone and I still had a couple more stops before transferring to my final metro line.

My blood was starting to boil, but I wasn't doing anything to relinquish the bubbling heat. I didn't try to meditate or close my eyes to relax. It was as if the rage had taken over and I was allowing myself to be kidnapped by the negative forces.

I didn't like the feeling, but at the moment, I felt too weak to try to fight it, so I let it run its course as if it were a cold. If only fluids and rest were enough to get over these emotional highs I was having.

After letting my thoughts run rampant in my brain for the remainder of the journey home, my nerves were on edge. I knew drinking wouldn't solve anything, but something in the substance abuse ad was enticing me. It might have been the lifeless look in the guy's eyes. I wanted that look right now. I wanted to feel lifeless.

When I got home I found an old bottle of scotch in my closet floor given to me as a birthday present years ago. I had never opened it. I tore open the paper wrapper and poured a little into a coffee cup. I lifted up the cup and smelled the woodsy aroma as I sloshed it around, causing a whirlpool in my hand. I put the cup to my lips and tilted the cup back, but I wouldn't let my mouth open. It was as if I felt Chelsea standing beside me telling me to stop. I knew that was ridiculous. I didn't believe in spirits like that, but it was the only explanation for what I was feeling.

I didn't want to drink to lessen my feelings. I didn't want to end up like the ad. I didn't want Chelsea to be ashamed of me turning to a glass to solve my problems since her older brother battled the addiction until he lost the war in a single car crash when he was twenty-six, four years before her death.

I grabbed the bottle given to me four years ago and poured its contents down the drain, along with the liquid in the coffee cup. I didn't want to be the type of man relying on a drink to get him through the night.

I was tired as it was.

Friday
CHAPTER 130

Simon laid on his hard thin mattress that thousands of other inmates had slept on in the last ten years. He thought any minute he would drift off to sleep and wake up refreshed from this nightmare.

Sadly, he had pinched himself until his arms looked like a heroin addict's with tiny pricks where the blood started to flow. Every time he saw a droplet of blood spill from his cut he knew he was never going to wake up from this nightmare. He knew his past had finally caught up with him.

He heard a faint muffled cry in the distance. Another prisoner whose life didn't end up the way he hoped was succumbing to the realization he was now a caged bird without a reason to sing. He marginally felt sad for the grown man shedding a few tears alone, but he mostly felt embarrassed for him. He knew he stupidly confessed to raping Fiona and there was a bleak glimmer of hope of escaping repercussions for that indiscretion. Prison was in his future. Orange jumpsuits were going to be his fashion, and his name was going to be replaced with a number.

He had thick skin. He had manipulated people enough in his past that he had hardened himself against worrying about ever getting caught from the many felonies he had committed. Rape was just a notch on his demented belt that had holes from battery, harassment, fraud, theft, and indecent exposure.

But murder wasn't one of his vices. He had thought of killing people in a drunken stupor or in patches of unemployment, but the thought was only merely a thought. Never an intended action. They were just a means of passing the time in his lonely existence. But now, his lonely existence was about to get very populated with a motley crew of delinquents he used to mock behind their backs.

Now he was going to have to watch his back, not from snide remarks or a jaded backhanded word. No, he would have to trust no one to make it through this period and come out again unscathed.

Only sixteen hours had passed since he was arrested for the murders of his exes, but it seemed like sixteen years. His attorney never returned. His family was undependable. His friends were few. He couldn't think of anyone he would reach out to for a kind word.

He stared out the steel bars into the cell across from him and saw a man snoring, curled up with a worn blanket. He was going to have to learn to fall asleep without his white noise machine.

Deep down he knew he was guilty of many things: crimes too many to count in the last ten years. He didn't understand the eastern notion of karma, yet as he looked over in his corner where his filthy toilet was, he knew he didn't need to understand karma to believe in it. He had done many things to deserve a punishment such as this.

Just as his moral compass was leaning to a graceful position of acceptance, a rise of unfairness seeped into his cold heart.

"I should have killed Fiona that night ten years ago," he mumbled to himself. "I should have killed her when I was done with her."

He closed his eyes, listening to the man snoring across from him. It wasn't a sleep machine, but it was still something to drown out the silence. He started to drift into a sleep as he mumbled to himself.

"I'll get you someday, Fiona," he said with a twisted smile. "Then I'll be a murderer."

CHAPTER 131

"I'm going to New York City this weekend," a man's voice said in the darkness as the sound of clattering cups and forks scraping the bottom of plates filled the background noise. "Whitney is gone for a few days, and I need to get rid of something. Want to have a guys' weekend?"

"I'm down," another voice answered with a mouthful of food.

"I'm free," a man with a British accent said. "I haven't had a holiday in some time."

"Stewart, you've lived here for years," another voice said with a laugh. "When are you going to start talking like the rest of us?"

"Pardon me," the British voice answered. "Do you want me to stop talking to my mum, Collin?"

"Fine," the voice uncaringly answered, "keep looking like a tourist."

The conversation continued, but the words weren't audible. The sounds of the diner atmosphere overtook the dialogue until the sound of bubbling water overtook the chaos.

The water bubbled as if in a peaceful brook in a meadow as a woman started humming softly. Nothing was seen, but the humming continued. The sound was relaxed and cheerful.

A door creaked open, allowing a sliver of light to enter a room. It was too quick to see anything other than a shadowed figure walking away from the door and coming closer to the bubbling water and gentle humming.

"Hey sis," a voice said before a loud thud and the sound of a body dropping to the ground. The humming stopped. "I wonder if Luther will take off for your funeral."

A fragile moan collided with the bubbling water.

"I doubt it," the same voice said. "I bet he'll even give me a raise for getting rid of you. You know me, employee of the year."

The moan dwindled until the only thing heard was the bubbling water. A light flashed, as if a snapshot was taken, hitting the woman's face.

"Jenny!" I screamed as I bolted up from my bed. I reached for my phone to call Wint only to realize I still didn't have one.

CHAPTER 132

I knew it was early. My clock radio shined 5:57 a.m., but I had to tell Wint. There was no telling when Jenny was going to attack Veronica. My dream didn't give any specific time, only bubbling water and humming. Also, there was a good chance it would happen indoors.

I put on an old pair of blue jeans, a worn out Nationals t-shirt, and a gray zip-up hoodie. I was out the door a few minutes past six. I hated to admit to Wint he was right about getting a new phone. Being disconnected from everyone was good on short trips and random days, but not every day. *Note to self, go to the cell phone store as soon as it opens.*

I drove my beat-up Honda Civic as fast as it could go, pressing down the gas pedal until I thought my foot would go through the floorboard. I considered stopping to pick up some breakfast to take with me so I didn't look crazy, as if a bag of chocolate chip muffins would sidetrack Wint's mind from asking a hundred questions.

"When's it going to happen?" or "Where's Jenny going to attack?" or "How will she do it?" and the hardest question to answer: "Why do you think Jenny is going to try to kill Veronica?"

I didn't know how to answer any of these questions. I didn't know when, where, or how. But I did know why. But the honest answer wasn't one I was ready to share at this time. I wasn't ready to see my best friend look at me with disbelief. I wasn't ready to watch the guy who was the best man at my wedding doubt me and my dreams. I wasn't ready to open myself up and be raw with someone else. That first person hurt me too deeply to consider sharing my secrets.

I inhaled a deep breath as I turned down a street entering his quiet neighborhood of million dollar homes. I often wondered if I was jealous of his lifestyle of driving nice, foreign, fast cars, eating at the ritziest restaurants on a whim, and living in a place resembling the size of some small castles in Ireland. I often wondered -- and if I was truly honest with myself, I would conclude--I was.

But the thing that made me most jealous of Wint was his relationship with Veronica. Not that I wanted to have a romantic fling with her, but I missed the times I had with Chelsea, whether it was walking hand in hand at a park at dusk, laughing wildly at the goofy politicians we used to see on the streets, or the way she always stood her ground and encouraged me to be the brave man she knew I was but I couldn't see. I missed her optimism.

I pulled into their driveway and parked in front of their garage. Immediately, I saw a familiar car beside mine. Elizabeth was here.

I shook off the disdain and marched up, empty-handed and empty-minded and rang the doorbell. Wint came to the door still in his pajamas, scratching his head and yawning.

"Solo? What are you doing here?"

CHAPTER 133

He invited me into his house and I gladly accepted. This wasn't the type of conversation to have on a welcome mat.

"How's Veronica?" I asked as we walked through the foyer into his classically decorated living room. Everything matched the blue and gold color scheme, from the couch and loveseat to the lamp stand and chandelier.

"She finally went to sleep around two this morning," Wint answered sleepily as he plopped down on the couch as I followed beside him.

"Glad she's getting some rest," I added.

"I'm glad to see you man, really, but is there something wrong?" Wint asked compassionately, but with tired eyes. "It's six o'clock in the morning."

"I needed to talk to you and I didn't go and get a phone yesterday," I started as Wint jumped in.

"You need to get one today, Solo," he said paternally.

"Yes, yes," I nodded, "I know, but anyways, I had a feeling when I woke up that something wasn't right." Technically, this wasn't a lie. I did have a bad feeling when I woke up.

"Bad feeling?" Wint questioned, looking confused. That was the look I was fearing, and all I had said was I had a feeling. How would he look if I told him I had dreams each night that always happened?

"Call it a gut, or a friend's intuition, but you need to stay with Veronica all day," I said sanely.

"Yes, I already called in to work and told them I was taking the day off to be with her," he said, finding a decorative pillow and hugging it.

"No, I mean, do not leave her side," I said slowly. "You got me?"

"Solo, everything is going to be okay," he said optimistically. "Elizabeth and I are here. Veronica's going to be okay."

I quickly thought of a new way of saying it to get it through his brain. "I just have a bad feeling Jenny is going to try to do something."

"Don't worry about Jenny," Wint said, brushing my comment away. "She's been in jail for six months, and she's not stupid enough to try something now."

I huffed in defeat. "I'm not so sure about that, man. She's loco. Just please promise me you will be with Veronica all day. If she takes a bath," bubbling water, "if she goes for a walk," possible streams in a park, "if she does anything or goes anywhere, promise me you'll stick beside her like a peanut butter and banana sandwich."

"You need a new lunch, Solo," Wint said with a laugh, as I had been eating the same sandwich since elementary school.

"Promise me, please," I urged as I leaned over to look him in the eyes. "I don't want you to go through what I went through with Chelsea."

That got him. It got me too.

"Yes, man, I promise. I won't let Veronica do anything without me," he said. "Can I ask you something?"

I took a deep breath and quickly tried to come up with an answer to the question I knew he was going to ask.

"What happened between you and Elizabeth?"

"Oh…uh…" I stammered, not thinking he was going to ask me that question. "She said something to me that stung."

"What did she say?" he asked.

"I already forgot it," I lied.

He looked at me with a disbelieving gaze. If he was my father, he would have called me out on that lie. But since he was my best friend, he let it slide.

"You know, if you ever want to talk to me about anything," he started as I stopped him.

"I know, I know," I answered graciously. "Maybe I'll be ready one day."

CHAPTER 134

I stuck around the Cooper house until the women starting waking up. I didn't want to see Elizabeth, so I quickly departed before she came out from the guest bedroom. I once again begged Wint to stick beside Veronica all day long, and he assured me he would.

I walked away relieved I had settled that crisis because I was positive if Jenny came around Veronica, Wint would do anything to keep his wife safe. Anything.

I looked down at the watch I'd had since middle school and thought the cell phone stores should be open by then, so I made my way to the closest one.

I almost vomited when I saw the prices for the latest iPhone, so I cheapened it by buying one three versions old, still feeling cheated. The store was kind enough to log into my account and restore all my contacts in my phone. I lost some things from my phone being stolen, but as long as I had all my contacts again, I felt much better.

I texted Wint to let him know all was well in the world, and I had gotten a new phone. He texted back a thumbs up, and we both carried on in our daily routines.

I hadn't spoken to Jeremiah since yesterday's coffee, and I wanted to check up with him and see how he was doing with the news of Eugene. He gladly took me up on my offer of meeting for a late breakfast at a little diner near his work, American University.

I got there first and ordered my tea and water and waited for my friend to arrive. He did as punctual as ever, ten a.m. on the dot.

"I hope you haven't been waiting long," Jeremiah said apologetically as he removed his messenger bag from his side and sat down across from me.

"We said ten," I said smiling trying to remove any guilt Jeremiah might be holding. "You are right on time."

"Good," he said, breathing a sigh of relief. He ordered his black coffee with a slice of cheesecake.

"Cheesecake?" I remarked surprised as this was totally out of the norm for him.

"Well," he said thinking for a proper response. "Many people eat cheese for breakfast, so why not join that majority?"

"Oh, I'm not judging," I smiled as I asked the waitress for a slice of their strawberry pie. "I'll just think of this as toast and jelly."

"Very sensible of you," he smiled as we sat in the quiet diner. The breakfast crowd had faded, and it was too early for lunch.

"How are you doing?" I finally asked, stirring in another packet of sweetener for my tea.

"Eugene seems to be taking the news rather well, which gives me both relief and concern," Jeremiah said honestly.

"Relief and concern?" I asked shocked.

"He's known about this for a few weeks and has kept it a secret from me. So, I'm not sure if he's in the denial stage or acceptance stage of grief," he said as the waitress brought us our sweets. "He just keeps telling me it's going to be okay, and my mind keeps thinking he's in denial."

"But you have to think of it from his vantage point," I spoke confidently.

"And what's that?" Jeremiah countered.

"He's a man of faith," I said shrugging my shoulders.

"And men of faith can't lose it sometimes?" Jeremiah asked. "I recall many sermons he's preached on the suicidal prophet Jeremiah."

"Yes, but those were during the weakest moments of his life when he was crying out to God. He then picked himself up and carried out his mission even in those dark moments," I said joyously.

"So, are you saying people of faith shouldn't show their weaknesses to the public but only in secret to God?"

I let the question marinate for a few seconds. "I know from personal experience I tried to hide my pain, but it eventually seeped through to my daily life. I tried to be strong and put together, but I was cracking and everyone could see it but me," I said showing my wounded heart from my past. "But I wouldn't worry about whether he is in the denial or acceptance stage. I would just be there for him no matter what stage he is in."

"Hmm," he said, taking a nibble of his cheesecake. "But he needs to go through all the stages," he brought up defensively. "Or he will just be--."

"Be surrounded by friends and family who will do anything for him," I said digging into my strawberry pie. "Miss," I said to the waitress, "can you bring some whipped cream out too," I asked with a wink to Jeremiah. "Got to get my dairy."

We both continued to eat our breakfast, but I still never got a definite answer out of Jeremiah. "But, really, how are you doing?"

"I think I am in the denial stage," he said. "When I sit and talk with him, I don't see him as a dying man, so I tend to think, maybe it's a mistake."

"But we are all dying," I flatly said. "Eugene could live another ten years, and you could die tomorrow of a heart attack with your gluttonous cheesecake," I said with a laugh.

"So, what would you rather have?" he asked intently. "A time table of your death or a surprise?"

I stared down at my water with the melting ice cubes. "See my cup of water?"

"Yeah," he nodded.

"Well, my ice cubes are disappearing. Where are they going?"

"Solomon, are you really asking, or are you making a point?" he asked bewildered.

"Just answer it. Where are the ice cubes going?" I asked once again.

"Well," he started in a lecturing tone, "they are melting from their solid state to a liquid state. They are just becoming water like the rest in your cup."

"Exactly," I said with a grin as he cocked his head at me slightly confused. "No matter what form the water is now, it keeps changing from solid to liquid to gas back to liquid and so on. I feel that's how life is. I am living life like an ice cube, and when I eventually melt away, I'm not really vanishing, but I'm just moving into a different form. When I die, I may be dead here, but I will still be alive in some form somewhere. Hopefully in Heaven. And when you die, even though you don't believe it, your soul will be existing somewhere."

"In Hell," he facetiously winked. "I understand your concept. I see the parallels in it. I can read books and watch documentaries on it, but at the end of the day, I can't believe it. There is a great chasm between understanding and belief. I have the understanding down to a science. I can recite excerpts from the Bible, Koran, Book of Mormon, and so forth, but at the end of the day, when you melt, Solo, you melt."

"And isn't that a depressing concept?" I asked sincerely. "Is that really what you want to fall sleep thinking about?"

"I've fallen asleep to it for this long, and it's never given me a nightmare," he said taking a last bite of his cheesecake. "But if you believe it, that's your stance."

"Do you think me simple-minded for taking such a stance on faith?" I asked delicately.

"Simple-minded?" he asked and shook his head no. "I know many great minds much wiser than me that follow the same belief as you, and I wouldn't dare say they are simple-minded."

"So, there's hope for you yet?" I winked as I licked the last remaining dollop of whipped cream from my plate.

"Hope is a funny thing," Jeremiah said playfully. "Just be careful what you hope for. You may get what you've hoped for but not see it because it's not packaged in the container you were imagining."

I shook my head at such a profound thought. "You are something else, Jeremiah. Truly."

"Nah, I read it on someone's Facebook status yesterday."

CHAPTER 135

"I'm going to New York City this weekend," Grant said at Gus', a mom and pop diner two blocks from the Department of Transportation. "Whitney is gone for a few days, and I need to get rid of something. Want to have a guys' weekend?"

"I'm down," Jordan said as he chewed one of his honey-mustard-covered chicken strips.

"I'm free," Stewart said staring sadly at his half eaten salad while looking at everyone else's fried food. "I haven't had a holiday in some time."

"Stewart, you've lived here for years," Collin said with a laugh and a cheeseburger in his hand. "When are you going to start talking like the rest of us?"

"Pardon me," Stewart answered. "Do you want me to stop talking to my mum, Collin?"

"Fine," Collin uncaringly answered. "Keep looking like a tourist."

"I don't look like a tourist," Stewart interjected, looking around the table for confirmation from the others.

"You sound like a tourist, but you look like one of us," Grant said with a British accent, smiling as he popped a sweet potato fry into his mouth.

The guys continued eating their lunch and started planning their trip.

"Okay, you three take the train up to New York, and I'll drive up there, and then we can go do whatever."

"No Broadway," Collin said, pounding his fist on the table.

"What's wrong with a show?" Stewart asked amazed. "It's just like a movie but live."

"And a lot more expensive," Jordan said, agreeing with Collin.

"Fine," Stewart said, sinking back into a bowlful of rabbit food.

"What about a Yankee's game?" Grant asked, popping a few more fries into his mouth.

"Boo!" Collin roared. "Yankees suck! See, I knew you weren't a true Nationals fan."

"Get off it," Grant laughed. "I was just trying to think of something we all would want to do."

"Let's just play it by ear," Jordan reasonably commented. "I'll buy three train tickets going and four coming back when I get back to the office."

"I'll look for the hotel," Collin chimed in as the rest of the guys moaned.

"How about letting Jordan plan that?" Stewart kindly suggested.

"Why?" Collin asked deflated.

"Remember when we went to Miami and we stayed in a roach-infested, drug dealer central, slum lord motel? You lost the privilege of booking hotels after that," Grant said enthusiastically. "Learned that mistake."

"It had good reviews on the internet," Collin defended.

"Fake," Stewart chimed in. "They were all fake, probably written by the hotel owners using fake names."

"Fine. Book it, Jordan," Collin said taking a big bite of cheeseburger. "But it better not cost me a fortune," he said with his mouth full. "When I get my refund check, then I can pay you back."

"You've already done your taxes?" Grant asked shocked. "I just gave you the K-1 yesterday."

Jordan shrugged his shoulders cutting into the conversation. "That was the last thing I was needing, so I finished it last night. Getting back a nice chuck of change," he grinned.

"Wait, you had to use that K-1 thing on your taxes?" Collin asked amazed. "I filed my taxes a month ago."

"Collin," Grant said rolling his eyes. "Every year I tell you, you have to wait until the partnership tax return is done before you can file your taxes."

"Wait, are you saying that K-1 is supposed to go on my taxes every year?" Collin asked lost. By the expression on everyone's face, he knew he should have never said a word. "I know now," he muttered to himself as the rest of the guys roared in laughter.

"Don't be shocked when the IRS sends you a nice little love letter," Grant laughed, and Collin's eyes widened in dread.

"Go home and pack after work and meet back at Union Station at 6:30," Jordan stated as he looked on his phone for the train departure times for New York. "You got that, Collin? Train leaves tonight around seven."

"I got it," Collin grinned as he took another bite of his burger. "Thanks for dumbing it down for me." He laid his burger down and raised his hands. "You said six?" he asked raising five fingers with one hand and a lone middle finger on the other.

"Not exactly," Jordan smiled. "Seven," he said raising his hand and flipping Collin off. "You forgot one."

CHAPTER 136

"You asked me earlier this week if I believed in absolute truth," Jeremiah stated as he finished his second cup of coffee and I my third tea.

"You have an answer for me?" I asked, eager to hear his response.

"I believe you were meaning what is my belief in absolute moral truths because absolute truths are common every day. Like, I am certain in all scenarios there are no round squares and every square is a parallelogram, so scientifically speaking, I believe in absolute truth."

"Yeah, yeah," I said waving him off. "But you know I wasn't meaning that."

"That I do," he smiled as he picked up his messenger bag and pulled out a book.

"Are you going to read to me?" I asked as he opened a tattered old book aged through years of reading.

"Just a little," he said flipping through the pages until he stopped on a highlighted passage. "'Jesus said to him, 'I am the way, and the truth, and the life. No one comes to the Father except through me.' John 14:6.'"

"Is that your Bible?" I asked amazed.

"I told you I can recite passages from many religious texts. Why does that flabbergast you so? I'm a man of anthropology, and religion is an important foundation of civilizations."

"But it's so used," I said mesmerized. "It looks like you read it more than I do."

"And isn't that sad?" he said wide-eyed. "An atheist knowing the Bible backwards and forwards whereas most Christians can only paraphrase a few verses out of their beloved word of God."

I nodded my head in agreement as if being penalized for being a fake follower of Christ.

"I'm not trying to degrade you, Solomon," he said tenderly. "I'm just showing you in your faith you have to believe in absolute moral truths because if you don't, your faith would implode on you, whereas I don't hold such a high esteem on these words as a word of God, but as an author's take on life."

"So you don't believe in absolute truth?" I bluntly asked.

"I believe many people believe in absolute truth without thinking they believe in it, and from their points of view it would appear reasonable. But from the lens I see the world through, I don't believe in absolute moral truth. There are too many scenarios where one little thing could change the whole outlook and shift the entire question on the size of a pin." He stopped and placed his Bible back into his messenger bag.

"Wait," I said. "I just called you a little while ago when you were already away from your office. Do you keep a Bible on you all the time?"

"Don't you?" he returned. My expression must have told him. "Tsk-tsk."

"You know what?" I said, forming a new oath in my heart. "You just made me a better person. I want to be like you and know what I believe backwards and forwards."

"Glad I could be of some help on your journey," he said as he asked the waitress for the bill. "So, did you ever solve your problem of doing something or doing nothing?"

I thought back on our conversation pertaining to the shooter. "Yes," I nodded.

"Is it an absolute answer, or will you switch it up?" he grinned as he picked up his messenger bag and paid the waitress.

"Not all questions have an absolute," I stated precisely as I paid the waitress my bill as well.

"Oh, it doesn't?" he asked shocked. "I thought the words of Jesus plainly point out it does."

"But Jesus was just speaking of salvation," I reiterated as Jeremiah gave me a quizzical look.

"Really?" he asked like a teacher speaking to his pupil. "You think that verse is just about one situation and not all of them? Doesn't salvation for you encompass everything? In your faith you are all about absolutes. Absolute love. Absolute grace. Absolute forgiveness. Jesus was all about absolutes. There is nothing that separates a believer from Him. Nothing per your scripture. And aren't you supposed to mimic that? That's a tough life to follow, but as a follower of Christ you are called to follow it. On good days and bad ones. Sorry."

I didn't know how to respond. Once again, the atheist silenced a follower in a theological debate.

"I'm really glad I met you, Jeremiah."

CHAPTER 137

"You didn't have to drive me to the spa," Veronica said to Wint as she reclined the passenger seat and closed her eyes.

"Sure," Wint said as he looked over at his napping wife. "You just rest."

"How does Cooper Law sound?" she asked, raising up from her catnap.

"What are you talking about?" he asked with a shocked laugh.

"I'm asking how does Cooper Law sound?" she repeated, inclining the seat to its proper position.

"I heard you the first time," Wint said as he looked over at his bright-eyed passenger.

"So, what do you think?" she beamed at him with a bright smile, a smile he hadn't seen in quite some time, maybe years.

"Are you saying what I think you're saying?" he asked seriously.

"I want to start my own law practice," she said defiantly. "I don't want to be associated with my father anymore. I don't want to be known at Veronica Hyde-Cooper. I want to be known as your wife. Not his daughter."

"I'll support you with whatever you decide," he said, taking his right hand off the steering wheel to grip hers.

"Our lives are going to be dramatically different," she said point-blankly.

"I know."

"We are going to have to start watching our spending," she said authoritatively.

"I know."

"We are going to have to start buckling down and living on a budget."

"Okay," Wint nodded.

"We are going to have to sell our house and use it as equity."

"Fine," Wint replied.

"Doesn't this scare you any?" she asked stupefied.

"Nope," Wint said, holding her hand even tighter.

"We may lose everything if this idea fails," she said tragically.

"Not everything," he said as he lifted her hand to his lips. "Not everything."

"What did I ever do to deserve you?" she blushed like she did in college.

"Just being you, I guess," he said romantically.

Given any other man, Veronica would have thought that was a line for some intimacy later in the evening, but she knew Wint's true character. He was one of the good ones.

CHAPTER 138

"Hey Wint," Elizabeth said from Wint's kitchen. "Can you bring home some Italian bread on your way home?"

"Sure thing," he said. "Need anything else?"

"A tall, dark Italian would be nice," she laughed.

"I can't help you there," he laughed.

"What are you up to?" she asked as she rustled through the cabinets to find some pasta.

"Just sitting in the waiting area," he said, grabbing a nearby magazine to flip through. He picked up *Home & Garden* and rolled his eyes.

"You don't have to wait there," Elizabeth said harshly. "She's a big girl. You can go get a drink or something while you wait. The spa usually takes a couple of hours for a good session," she said as she finally found a small box of angel hair pasta. "Can you bring home some more angel hair pasta?"

"We have some spaghetti noodles in the pantry," he said. "Just use those."

"I don't like spaghetti noodles as much as angel hair," she said. "They are just too thick for me."

"Noodles are noodles," Wint smiled as he looked up at the television and saw it was a soap opera, causing him to once again roll his eyes.

"Not to my delicate pallet," she said playfully. "It's the least you can do since I'm slaving away in the kitchen for your supper."

"Slaving away?" he laughed. "It's pasta. You boil some water, drop in the noodles, warm up the sauce. Bam! Supper."

"I know Veronica prefers angel hair pasta," she said girlishly.

"Fine," he resigned. "I'll get you your pasta."

"Okay, good. Go get it now while she's in the spa so you can get home quicker," she said as she bent down to find a couple of large pots in the cabinets for the noodles and sauce.

"I can't," he sighed. "I promised Solo I wouldn't leave Veronica today."

"Wait. Repeat that," she said, stopping what she was doing and giving her undivided attention to the conversation. "Solo said what?"

"He told me to not leave Veronica at all today," he said curiously. "He drove over this morning and woke me up to tell me to stay by her side all day. You know Solo."

"Yes, I do," she said with a trembling tone. Her heart started to pound deep into her chest. "Then why aren't you in there with Veronica now?"

"I'm in the waiting area," he answered. "If anything happens, I am right here watching the door. Nothing is going to happen. He's just being overly dramatic."

"You get your butt in there now, Wint!" Elizabeth screamed into the phone. "I don't care if Veronica is taking a piss. You march your cute butt to my sister and watch her every move."

"Really?" he asked shocked.

"Now!" she billowed as her legs started to go weak. She knew Solo had a very good reason for being so adamant about Veronica's security. "Go Wint! And call me to let me know everything is okay!"

"Did you say cute butt?" he kidded.

"If you don't move, I will beat that butt so hard it won't be cute anymore! Go on! Move boy!"

402

CHAPTER 139

Veronica was lying peacefully on her back in total darkness. She listened to the water cascading off the wall fountain as meditation music played softly in the background. She continued to breathe deeply as her masseuse recommended to help alleviate some of the stress before the massage.

She deeply inhaled the aroma of the cucumber slices on her eyes to help with the swelling. The last few months had been incredibly stressful and this may be her last spa visit in quite some time, so she was doing everything to counteract her past and help rejuvenate her future.

There was a knock on the door. "Can I come in?" a woman's voice asked.

"Come in," Veronica said blindly.

"Veronica, your normal massage therapist had a family emergency, and someone new will be doing your massage today. Are you okay with that change?"

"Oh, yes, Tamara, that's fine," Veronica said unfazed. "With the months I've had, I would let Captain Hook massage me."

"Perfect," Tamara replied. "It will be a few more minutes, but someone will be in here soon. Just relax and enjoy the tranquility."

"Take as long as you need," she said as she continued to rest in this state of utopia.

The door closed and she tried to let all the thoughts of Jenny, Milo, her father, and Rosenburg drift away like the sound of the water. She was confident in starting Cooper Law, but she was also confident in the struggles she would be facing. She knew the next year was going to be bittersweet, but this change would hopefully bring more sweetness at the end than bitterness. If she remained with Manfield & Hyde, she would probably fall back into the rut of being a heartless attorney. She didn't want to be that woman anymore. She wanted to be a woman Winston would want to stick beside through better and worse.

She started to smile at the thought of telling her father she quit. She was basking in the moment when she could tell Jenny she would never see her again and get a restraining order to keep it that way. She was awaiting the day until Rosenburg would be a distant memory, but after she told Winston everything, and he still remained on the bathroom floor consoling her, she knew. She knew she would rather give herself to him than anyone else.

As a feeling of pure joy filled her spirit, she heard a light tapping on the door. The door creaked open and then closed. She heard a pair of footsteps walk into the room and come closer to the table.

"Ready for your massage, Veronica?" a woman's voice asked as she walked around the table, placing her hands around Veronica's neck. "Just relax."

CHAPTER 140

"Where's Veronica's room?" Wint asked the attendant. "I need to see her now!" He was confused when Solo came over this morning, but now that Elizabeth's mood changed when Solo was mentioned, he knew something was up. He didn't know how to explain it, but there had been a few unexplainable things happen when Solo and Elizabeth were together. Most recently, the shooting the other night where the woman's life was spared because they were there.

"Her massage therapist should be in there now," Tamara said as she looked up with a pleasant smile. "It's not customary to interrupt a session."

"I'm her husband, and there's an emergency!" Wint ranted. "What room is she in?"

"Please sir, sit and have some water while I get her," Tamara requested, pointing to a pitcher of water with lemon and lime wedges.

"No! Take me to her room now!" he demanded. "I promise, it's urgent!"

"Let me look it up," she said typing on her computer.

"If you don't tell me in two seconds where my wife is, I will start opening every door until I find her."

"She's in Room 16, through that door, down the hall on the right," she said as she hurried around her desk.

"Thank you!" he said as he darted through the door, running down the dim hallway watching the even numbers rise on the right.

Tamara quickly followed, afraid of the endless possibilities. Was he a deranged abusive husband? Was there really an emergency? If he had a gun, what was she going to do?

Wint reached Room 16 and burst open the door. "Veronica!" he yelled as he saw a woman holding onto his wife's neck. "Let go of her!"

CHAPTER 141

"How are you doing?" I asked driving away from school. I only had one class this week, and it was on a Friday afternoon.

"Well," Wint said a little on edge. "I'm sitting against the door of the room where Veronica is getting a massage."

"Bet that's the first time anyone has done that," I said casually.

"Well, I ran down the hall and barged into the room while I was talking to Elizabeth."

"Really?" I said amazed, but I was secretly thankful.

"Yeah, I was in the waiting room talking to her, and she was telling me a list of things to buy for supper, and I said I couldn't go run any errands because I needed to stay here and keep close tabs on Veronica because you said so. She instantly changed and said I needed to go check on her," he said, rubbing his forehead, embarrassed of the show he became a part of. "So I ran and flew into the room and found her getting a massage from a small Asian woman."

"I bet you freaked her out," I said with a laugh.

"She started screaming something in Chinese or Vietnamese or something, but freaked out was an understatement," he said stretching his legs on the floor, almost touching the other side of the wall.

"I'm sorry I caused you to look crazy, but I'm glad Veronica is safe," I said.

"No problem, man," he said with a slight chuckle. "It will be a funny story someday."

"Tomorrow maybe?" I chimed in.

"Yes, tomorrow we will all be laughing about it. Who knows, maybe even tonight over supper? Want to join us? Elizabeth is making pasta."

"I'll pass," I said. Hearing her name just made my insides churn.

"I don't know, apparently angel hair pasta is so much better than spaghetti noodles, so I have to go and get some after we leave here. We're having garlic bread too," he rambled on. "At least I think it's garlic bread. She wanted me to pick up some Italian bread."

Suddenly a chill filled my entire body. It started at my toes and quickly moved up my legs until my ears felt the cold. "Did you say she's making pasta?"

"Yeah, are you coming?" he asked. "Come on, the more the merrier."

"Wint, I have to go!" I said as I hung up in mid-sentence.

"Really?" I shouted at the top of my lungs as I started speeding home.

My dream I thought was about Veronica wasn't about Veronica. When pasta is cooked, hot boiling, bubbling water is used. And many people sing while they cook. Or hum. "Really God? Really?" I screamed, rattled and agitated.

I drove like a madman. I couldn't help but pray, "Really God? Really? You want me to save the woman who could have saved my wife's life? Is this some twisted joke, and I am just a muse for Your entertainment?"

In the middle of my prayer, something Jeremiah said earlier hit me at full force.

You think that verse is just about one situation and not all of them? Doesn't salvation for you encompass everything? In your faith you are all about absolutes. Absolute love. Absolute grace. Absolute forgiveness. Jesus was all about absolutes. There is nothing that separates a believer from Him. Nothing per your scripture. And aren't you supposed to mimic that? That's a tough life to follow, but as a follower of Christ you are called to follow it. On good days and bad ones. Sorry.

I looked into my rearview mirror and looked into my eyes. Those weren't the eyes of someone who didn't need absolute love. Absolute grace. Absolute forgiveness. Those were the eyes of someone who desperately needed to believe in this form of absolution. They were the eyes of a wounded man needing healing, and sometimes forgiveness heals.

I pressed my steering wheel for voice dial, "Call Elizabeth!"

My phone started searching. "No Elizabeth found," the robotic voice answered back.

I forgot I had deleted Elizabeth's contact in my phone two nights ago. I quickly called Wint back. "This is Officer Winston Cooper, leave a message."

I was about to go straight through a light to head home, but I knew I had somewhere else to go.

Elizabeth needed saving, and I was the only one who could save her. Maybe Jenny hadn't gotten there yet.

Maybe there was still time. I pressed the gas pedal harder.

CHAPTER 142

"Diddle, diddle, diddle, diddle," Elizabeth softly sang as she watched her water start to boil. She thought she would make Wint some spaghetti and then some angel hair pasta for the women when they arrived home with the container of processed noodles.

She danced around the kitchen, relieved Veronica was safe. She thought about texting Solo, but she knew what the cold shoulder treatment felt like. She just hoped it wouldn't last forever. She had grown close to Solomon over the last six months. They had an unlikely bond that was intertwined supernaturally. A bond like that didn't break easily, or she hoped it wouldn't.

She opened the refrigerator door to find some broccoli to cook as the power went out.

She closed the door and continued to lightly hum as she turned back to stir her pots. She thought the power would come back on at any second. After a minute of stirring the boiling pasta, she peeked her head out the window to see if it looked like it could be storm-related. She saw a cardinal flying by in sunny blue skies.

She returned to her meal preparation and stirred the homemade sauce and noodles a few more times. She reached for her phone to call Wint, wondering if something happened with the breakers, and she didn't even know where to find them in the house.

"Hey sis," an eerie voice said from behind. Elizabeth's heart stopped. She recognized that voice. She quickly turned to see Jenny holding a candlestick from the living room mantle. Elizabeth reached for the pot of boiling water, but she was too late. Jenny swung and hit the side of Elizabeth's face with the golden heirloom.

Elizabeth went down to the hard tiled floor. She was unconscious.

Jenny stooped down to whisper in Elizabeth's ear, "I wonder if Luther will take off for your funeral?"

CHAPTER 143

Jenny grabbed Elizabeth by her hair and pulled her through the kitchen. A few clumps of her hair broke, so she grabbed another two handfuls. She strained with the lifeless weight. In the past she'd always had the strength of her brother, Alexei, but now she was on her own. She left Elizabeth on the carpet beside the kitchen floor. She bent down to make sure she was still unconscious by kicking her in the ribs.

Elizabeth didn't flinch.

Jenny went into the dining room and grabbed one of the chairs. She saw the neatly placed china table settings and swiped her arm down the middle. Plates and saucers collided with the ground, smashing to bits. She picked up some crystal goblets and threw them across the room, watching the glass burst into a million pieces as they hit the wall. She laughed at the mess of this once pristine room.

She dragged the chair across the hardwood floor, scratching the wood. She didn't know what she enjoyed more, knocking out Elizabeth or destroying Veronica's precious dishes. It was a dead-heat race, but she thought killing Elizabeth would raise the scales from just smashing a gravy boat.

She placed the dining room chair in the middle of the living room. Elizabeth's lifeless body still laid beside the kitchen. Grabbing two new handfuls of hair, she pulled with all her might until she finally reached the dining room chair. Heaving Elizabeth's limp body, she sat her upright on the hard wooden chair.

She needed her to sit still and not fall over, so she pulled out a roll of gray duct tape from her backpack. Elizabeth kept falling forward, so she circled her chest and the chair backing with the duct tape a few times until she remained seated. She placed Elizabeth's legs next to each of the chair legs and started taping them together. Lastly, she grabbed Elizabeth's arms and forced them behind her back, taping them to the chair's back railings. In a matter of a few minutes she had Elizabeth fully secure. She only needed one more piece of tape to cover her mouth. She didn't want her to scream for help.

Yet, she wanted to hear her beg and plead for her life. She decided when the time came, she would remove the tape for a few minutes before her execution.

She patted Elizabeth's face, trying to wake her up. "Wake up, sister," she said welcomingly, but Elizabeth never opened her eyes. Jenny hit Elizabeth's face harder, but she still didn't budge. "Really? When I say to wake up, you better wake up!"

She walked into the kitchen and grabbed the pot of pasta sauce. Stomping back into the living room, she dumped the red sauce on top of Elizabeth's blotchy hair. The heat from the sauce started to seep into her bangs, running down her face.

Suddenly, moans started to escape from Elizabeth's duct-taped mouth. She carefully opened her right eye, and panic filled her vision. It was as if a burst of adrenaline surged through her body as both of her eyes opened wide when she tried to move her arms and legs. Leaning her head forward she saw the predicament she was in: duct-taped to a chair staring eye to eye with a sadistic killer.

"Hey sis," Jenny grinned, scrapping the pasta sauce out of Elizabeth's eyes. She popped her fingers into her mouth and moaned in ecstasy. "This sauce is really good. Do you want one final taste before, you know, I kill you?"

CHAPTER 144

I drove through Wint's yard. I didn't care about the driveway. My speeding car had a mind of its own. I ran up the driveway, passing Elizabeth's car to find the garage door open. I looked around the front of the house and noticed their security yard lights weren't working.

I quietly opened the door in the garage that connected the house to their mud room. It was dark, and I could barely see anything. In the darkness my other senses started to ramp up. The smell of garlic and tomato sauce found my nostrils. I walked cautiously through the kitchen, and a frightening voice caught my attention.

"This sauce is really good. Do you want one final taste before, you know, I kill you?" I heard Jenny say.

I looked around the darkened kitchen. I saw knives, butcher mallets, and skillets, but I didn't know what would be best. The pot of simmering pasta noodles caught my attention. Touching the side of the pot, I noticed it was still hot. I grabbed the handles and tiptoed through the kitchen and down the hall. I looked both directions in the dark, but I couldn't tell which room they were in. I listened intently and turned left towards the foyer. A small amount of light trickled through the room from the slim windows framing the front door.

Jenny started getting louder as she ranted and degraded Elizabeth, telling stories of their past when Elizabeth was just a spoiled brat. "You always got what you wanted while I had to watch. I watched as you received everything you asked for, and you never appreciated any of it. Any of it!"

I slowly walked down the hall and stopped when the screaming seemed close. I poked my head around the corner and vaguely saw Jenny holding what appeared to be a knife to Elizabeth's throat.

"Where should I cut first?" Jenny asked wickedly. "I bet you would die…" she stopped and started laughing. "I'm sorry, that was just too good, and I didn't even plan it. As I was saying, I bet you would die if I cut off one of your ears. I mean, your mother would have to bury you with only one diamond or pearl earring. I mean, how sad would that look to not be symmetrical?"

She raised up the knife, about to slice off Elizabeth's right ear as I jumped into the room with the pot of boiling water.

"Jenny!" I screamed as she quickly turned, slicing Elizabeth's right cheek causing some of the duct tape to open.

Elizabeth screamed from the pain as I came running forward.

"This is interesting. Let's do this again, but this time, you're not going to make it!" she screamed.

I thought Jenny would have run away, but she started running toward me. I quickly threw the contents in the pot forward, hitting Jenny in the face. The hot water scorched her skin as a cloud of steam rose from her head, but she didn't make a sound.

She merely smiled with a butcher knife in her hand.

I threw the pot in her direction, but she ducked under the flying object. I turned and ran out of the room, hearing Jenny following behind.

I darted into the closest room and snuck behind the door. I heard Jenny wheeze as she passed the room. I thought she was going to keep going, but she returned to the room I was hiding in. She was about to enter the room as I forced all my body weight into the door, trapping her body between the door and its frame.

She must have hit her head because she collapsed into the hall. I looked around the room, but it was just a spare bedroom with nothing to hit her with. I didn't realize the force of my body weight was that strong, but she was out cold. I opened the door and found Jenny lying lifeless. Her nose was twisted from her face getting slammed into the door and a stream of blood was escaping the broken appendage. I stooped down to get the knife out of her hand when her eyes opened.

Jenny wasn't unconscious. She was pretending.

She raised her hand up swiftly, and I felt my right leg buckle.

She had just stabbed me.

CHAPTER 145

"Help! Help!" Elizabeth screamed from the living room as I started to moan in pain in the hallway.

I fell backwards as my right leg collapsed from getting stabbed in the calf. I felt the knife sink in as she dragged the blade down.

I instantly used my left leg and kicked her in the side. She continued to swing her knife-holding arm in my direction, but I just kept kicking wildly. I got some momentum and plunged my heel into her stomach. She flinched, allowing me to give her another kick, but this time I aimed for the location of her face. I heard the back of her head hit the hardwood floor. So for good measure, I went in for another kick.

"Argh!" I screamed as the blade of the knife went through the sole of my left foot.

She merely laughed wickedly as I started scooting down the hall, away from her.

"You think you can get away from me?" she asked dementedly. "You can't!"

She stood up wobbly as I, too, tried to stand on my wounded legs. I was ten feet away from Jenny as I started hobbling down the hallway, holding onto the walls for support. I entered the foyer and grabbed a large vase sitting on the table.

Instantly I threw the object with all my might, but she easily dodged it. I grabbed more knickknacks, priceless snow globes, crystal figurines, and framed photos, and chucked them in her direction.

I hit her twice, slowing her down, but it didn't stop her. She looked at me like a lion chasing down an injured antelope. She smiled wickedly before she turned around.

She was returning back to Elizabeth.

"Solo! Solo! Help!" Elizabeth screamed as Jenny almost skipped into the living room.

"Miss me, love?" she asked cruelly holding out the bloody knife for Elizabeth to see.

I looked around the foyer and saw a wooden coat rack. I picked up the long object covered with jackets like a jousting stick and ran with all my might into the living room. I didn't care about the pain I was feeling. Death was going to feel much worse.

"Jenny!" I yelled as I ran full force like a knight, smashing her back with the sharp top.

Falling forward, Jenny screamed for the first time. I threw the solid wooden oak coat rack onto her back.

I looked around the room for something, but my mind wasn't working too clearly. I picked up the coat rack and kept whacking her with it as the coats started flying off the top.

Jenny stopped screaming but started to laugh as if my actions weren't hurting her but tickling her. I was fuming with rage as she looked up at me and smiled. I didn't know what else to do, so I jumped on her back. I know my mother told me to never hit a girl, but this wasn't a girl. This was a killer.

I started throwing punches at her side and smashing her head into the floor. I thought my strength would overpower her, but she quickly raised her hand and sliced my right bicep.

"Argh!" I yelled as I kept getting stabbed. I tried to force her knife-holding hand to let go, but she wouldn't.

"Isn't this romantic?" she laughed villainously as the strength in her arms started to out-do mine. I threw one more punch into her face and then scooted back to quickly regroup.

I picked up the coat rack and slammed the legs into her chest. I wiggled and pressed all my body weight into the wooden frame as another object fell from the top of the coat rack.

I watched as Elizabeth's purse collided with the ground.

I took my eyes off of Jenny for one second too long because she slashed her knife into my upper thigh. I screamed out in pain. I scooted back on my butt, trying to get away from her reach. I rolled over onto my belly to grab for Elizabeth's purse as I felt another knife wound to my leg. And then another.

I was inches from her purse, and I hoped with every breath in my lungs I was right. I grabbed her purse strap and pulled it into my reach. I felt the knife slice through another layer of skin as Jenny started working up my leg. In a few more seconds she was going to be near some of my vital organs.

I reached into the purse and rolled onto my back and pointed.

Jenny stopped and looked quizzically up at my hand in a purse. She raised her hand one more time when I found what I was looking for.

The trigger.

I squeezed and a bullet whizzed through the bottom, hitting Jenny in her right shoulder.

"Kill her!" Elizabeth screamed. I knew she had been screaming the whole time, but I wasn't listening. I was more focused on Jenny.

Jenny looked stunned as her shoulder started to ooze red liquid. She didn't let go of her knife, so I fired again.

And again.

And again.

CHAPTER 146

I laid wounded, with blood pouring out of my legs and arm. I reached for Jenny's knife laying beside her hand, but punched her in the side first to make sure she was dead.

I wiggled around on the ground cutting through the tape binding Elizabeth's hands.

"Solo, thank you," Elizabeth gushed as she grabbed the knife and cut through the remainder of the tape. Once she was free, she ran to her phone and called for the police and paramedics.

"They're on their way, Solomon," she said, kneeling down beside me. "How'd you know?"

"You were cooking pasta," I casually said as I laid back down and closed my eyes.

"Solomon, don't die on me!" she screamed. "You better not die on me!"

I just smiled a tired grin. "I hope I'm not dying. I'm resting."

"Well, you can rest later," she commanded. "Just keep your eyes open until they get here."

"Fine," I said rolling my eyes.

"There's the Solo we all know and love," she said playfully as she left.

"I'm still mad at you," I finally said as she came back with towels to stop the bleeding.

"I know."

"No, I'm really mad at you."

"I know."

"Elizabeth, I don't think you truly understand. I'm really mad at you. Really mad."

Elizabeth's eyes started to well up with tears. "I know because I'm mad at me too!"

I didn't expect her to say that. I looked up at her and realized the pain I had been feeling the last few days she had been feeling it too. I had the pain of a loss, but she had the pain of regret. I had the pain of deceased love, but she had the pain of lost friendship. I had the anger of revenge, but she had the anger of self hate.

"You may not believe me, Solomon, but I'm so, so, so, sorry."

"Don't ever say that to me again," I said flatly.

"Oh, Solomon," she moaned and started to cry.

"Call me Solo," I said with a smile. "It just sounds motherly when you call me Solomon. And I can't picture you as a mom. It's just a scary image in my head."

"I'm keeping you from bleeding out and you say that to me," she said as she pressed into my thigh a little too hard.

"Ouch!" I screamed out in pain.

"Serves you right!" she laughed at my agony. "So, why did you come to save me?"

"It was something Jeremiah said," I said shrugging my shoulders.

"Jeremiah?"

"Yeah, so you should thank him sometime," I said with a wink. "Because if this had happened yesterday, I wouldn't have come to save you."

"Thanks," she said sarcastically. "Good thing Jenny wanted to kill me today and not yesterday then. Maybe I'll send her some nice flowers to her funeral for coming a day later."

"I think that's a good sentiment," I smiled as I heard the sirens coming in the distance. "I think they're here."

She jumped up and ran out the front door, motioning the police and paramedics into the house.

"He's right here; he needs your help," Elizabeth said as a group of men and women came rushing into the darkened living room.

419

They lifted me up onto the gurney and placed me in the back of the ambulance as Elizabeth followed, never letting go of my hand.

Two more paramedics wheeled Jenny's body toward the ambulance as I heard one of them shout, "She's still alive."

"What? I shot her four times," I said shocked. "She looked dead to me."

"Evil doesn't die easy," Elizabeth said. "It's going to take a bomb to get rid of me."

"I should have shot her in the head," I said a little too loudly as one of the paramedics looked up, baffled at my comment. Luckily, Elizabeth was there to defend me.

"Hey, she tried to kill us, sir, so don't give us that look of judgment. Do you see his stabbings all over his body? She did that to him. And I usually don't have spaghetti sauce in my hair or a sliced cheek. But she bound me up and was about to kill me. If Solo didn't come rescue me, I would be dead now. So, I hope she dies." She stopped and looked down at me as I smiled at her in appreciation. "And if you make sure she doesn't make it, I'll put a little extra in your bank account."

"Elizabeth!" I said shocked as the paramedic just shook his head.

"What's wrong with the world when money can't buy someone's death anymore? Where's a hit man when you need one?" she continued to rant as Jenny was placed in the back of our ambulance.

I looked over at her motionless body as the paramedics continued to work on her to save her life. I think Elizabeth felt my angst.

"I'm being serious," Elizabeth added. "How many zeros do you need?" As she continued to rant and beg for the paramedics to stop, she never stopped holding my hand. Even after I told her I would have let her die yesterday.

CHAPTER 147

The hospital was peacefully quiet. The doctors had stitched me up from the numerous wounds Jenny had inflicted. They told me how many stitches they had to use to sew me up, but I didn't remember. I just knew my legs looked like the monster of Dr. Frankenstein now.

Elizabeth left my side and went for a cup of coffee, but when she returned, my empty room was filled with friends I would have died for.

"Solo," Veronica feebly said as she walked in with Wint by her side. She rushed to my bed and hugged me, wrapping her hands around my body, squeezing where the knife sliced my arm.

I winced in pain as Veronica quickly let go.

"I'm sorry," she said giving me a quick peck on the cheek. "Thank you for saving my sister."

"Yeah, Solo, thanks for saving Elizabeth," Wint said as he reached out his hand to shake mine. "I still don't understand it."

"I don't either," I said casually with a grin.

Wint leaned down to give me a hug and whispered in my ear, "You know you can trust me with anything."

"I know," I said back with a wink. "One day I will."

Elizabeth walked into the room holding her coffee, "Finally get done with your spa?"

"Well, I already interrupted her massage once, so I didn't think your life and death matter was a reason to stop it again," Wint kidded as he looked over at me before I glanced up at Elizabeth.

Wint saw the glance and looked over at Elizabeth who merely shrugged her shoulders, pretending to not understand either.

Wint walked over to Elizabeth and whispered into her ear, "I don't believe you. You know what's going on here too."

"I don't know what you're talking about," Elizabeth said with a smile. She leaned over and whispered in his ear, "One day," then kissed Wint on the cheek.

Wint looked at Elizabeth quizzically and then at myself. I wasn't tired, but I didn't want to talk about the dreams Elizabeth and I had, so I pretended to fall asleep.

"The doctors gave him a lot of medicine," Elizabeth said as she started to push Wint and Veronica out the door. "We need to let him get his rest."

Elizabeth turned back to me, "Good night, Solo." She grabbed my hand and squeezed and I squeezed back. Opening one of my eyes, I let her know we may have had a hard last few days, but we would get through it. God put us together for a reason.

"Hey, uh," I whispered so no one else could hear. "Can you get my phone out of my pants pocket over there?"

"Sure," she said.

She handed me my phone. "Um, can you tell me your number?"

"Did you delete me from your phone?"

"I was upset," I rebutted.

"I'll just text it to you," she said.

"Well, I blocked you too, and I'm not sure how to unblock you."

"Really?" she asked, sounding shocked.

"Whatever," I said with a grin. "Just put it in yourself and remove the blocks too."

She quickly fixed my phone and laid it on the table beside me. Then she turned off my light and walked out the door. I turned on the television as my phone vibrated.

Wint's on to us, Elizabeth texted with a smiley face.

Yep, I texted back. Yes he was.

Saturday
CHAPTER 148

An abandoned warehouse building next to the water was illuminated from the lights from the city skyline under a black sky with hundreds of shining stars. Three men walked up to another sitting on the hood of a black Ford Fusion.

"So, how are we going to do this, Grant?" a fit looking man asked.

"I thought about torching the vehicle, but then, what if we just dump the car in the harbor? It will sink to the bottom, and no one will ever find it," the handsome man on the hood said.

"Are you sure it will sink?" asked a man in a British accent.

"I filled the trunk and inside with bricks, Stewart," Grant answered. "The car will sink."

"Okay, let's push it in and get out of here," the last man nervously said.

"Don't tell me you're scared, Jordan," said the first man.

"At least I killed the girl I planned to kill, unlike you, Collin. If you had just killed Fiona, we wouldn't have to be doing this," Jordan said. "There were still many other people we each wanted to kill."

"I didn't even get a chance to do anything," Stewart said in his British accent. "I was just questioned by the police. How fair is that?"

"Don't worry, Stewart. I'm already thinking of how we can do this again," Grant said. "Next time you can start the kills, and we will go in reverse. Then Collin, then Jordan, then me."

"Since no one is around, you guys can finally tell me. How did it feel to watch Sabrina die?" Stewart asked.

"I don't want to lie, but it felt great," Grant smiled. "All those memories of high school came flooding back."

"What about you, Jordan? When you shot Piper?" Stewart asked.

"I guess it's just like Grant said," Jordan answered. "It felt like I was righting a wrong. She finally got what she deserved."

"Don't you want to ask me?" Collin asked, trying to get into the conversation.

"But you didn't kill Fiona," Jordan mocked. "You missed her completely."

"Yeah, but I still shot at her," Collin defended. "Two people startled me and caused me to miss."

"Seems like you needed to plan a little more," Grant said disapprovingly.

"I planned enough," Collin said raising his voice. "Come on, let's sink the car and get out of here."

"Who's scared now?" Jordan mocked.

The four men pushed the black vehicle until it toppled into the water, quickly sinking beneath the waves.

"And there's no way they can track us down from this car?" Stewart asked for the fifth time since they'd started this plan a few years earlier.

"The car is set up in a partnership headquartered in Nevada. Taxes are paid to Nevada. It's licensed in Nevada. The D.C. cops wouldn't think of looking for a Nevada vehicle. Anyway, they already arrested that backstabbing Simon. We are in the clear now that we have the car out of the way," Grant explained. "So, ready for a midnight snack somewhere?"

"I'm always up for food this time of night," Jordan grinned.

"So, who are you thinking as the scapegoat for the next round of kills?" Collin asked.

"Actually, it's you," Grant said with a hearty laugh.

"What? Me?"

"I'm messing with you, Collin. The four of us are in this until the end, right?" Grant said, sticking his hand out in the middle of the group.

"I'm in," Jordan agreed, placing his hand on top of Grant's.

"Me too," Stewart said, putting his hand on top.

"As long as you're not going to pin the murders on me, I'm in," Collin unconvincingly replied, throwing his hand into the mix.

"This is just the beginning, boys," Grant smiled as he placed his arms around his best friends. "Plan B will be here before you know it."

"Let the fun begin," Stewart grinned.

The scene faded as the group of men walked off into the distance leaving the darkened warehouse and heading toward the Big Apple.

"We got the wrong guy!" Elizabeth said, gasping as she shot up from her dream state. She quickly started typing all the details of her dream. The names, places, and descriptions were flowing effortlessly. She looked at the time: 4:16 a.m.

She thought she would send a text later, but suddenly she received one. She smiled as she read it. She didn't know what made her smile more, what she read or who it was from.

Four guys tag-teamed the shootings this week. Not the guy they arrested! How are we going to handle this?

I was about to tell you the same thing, Solo, she texted back.

She put her phone back on the nightstand and fell back to sleep. She had missed getting these texts in the middle of the night. She had a hunch the next six months were going to be better than the last.

And her hunches were usually right.

ADDITIONAL BOOKS

Mystery and Suspense

Intertwined

Bethany, Mississippi, is a quaint, step-back-in-time type of town, where its only protection is the symbolic white picket fences. But even small communities have big secrets. Even the perfect family. And their white picket fences can't protect them from the tragedies that lurk around the   corner.

When a mysterious stranger saves a young girl from drowning in a secluded river, the question rises is he trustworthy or not? Where did he come from? Why does he keep hanging around the twelve-year-old girl he saved?

This tight-knit community is connected by more than their zip code. Their lives and secrets are woven into a tapestry of heartache and pain. As life unravels, there is a common thread that holds them all together. It's their decision to grab onto it or let it choke them.

What other secrets are they hiding?
Are any worth killing or dying for?

Inspirational

Dream Chases: A Journey of Faith

We all have a dream
We all have a purpose
It's time to use your dream to fulfill your purpose

We were created to dream, but so often we lose the childlike innocence of dreaming of things to come. This book is a compelling reminder that God has an incredible purpose for everyone's life. The Bible is filled with stories of people following their dreams – walking to freedom through a sea, defeating giants with mere pebbles, or watching loved ones be healed. These people dreamed big dreams, but not from their own imagination or merit. No, God ordained these great men and women of faith to chase their dreams, just as He still does today. In this captivating book, mystery and inspirational author, Eric Suddoth engages dreamers to begin a journey they were destined to walk.

First steps are always scary, but we are on this journey together. It's time to be Dream Chasers.

Unsung

Within these pages is a deeply intimate work of praise-filled poems, heartfelt prayers, reflections on hard lessons learned and hopeful reminders of God's infinite love and mercy. Each of these writings may not have been intended to become songs, but somehow found themselves, sometimes years later, sung behind my piano or guitar. The majority of these songs have only been sung from the safe confines of my home. Until recently, I believed these writings were just cherished moments between me and God. That is until now.

This book is decades in the making.

A book I never intended to publish.

Come and prayerfully meditate over these words. I pray that this book will bring a blessing to you and that God will sing over you as He originally sung them over me.